Praise for the Novels
of Brenda Scott Royce

Monkey Star

"To say that Holly Heckerling is one of those quirky characters with a heart of gold might sound like a cliché, but there is nothing clichéd about Brenda Scott Royce's writing. *Monkey Star* is funny—really and truly funny—and it is also a novel in which everything and everyone rings true. Royce has a great ear for how people—funny people—talk and think, but she also has a true understanding of how people feel, which comes through on every page and which makes *Monkey Star* such a satisfying read. Plus, any novel with 'monkey' in the title has to be good."

—Laura Zigman, author of *Animal Husbandry*

Monkey Love

"Delicious as a jelly doughnut. . . . Juggling life, love, and loony relatives, Holly Heckerling is a lot like Stephanie Plum—only nobody's shooting at her."
—Janet Evanovich

"A hilarious romp of a novel. If you've ever felt like a monkey in the middle, you'll love this book!"

—Sarah Mlynowski, bestselling author of *Milkrun* and *Monkey Business*

"*Monkey Love* is charming in both its oddity and originality, with characters that jump off the page and wind their way into your heart. Royce's writing is read-out-loud-to-your-friends hilarious; I'm a fan!"

—*Lani Diane Rich, author of *Time Off for Good Behavior* and *Maybe Baby*

continued . . .

Monkey Star

Brenda Scott Royce

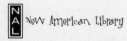 New American Library

New American Library
Published by New American Library, a division of
Penguin Group (USA) Inc., 375 Hudson Street,
New York, New York 10014, USA
Penguin Group (Canada), 90 Eglinton Avenue East, Suite 700, Toronto,
Ontario M4P 2Y3, Canada (a division of Pearson Penguin Canada Inc.)
Penguin Books Ltd., 80 Strand, London WC2R 0RL, England
Penguin Ireland, 25 St. Stephen's Green, Dublin 2,
Ireland (a division of Penguin Books Ltd.)
Penguin Group (Australia), 250 Camberwell Road, Camberwell, Victoria 3124,
Australia (a division of Pearson Australia Group Pty. Ltd.)
Penguin Books India Pvt. Ltd., 11 Community Centre, Panchsheel Park,
New Delhi–110 017, India
Penguin Group (NZ), 67 Apollo Drive, Rosedale, North Shore 0745,
Auckland, New Zealand (a division of Pearson New Zealand Ltd.)
Penguin Books (South Africa) (Pty.) Ltd., 24 Sturdee Avenue,
Rosebank, Johannesburg 2196, South Africa

Penguin Books Ltd., Registered Offices:
80 Strand, London WC2R 0RL, England

First published by New American Library,
a division of Penguin Group (USA) Inc.

First Printing, August 2007
10 9 8 7 6 5 4 3 2 1

REGISTERED TRADEMARK—MARCA REGISTRADA

LIBRARY OF CONGRESS CATALOGING-IN-PUBLICATION DATA:

Royce, Brenda Scott.
   Monkey star/Brenda Scott Royce.
      p. cm.
   ISBN: 978-0-451-22126-1
   1. Women animal trainers—Fiction.   2. Natural childbirth—Coaching—Fiction.
3. Hollywood (Los Angeles, Calif.)—Fiction.   4. Motion picture industry—Fiction.   I. Title.
   PS3618.O895M665 2007
   813'.6—dc22   2007007613

Set in Simoncini Garamond
Designed by Elke Sigal

Printed in the United States of America

For Nicholas,
my monkey star

Acknowledgments

When I was young, I desperately wanted a pet chimpanzee. While my friends collected Barbies and dreamed of owning ponies, I covered the walls of my bedroom with posters of monkeys and apes, and fantasized about joining Jane Goodall in the wilds of Tanzania. My mother judiciously supported my dreams while steadfastly refusing my demands that we adopt a chimp. She remains a source of encouragement and good judgment to this day.

My editor, Kara Cesare, is the person most responsible for this book. I had begun writing an entirely different novel—this one involving an unruly duck—when she urged me to consider continuing Holly's adventures. Her love for the characters and belief in my abilities spurred me to ponder what might have happened after the close of *Monkey Love*—and I quickly agreed that Holly had more tales to tell.

Miriam Kriss, agent extraordinaire, was a source of sanity along the way, providing support and encouragement when I was facing down the "second-book syndrome" that plagues so many sophomore authors.

My friends Daphne Ashbrook and Vikki Young were my first-line readers, eagerly grabbing up chapters as soon as I finished them and providing helpful feedback. Daphne, Jodi Gottlieb, and John Landis ensured that my depiction of life on a movie set was believable. Other friends and early readers offered insightful comments: Corinna Bechko, Lanette Hohl, Madeline McGrail, Krissy Parada, and Lauren Royce. My husband, Ramón, not only read early drafts but offered to act out the sexy parts. Thanks, honey, for going the extra mile.

The long list of individuals and organizations that provided inspiration, information, advice, or assistance includes Norm Abbey, Angela Adams, the American Humane Association, Anthony Vincent Bova, Andrea Campbell, Dan Cubias, Janet Evanovich, Kristan Ginther, Gabriel Hardman, Tony and Marianne Hudz, Tricia Kokoszka, Deborah Landis, Connie Morgan, Jennifer Owens, James Robert Parish, Jamie Pham, and David Mascarina.

Anyone interested in learning more about the fate of post-retirement performing apes should visit the Center for Great Apes' Web site at www.prime-apes.org or spend an hour in the company of its intrepid director, Patti Ragan.

Extra brownie points go to my grandmother, Helena Mete, the inspiration for Aunt Betty. She doesn't share Betty's habit of biting people, but she does possess her fictional counterpart's innate goodness and devotion to her family—a devotion that led her to purchase an obscene number of copies of *Monkey Love* and distribute them to friends and relatives far and wide.

Most of all, I am grateful to my family, especially my husband for helping me find time to write when I barely had time to breathe, and Emmanuel, Daniel, and Nicholas, for sharing their lives and their laughter with me.

1

Baby on Board

The smell of stale coffee and industrial-strength antiseptic permeated the community room in the basement of Bensonhurst Memorial Hospital. I followed the scent to a cafeteria table on which sat a pitcher of punch, a plate of cookies, and a sign-in sheet. But no coffee. I should have stopped at Starbucks, I chastised myself as I wrote my name at the bottom of the page and snatched a sugar cookie from the plate. It was only six p.m., but after a long day of wrangling thirty children and almost as many animals, I was exhausted.

A dozen women in advanced stages of pregnancy were seated in a circle on the floor, surrounded by mounds of pillows. At their sides, a dozen men in the advanced stages of get-me-out-of-here exchanged furtive glances at the overhead clock in between patting their mates' tummies, rubbing their shoulders, and whispering soothing words into their ears.

Most of the women had their eyes closed and were practicing the kind of deep breathing that I'd failed to master in my last disastrous attempt at yoga class. My best friend, Carter—a yoga instructor who's ordinarily a nice person but who gets some kind of sadistic pleasure out of watching women contort their bodies into gravity-defying poses—had chosen me to demonstrate a position that not only defied gravity, but several other laws of nature, as well. I'd nearly dislocated my pelvis in the process. Even though my pelvic ligaments had healed completely, the memory sent a stab of pain shooting through my groin.

Hovering around the expectant couples was a tall, muscular woman wearing a sweatshirt that read COACH, a whistle dangling from a chain around her neck. She looked up when I entered, giving two quick bursts on the whistle that cut through the soothing sounds of nature emanating from the CD player.

"Continue your cleansing breaths," she said as she crossed the room in three quick strides and extended her hand. "I'm Maya."

"Holly Heckerling," I said. "Sorry I'm late. I missed the subway stop and had to double back."

"Don't worry about it," Maya said, scribbling my name on a sticker. She peeled off the backing and slapped the sticker just above my right breast with a force much greater than the task required. "Happens to all of us." She looked down at my midsection. "You're really on top of things. Most of my moms don't even think about Lamaze until they're just about ready to pop. You're barely showing. Good for you!"

My head sank as I followed her gaze down past my red HI! I'M HOLLY sticker to my stomach, which was protruding slightly over the waistband of my jeans.

I nearly choked on my half-eaten sugar cookie. "I'm not pregnant," I sputtered, brushing cookie crumbs off my T-shirt. "I'm the coach."

"Oops, my bad." Maya ripped the red sticker off my shirt and scribbled a new one. This one was blue. She slapped it on my breastbone with even more force than the first time. "Where's your partner?"

I glanced at the door. "She should be here any minute. She had to use the restroom."

"Of course." Maya nodded knowingly. "Why don't you just take a seat in the circle?"

I shoehorned myself into a space between a tiny Asian woman

whose stomach looked like a perfectly formed basketball and a red-head who looked about thirteen months pregnant. I hoped if I ever actually became pregnant, I'd look more like the Asian.

The redhead, whose name was Lynda according to her tag, waved a plump hand and smiled. "First time?"

"I'm *not* pregnant," I said through gritted teeth.

"I know." She pointed to my sticker. "Blue is for the coaches. I meant, is this your first class?"

"Oh, um, yeah. Sorry for jumping on you. Must be the hormones." Who says you have to be pregnant to use the hormone excuse? I have hormones, too, and lately they'd been running amuck.

She gave me a curious stare, then turned back to her husband, who looked like he was half her size and lived in fear of her rolling over in the night and crushing the life's breath out of him.

The door burst open and my aunt Betty pushed through. She set her pocketbook on the cafeteria table and waved me over. "Holly, honey, you gotta see this," she said, unbuttoning her blouse.

I uncrossed my legs and struggled to get to my feet. Aunt Betty suffers from psoriasis, a condition that causes her skin to break out in scaly red patches. During particularly severe outbreaks, her skin itches so badly that she can't stand to wear clothing. Fortunately, the family has learned to avert their eyes when Betty decides to air her wares at home. Unfortunately, she isn't averse to an occasional public airing.

Any one of the pregnant women could probably have made it across the room quicker than I managed to stumble over to Betty. I shuddered to think of how ungainly I'd become if I was ever actually with child.

"Stop!" I yelled, but it was too late. Betty had unfastened the last button of her blouse and was yanking it off.

To my horror and relief, underneath the blouse she was wearing a bright yellow T-shirt that read BABY ON BOARD, with a giant arrow pointing at her stomach. "Isn't it something? I bought it at BJ's."

Maya was gaping at Aunt Betty, eyebrows raised but saying nothing. Betty scribbled her name on the sign-in sheet and shuffled toward the circle. "Where do I sit?"

The women had stopped their deep breathing and were staring at Betty. "What's the matter?" Betty asked the tiny Asian woman. "Never seen a late-in-lifer before?"

I know I could have put an end to the wide-eyed stares and whispered comments by explaining that my octogenarian aunt was merely standing in for my pregnant best friend. Carter had moved to California with her boyfriend, Danny, my former comedy partner, and she wanted me to fly out to be her labor coach. I thought she was making a huge mistake, since I have a habit of fainting when I see blood—and while I'd never witnessed childbirth, I was fairly certain there'd be some blood involved. But she insisted. She also insisted I take Lamaze classes and balked at my suggestion that I could learn all I needed from a DVD or an online class. Carter, who'd undoubtedly mastered eighty-seven different ways to breathe, wouldn't allow me to get by with just the one.

So here I was, in the community room in the basement of Bensonhurst Memorial Hospital, taking the first in a series of six Lamaze classes to help ease Carter through the pain of childbirth.

I had tried to find an actual pregnant woman to go through Lamaze with me, but my "seeking single pregnant woman" flyer was removed from the bulletin board of my local Starbucks by the new manager, who suspected nefarious motives on my part.

In a moment of desperation, I had even asked my cousin's fiancée, Monica Broccoli, though I'd rather endure a painfully protracted labor with no anesthesia than spend six weeks straddled behind Monica and telling her to push. Monica was a dancer-actress with the legs of a Rockette and the personality of a pit bull. Though we'd never been friends, lately I was trying to make peace with

Monica for the sake of the family. To her credit, she'd declined to press charges when I inadvertently caused her to break her leg. But she did walk with a ridiculously exaggerated limp whenever I was around.

"Think of it as an acting assignment," I'd told her. "You play the part of the pregnant woman and I'm your coach."

"Is it a union job?" she'd asked. "Does it pay scale?"

"Okay, forget acting. Think of it as female bonding."

"If you wanted to bond with me, you'd have agreed to be in my bridal party."

I'd seen the sequin-studded sofa covers she'd selected for her bridesmaids' gowns. No favor was worth seeing myself in that dress staring back at me in family photographs for the rest of my life.

When I reached the group, the women were commiserating over their ever-worsening pregnancy symptoms. "My breasts are so tender," Lynda said, squeezing her oversized orbs for emphasis. Her husband went pale. The other mates respectfully checked their watches or adjusted their ties, making sure their gaze was directed at anything except for Lynda's overblown breasts. "And my ankles are swollen."

They continued to compare notes—heartburn, varicose veins, and stretch marks, along with the effectiveness of various remedies for each. "I tried Bertha's Belly Cream," said a middle-aged blonde whose name badge read KENDRA. "But nothing works." She unbuttoned her blouse and outlined the offending marks with her finger.

"Think that's bad?" Betty hiked up her yellow shirt to reveal an oasis of scaly red patches. "Look at these."

I leaned over and tugged Betty's shirt back down. "Those aren't stretch marks," I whispered. "It's psoriasis."

She hmphed. "I'm just trying to fit in."

Betty grabbed two pillows from the center of the circle. She propped one behind her back and stuffed the other under her T-shirt. Then she patted her tummy and smiled. "I always wondered

what this would feel like," she told the redheaded woman. "My husband, Bernie, and I never had kids." She looked over at me and
smiled. "But Holly's always been like a daughter to us."

As if to prove her maternal devotion to me, Betty proceeded to
boast about my accomplishments, from my first ballet recital to my
brief career as a stand-up comic. "She's really funny," she told the
Asian woman. "At one of her shows, I laughed so hard I wet my
pants."

Only Betty would find a lapse in bladder control something to
brag about.

Maya kept shushing Betty, eventually resorting to blasting on
her whistle and giving her a warning gesture whenever Betty opened
her mouth.

Betty finally stopped gabbing and focused on the exercises.
Pretty soon she was on a roll, not only going through the motions
but fully enacting the labor process. At one point, she gripped my
hand so hard she cut off the circulation to my fingers.

"Ouch!"

"Sorry, sweetie," she said, releasing her death grip. "Contraction."

Two hours, three breathing techniques, and one disturbingly
graphic childbirth video later, class ended.

As the husbands and other assorted life partners helped the
pregnant women to their feet, I struggled to stand, then turned and
reached a hand out to Betty.

As she grabbed my hand, I noticed Betty had an uncharacteristically sheepish expression on her face. As she pulled herself up, I
saw the cause of her sheepishness trickling down her leg and forming a puddle at her feet.

I froze in place, hoping that if we didn't move, no one would
notice. Then when the room cleared out, I could mop the floor and
find something dry for Betty to change into.

But the art of nonchalance was lost on Betty. She stared down at the widening pool of liquid and pointed, attracting the attention of everyone who hadn't already bolted for the bathrooms. As the crowd gathered around her, Betty said, "I think my water broke."

I helped Betty up the stoop of her brownstone and waited while she fished her keys from the bottom of her cavernous handbag.

She unlocked the door, then untied the oversized NYU sweatshirt I'd wrapped around her waist for the cab ride home—a gesture I'd almost instantaneously regretted. After all, the backseat of a New York City cab was surely no stranger to urine, whereas the sweatshirt had been a gift from my boyfriend, Tom, an English professor at NYU.

Boyfriend. Even *thinking* the word made my cheeks flush. Tom was the first guy who'd made it past the dreaded three-month marker that had previously sounded the death knell of my romantic relationships. The sweatshirt had been his; he'd draped it over my shoulders on a chilly night as we walked through the Village. I'd adopted it and worn it often, loving how his scent still faintly lingered on the soft material.

Betty held it out to me. "Don't forget your shirt."

I eyed the soaked sweatshirt uncertainly, wondering if I could ever bring myself to wear it again. Even if multiple launderings managed to take care of the smell, Betty's bum bladder had surely killed whatever sentimental value it once possessed.

"Keep it," I said. "It's yours."

"Gee thanks. NYU. Maybe people will think I'm a coed."

"Yeah."

"That was something," she said. "We should practice those breathing exercises so we'll do better next time."

"Next time?" I sputtered. "You peed in class. We're not going back."

"It's not my fault. All that pushing and deep breathing loosened things up down there. Besides, it's a hospital. They must be used to people having little accidents."

"Not in the classrooms!"

She shrugged. "We'll talk about it on Sunday."

"Sunday?" I scrunched my forehead.

"Ronnie's birthday dinner. Kuki's gonna make her marinated meatballs."

I rolled my eyes. My cousin Ronnie, short for Veronica, was the younger of my aunt Kuki's two kids. Being the only girl, she'd gotten the dubious honor of sharing her room with me when my mother died and my father dumped me on Kuki's doorstep. For the rest of our childhoods, Ronnie treated me like a giant invasion of her personal space.

"Yeah," I sighed. "I might be busy on Sunday." Ronnie never liked my gifts, anyway. Maybe this year I'd give her what she always wanted: my absence.

I knew I should stay and help Betty change into dry clothes, but I had to draw the line somewhere. Besides, I had a big date with Tom in an hour, and it'd take half that long just to get back to my apartment in Manhattan.

I helped Betty inside and was turning to leave when I saw my cousin Gerry walking up the street, arm in arm with his fiancée, Monica. They looked happy together, laughing in unison and striding purposefully toward Betty's stoop.

I shouted "hey" and waved in their direction.

Monica's smile fell abruptly when she saw me. Her pace slowed and she allowed her left leg to drag behind her with each halting step. I rolled my eyes, knowing the limp was purely for my benefit.

Gerry bounded up the steps and wrapped me in a bear hug. Thankfully his affection for me was unaffected by his fiancée's and sister's personal grudges.

"You comin' or goin'?" he asked.

"Going. Betty and I just came from Lamaze class."

He nodded as though this made perfect sense. "Monica and I came to get a second opinion on the wedding invitations."

"*Second* opinion?" I arched one eyebrow. It was a safe bet the first opinion belonged to Gerry's mother, my extremely opinionated aunt Kuki.

"Ma thinks they're too . . . distracting." He nudged Monica. "Show Holly."

Monica reached into her purse and pulled out a thick envelope. I could tell by her expression that she wasn't really interested in my opinion.

I slid the invitation out of the envelope and blinked. Neon pink lettering stood out against a lime green background. The text was composed of at least twelve different fonts. Dotted all around the text were little illustrations—a bride and groom, a heart, a cake, champagne flutes, a pair of socks, streamers, and something that looked like a Brillo pad. I could understand the wedding graphics— and even the socks made sense, considering Gerry's near-fanatical obsession with building his celebrity sock collection—but even I was stumped by the Brillo pad.

"It's great," I said, smiling. Okay, the colors were garish and the text was indecipherable, but I had nothing to gain by telling the truth. It was Monica's wedding, and if she liked the invitations, that was all that mattered. Besides, the invitation seemed appropriate since the event itself was destined to be a train wreck. "I see you used your real name."

"Of course. Except for your family, everyone knows me as Esther. If I put 'Monica Broccoli' on the invitations, nobody'll show up."

"But she's gonna let me call her Monica during the ceremony," Gerry said.

She shot him a look that would have emasculated Superman. "I'm still thinking about it."

"That might not be—" I stopped short. I was going to protest that using an alias during the ceremony may invalidate the proceedings, but then I thought better of it. One day my cousin might need a legal loophole to free himself from his folly of marrying Monica Broccoli. "That might not be a bad idea," I said instead. "Gerry will be nervous enough trying to remember his vows. Maybe he shouldn't have to remember to say your real name, too."

They both cut their eyes at me. I guess Monica's name was still a sensitive subject, since it had nearly ended their relationship. Gerry, who is notoriously bad at names, had begun calling his girlfriend Monica Broccoli at the beginning of their courtship. Bizarrely, she didn't complain *for two years*. Then Gerry popped the question, and Monica put him on the spot, asking him—in front of the entire family—to call her by her real name. Which he couldn't remember.

They'd eventually patched things up, thanks to me. And while my attempts to discover Monica's true identity ultimately resulted in her hospitalization, I thought they both owed me a debt of gratitude.

"I know your name is Esther," Gerry was saying to Monica. "But you'll always be my Brockly Wockly."

"Awww," she said, leaning in for a kiss.

Gag.

I returned my attention to the invitation, just so I'd have somewhere else to look. "The pictures are . . . cute," I said.

Monica came up for air. "They're symbols of our love."

I pointed at the Brillo pad. "What's that?"

"It's broccoli."

The front door opened and Aunt Betty emerged, now dressed in a floral housedress and slippers. "I thought I heard voices out here."

Gerry kissed her on the cheek. "We came to show you our wedding invitation," he said, taking the neon monstrosity from my hands.

"Go on inside," Betty said, stepping aside to let him pass. "There's snickerdoodles on the counter."

Monica followed, stopping to give Betty a halfhearted hug and yelping when Betty bit her on the cheek.

In addition to being a flasher and a public urinator, Aunt Betty is also a biter. Thankfully she mostly refrains from biting strangers. Inflicting little nips, tweaks, pinches, and punches is her way of expressing affection. I suspect she wasn't hugged much as a child. I'd grown used to her assaults—and the bruises they invariably left behind—but Monica obviously hadn't warmed up to them yet. She dashed after Gerry, her hand clutching her cheek. I could hear her yelling something about having my aunt fitted for a muzzle before the wedding.

Betty looked down at me. "You're still here? I thought you had a date with your young man."

Tom! I glanced at my watch. If the subway gods were with me, I'd just barely have time to shower and change before he was scheduled to arrive. I'd wanted to spend extra time getting ready since it was a special occasion—exactly six months since our first date, a major milestone in my dating history—and I hoped to celebrate it by finally finding out if Tom was as good in bed as he was in everything else.

While we'd had several hot-and-heavy romantic encounters, we hadn't slept together yet. Part of it was timing—Tom's divorce had just been finalized and he shared custody of his eight-year-old daughter with his ex-wife. Invariably, the nights I was available, Tom had Nicole. But the other part was we were both gun-shy. I'd had many relationships start off hot and quickly fizzle, so I was all for taking it slow. And Tom had to be cautious because he had his daughter to consider. But enough was enough. After six months of long, deep kisses that curled my toes and made my insides turn to melted butter, I was ready to take the next step. I had a feeling Tom was ready, too, but just in case, I'd bought a red-hot body-hugging dress that would help convince him to take the plunge.

The thought of Tom finally taking the plunge sent a hot rush surging through my veins.

I squeezed Betty's hand and said, "Gotta dash," before power-walking in the direction of the subway.

The subway gods were on my side—an express train arrived just as I got to the platform and got me back to the Village so quickly I didn't have time to read all the ads for abortion clinics and personal-injury attorneys before reaching my stop—but the Great Deity of Manhattan Apartments was definitely against me.

I unlocked the front door to my building and charged up the stairs toward my sixth-floor apartment, darting a quick glance at my watch between floors. Tom was due to arrive in fifteen minutes. My shower would have to be a quick rinse and dry; makeup and hair would be minimal at best. My pace slowed by the fourth floor, as gravity and the steamy heat of the enclosed stairwell conspired to knock the wind out of me. I was huffing and puffing by the time I reached my landing, rivulets of sweat streaming down my face and soaking into my bra.

I grimaced when I saw the familiar red flyer tacked to my apartment door. It read FINAL NOTICE, but I knew this was far from the last time I'd come up a little late and a lot short with my rent money. The nature of my business—Holly's Hobbies—is such that work, and the income it produces, is irregular. Under the Holly's Hobbies banner, I do a number of odd jobs—mostly typing, hairstyling, pet-sitting, babysitting, and tax preparation, but I'm open to just about anything that's not illegal, immoral, or injurious to others.

Aside from tax season, when I tend to get a nice influx of cash from last-minute filers who don't mind selecting their tax professional from a Laundromat flyer, my cash flow is extremely erratic.

My new sideline profession as an animal educator for the elementary school set is emotionally rewarding but not financially so. I only make about fifty bucks per presentation, and this morning's gig at PS 118 had been my first in two weeks.

Unfortunately, the company that owns my apartment building prefers their tenants to pay up promptly on the first of every month. And today was the fifth.

I ripped the red notice off the door and tucked it into my purse. Then I stuck my key in the lock and leaned on the door as I turned the key.

But something was wrong. They key wasn't turning. I eased up on the door, said a silent prayer, then tried again. Nothing. The key wouldn't budge.

I kicked the door and cursed. It was futile, but felt good, so I did it again. Kick, curse, repeat. When my big toe was numb, I banged my head against the door and cried.

I used to be better at stretching my meager income to meet all my expenses and still leave room for an occasional Mocha Frappuccino. But as computer prices kept dropping, fewer people hired me to do their typing, and that part of my business had been declining steadily. I'd lost a few of my regular hairstyling clients when a SuperCuts opened down the block, and some of the kids I used to babysit stopped coming after their moms found out I had acquired a pet boa constrictor. Go figure.

I was still much in demand as a pet-sitter, but that didn't pay enough to cover my bills.

Even with these setbacks, I could have scraped enough together to pay rent this month, but I'd splurged on my new red dress for tonight's date with Tom. *What was I thinking?* I wondered as I banged my head against my unyielding front door. The dress was fabulous, but was it worth getting tossed out of my apartment? It was stunning and slimming and sexy and would probably help seal the deal with Tom, but it was too expensive and I should have known better.

And more important, it was on the other side of this locked door.

I charged back down the six flights and pounded on the door of the super's apartment. No answer. I pounded harder. "Pete! Open up!"

Still no answer. I pushed my ear against the door and strained to hear what was going on inside the apartment. For a moment I thought I could hear angry voices shouting obscenities about evil, heartless, moneygrubbing landlords, but then I realized those voices were coming from inside my own head.

I tried another approach. I knocked again, firmly but not impatiently, and said, "Pete? It's Holly Heckerling. I really need to get inside my apartment. I'll straighten out the rent in the morning, I promise. But I need to get in there tonight, because I—"

I stopped short, realizing my desperate plea to make myself pretty for my date probably wouldn't elicit much sympathy from Pete, a divorcé with barely concealed bitterness toward all womankind. "My animals are inside," I said. "My cat, Grouch, is probably starving. And Rocky—"

Oops. I stopped myself short, remembering that snakes were not allowed in the building, and I'd thus far successfully hidden Rocky the Boa's existence from building management.

"And *Rocky*'s on TV tonight," I said lamely. "I gotta see it. I love that movie," I lied.

I listened at the door again, heard nothing, and decided maybe Pete wasn't home after all. I pulled the red flyer out of my purse, flipped it over, and rooted around in my purse for a pen. Finding nothing, I uncapped a tube of lipstick, wrote a two-word message on the back of the flyer, and slipped it under Pete's door.

I checked the time. Five minutes until the date that could potentially change my life. And I was a sweaty, grubby—and potentially homeless—wreck.

Get a grip, I told myself. Tom wasn't like my previous boyfriends.

He'd understand my little screwup. So I was the epitome of fiscal irresponsibility. He still loved me, right?

Okay, so he hadn't actually ever *said* that he loved me. But it was coming—I could feel it.

I looked down at my sweat-stained T-shirt and jeans and felt a renewed sense of panic. I had to get inside before Tom arrived. Even if a shower was out of the question, I could at least change into my dress and run a brush through my hair.

In a rush of adrenaline, I ran up all six flights, brainstorming all the way. If I couldn't get in through the front door, I was going to find another way.

When I reached my landing I kept going. My neighbor Brian's apartment was one flight up, directly over mine. I knew from experience that we shared a fire escape. If he was home, he'd surely let me climb through his window. I couldn't remember if I'd left my window open, but I'd break the glass if I had to. I knocked, but there was no answer, and no sounds emanating from the apartment.

Damn. I ran back down to my floor and gave my front door another kick. It didn't yield. Then I spotted the little latched milk door that led to a cubbyhole in my pantry. One of few reminders of the building's 1940s origins, the milk doors once allowed the milkman to make early-morning deliveries without disturbing the residents. Most of my neighbors had boarded over theirs, but I'd put mine to practical use. If I wasn't home, my typing clients could drop off or pick up work. The cubby was just large enough for a few bottles of milk, or, in my case, envelopes containing manuscripts or tax returns.

Unfortunately, many of my clients had gone the way of the milkman, which is why I didn't think of the cubby sooner. The milk cubby might be big enough for a small person to squeeze through. I unlatched the outer door and gave the inner one a sharp shove. It popped open. So much for the security latch I'd installed on the inside.

I opened both doors wide and sized up the opening. It was maybe ten inches square. I looked down at my midline and reminded myself that just a few short hours ago I was mistaken for a pregnant woman. Maybe this wasn't such a good idea.

Too bad Tallulah isn't here, I thought. Tallulah was a capuchin monkey who accompanied me on my Critter Comedy classroom visits. Along with my bunny rabbit, snake, tortoise, and assorted other creatures, Tallulah helped me educate schoolkids about animals.

Tallulah first entered my life when her owner, a quadriplegic named David, needed surgery, and since I had both pet-sitting experience and a degree in primatology, I got the job. Neither of those qualifications had prepared me for life with a monkey, and within days, Tallulah had turned my life upside down, stealing Monica Broccoli's engagement ring, dismantling my phone, humping my television set, and escaping through the milk door.

If she'd gotten out that way, there was no reason she couldn't get back in, I thought, dashing down the stairs and out the front door.

A Tight Spot

David Marquette lived just four blocks away, which made our working arrangement convenient. He'd given me a key to his apartment so I could enter when I pleased, but I still rang the buzzer downstairs—three short bursts—to signal him that I was on my way up.

"Is that you, Holly?" he said when I poked my head in the door.

"Yeah, are you decent?"

He laughed. "You know I can't get myself indecent without help. And Margie just left, so you're safe."

Margie, David's nurse, left at six each day. David's sister, Paula, who lived in the building, would stop in with his dinner when she got off work. Between the two of them, David had nearly round-the-clock care. For those times when he was alone, Tallulah was trained to perform tasks for David, such as turning on or off the TV, opening bottles, fetching various items, and more critically, dialing 911 in case of an emergency.

"One of these days I'm gonna catch you in a compromising position," I teased as I entered the small apartment and found David in front of the TV, Tallulah sitting on the arm of his wheelchair. She was wearing a pink-and-green plaid dress over a preemie-sized Pamper with a hole cut out for her tail.

"I hope so," David said.

Tallulah leapt onto my shoulder and began grooming my hair.

"She's always so happy to see you," David said.

"The feeling is mutual." I reached into my purse and pulled out a Ziploc bag, from which I extracted a few gummy bears, one of Tallulah's favorite treats. She took one and popped it into her mouth, then hopped back down to her usual place on the arm of David's chair.

"What's going on? We didn't have a date, did we?"

"I need to borrow Tallulah for a few minutes. That is, if it's okay."

He glanced at the wall clock. "Sure. Paula will be here any minute. What are you girls going to do?"

Just a little breaking and entering, I thought. But I said, "I know this is gonna sound crazy, but—"

He interrupted with a short burst of laughter. "You know how many of your sentences start that way?"

"I lost count," I admitted. "Anyway, I locked myself out of my apartment. I thought if I send Tallulah in through the milk door, she could unlock the front door and let me in." Now that I was saying it out loud, I realized just how crazy it actually sounded. Tallulah was smart, but would she understand what I wanted? Or would she just enter the apartment and run amok?

"Doesn't anyone else have a key who could let you in?" David asked.

"The super's not home, and I don't know when he'll get back. I've gotta get inside to feed my animals, and get ready for my—" I cut myself short, realizing how petty my needs were compared to David's. I was desperate to get inside my apartment to change into a slinky red dress and seduce my boyfriend. David couldn't dress himself and had probably never been on a date. And here I was, trying to take his companion animal from him.

"Never mind," I said, backing away. "It was a stupid idea."

"It's okay, Holly. I trust you. If you need to borrow Tallulah, she's yours. No questions asked. That is, if she wants to go."

As if in answer to the question, Tallulah leapt onto my shoulder and bobbed her head up and down excitedly, the way she does whenever we leave the apartment. While she's content to spend most of her time perched on the arm of David's wheelchair, she's a people monkey—she loves to go out and mingle with the masses.

I hesitated. Then the buzzer sounded—two long bursts, Paula's signal. If she was here, there really wouldn't be any harm in my borrowing Tallulah, would there?

When I opened the front door to my building, Tallulah hopped down and tugged at her leash. I unclipped it and she skittered up the stairs. By now she knew which apartment was mine, and when I reached the sixth-floor landing, huffing and puffing, she was sitting patiently at the door.

"Not that way," I said, taking her by the hand and leading her to the milk door. I opened the outer door and pushed the inner one open as far as it would go. I reached into my pocket and pulled out the laser pointer I'd borrowed from David. Most of the commands Tallulah performed were in response to the laser. Train the red dot of light onto an object and Tallulah would retrieve it, expecting to be rewarded with a treat for her efforts.

I thought for a moment about how to best communicate my needs to Tallulah. She was adept at unlocking doors, so that part wouldn't be a problem. I shined the laser on the front-door lock. Then I pulled the Ziploc baggie of treats out of my purse and set it in front of the locked door. She started toward the baggie, but I held her back.

I pointed to the open milk door. "Okay, Tallulah, I need you to go in through here, then go unlock the front door." I repeated the instructions several times, shining the laser first through the milk door, then at the front-door knob, and finally on the baggie of gummy bears. I hoped the repetition would serve to reinforce the command, rather than confuse her.

"Ready?" I asked her.

She bobbed her head up and down rapidly, a gesture that seemed to me to convey not only understanding but impatience.

I took a deep breath and helped her through the little opening.

Tallulah hopped onto the floor of my pantry and turned to look back at me.

"Good." I nodded my approval. "Now go!" I pointed in the direction of the living room.

Tallulah started toward the dining room but then stopped as though something had caught her attention. Her gaze fixed on an upper shelf of my pantry, on which sat an economy-sized bag of gummy bears.

Damn. I'd forgotten that I was sending Tallulah in through the pantry, which, aside from a few cans of soup for me, primarily held pet food and treats for Tallulah. How would I lure her back outside with a few paltry gummy bears when she was sitting on the mother lode?

Tallulah's gaze swept around the little pantry, taking in the boxes of cereal, raisins, and jellybeans. Her eyes were wide, and she was making happy little tittering noises. She looked like the proverbial kid in a candy store.

I was sunk.

I called her name and flashed the laser pointer back to the milk door. If she wouldn't unlock the front door, I had to get her back outside with me.

She cast an indifferent glance at the little red dot and returned her attention to the jumbo bag of gummy bears. Then she jumped up and careened from one shelf to another until the gummy bear bag was in reach. She reached for it and the bag toppled to the floor. The impact caused one side of the bag to split open. Gummy bears flew everywhere.

I heard my cat, Grouch, hiss from somewhere inside the apartment—his usual response to having his space invaded by the monkey.

Tallulah sailed through the air, landing in the middle of the mess and cackling in glee as she used both hands to fill her mouth with treats.

I kept calling her name, but she ignored me. I stuck one arm through the door up to my shoulder. Tallulah was out of my reach. I withdrew my arm and pointed the laser light at her shoulder. She brushed at the spot as though it were a pesky mosquito. She didn't look up at me.

I had to face it: she was lost to me. At least until she'd had her fill of gummy bears, at which point she'd probably be in a sugar-induced coma and unable to help me.

I sank to the ground, my back against the wall. I checked my watch. Five minutes to eight. Tom would be there any minute, but prettying myself up for our date was no longer my most pressing problem. I needed to get Tallulah back to her owner. I'd promised to have her back in time for *Grey's Anatomy*, and while I knew Tallulah was a TV addict, for David the issue was far more serious than having someone to watch Meredith and McDreamy with. Tallulah was his best friend and constant companion, and I—and my trifling tribulations—had taken her away.

I heard a crash and turned to look through the milk door. The mound of gummy bears was still there, but Tallulah wasn't. She'd left the pantry and was out of sight, somewhere within my apartment. There was another crash, then some banging. The good news was that few of my belongings were actually worth anything. The bad news was my apartment wasn't monkey-proofed. She had easy access to knives and other sharp instruments, not to mention medicine, household cleaners, and other toxic substances.

I raced to the front door and knocked sharply, calling her name. I twisted the doorknob. "Let me in, Tallulah!"

Crash, bang, splat. Tallulah was having a field day.

I ran back down to the first floor and pounded on Pete's door. "Pete, open up! It's an emergency!"

I pounded until my hand was numb. Then I ran back upstairs, past my floor, and rapped hard on Brian's door. No answer there either.

In desperation, I even tried Mrs. Mete, the building's resident busybody. She spent her days spying and spreading gossip. I hated bringing her into my problems, because I knew within minutes all my neighbors would not only know about the monkey ransacking my apartment, but my money problems and sex life, too.

Mrs. Mete didn't answer, which was odd because she rarely left her apartment due to rheumatoid arthritis. I had the urge to bust down the door to make sure she was okay, but it stood to reason if I couldn't knock down my own door, I wouldn't get anywhere with Mrs. Mete's.

I headed down the stairs toward my floor, speeding my pace when I heard voices coming from the vicinity of my apartment.

No one was on the landing, and my door was still locked tight. I stuck my head through the milk door and realized the voices were coming from my television set. Tallulah must have switched it on. Someone was yelling, "Stat," over the beeps and blips of surgical equipment. The monkey had managed to find *Grey's Anatomy* after all. Which made me think of David again, watching alone in his apartment.

I pulled my head back and appraised the little opening once again. It was more than ten inches wide, I told myself. Probably a good foot across. I sucked in my stomach and tucked my butt under, trying to make myself pencil-slim. I had no doubt I could squeeze my upper body through the opening, but wasn't so sure about my hips. *Childbearing hips,* Aunt Kuki often called them, adding with a cluck that it was a shame I wasn't putting them to their God-given use.

Maybe I could borrow a neighbor's phone to call a locksmith and convince them that I'd locked myself out. Or maybe my cousin Gerry could come over with his toolbox and break the door down. As I sat contemplating my options, I heard more noises emanating from my apartment, not all of which I could identify. If only I could be sure Tallulah would sit patiently in front of the tube while I went for help. Then I heard her shriek, a hair-curling sound that usually meant she'd come face-to-face with Rocky the boa constrictor.

I sucked in a breath, raised my hands over my head, and pushed myself into the opening.

Tom arrived for our date shortly after eight o'clock. I heard my intercom buzz, but I couldn't press the button because I was wedged half in, half out of my pantry. My head, arms, and upper torso were hanging into the pantry, while my hips, ass, and legs dangled into the hallway.

My buzzer sounded again. Tom probably thought he'd been stood up. I wondered what he was thinking as he repeatedly pressed the buzzer and got no response. "My date's wedged into a hole in the wall" was probably far down on his mental multiple choice list.

I wriggled my body some more but it was no use. There was no moving forward or back. I felt like Winnie-the-Pooh, stuck in the rabbit hole. But while he had the gang from Hundred Acre Woods pitching in to help him out of any old jam, there I was, all alone.

I heard something smash and was reminded of Tallulah's presence in my living room. The pint-sized primate surely lacked the strength to pull me free, but perhaps there was another way she could get me out of my current predicament. Capuchin monkeys are very intelligent—perhaps the smartest of all the monkey species, which is why they can be trained to act as helper animals for the disabled.

I called her name and added a few clicking sounds to get her attention. I heard her drop the remote; then she popped into view. She stood in the doorway of the pantry and stuck her tongue out at me—a gesture I'd learned was an expression of affection in Tallulah's world.

"Hey, Tallulah," I said to the monkey. "Unlock the door. Go get help."

She cocked her head quizzically to one side, the monkey equivalent of a shoulder shrug. I could tell she was thinking, *What did you get yourself into now?*

"Get help," I repeated. "Holly's stuck in the wall."

But she just sat there. She might be smart, but she's no Lassie.

Tallulah cast a glance back toward the living room as though wondering if her show was back from commercial break. I was losing her attention.

"Phone," I shouted. "Bring me the phone!"

Tallulah was trained to retrieve objects, like telephone receivers, and she responded to several voice commands in addition to the laser pointer.

She pranced away and returned moments later with the TV remote, which she put in my hand.

"No, not the remote, the phone. *Telephone!*"

She took the remote and was gone. Instead of returning with the phone, she cranked the volume up on the TV and began shrieking in concert with a car commercial.

Ten minutes earlier, I had thought that being stuck in the wall of my apartment was the worst thing that could happen on my six-month anniversary. Now I knew better. The worst thing that could happen was being stuck in the wall of my apartment and having to pee.

I sucked in my stomach and tried to wriggle around to find a more comfortable position. I took some shallow, panting breaths, which Maya the militant Lamaze instructor had said would ease the pain of contractions, but they just made me light-headed. I closed my eyes and prayed for a miracle.

After three tries, whoever had been ringing my buzzer had given up. Tom wouldn't have just gone home, would he? On our anniversary? After I'd gone to so much trouble to prepare the perfect night of seduction? My indignation was almost enough to take my mind off my ready-to-burst bladder.

I'd tried screaming for help, but either no one heard me or nobody cared. This was Manhattan, after all. Screams for help were routinely ignored. My college psych instructor had called it by-stander apathy. I called it a real sucky attitude.

I tried a different approach. "Free pizza in 6B," I screamed at the top of my lungs. "Extra pepperoni!" It wasn't an empty promise, either. I'd gladly buy pizza for the entire building if someone would get me out of this damn hole.

The thought of pizza made my stomach growl. I hadn't eaten in hours. I reached for the mound of gummy bears, but they were beyond my grasp.

Moments later I heard a door open and the sound of little feet running on my landing. Then I felt a tap on my right foot. "Is this where the pizza is?" a boy asked. Probably one of the kids in 6D, whose names I could never remember.

"Kevin?"

"Kyle," he corrected me. "Is the pizza in there? I don't smell pizza."

"Is your mommy with you?"

"No. She said to get the pizza and bring it back to her. She has a head egg and don't feel like cooking."

"A head egg?"

"Yeah. It's like when you get a stomach egg except it's in your head. Where's the pizza?"

"It's not here yet. You have to get someone to help me out of here. Then I'll call and order it."

"That's so retarded." He ran back down the hallway. "Come get me when the pizza's here!"

"Wait! Tell your mommy I need help!"

The phone rang. I hung my head, knowing it was futile to ask Tallulah to bring it to me.

And then she appeared in the pantry, cradling the receiver against her ear and making tittering sounds into the mouthpiece.

I reached out one hand. "Give me the phone."

Tallulah paused only momentarily to glance at the heap of gummy bears on the floor before placing the phone in my hand. *Yes!*

"Hello!" I shouted to my potential rescuer. "Whoever you are, I love you."

"I guess that means you're not mad at me," Tom said, his voice low. "Was that Tallulah?"

"Yes. You'll never believe what happened. Mad at you? Why?" I was rambling, so relieved to have contact with someone who could save me. "You're the one who should be—"

Tom broke in. "I can't make it tonight. It's Nicole. Well, actually, Bianca."

Something about the way Tom said his ex-wife's name sent chills up my spine. He rarely mentioned her at all, and when he did talk about her, he had a way of saying her name as though he was discussing a hemorrhoid remedy. But even in my current distressed state, I detected something softhearted in the way he'd just said it.

"Bi-an-ca?" I repeated, slowly, my ears poised on high alert.

Tallulah, who had settled near the pile of gummy bears, pricked up her ears. Even the monkey sensed danger.

There was a moment of silence on the other end of the phone. When Tom spoke, his voice was low, barely above a whisper.

"She's here," he said. "She wants to talk."

"Nicole?" I asked, deliberately misunderstanding.

"Bianca," he said, and the tenderness with which he said it sent a stab into the center of my heart. "She's upset. It's about Nicole."

"Is she okay?" I asked, then added quickly, "Nicole, I mean," to underscore the fact that I didn't give a damn about Bianca's well-being.

"She's fine," he said. "One of the teachers at her school said something to Bianca about children of divorce, and it got her thinking that we should all go to family counseling."

"All of us?"

"Well, no." Tom hesitated. "Just Nicole, Bianca, and me."

Duh.

I let this sink in for a moment. My boyfriend was going to see a family counselor with his ex-wife and their daughter. I had blown my rent money on a dress I would never be able to afford, to seduce a man I would never be able to call my own. Suddenly, being stuck in my milk door didn't seem like my biggest problem.

"I just wanted to let you know I can't make dinner," Tom was saying. I wondered who had been ringing my buzzer, if not him. "I'll come by later. You'll be there?"

"I don't have much choice," I said. "I'm kind of . . . stuck."

"Babysitting Tallulah again?" he asked, but didn't wait for my answer. "Well, you girls have fun. Tell her I'll bring her something later."

Then he was gone and I was listening to the dial tone.

3

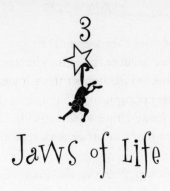

Jaws of Life

The urge to laugh almost overpowered the need to cry. But not quite. I bit my lower lip as tears spilled down my cheeks. Tallulah hopped to my side and swatted my face with her slender fingers in an awkward attempt to wipe my tears away.

I took a deep breath and told myself to get a grip. There'd be plenty of time to cry later. First I had to get myself free. At least now I had a phone.

"Who should I call?" I asked Tallulah as I ran through a mental list of friends and family. I probably should call David to explain why I hadn't returned with Tallulah yet, but I didn't want to alarm him when there was nothing he could do to help. Best to wait on that one.

Aunt Kuki was out of the question. To her, my entire life was a series of missteps and disasters that had begun the day I left her home for my apartment in the big, bad city and a misguided career in stand-up comedy. My current predicament would become just one more piece of evidence she'd trot out at family dinners to prove my incompetence at living on my own.

My cousin Gerry would rush to my aid, no questions asked, but since he couldn't keep a secret, he was out.

Ditto Aunt Betty. Besides, even if Betty was up for a late-night cab ride into the city, she had the upper-body strength of a gnat and would never be able to dislodge me from my present position.

Monica Broccoli could undoubtedly free me from the wall with one well-placed kick from her size nine stilettos, but she harbored so much hostility toward me I didn't think it wise to let her see me in such a vulnerable position.

For a brief moment I contemplated dialing 911, but I cringed at the thought of having yet another accident report on file somewhere. If the emergency medical technicians gave out frequent-customer points, I'd have earned myself a free toaster oven by now. It was embarrassing how often I'd utilized their services. Since I couldn't think of a reason for being stuck in the wall that would look good on paper, I opted to keep the uniforms out of it.

I also hated having to explain why I had a monkey, a boa constrictor, and numerous other small creatures in my apartment, unbeknownst to my landlord or the city authorities.

I banged the receiver against my forehead in frustration. In the past, I'd always called my best friend, Carter. But she and Danny had abandoned me for life in Los Angeles. True, they'd asked me to go with them, but I didn't want to be a third wheel, and besides, I really loved my life in Manhattan.

Most of the time.

Without thinking I dropped the phone, and Tallulah snatched it up before I could react. She scooted just out of my reach and sat with her back to me, pushing buttons.

"Stop playing with the phone!" I scolded her, worrying that she'd accidentally call the operator. Or worse, that she'd hit the speed-dial button I'd programmed with Aunt Kuki's number. "Give me the phone," I commanded in the sternest tone I could muster.

Tallulah turned around and looked at me, then cradled the phone to her chest and skipped away, out of sight.

"Holly? Is that you?" My neighbor Brian's voice interrupted my tortured reverie.

"Brian!" I shouted, waves of relief washing over me. "Thank goodness you're here."

"It *is* you," he said. "I didn't recognize you from this angle."

It wasn't surprising that Brian couldn't ID my backside. He was gay, after all, and probably not accustomed to checking out women's butts. But it was nonetheless comforting to know that when he saw a body protruding from the wall, I didn't immediately jump to mind. "Do you think you could pull me out?"

"Sure." He grabbed both legs and tugged. "What happened?"

"I locked myself out of my apartment and thought I could get in this way."

Brian let out a bark of laughter. "Someone miscalculated her girth."

"It's not funny," I said. "I have to pee, I was stood up by my date, and Tallulah is in the next room, most likely calling Brazil."

"Monkey girl's trapped in there? Why didn't you tell me?" He yanked my legs much harder this time. The steel sides of the milk doorframe cut into my rib cage.

"Ouch!"

"Sorry," Brian said. "But you're really wedged in tight."

I sucked in my breath and willed myself skinny as Brian tried again. My breasts, which hadn't been much of an obstacle when I'd pushed through the opening, were now putting up a protest. As he pulled my lower body, my upper body became like an over-inflated balloon.

"My boobs are in the way," I yelled.

"Since when do you have boobs?" Brian said, yanking with all his might. It seemed like he was making progress, but all he managed to do was inch my jeans down over my hip bones.

"Maybe I should go upstairs and get some shortening. I bet if we grease up your midsection, you'll slide right out."

Getting greased up by my gay neighbor was not how I'd envisioned spending my six-month anniversary, but what the hell?

"Maybe you should try from inside the apartment," I suggested. "Come down the fire escape and let yourself in through the window."

"Good idea," he said. "That way I can talk to your face instead of your ass."

For the first time since Danny and I broke up our comedy act, I regretted leaving stand-up comedy. In the past, I'd been able to take whatever went wrong in my life—bad breakups, accidental injuries, humiliating family gatherings—and, once the pain subsided, milk it for laughs onstage. But instead of the club scene, my comedy now catered to six-year-olds. My personal life was of no interest to them, but they howled with glee whenever one of my animals went wee-wee in the classroom.

I heard a crash coming from the living room. Tallulah gave an alarmed shriek.

"It's okay, monkey girl. It's just me," Brian said. There was some more smashing and cursing, and then Brian appeared in the pantry. "Sorry. I tripped and knocked over a lamp on my way through the window."

"I don't care. Just get me out of here."

"Mmm, gummy bears." He kicked the candies aside to clear a path to the milk door. "I couldn't find any shortening, but I have this." He held up a plastic bottle whose hot pink label read MR. SLICK'S LOVE GEL.

My lip curled involuntarily. Beggars can't be choosers, I suppose.

"It was a gag gift," Brian said, swatting my head playfully. "It's not even opened."

"Uh-huh."

He uncapped the bottle. "Mmmm. Cinnamon scented."

Tallulah rounded the corner, still holding the telephone. She dropped it and leapt onto Brian's shoulder. She reached for the plastic bottle.

"You wanna try some?" Brian asked, squeezing a dollop onto the monkey's outstretched hands before I could protest.

"Great. How am I going to explain to David why she came home smelling like Mr. Slick's Cinnamon-Flavored Love Gel?"

He tossed his head dismissively. "Let him wonder."

Tallulah rubbed the gel all over her face and head. Now her hair was sticking up in a little monkey Mohawk.

Brian tugged my T-shirt until my midriff was exposed. "This might be a little cold," he said. A big blob of gooey gel landed on my lower back.

"Yikes! Do you keep it in the freezer?"

"Don't worry. It warms on contact"—he cleared his throat and added—"according to the label."

Brian began rubbing the gel onto my back, sliding his hands as far as he could into the doorway. Within seconds, my skin was sticky and tingling hot, and my pantry smelled like the inside of Cinnabon. Tallulah was licking her lips and salivating.

Brian squeezed another glob of gel onto his hands, then crouched down low to slather it onto my stomach.

"Suck in," he said, and I did as instructed. I gave a yelp of surprise as his hands slid underneath the waistband of my jeans. "Don't get any ideas, princess," he said. "Just doin' a job here."

I'd started out the evening hoping a man's hands would end up in my pants, but this wasn't what I had in mind. I closed my eyes and tried to remember the breathing exercises I'd learned in Lamaze class.

"What are you doing?" Brian asked.

"Lamaze," I said.

"Oh, my God, are you pregnant? I thought you seemed a little bulgy around the middle."

I contemplated smacking him, but resisted the temptation since at the moment he was my only hope for rescue. "No, I'm not pregnant. I'm Carter's coach."

"Thank God," Brian said. "I was afraid we might be squishing little Tommykins in there."

"No. Just big Hollykins and a bladder that's about to burst."

Brian grabbed a towel from the counter, wiped his hands, and recapped the bottle of love gel. "You're all lubed up and ready to roll."

"Uncle, uncle!" I cried. "I can't take it anymore."

Brian had been pulling for several minutes. My exposed skin was covered with scratches where it had been scraped against the steel door. He'd gotten me a half foot farther through the opening, but my hips were unapologetically stuck.

"I think we need help. Someone to push from the outside while I pull from in here," Brian said. "Where's that hunky boyfriend of yours?"

"On a date with his wife," I groaned.

Brian patted the top of my head. "Not your day, is it?" He pulled a cell phone out of his pocket. "I'll call Pete."

"He's not home. I tried him already."

"It's ringing . . . ringing . . . ringing . . . voice mail." He hung up without leaving a message.

"Is Mrs. Mete home?" I asked.

"Mrs. Mete can't open an aspirin bottle without assistance. Think she can get you out of here?"

"No. I was just wondering if you'd seen her. She didn't come to the door before."

"Maybe *Wheel of Fortune* was on." He was scrolling through numbers on his cell phone. "I'd call Andrew, but it will take him too long to get here," Brian said. "Ditto Darryl." He flipped his phone closed. "I know you don't like paramedics, but I think it's time to call nine-one-one. Maybe they'll use the jaws of life on you."

"No paramedics, no police. I didn't mention this before, but I'm behind in my rent, my locks have been changed, and this may actually be considered breaking and entering."

Tallulah had been quietly chomping on some cashews she'd raided from a top shelf. She tossed them aside, reached for the phone, and punched in three numbers. Then she began screeching into the mouthpiece.

Realization hit me and I shouted, "No!" Tallulah shrieked and dropped the phone. Her expression registered hurt and surprise. "Call nine-one-one" was one of her voice commands, after all, and she'd just done as she was told.

"Damn," I told Brian. "She just dialed nine-one-one."

Brian bent to retrieve the phone. "We should get her on *Letterman*," he said. "Don't worry. It disconnected when she dropped it."

I heard footsteps pounding their way up the stairwell. "There's someone on the stairs. Go see who it is."

Brian flung the phone aside and dashed out of the pantry. I heard the dead bolt on my front door click open, and he was out the door.

It was Pete, the super, and he was superpissed. He'd gotten my note. Though I hadn't signed my name, he had a hunch it was from me, since I'd written it on the back of my red eviction notice.

"This is the thanks I get for standing up for you?" he asked from the hallway. "They wanted to boot your butt out of here last month, but I said you were a sweet kid who deserved another chance." I heard the flyer flap around and imagined him waving it angrily to punctuate his sentences.

"If I'm such a sweet kid, why'd you change the locks on me?"

"I didn't change the locks."

"Then the owners must have changed them."

"No way," he said, slapping the flyer. "See here? Forty-eight hours' notice. They can't change the locks without a court order. Which they'd probably get first thing Monday morning."

"She can't see that," Brian pointed out helpfully. Then to me, he said, "He's holding a red piece of paper that says 'Final Notice' on it. Let me see that." A moment later, Brian said, "He's right. This says you have until Monday to pay up or quit the premises."

"Then why won't the lock work?"

"Where's your key?" Pete asked. Without waiting for an answer, he felt my back pockets like a cop doing a pat down.

"Hey!" I shouted as his hands slid around my front. He thrust his fingers into my right front pocket and wriggled my keys out.

Damn. The second time in one night a man had had his hands in my pants, and it was still the wrong man.

Pete marched to my front door and turned the knob. "It's not even locked," he shouted.

"I opened it," Brian said, "I went down the fire escape and came in through the window." Then, to preempt Pete's next question, he said, "She was already stuck when I got here."

I heard Pete mumble something that sounded like "dumb chick" as he fumbled with the keys. "Key's bent a little," he said, "but it works."

I was baffled. "It probably got bent when I was trying to force it. But it wouldn't turn before, I swear."

"Locks stick," Pete said on a grunt, "especially in summer. No reason to write nasty notes."

Some people have all the luck. They find quarters in pay phones and arrive at the subway platform just as their train is pulling in to the station. Vacant cabs materialize out of thin air the moment they stick their arm into the air to hail one. They never break a heel in the subway grate when running late for a job interview or accidentally squeeze Binaca instead of Visine into their eyes moments before going onstage.

If those people have *all* the luck, it stands to reason that an equal number of people have exactly *none* of the luck. And I was obviously one of the unlucky souls that had been sacrificed by fate to endure a life of unrelenting ill fortune and bad timing. The lock stuck. I'd gotten myself into this predicament because the *freaking lock stuck?*

"She'll be more patient next time," Brian told him.

"There's not gonna be a next time," Pete said, firmly slapping my behind. "Unless she comes up with two grand by Monday morning."

I kicked out reflexively but didn't connect. "Just 'cause I'm trapped doesn't mean you can take a free grope!"

"He just affixed the eviction notice to your ass," Brian explained. "It's quite a visual."

"I'm outta here," Pete said.

"Wait," Brian called. "Can you help me get her out of the wall?"

There was a long pause. Then Pete said something about a sledgehammer and stomped down the stairs.

"Did he say *sledgehammer?*" I asked Brian.

"Heave!" Pete shouted as he shoved my lower body toward the door with unrestrained zeal.

"Ho!" Brian responded as he pulled with equal fervor.

The sound of sirens in the distance made me question my decision to forgo calling for professional help. If I'd called 911 when I first got hold of the telephone, I'd be free by now. On my way to the pokey perhaps, but I'd still have my internal organs intact, and they'd probably let me use the bathroom before putting me in lockup.

"Ouch," I squealed. "Could you heave a little harder, and ease up on the ho?"

They ignored me and continued heaving and hoing. They'd

loosened the plaster around the doorway, and with each heave-ho, more chunks fell from the opening and landed on the floor. Unfortunately, they'd been unable to make a dent in the steel doorframe, so they were back to trying to shove me through it. I was no longer worried about surface scrapes and scratches; I now feared I'd sustained internal injuries.

"It'll go quicker if we take your jeans off," Pete said, tugging at my pant leg.

"No!" It was bad enough I'd heard a handful of neighbors stop on the stairs to gape at the six-car pileup otherwise known as my life. If my half-naked lower half was hanging out in the hallway, there'd be no end to the gawking and squawking.

"Just a thought."

One last ho and I was through the opening. Brian toppled backward and I landed on top of him.

"Ooof." Brian rolled me off him, and we both lay sprawled on our backs, trying to catch our breath. Tallulah bobbed her head excitedly, then settled at my side and popped a gummy bear into my mouth.

A little blond head popped through the opening. "Is the pizza here yet?"

"Kyle?"

"Kevin. Kyle's my brother." He didn't question the mess, the three adults panting and sweating, or the monkey in the middle of it all, noticing only the candy that was spilled all over the floor. "Did you break a piñata in here?"

"Yeah," I said. I handed him the remains of the plastic gummy bear bag and said, *"Feliz Navidad."*

He grabbed the bag and ran in the direction of his apartment.

The sirens grew louder. Brian and I exchanged a worried glance as my buzzer sounded and the downstairs door was kicked in.

"What the hell?" Pete said as he charged down the stairs.

"How do I look?" Brian asked, brushing plaster pieces off his pants and running his fingers through his hair.

Brian, a soap opera star, looked none the worse for our adventure. If anything, his faintly glistening forehead and rolled-up shirtsleeves made him all the more attractive. He looked ready for a photo shoot, while I looked like I should be shot.

"Quick, what's our cover story?" he asked.

My mind was racing. I couldn't think of anything except my urgent need to urinate. Then I remembered something that had been nagging at me since I got home. "Mrs. Mete."

"What?" he asked, the question drowned out by the sound of at least a half dozen men stampeding up the six flights of stairs leading to my apartment.

I pushed him toward my front door. "I think something's wrong with her."

The stampede was getting closer. I unbuttoned my jeans, yanked the eviction notice off my butt, and raced toward the bathroom. "Hurry, bring them up to Mrs. Mete's."

"You'd think with all this pounding and screaming, the nosy old biddy would have been down here by now."

"Exactly." I burst through the bathroom door as Brian raced out of my apartment, slamming my door behind him.

An emergency medical technician named Eddie was nodding his head but looking like he didn't believe a word I'd said. His pen was poised over his clipboard, but he wasn't writing anything down.

Two other EMTs had carried Mrs. Mete down on a stretcher, with Pete leading the way. She had taken a fall that morning and most likely broken her hip, Eddie said. She was pale and her blood pressure was dangerously low, but she was alive. As they passed my floor, she pulled off her oxygen mask and thanked me for calling the paramedics.

"I screamed *help* for hours, but no one came," she said weakly.

"Next time, try yelling 'pizza,'" I'd said as the EMTs repositioned the mask and continued down the stairs.

Brian followed behind them. "I'm gonna go to the hospital and make sure she's all right," he said. He tossed me an I♥NY key chain with a single key on it. I recognized it as the spare he'd give me whenever he left town and needed me to feed his cat. "Just in case." He winked and trotted down the stairs.

"Thanks," I said, pocketing the key and turning back to Eddie, who was regarding me dourly. "The call came from this apartment, but the nine-one-one operator just heard some screaming before the line went dead." He craned his neck to see around me into my apartment. "She said it didn't sound human."

As if on cue, Tallulah came up behind me and climbed onto my back. She loved meeting new people, especially men in uniform. I tried to restrain her as I explained to Eddie that she was a licensed helper monkey temporarily in my care. "She made the call," I said. "She's trained to dial nine-one-one in an emergency."

"Why didn't you make the call yourself?"

"I was . . . unavoidably detained."

Tallulah made a clucking sound with her tongue, as though she found my explanation to be woefully inadequate.

Eddie's eyes were set to grim but the edges of his mouth turned up in a barely perceptible smile. Sensing that the monkey might be the key to winning his understanding, I nudged her toward him. "Say hello to the nice man," I encouraged.

Tallulah took the bait, leaping from my shoulder to his. She rubbed her head against his cheek, and he looked like he was going to melt.

"She's so soft," he cooed.

I smiled. "She likes you, I can tell."

As if to prove her adoration, Tallulah began combing her fingers through his hair and making chattering sounds in his ear.

"Your wife's gonna be jealous," I teased.

"I'm not . . . married," he said, giving me a meaningful look. Suddenly self-conscious, I glanced down at my torn-and-bloodied T-shirt and my jeans, which were stained with body oil and coated with plaster dust. I didn't need to look in a mirror to know that my makeup had worn off and my hair had seen better decades. Either Eddie was hard up or I was misreading his signals.

"Can I come in?" Eddie asked, taking a step closer. "Is that cinnamon?"

I held my ground, blocking his entry. While the EMTs were upstairs with Mrs. Mete, I'd made a quick pass through my apartment, sweeping up plaster and candy, uprighting lamps, and trying to undo the worst of the damage from Hurricane Tallulah. I'd hidden Rocky and the rest of my undocumented pets in the bedroom. Still, I didn't want to risk letting anyone remotely affiliated with the city of Manhattan into my apartment.

"Of course I don't mind," I lied. "But I really have to get Tallulah back to her owner. He's probably worried sick."

Eddie furrowed his brow. "Her owner?"

I nodded. "He lives on Eighteenth Street. He's paralyzed and—"

"Then let's go!" He turned and charged down the stairs, Tallulah clinging to his back and chattering excitedly. A man and a monkey on a mission.

I scooped up Tallulah's laser pointer and leash, stuck my keys in my pocket, and shut the door behind me.

4

Some Enchanted Evening

It was after eleven when I let myself into my building and staggered up the stairs to my apartment. Normally the six-flight hike takes less than two minutes, but I was physically and emotionally spent. I could barely muster the energy to reach into my pocket for my keys. Then I remembered I hadn't locked the door, a realization that would normally send me into paroxysms of panic, but in my bruised-and-battered state barely registered as a footnote to my disastrous day.

Besides, if my apartment had been looted while I was gone, there'd just be less junk to cart to the curb when my eviction became final. As long as my animals were safe inside, who cared about the rest of it?

The smell of fresh plaster greeted me when I reached my landing. My milk cubby was gone, a large plaster patch in its place. I groaned. I supposed I couldn't blame Pete for getting rid of my milk cubby, but not having it was going to put a crimp in my business activities.

I took a moment to mourn its loss before trudging to my front door. I pushed the door open and found Tom sitting on my sofa, a take-out bag from Hong Kong Palace on the coffee table in front of him.

He stood when I entered. "The door was unlocked," he said, crossing to me. "What happened here?"

I looked around and saw that despite my quick cleanup job, there was still plenty of evidence of the evening's mayhem—including the now-empty bottle of Mr. Slick's Cinnamon-Flavored Love Gel, which was lying in the middle of the dining room floor. I kicked it aside, preferring not to explain its presence at the moment. "It's a long story."

I hurried to my bedroom and opened the door. Grouch jumped off the bed and ran past me into the kitchen, where he began howling mournfully at the sight of his empty food bowl. I did a quick head count of the rest of my pets before hobbling to the kitchen to feed Grouch.

Tom came up behind me as I filled Grouch's dish. "Thank God you're all right," he said. "The place is a mess. The phone was off the hook. I was worried."

"Tallulah and I had a slumber party. It got a little out of hand."

He wrapped his arms around me and I let out an involuntary yelp.

"What is it?" he said, taking in the blood and crud on my clothes and the gauze peeking out from the rips in my shirt. "Are those bandages?"

I nodded and lifted the front of my shirt.

After Eddie had returned Tallulah to a much-relieved David, he'd tried to take me to the emergency room at St. Vincent's. Finally noticing my blood-soaked shirt, he felt duty bound to help me, despite my assurance that my wounds were superficial. I'd broken down and told him the whole stupid story, including my inability to afford either rent or emergency medical treatment.

"Go rescue someone who really needs it," I'd told him.

"You need it."

"Maybe. But I can't pay for it."

He'd taken pity on me and agreed to let me go home, but only after he and his partner had examined my cuts and bruises and were convinced the damage wasn't serious.

"Where does it hurt?" he had asked.

"Everywhere," I complained, "but especially my hip bones."

"I don't think you fractured anything," Eddie said, just after becoming the third man to have his hands in my pants that night. "But you have some second-degree bruising." He applied ointment to my cuts and wrapped gauze around my rib cage. "If the pain worsens, I want you to go to the hospital."

After extracting my promise, and agreeing to leave any incriminating details out of his official report, Eddie had dropped me in front of my building.

Now I was repeating the story to Tom, who was regarding me with a mixture of shock and regret.

"You mean you were stuck in the wall when I called?" he asked. "Why didn't you say something?"

"Because you were with Biaaaaanca," I said, knowing I sounded like a whiny six-year-old and not caring.

My stomach growled. Aside from a few sugar cookies at the Lamaze class and the single gummy bear Tallulah had fed me, I hadn't eaten anything all evening. I turned my attention to the bag of Chinese food on my coffee table, the thought of moo goo gai pan lightening my mood and almost making me forget about Bianca.

"Is that for us?" I asked Tom. "I hope you got extra egg rolls, 'cause I'm starving."

He shook his head. "I already ate with Bianca," he said. "I brought you the leftovers."

The male mind is truly astounding. His voice devoid of any trace of irony, Tom had suggested that I eat leftovers from his dinner with his ex-wife, as though it was the most reasonable thing in the world. After all, food is food, and I was hungry, and we were all mature adults, right?

Wrong.

I stormed into my bedroom, tore the slinky red overpriced dress off its hanger, and returned to the living room. I opened the bag of leftovers, stuck the dress inside, and handed the whole package to Tom. "Happy anniversary," I said.

I could tell by his expression he was mentally backtracking, trying to determine what he had said that set me off. He opened the bag and looked inside. "Nice dress," he said, lifting it out.

"Maybe it will fit Bianca," I pouted.

It was frightening how quickly I was regressing into early childhood. A little while ago I was acting like a six-year-old. Now I felt all of four. Any minute now, I'd stick my tongue out and call him a poopy head.

"Hold on," he said. "You're not jealous, are you?"

I folded my arms across my chest but didn't say anything. Truth is, I didn't know the answer to his question. I couldn't pinpoint my feelings. Exhaustion, frustration, and fear were roiling around in my chest, along with a dash of rage and a whole lot of hurt. Jealousy might be mixed in there somewhere, but I couldn't be certain until I sorted the rest of it out. I felt tears welling and bit my lower lip to keep myself from crying.

Tom put one arm around my shoulder and pulled me toward him. My resolve crumbled and I snuggled into his embrace.

"You're greasy," he said, stepping back and examining the residue on his hands. "Why don't you shower? And then we'll talk."

I nodded numbly and let him lead me to the bathroom.

Showering was out of the question due to my bandaged ribs, but I took a shallow bath, gingerly washing my skin until my lavender-scented soap began to obscure the cinnamony smell. I was carefully picking plaster out of my hair when I heard the buzzer ring.

I glanced at the wall clock. It was five to midnight. I couldn't imagine who would be ringing my buzzer at this time of night—unless Eddie the EMT was returning to fill in some more blanks on his official form.

"Ignore it!" I called out to Tom, but it was too late. I heard Tom say, "Yes?" and then a voice crackled through the speaker. I strained to hear, but from my spot in the tub, I couldn't identify the voice or make out the words. *Definitely male,* I thought, suddenly wishing I could slip down the drain with the bath water.

If it *was* Eddie, I hoped he wouldn't mention anything to Tom about having his hands in my pants earlier in the evening. While it had been a purely professional act—he was palpating my pelvis to check for broken bones—I had to admit that my blood pressure had shot up and my heart had skipped a beat during the brief examination. Under the circumstances, I was certain both reactions were perfectly normal, medically speaking. I wasn't so sure about the tiny tingle I felt when Eddie's fingers brushed the top of my underwear.

Tom knocked on the bathroom door as I was stepping out of the bathtub. Before I could reach for a towel, the door opened and our eyes met. He lowered his gaze and let out a single, startled utterance. "Ugh."

Not exactly the reaction I'd wanted when my boyfriend saw me completely naked for the first time.

He quickly realized his mistake and began sputtering apologies, his ability to form complete sentences apparently suspended the moment he saw my battered body in the buff. "I didn't mean . . . wow . . . bruises . . . are you . . . can I . . . zowie . . ." He trailed off, causing me to wonder how bad I must look to have rendered an NYU English professor incapable of comprehensible speech.

I bundled myself in my bathrobe. "Who was at the door? And please tell me you didn't let them up."

He nodded, still speechless, and followed me into the living room. From the amount of noise coming from my staircase it seemed Tom had buzzed a herd of buffalo into the building.

I opened the door to my apartment and leaned over the railing. My cousin Gerry's face came into view, as he rounded a corner a few flights down. Someone, most likely Monica Broccoli, was stomping up the stairs behind him.

My relief that my gentleman caller wasn't Eddie the paramedic dissipated the instant I saw that not only Monica but also my aunts Betty and Kuki and my uncle Leo were trailing behind Gerry. They followed him single file, convoy-style, Betty pulling up the rear, red-faced and grasping the railing for support.

"Holy cow," I said, dashing to my bedroom, "what are *they* doing here?"

"I called them," Tom said.

I stopped at the door to my bedroom, dumbstruck. "You *called* them? You called *them*?"

I marched to my dresser and pulled out a clean T-shirt and jeans. I let my robe fall to the floor and quickly shimmied into the jeans. I no longer cared about Tom seeing me naked—the important thing was getting dressed before the convoy arrived.

"I didn't know what else to do, so I called everyone on your speed dial, asking if they'd seen you." He shrugged his shoulders helplessly. "I was worried. There was blood in the pantry, a sledgehammer in the hall, and one of your neighbors said he'd seen ambulances out front."

I yanked the T-shirt over my head. "You talked to my *neighbors,* too?"

"Just the ones that were home. The kid next door says you owe him pizza."

Gerry was first to burst through my door. "Holly!" he said, wrapping me in a bear hug. "Thank God you're okay."

"I'm fine." I winced, as pain stabbed my ribs. "I got stuck in my milk door. No biggie."

Monica Broccoli limped in behind him, dragging her left leg dramatically across the threshold even though we both knew she'd just charged up six flights of stairs like a linebacker on steroids. "What's going on?"

Kuki was next. She marched toward me with one finger extended. "I told you something like this would happen."

"You did?" I remembered Kuki warning me against rapists, robbers, muggers, and flashers, but she never said anything about wedging myself into ten-inch steel-rimmed openings.

"Don't be sarcastic." She bent to retrieve something from the floor. "Mr. Slick's Love Gel?" she read, then dropped the bottle as though it was on fire. She turned and gave Tom a long head-to-toe appraisal. "What in God's good name is going on here?"

Tom looked at me, unsure how, or if, to respond to Kuki's question. I opened my mouth to speak but was cut short by my uncle Leo, who burst through the door and ran directly into my bathroom shouting something I couldn't understand.

"What did he say?" I asked Aunt Kuki.

She pursed her lips. "He took a"—her voice dropped to a whisper as she uttered the last word—"*laxative.*" She looked around to make sure Tom hadn't heard, but he'd been cornered by Gerry and Monica, who were volleying questions at him. "Before we got the call," Kuki said, leaning in close. "It started kicking in on the ride over."

"Yeesh," I said, wishing I hadn't asked. "Why didn't he just stay home?"

"He wanted to, but I needed him to drive the station wagon. I can't drive that boat in the city. People drive like maniacs here."

My eyes bugged. "You brought the wagon? Why didn't you just take a cab?"

"I figured we'd need the station wagon to load up all your stuff and move you back home."

Betty appeared in my doorway, huffing and puffing and clutching her handbag. She sucked in air and headed straight for my sofa, where she plopped down with a sigh.

It was official. Every person I had intentionally not phoned for help was now in my apartment, all raising their voices to be heard over the others. Despite my attempts at subterfuge, my secrets were out in the open. At least they didn't know about my money troubles, I told myself. That would be the last bit of ammo Kuki would need to put me over her shoulder and carry me kicking and screaming back to Brooklyn.

"Where's Uncle Bernie?" I asked Betty.

She stuck a finger in the air and made a circular motion. She was still struggling for breath, so I hurried to the kitchen and returned with a glass of water. After taking a few gulps, she said, "He's circling the block looking for a parking space."

In my neighborhood, parking spots were rarer than heterosexual hairdressers. I doubted we'd be seeing Bernie anytime soon.

"Why's your milk door boarded over?" Gerry asked, returning from the pantry.

"And why is there blood on the floor?" Monica added.

"Blood?" Kuki asked. "What on earth?"

"It was nothing," I yelled above the clamor. "The lock was stuck and I really wanted to get in my apartment to get ready for my date." I shot Tom an accusing look. If I'd known he'd break our date, I wouldn't have felt such urgency to break in. "I thought I could get in through the milk door."

Monica arched one eyebrow. "With *those* hips?"

"She's right," Kuki said. "You have childbearing hips." She shook her head sadly, but thankfully said nothing about my failure to test my hips' ability to bear large and plentiful babies.

Tom looked apologetic. "I was just trying to find out if you were all right. I wish you had a cell phone. Then I could have reached you."

"Yeah," Monica said. "You're like the last American under thirty who doesn't have a cell phone."

I rolled my eyes. Most months I could barely afford rent and my daily dose of Starbucks; there was seldom money left over for non-essentials like cell phones and groceries.

"Even *I* got a cell phone," Betty announced, lifting up her sweater to reveal a phone clipped onto the waistband of her skirt. "Of course, it's just for emergencies."

Okay, so maybe I was the last American under *eighty* without a cell phone.

There was a moment of silence, and I knew what everyone was thinking: I had more emergencies than both my elderly aunts combined, and while they never left home without their cell phones, rape whistles, medic-alert bracelets, laminated emergency contact cards—perhaps even flare guns and antivenom kits—I'd be shocked if my first-aid kit had so much as a Band-Aid in it.

"It's a camera phone," Betty continued. "But I can't figure out how to use the darn thing. It keeps taking pictures all on its own. I got seventy-three photographs of the inside of my pocketbook."

My phone rang and I lunged for it, eager to talk to anyone besides my family, and not even questioning who would be calling me after midnight.

"Hello?"

"How's Lamaze?" Carter asked.

"Fine," I said. "Aunt Betty really made an impression on the class."

Betty smiled and wiggled her fingers.

"Good. I can't wait for you to get here. Danny's driving me crazy with his idiotic baby name suggestions."

"What is it now?"

Carter and Danny had been battling over baby names ever since they learned they were having a boy. The only thing they agreed upon was that their child would not have an ordinary name—no John or David or Robert or Mark for the son of Carter the punk-haired yoga instructor and Danny the wise-ass stand-up comedian. Now that they'd gone Hollywood, the poor kid would probably be saddled with a highly symbolic and utterly unpronounceable name.

They each had been calling me periodically, trying to enlist my support in the baby-naming war. A few days ago, Carter had phoned in tears. She wanted to name the baby Mahatma, in honor of Gandhi, one of her spiritual heroes, but Danny wanted to name him after one of his own idols, Shecky Greene. "Can you imagine me at PTA meetings? 'Hi, I'm Shecky's mom,' " Carter had cried. I didn't have the heart to tell her I couldn't imagine her at a PTA meeting, period.

Shecky versus Mahatma had ended in a stalemate, and now Carter's top choice was Harm, short for harmony. Danny had different ideas.

"Ling-Chao-Kim or Juan Felipe," Carter wailed. "Can you believe—"

Then Carter was gone and Danny's voice was booming over the line. "Picture it, Holly. A bunch of kids on a playground. Someone yells 'Ling-Chao-Kim' and our little white-bread kid comes running. It'll be hysterical."

I heard Carter screaming in the background, "Our baby is not a punch line!"

Monica had disappeared into my bedroom and returned with Rocky, my boa constrictor, wrapped around her shoulders. Rocky had once been Monica's pet, but when the snake had threatened her relationship with Gerry, she'd foisted it upon me. I'd been terrified of Rocky at first, but we'd since settled into a peaceful coexistence. I could even handle him without trembling too much—a good thing since he was one of the stars of my Critter Comedy classroom presentations.

No matter how comfortable I became with Rocky, I doubted I'd ever express anywhere near the level of affection that Monica still displayed toward the snake. She was making kissy sounds and stroking his body. "Did wittle Wocky miss his mommy?"

"When are you coming?" Danny asked.

I surveyed my apartment. Kuki had backed Tom into a wall. She was pointing at the bottle of Love Gel and saying something about my Catholic upbringing. I couldn't make out her words because Monica and Gerry had launched into a heated argument over whether Rocky should be a member of their wedding party. Betty had made her way to the bathroom and was pounding on the door and pleading with Leo to hurry up.

"Not soon enough," I said before hanging up.

With Leo refusing to vacate the bathroom, and Betty's pleas growing more insistent, I knew I had to act fast or risk a repeat of the Lamaze incident. In my own apartment. I'd given up my pee-soaked sweatshirt because I knew I'd never be able to forget what it had been through. If Betty wet herself in my apartment, I'd probably have to move.

"Let's run down to the corner," I said to Betty. "You can use the restroom at Village Pizza."

"At this hour?" she complained.

"They're open twenty-four-seven," I said, grabbing my purse and opening the door wide. "And I haven't had dinner. So let's all go."

Betty shuffled lock-kneed out the door, followed by Gerry and Monica, who still had Rocky wrapped around her shoulders.

"No pets allowed," I pointed out.

She shrugged and disappeared into my bedroom with Rocky.

I heard more kissy sounds as she told the snake to "be a good boy for mean old Holly." She returned and darted out the door to catch up with Gerry. I raised one eyebrow but didn't say anything about her lack of a limp.

Tom was clutching his bag of take-out Chinese food. He stopped at the door, kissed my cheek, and said, "I have an early class tomorrow, and since you're in such good hands—"

I nodded. I didn't want him to go, but there really was no point in him staying. If there'd ever been any chance of us having the magically romantic evening I'd hoped for, it had evaporated the moment I'd plunged headfirst into my pantry. Or maybe it had been doomed from the start. After all, fairy tales rarely include ex-wives and eviction notices.

He pulled a few fortune cookies out of his coat pocket and handed them to me. "For Tallulah." Like nearly everyone who knew her, Tom had a soft spot for Tallulah. Which was surprising since the first time he'd tried to kiss me, she'd attacked him, forcibly prying his lips off mine. But while being mauled by a monkey might have frightened most men off, it didn't faze Tom. He'd even gone out of his way to win her over, as though he suspected the way to my heart was through the monkey.

"Happy anniversary," I muttered to his departing back. Betty was already a half flight down. Tom took her by the arm and offered to help her the rest of the way. Always the gentleman, even in retreat.

"I'll stay here with your uncle," Kuki said, gesturing toward the bathroom, where Leo had ensconced himself.

I considered the wisdom of leaving Aunt Kuki alone in my apartment. I knew from experience that she had no regard for my privacy and wouldn't hesitate to search through my belongings looking for any evidence that I wasn't living my life as she, God, and my dearly departed mother had intended. (She used that line so much during my teen years that I often envisioned the three of them convening weekly to discuss The State of Holly's Moral Development.)

Kuki could toss a room like a CSI tech, only she wouldn't leave crime-scene tape behind to advertise her actions. During the years I lived with Kuki, I'd gone through a series of hiding places, but it never took her long to ferret out my secret stashes of candy or romance novels or the succession of diaries in which I'd detailed the desperate crushes I'd harbored throughout junior high and high school.

Leaving her alone in my empty apartment would be an invitation to snoop. And there was more at stake now than her discovering my seventh-grade crush on Robby Francomano. I'd recently stocked my nightstand with various forms of birth control so that, when the time came to discuss safe sex with Tom, I'd have plenty of options on hand. Not that I'd be needing them tonight.

I shook my head. "He brought the paper in with him. He could be in there all night."

She crossed her arms and refused to budge. I was about to give in and leave her behind when I caught sight of the red eviction notice on the floor, where I'd haphazardly tossed it earlier. It was a cinch Kuki would find it and read it. By the time I made it down the stairs, Kuki would discover that not only was I mismanaging my money, but I was no stranger to the F word.

Damn, I thought. Then, just in case her powers of telepathy were as well-honed as I'd always feared, I mentally corrected myself. *Darn.*

She'd followed my gaze and seemed to be eyeing the red flyer on the floor with mounting interest. She took a step closer to the living room. I had to think fast.

"I'll move home," I blurted.

Her face beamed. "You will?"

I crossed the fingers of my right hand behind my back, already envisioning how this act of deception would go over at the next meeting of the Moral Development Squad. I nodded. Not so much because I wanted to, but because I had lost the power of speech.

Aunt Kuki clutched my arm. "That's wonderful, honey. Let's go tell everyone the good news."

5

Bingo With Betty

The phone roused me from sleep the next morning. As I reached across the bed, pain ripped through my rib cage, reminding me of the prior night's activities. As if I could ever forget.

All night long, I'd tossed and turned, thinking about Tom and his guttural reaction to seeing me nude. Had he really said "Ugh"?

Prior to meeting Tom, I'd never had a relationship that lasted more than three months. When Tom and I sailed past that marker, I had begun entertaining notions that he was *The One*. Now he was *The One Who Said Ugh*.

And had I really agreed to move back in with Aunt Kuki? How was I going to get out of that one? I'd managed to stall her last night, insisting that it was too late to start packing my belongings and promising to talk to the building manager first thing in the morning.

By the time we finished our pizza and returned to my apartment to find Leo and Bernie snoozing side by side on the sofa while *Nightline* blared in the background, Kuki had already planned the next twenty years of my life—moving back home, working alongside her in the barbershop, marrying one of the Balducci boys down the block, and bearing large and plentiful children.

I'd protested that even if I *did* move back to Brooklyn, the rest of my life would remain unchanged. She'd said, "Of course it will," through a smirk that betrayed her true feelings. She'd spent the next fifteen minutes surveying my apartment, noting which items I should pack, which I should sell, and which I should leave on the street on garbage day. Not surprisingly, she earmarked nearly all my earthly possessions for the trash heap.

The phone rang again. I lifted the receiver to my ear and grunted into the mouthpiece.

"Holly? Is that you?"

I didn't recognize the voice. I grunted again.

"When's your flight?"

"Carter?" My best friend's voice sounded unusually agitated. Even when she was a caffeine addict with a six-espresso-a-day habit, Carter never sounded this high-strung.

"The thing is, I need you here. I feel like a sumo wrestler on steroids. I'm humongous and nothing fits and I can't get comfortable and my feet are swollen and my belly itches, and this baby has a mind of his own—"

"Well, let's hope so," I interjected.

"When I finally get a chance to relax, he decides to do jujitsu in my uterus. Do you know what it's like to try to sleep with someone doing the Hokey Pokey on your bladder?"

"Uh, no."

"And cravings. You know how I said I didn't have any cravings? Well, they all hit at once. First seven months, I'm a normal person. Then month eight comes, and I'm a freak who wants to smear peanut butter on steak and eat it with a jar of green olives."

I suppressed a gag. "Gross."

"I'm getting hungry just thinking about it. And Danny is never home. Most pregnant women get to send their husbands out to the grocery store at midnight for pickles and ice cream, but Danny's always working. And when I call him he says he can't leave the set. Ever since he got this film—"

"Danny got a film role?" This was news to me. I felt slighted. Danny used to tell me everything. He was my friend and comedy partner long before he and Carter hooked up. I had been thrilled when my two best friends first started dating, naively thinking I'd see more of both of them. Instead they moved across country and started a family without me.

"Oops," Carter said. "I forgot. Danny didn't want me to tell you. He thought you'd be upset. That's another thing about pregnancy—it totally zaps your brain cells."

I let out a sigh. Danny hadn't told me because he thought I'd be jealous of his success. We'd struggled together for years, and things were finally happening for him. He'd filmed two commercials and now this. He probably felt guilty about leaving me behind. "I'm happy for him," I said with all the sincerity I could muster. "What's the film?"

"It's a chick flick. *Vets in the City.* Jennifer Aniston and Kelly Ripa are veterinarians in love with the same guy."

I groaned inwardly at the corny title even while admitting to myself it was the kind of film I'd eagerly shell out ten bucks at the box office to see—even if Danny wasn't in the cast. "Don't tell me Danny's the guy."

"No," Carter snorted. "I love Danny, but even *I* can't see Jennifer Aniston and Kelly Ripa fighting over him."

"Heather Locklear hooked up with David Spade," I countered. "Anything is possible."

"Hugh Jackman's the guy. Danny plays Kelly's kid brother."

I could see that. They were both petite, blond, and perky. "David will flip when I tell him Danny's working with Kelly Ripa," I said. "You know how Tallulah loves *Regis and Kelly.*" More specifically, Tallulah loves Regis Philbin. Among the more revelatory experiences I'd had while babysitting the monkey was watching her attempt lewd acts with my television set whenever Regis came on-screen. "Hey, maybe Danny can get Kelly's autograph for Tallulah," I suggested.

"Um . . . maybe," Carter said.

Then I had another idea. Ever since I'd helped him acquire several specimens for his celebrity sock collection, I'd become a hero in my cousin Gerry's eyes. While I thought he was crazy for trying to turn his sock thing into a paying proposition, I couldn't help wonder how thrilled he'd be with some A-listers in his collection. "You think Danny could get me a pair of her socks?" She was silent for a moment and I reconsidered my request. "Or is that too strange?"

"No stranger than asking her to sign an autograph for a monkey."

A few minutes later the conversation turned to Los Angeles. While Danny, who'd grown up in Houston, had immediately adapted to their new surroundings, Carter, a native New Yorker, was feeling like a fish out of water. "I'm stuck in this apartment all day," she complained. "I can't drive. And even if I could, I can't fit in our car. It's a freakin' VW Beetle. I'm stranded in Hollywood, with a little clown car. LA's not like Manhattan, Holly. The subway system's a joke, and everything is all spread out. When are you coming?"

"The thing is . . ." I sucked in my stomach, steeling myself for what I had to say next. If I'd learned nothing else from the past twenty-four hours, I'd at least realized I had to regain control of my finances. No more overpriced coffee drinks, no slinky red dresses, and definitely no plane tickets. If I couldn't afford to pay my rent, I certainly couldn't afford a trip to LA.

"As much as I'd love to be anywhere but here at the moment, I . . ." I trailed off, knowing that what I had to say would devastate my best friend.

"You what?" Carter prodded.

"I . . . can't . . . go."

I held my breath, waiting for the sounds of Carter's spontaneous combustion to reach through the phone lines. But all I heard was familiar-sounding rhythmic breathing.

"Carter? Are you there?"

More breathing. "Hee-hee-hoo, hee-hee-hoo."

I finally recognized the pattern I'd learned with Betty in Lamaze class. I experienced a twinge of guilt at not having practiced any of the breathing techniques. But then it passed. "Are you okay?"

Another breath and she said, "Contraction."

"You're in labor?" I screeched. Holy crap. I'd known my announcement would upset her, but I had no idea it would send her into premature labor.

"No," she panted. "Braxton Hicks. They're like practice contractions. I've been having them on and off for a few days now."

"Practice contractions? What kind of sadistic person dreamed up those?"

"The Divine Being is neither sadistic nor a person," Carter intoned, sounding like her old mellow self. "Everything happens for a reason. And I am in control. I am at peace. I am strong. I am centered."

I drew in a breath, relieved that she was taking my news so well. And then she started to cry.

Damn. I hated letting Carter down. She'd seen me through my mother's death and father's abandonment, not to mention several broken hearts and one severely bad perm.

I told her my whole sorry story, starting with the slinky red dress and ending with my promise to move in with Kuki. "I have two days to come up with rent money or I'll be evicted."

"We could loan you some money. We don't have much, but—"

"No way," I interrupted. "You have a baby on the way. I couldn't take money from you guys."

"Maybe you should try—*oww*," Carter said, before resuming the *pant-pant-pant*ing that signaled another Braxton Hicks thingy.

"How do you know you're having practice contractions and not the real thing?"

"I don't know," Carter said. "The doctor said when the time comes, I'll know."

"But how will you know?" I asked.

"I'll just know." She took a deep, cleansing breath and added, "And you'll be there. Holding my hand."

I exhaled deeply, matching her rhythm. "Okay."

There was a knock on my door and I climbed out of bed, feeling decades older than my chronological age. Everything ached. Grouch scampered to the kitchen the moment my feet hit the floor. He skidded to a stop at the cabinet where his food is stored. When he saw I hadn't followed faithfully behind him, he began wailing and rubbing his head against the cabinet.

I peered through the peephole and saw Brian's miniaturized face smiling back at me.

"Howdy," I said, opening the door.

"Just thought I'd pop in and give you an update on Mrs. Mete."

"Oh, yeah." I'd nearly forgotten that in the midst of my overblown drama, someone in the building had been suffering an actual emergency. "How is she?"

"Fine. They're going to keep her for a few days. She couldn't stop talking about how you'd saved her life."

"It was no big—"

"It *is* a big deal, Holly. No one knew she was hurt. No one but you noticed she hadn't been sitting in her window all day as usual. No one else cared enough to call nine-one-one."

"Tallulah made the call," I pointed out.

I was shuffling my feet and staring at the ground, guiltily. I was no hero. If indeed I had saved her life, it was only by default. He reached out and lifted my chin so that I was forced to look in his eyes.

"I know how it happened, Holly. But still . . . you noticed. You cared." He let go of my chin and my eyes sank to the ground again. "You're a good person. Too bad we don't have more like you in this building."

The thought of more than one of me in the building caused me to shudder.

Brian gave me a playful punch on the shoulder, then dashed down the stairs, a gym bag slung over one shoulder.

I shuffled to the kitchen and filled Grouch's bowl with Friskies, then made my way to the bathroom to shower.

Eddie the EMT had warned that my bruises would look worse before they got better, and he was right. Last night's bruises had sprouted bruises of their own. My midsection vaguely resembled Van Gogh's *Starry Night*—a series of whorls in blue and yellow, with staccato slashes of purple here and there for dramatic effect. There were new bruises, too, including two on my ass that were probably a match to Brian's handprints.

When I removed the last of the bandages and stared at myself in the bathroom mirror, I could think of only one thing to say.

"Ugh."

As I showered, I made a mental checklist of possible sources of income. Too bad tax season was still several months away. It was the only time of year when my income was limited only by my ability to forgo sleep.

After dressing in baggy sweats and an oversized T-shirt, I sat at the dining room table with my DayPlanner and phone and began making calls.

"Mrs. Toback? It's Holly Heckerling. It's been a few months since your last perm. How about setting another appointment? Like, say, today? No? Does tomorrow work? Next Thursday. Sure, I'll pencil you in."

After exhausting my hairstyling clients, I moved on to the baby-sitting list. "Hi, Ellen. I was just thinking, you and Drew probably don't get out on a Friday night very often. How 'bout I watch Tyler tonight? I'll give you my Friday-night special—fifty bucks for five hours and I'll throw in a free haircut."

There were only a handful of people who still paid me to do their word processing. I left a message on Dr. Handelman's service imploring him to send some patient files my way and moved down the list.

The least lucrative, but perhaps most rewarding, of my paid positions was pet-sitting. I was mostly charged with caring for cats and dogs, but I'd also tended a few more exotic animals—including a tarantula and a lorikeet. I'd met some of my best friends via their pets, including Brian, whose cat, Kramer, was one of my favorite clients.

Of course, pet-sitting sometimes went awry, as evidenced by the boa constrictor currently taking up residence in my bedroom. And, because I'm a sucker for animals, I often take on pet-sitting jobs free of charge. I met Tallulah and David through a charity named Pets and People Support Network, which provides free pet care to animals whose owners are in the hospital.

Though I was unlikely to pull in big bucks with any of my pet-sitting clients, I called them all, offering to walk, groom, or play with their animals.

I'd worked my way through the ledger in which I'd listed every paying transaction of the past year. There were only two left: Monica Broccoli and my father. Of course, at the time I was doing his typing, I didn't know he was my father. I'd listed him simply as "The Writer." He'd posed as a client in need of my typing services, presumably as a way to ease his way back into my life. But once I discovered his identity, he retreated back into the woodwork. I didn't even have his phone number or address. Not that I had any intention of contacting him.

Nor was I desperate enough to call Monica Broccoli. Doing her hair was rarely worth the money, especially now that she felt her status as my future cousin-in-law entitled her to a hefty discount. The little profit I made wasn't worth subjecting myself to two hours of Monica.

I rarely had success cold-calling elementary schools to book my Critter Comedy act. My gigs either came from word-of-mouth referrals or in response to the brochures I'd had printed with Tallulah's face on the cover. It couldn't hurt to mail another batch out, I reasoned, retrieving the brochures and a box of envelopes from a desk drawer. This time, I'd target schools citywide, not just in lower Manhattan.

David had recently bought a van and had it specially outfitted—not only for his wheelchair, but also to carry the various cages and creatures we used in our presentations. Ideally I would drive the van with David riding shotgun, but since I hated driving in the city, I usually persuaded David's nurse, Margie, to act as chauffeur, while I rode in the back with the animals. All except Tallulah, that is, who loved sitting on David's lap and watching city life whiz by through the window.

I was hand addressing envelopes when the phone rang. "Hello?"

"Your uncle is a nincompoop," Aunt Betty announced. "I need a favor."

I had a sinking feeling in the pit of my stomach. The last time Betty and Bernie had had a fight, Betty ended up moving in with me. I wasn't eager to repeat the experience. My sofa still reeked of Bengay.

"What is it?" I asked, fingers crossed.

"It's bingo night at the senior center," she said. "We always go, Kuki and Leo, Bernie and me. Kuki's not coming because she has to set her hair and make hors d'oeuvres for Sunday night."

"What's happening Sunday?"

"Ronnie's birthday dinner," Betty reminded me.

"Oh, yeah." Why did I keep forgetting that?

"Leo says he won't go without Kuki. And Bernie won't go without Leo. He says he has no one to talk to."

"What about you? Can't he talk to his own wife?"

"I don't talk when they're calling numbers. I gotta mind my cards," she said. "He's too distracting. Will you go with me?"

"Me? Play bingo?" I tried to imagine myself in the senior center, the only person on the south side of seventy playing bingo on a Friday night in New York. "Gee, I don't think so. I should stay by the phone. I've been trying to drum up some business."

"This isn't about the incident the other day, is it? I promise I won't embarrass you. Not that they're not used to little accidents at the senior center. The only ones who don't wet themselves have catheter bags."

"It's not about the *incident*. I'm really busy. Why don't you ask Gerry to go with you?"

"He never goes anywhere without Monica. And she's a talker, that one. Last time the two of them went to bingo, I couldn't concentrate on my cards and I missed a number. Cost me a five-hundred-dollar jackpot."

Excuse me? "Five hundred dollars?"

"Yeah. If she wasn't about to become family, I'd have knocked her on her big broccoli booty."

Normally I would have taken a moment to savor the mental image of Monica being knocked on her big broccoli booty by Aunt Betty, but I was still stuck on the five hundred bucks. "What's it cost to play?"

"You can play Bernie's cards. And if you win, you keep the money."

I considered my options. Friday night used to be about going out on the town—club hopping, hooking up with friends, catching a movie. But since my best friends hightailed it to Hollywood and

I started dating a man who spent his Friday nights watching Disney DVDs with his eight-year-old daughter, my Fridays had become depressingly sedate. I hated to admit it, but bingo with Betty was the best offer on the table.

With any luck I'd win the jackpot, pay my rent, and tell Kuki I'd changed my mind about moving in with her.

"What time should I pick you up?"

When I was thirteen, Aunt Betty and Aunt Kuki brought me to Monty's Drugstore to purchase my first feminine-hygiene products. It was perhaps the single most mortifying moment in a childhood filled with mortifying moments. A few months earlier, Kuki had taken me bra shopping, pulling training bra after training bra on over my shirt in the middle of Woolworth's, while my cousins Gerry and Veronica watched and snickered. I thought I'd die from embarrassment.

But I survived, only to have that experience eclipsed by the great Maxipad versus Minipad debate.

"She's so little, she'll feel like she's got a mattress in her panties if she wears a maxi," Aunt Betty offered.

"But what about leakage?" Kuki complained. "I don't want her staining my new sheets."

"How about these newfangled things with wings?" Betty had asked, dragging a passing sales clerk into the conclave. "How do the wings work?"

After sizing me up and suggesting a box of slender tampons, the clerk was summarily dismissed by Kuki, who probably believed such a sinister product might prematurely relieve me of my virginity.

In the 1990s, Monty's was bought out by Rite Aid. The old soda counter where I used to sit and do my homework after school while waiting for Kuki and Leo to close up their barbershop had been transformed into a cosmetics counter, but otherwise the pharmacy was essentially unchanged.

Except the world had turned on its axis, and I was now standing in the same aisle, helping Aunt Betty select her first adult bladder control products.

Despite my aunt's assertion that incontinence was de riguer at Havencrest Senior Center, I didn't want to risk a repeat of the Lamaze incident, so I'd refused to be her bingo buddy unless she saddled up.

Now that our roles were reversed, you'd think Betty would be the one suffering the embarrassment. You'd be wrong.

I squirmed as Betty read aloud from package after brightly colored package. "Superior absorption and maximum odor control," she said as I mentally composed a list of a kajillion ways I'd rather spend my Friday afternoon.

Other shoppers cast amused and curious glances our way, but Betty was unaffected by their stares. She asked another woman, who had removed an economy-sized box of Depends from a lower shelf, why she chose that particular brand. The woman mumbled, "I dunno," and hurried down the aisle.

"I don't really need any of these," Betty said, her wave taking in the entire section. "Everyone has little accidents once in a while. Your aunt Kuki told me once that every time she sneezes, she pees a little."

I'm sure Kuki would kill Betty for passing on that little tidbit of information.

Betty picked up a slender package of I'm So Dry Adult Diapers. "I'm just doing this so you'll take me back to Lamaze class," she said. "I've been practicing." She gripped my arm for support as she demonstrated a rapid-breathing technique we'd learned. Her nails dug into my flesh on the final exhale.

"Ey-ouch!"

"Sorry, sweetie. That was a doozy of a contraction."

I led her toward the cash register. "Do I need to remind you that you're not actually pregnant?"

She laughed. "Me, pregnant? At my age?" She put her diapers on the conveyor belt. "Although I have had some strange cravings lately. And my ankles are taking on water."

As Betty paid for her purchase, I remembered that I had less than twenty-four hours to buy a birthday gift for my cousin Veronica. A present for Ronnie was not in my budget, but I knew I'd be raked over the coals if I showed up empty-handed. She was impossible to buy for—her tastes changed as often as her boyfriends, which was to say *a lot*.

I combed through the red-stickered items in the clearance bin near the register, eyeing each one critically. The only items in my price range were a package of scented soaps in the shape of ducks and a *Captain & Tennille Greatest Hits* CD. I sighed and grabbed the CD. *Maybe I can skip out before Ronnie opens the presents,* I thought as I hurried to the register.

Bingo was a bust. Not only did I not score a jackpot, but I spent most of the night turning down the advances of lonely old geezers, the youngest of whom could easily have passed for dead.

"Introduce me to your friend," one old-timer asked my aunt Betty.

"She's spoken for, Herb," Betty said, shooing him away with the back of her hand.

"I don't see a ring on her finger," Herb responded.

"She's still spoken for. Now stop looking at my cards. It's bad luck."

I soon learned that Betty was very superstitious when it came to bingo. We'd nearly had to cancel when she couldn't find her lucky bingo brassiere. Ever since she won the grand jackpot of a thousand dollars two years ago, she wore exactly the same outfit every Friday night—right down to the underwear.

She always sat in the same chair at the same table facing the same direction. She lined her cards up—twelve of them—in the same pattern, three rows of four cards each. She and Bernie had his 'n' hers personalized bingo markers, and she'd growled at me like a pit bull when I accidentally reached for the wrong one. Looking at her cards was another no-no. When I noticed she was nearing a win, I leaned closer to see which number I should be rooting for.

She squinted at me as though giving me the evil eye. "Jinx!"

I soon discovered there's a whole bingo subculture I know nothing about. It's a very closed community, and one that doesn't take to outsiders lightly. Oh, an occasional visiting family member is accepted, even fawned over, but interlopers from other neighborhoods or senior centers were regarded like rival gang members. If someone who wasn't a recognizable face to the regulars shouted bingo, a chorus of boos went up around the hall.

Then there were the shout-outs. When the bingo caller—a strapping young man who looked blatantly out of place in the senior center—called I-22, and my aunt squawked, "Quack, quack," I thought it was one more sign of her advancing age. Then I heard a chorus of quacks erupting from around the hall.

"What's with the quacking?" I asked Betty.

"I-twenty-two," she responded, shielding her cards from my view. "You say quack, quack."

I nodded uncertainly. "Why?"

She shrugged and went back to checking her cards, methodically running a finger up and down every row of every one of her twelve cards, quacking under her breath and bouncing with excitement when she found I-22 on the last card.

By the end of the night, I'd learned that several numbers get special responses. Some made sense, like B-4 ("and 'after' ") and

B-11 ("chicken legs"), but most had an etymology that could probably never be traced.

And like all subcultures, there was obviously variation between different bingo communities. At one point, a lone couple yelled, "Fiddledy-dee," in response to 73—a dead giveaway that they were from Park Slope, according to Betty. Havencresters observed a moment of silence when the same number was called, in respect for former bingo caller Madeline McNulty, who'd died of a heart attack after calling that number four years earlier.

"Her number came up," Betty solemnly explained, "and it was O-seventy-three."

In addition to the universal shout-outs, Betty observed a few private rituals, as well. She bowed her head and made the sign of the cross on hearing the year of my grandmother's birth. The year of her birth, marriage, and other significant dates also got special notice—a tug of the ear, a hand across the heart, a finger to one side of her nose, and so on.

When the caller read I-27, she thumped her chest with a closed fist.

"What's I-twenty-seven?" I asked, pounding my own chest in imitation. I wanted to play along, but I was beginning to feel like I'd wandered into an underground society with a panoply of secret codes and ritual handshakes.

"Heartburn," she said, repeating the chest-thumping gesture.

It took me a while to get the hang of playing twelve cards simultaneously. In the beginning, I barely managed to check half my cards before the next number was called. But midway through the evening, I was not only up to speed, but I was growing bored. Especially since Betty made it clear that casual conversation was verboten.

After tiring of the advances of wizened widowers, my attention turned to the only other person in the hall who probably thought AARP was something a seal says.

The bingo caller was tall and dark-haired, with broad shoulders and a stoic expression. If I would have ever taken the time to wonder what a professional bingo caller looked like, I'd never have conjured up this guy. He must have been someone's grandson or nephew, helping out as a family obligation. I could easily picture him on a firefighters' calendar or the cover of a romance novel.

I was in the process of so picturing him when he looked in my direction. I felt a shock of recognition. Eddie the EMT!

I nudged Betty. "That's the paramedic who came to my place the other night." I pointed discreetly with my bingo marker. "Is he always here?"

"There's a couple of regulars. But he's the best." She dabbed ink on three of her cards in rapid succession. "Some of them fumble with the balls, keep you waiting. Ralph Kleinman even dropped one once. We had to wait ten minutes for them to find where it had rolled behind the Coke machine. Almost caused a stampede. But this one's got a good grip."

"Good to know."

During a ten-minute bathroom break, Eddie made his way over to our table. "No monkey tonight?" he asked.

I shook my head. "No. I'm here with my aunt."

He gestured at my midsection. "How are those ribs?"

"Fine," I said.

"You want me to take a look?"

Medically speaking, it probably would have been wise to let him examine me, but I didn't feel like being groped in front of Aunt Betty and her bingo buddies. "No, thanks."

He nodded and fell silent, a man of many numbers but few words.

I stood appraising him and wondering how a hunky medical technician wound up calling bingo numbers at a senior citizens center. "Are you moonlighting, or do you just hang around here waiting for someone to have a heart attack?"

The corners of his mouth turned up slightly. "It's a fun way to spend a Friday night."

My eyes bugged. "Really?"

Now he let loose an actual smile. "Well, kind of. My uncle Angelo got me into it. He's been calling since I was a kid. I used to help out. Then, when his eyesight started going, he drafted me to fill in." He looked down at his feet. "Funny the things you'll do for family."

I looked over at Betty, who was making use of the break to adjust her adult diaper. At the table. "Yeah. Funny."

Another uncomfortable silence descended. Not surprising, since I sucked at small talk. What was surprising, however, was what I blurted out to break the silence.

"I hear you know how to handle your balls."

"You said *what* to him?" Carter shouted over the phone.

I sank down on my sofa, cradling the receiver against my ear as I pulled off my shoes and tossed them in a corner. Bingo had been a total bust. I did get to shout bingo once, but it was a low-stakes game, and three of us had to split the eleven-dollar prize, which meant that I didn't even make enough to cover my round-trip subway fare. Not a good trade for spending my evening rejecting lonely widowers and convincing my aunt that I wasn't a jinx. And then there was the whole ball-handling comment. "I wasn't thinking."

"He's going to think you were flirting."

I couldn't argue with that. As I replayed the conversation on the subway ride home, I kept coming to the same conclusion: he must think I was flirting. But of course, I wasn't flirting. I was just socially maladjusted, the kind of person for whom terms like "Open mouth, insert foot" had been coined.

"You *were* flirting," Carter accused, "weren't you?"

"No! Why would I flirt?" I asked. "I have an incredible boy-friend."

"Who spent your six-month anniversary with his *ex-wife*."

I blew out air. Maybe that was what this was about. I was still a little miffed about Tom's continuing involvement with Bianca. Of course, I knew what I was in for from Day One. Divorced men, es-pecially those with kids, come with baggage. Often in the form of an aggrieved ex-wife, whose sole mission in life is to make his life a living hell.

It was easy when Tom's only interactions with his ex were combative. But now they'd turned some kind of corner and were trying to mend fences for Nicole's sake. I told myself it was a good thing that Tom was mature enough to put his daughter's welfare above his grievances with his ex. But I couldn't help it. Whenever he spoke about Bianca as though she was a mature, levelheaded adult rather than a mutant two-headed alien, it made me want to gag.

"Okay, maybe on some deep, subconscious level I was flirting," I admitted. "But it was a mistake. I love Tom."

"The L word," Carter gasped. "Does Tom know?"

"I haven't said it yet." I'd envisioned us both declaring our love—him first, of course—on the night of our anniversary. But since we'd botched that big-time, I'd barely spoken to him. "Maybe Sunday night. We're having dinner at Aunt Kuki's for Ronnie's birthday. Then I'm going back to his place."

"Are you wearing the red dress?"

"I can't," I said. "It smells like Szechuan sauce."

Before climbing into bed, I hit the button on my answering ma-chine. First up was Kuki, reminding me about Ronnie's birthday dinner and asking what day she should arrange for the movers to come. Then came a message from Tom. His voice was hushed, which usually meant that Nicole was sleeping and he didn't want to wake her.

The message was brief. "Sorry to do this again, but I can't make dinner on Sunday. Nicole's got a recital. I forgot all about it until a few hours ago. Wish your cousin a happy birthday for me."

Normally such a call wouldn't have bothered me. It was part and parcel of dating a dad, but tonight, it just added to my bewilderment. Why, when I'd just reached a milestone unequaled in my dating history—six months with one guy—would I even momentarily entertain thoughts about Eddie the EMT? Why did my flesh tingle when I thought of his rough but tender hands dressing my wounds? Why could I not erase the mental image of him handling his balls? And was it just my imagination, or did he give me a flirty glance when calling O-69?

As I got undressed I vowed to banish all thoughts of Eddie from my head. Damn him and his bingo balls.

Grouch jumped onto my bed and curled up near my head. I scratched his belly and he began to purr. I drifted to sleep thinking about Tom, but sometime during the night, my thoughts shifted to Eddie, and I woke up even more confused than ever.

6

Pass the Potatoes

My stomach was grumbling as I rang Aunt Kuki's doorbell. I'd worked all day without stopping for lunch. My phone had begun ringing first thing in the morning, and by late afternoon, I'd managed to squeeze in two hairstyling clients, walked and groomed a cocker spaniel, and transcribed three patient files for Dr. Handelman. I'd even sold my stereo system at a rock-bottom price to two college students in the building.

Even after this flurry of productivity, I was forty bucks short on rent. And after stopping for my daily Mocha Frappuccino, I was forty-three in the hole. It was Sunday night, and I needed to come up with the full amount by morning. I was going to have to bite the bullet and ask for a loan.

But who? I couldn't ask Kuki. She'd just use my money troubles as further proof of my inability to live on my own. Betty and Bernie, both retired, were on a fixed income, and while they'd probably gladly offer me the money, I would feel terrible taking it. Gerry, whose career aspirations surpassed even mine for impracticality, had quit his catering job to focus on building his celebrity sock collection, which had yet to generate any income whatsoever. Monica probably raked in a decent amount from her sporadic modeling assignments, but her generosity toward me extended only as far as not pressing assault charges against me for breaking her leg.

Then there was Ronnie. At twenty-six, she still lived at home, which meant that whatever income she brought in was largely disposable. But how tacky was it to not only show up for her birthday with a crappy-assed gift, but to hit her up for a loan afterward.

I definitely couldn't ask Tom. I didn't want him to think I was some flighty young girl who blew her rent money on a slinky red dress. I wanted him to think of me as a responsible career woman—the kind of girl who'd make a good wife and mother.

Never mix men and money, my mother had once told me. At least I think that was what she said. My mother died when I was eleven, and my memories of her were hazy. Now that I thought about it, I had to admit it was unlikely my mother gave me dating or financial advice at eleven. She'd probably been warning me not to mix milk and honey. Or men and monkeys. The more I struggled to recall them, the more improbable her words became.

I clutched Veronica's present in my hands. I momentarily considered chucking it into the alley next to the house. Maybe it was better to show up empty-handed than with a lame-o bargain-bin gift.

It was too late. The door swung open and Gerry swept me into a hug. "Holly's here!" He yanked me inside, where I was greeted by the mouthwatering aroma of my Aunt Kuki's marinated meatballs.

Aunt Kuki came from the direction of the kitchen, wiping her hands on her apron. She looked around and behind me, then put both hands on her hips. "Where's your luggage?"

I willed myself to stand up to her, to tell her I wasn't moving home. Not today, not ever. But forty-three dollars were standing in the way of my resolve. I couldn't completely turn my back on her offer until my rent was paid. "I . . . uh . . . didn't . . ." I sputtered. "I haven't had a chance to pack."

The door opened behind me and Ronnie came blasting through the foyer. "Dinner ready?" she asked her mother.

"Ronnie will help you," Kuki said.

Ronnie shot her mother an oh-no-you-didn't look and pouted her lips. "Help her *what*?"

"Pack her things," Kuki said matter-of-factly. "She's moving back home."

If there was anyone less enthusiastic than me about the possibility of my moving home, it was Ronnie, who'd never warmed up to sharing a room with me the first time around. She'd allotted me one and a half drawers in the dresser and one-eighth of the closet space, and affixed labels to everything she owned, lest I forget I was a mere visitor with no rights of ownership over the room or its contents.

I smiled halfheartedly in her direction, hoping to convey, if not warmth, then a lack of hostile intent. "If it's going to cause problems," I said, spotting a possible out and grabbing it with both hands, "I don't have to—"

"She's not sharing my room," Ronnie said before stomping up the stairs that led to the bedrooms. I wouldn't be surprised if she was pulling the old label maker out of storage and once again marking her territory.

Her reaction did raise an interesting question. Where was Kuki planning on planting me? Gerry's old room had long ago been converted into a multipurpose room housing both Kuki's sewing supplies and Leo's collection of military memorabilia.

"Where will I stay?" I asked. Hypothetically, of course.

Kuki ignored the question. "Take off your shoes," she said, whirling on her feet and returning to the kitchen.

I removed my shoes and kicked them aside. Then I took a deep breath and strode into the parlor with Gerry trailing close behind. I slipped my gift in with the others piled on the side table, noting without surprise that I was the only one who'd used the Sunday comics as wrapping paper.

Monica Broccoli was in an overstuffed chair next to the window, flipping through a bridal magazine. Bernie and Leo were occupying their customary positions on opposite sides of the sofa. Bernie's eyes were open but they had a vacant look as though he'd fallen into a trance. He seemed almost as excited about this family dinner as I was. Leo managed a smile and wave in my direction. Betty, who had been sitting between them, used Bernie's leg for support as she pushed herself off the sofa.

She met me halfway across the room. "Holly, honey," she squealed, pinching my cheek between her thumb and forefinger and squeezing until I yelped. "I was just telling the boys about Lamaze class. Now that you're here, we can demonstrate."

Monica looked up from her magazine. "I gotta see this."

"I don't think—" I protested, but Betty grabbed my hand and lowered herself to the floor, pulling me down in the process.

Gerry plopped into a recliner and clapped his hands. "This is more fun than charades."

Aunt Betty stretched her legs out in front of her, slightly apart, and leaned back against me. Feeling ridiculous, I kneeled behind her with one knee on either side of her body. Then there was silence and everyone looked at me expectantly. For the life of me, I couldn't remember what I was supposed to do. I closed my eyes and tried to recall the techniques we'd learned in class. "Breathe in," I instructed vaguely. "Visualize a white light traveling up your body. Or down your body. Or hovering over your body."

Betty closed her eyes and inhaled through her nose.

I patted her shoulders reassuringly. "Good, good." I was drawing a blank about what to do next when I noticed her face begin to flush and her cheeks puff out like a chipmunk.

"Exhale!" I shouted.

She breathed out through her mouth, emitting a sound like a deflating balloon. "Whoooooo-oooo-oooo."

"Good," I said. "Um . . . now . . . I don't know. Do it again."

Betty repeated the pattern, a blissful look on her face. I was beginning to wonder if I might actually be good at this coaching thing.

Then she kicked her legs out in front of her and scrunched her face up. "Yow-eee-ka-zowee," she hollered.

Leo leaned forward to get a better view.

Bernie sat bolt upright, gaping at Betty, who was splayed out on the floor, gripping her chest and howling at the ceiling. "Kidney stone?" he asked.

Betty shook her head. "Contraction."

"Oh." He sank back into the sofa and instantaneously fell asleep.

"Dinner is ready," Kuki called from the kitchen. She appeared in the doorway, oven mitts on both hands. Her mouth fell open when she saw Betty on the parlor floor in the throes of faux child-birth. She made the sign of the cross, splattering pasta sauce from the oven mitt on her forehead in the process.

I hung my head in anticipation of the speech about minding my manners and comporting myself like a proper young lady that was surely forthcoming. Instead, she turned back toward the kitchen, calling over her shoulder for everyone to go to the dining table.

I struggled to my feet before helping Betty. "I was just getting into it," she said. "I hope we can do the rest after dinner. Like those skits you kids used to do when you were little."

Somehow I doubted that was how Veronica wanted to spend her birthday.

Betty nudged Bernie awake, and Gerry dashed up the stairs, shouting Ronnie's name. Monica set aside her magazine and strode toward the dining room. I fell into step behind her and nearly tripped over her feet when she stopped short, suddenly resuming her limp-gaited walk.

The delectable array of food spread out on Kuki's dining room table was almost enough to persuade me that moving back home might not be a bad idea after all. At least I'd be well fed. At my apartment, a typical dinner spread consisted of a jar of peanut butter and a spoon.

My reservations about moving home returned full force when Ronnie slunk into the dining room and took her customary seat across from me. She was always flippant toward me, but tonight she was downright surly, sneering at me throughout the meal. As her hostility intensified, I grew increasingly more thankful that I'd only dropped $4.99 on her gift.

At one point, Bernie asked how "that little dickens, Carter" was faring in Hollywood, and I told him about her frustration at being home alone while Danny worked on a movie.

Gerry had his head bent over his plate to minimize the mouth-to-mashed-potato distance his fork had to travel. His head shot up upon hearing about Danny's film.

"Your friend Danny? Your old partner? He's doing a movie?"

I blew out air and nodded. I could see where this was going. Gerry sniffed potential prospects for his celebrity sock collection. I'd already asked Carter to enlist Danny's help, but she'd called back to say he refused, not wanting to be labeled a foot freak so early in his career.

I mentally smacked myself for mentioning Danny's movie role. Gerry was tenacious when it came to his collection; he wouldn't give up as easily as I had. I really should learn to think before I speak.

"Big budget?" Gerry asked. "Who's in the cast?"

I shrugged one shoulder and tried to divert his attention by passing a dish of marinated meatballs down to his end of the table.

I shrugged one shoulder noncommittally. "I don't remember."

"What's it called?"

"*Vets in the City,*" I said, only because I couldn't think of a lie fast enough and I didn't think he'd know who was starring in a chick flick that had just started production.

Gerry scrunched up his forehead in thought. "Never heard of it."

That was a relief.

Then Ronnie piped in, "It's with Jennifer Aniston and Hugh Jackman. I read about it in *Style* magazine."

For the tenth time that evening, I resisted the urge to lunge across the table at Ronnie.

"Jennifer Aniston and Hugh Jackman!" Gerry's eyes were wide. "You have to help me get their socks, Holly. It would be such a coop for my career."

"That's *coup*," I corrected. "And I still don't understand how collecting socks constitutes a career."

"Stop belittling my brother," Ronnie hissed across the table. "You're always putting him down."

My eyebrows shot up. It was true I made the occasional joke at Gerry's expense, but he always enjoyed the attention. And so far, I'd helped him acquire the majority of his celebrity sock specimens. "I am not," I said, stabbing a marinated meatball with my fork for emphasis.

Aunt Kuki raised a hand in warning. The gesture wasn't directed at any one of us, but rather at all of us, and it worked. Everyone was silent.

Satisfied that order had been restored, Kuki went to the kitchen to fetch dessert.

When she was out of earshot, Gerry leaned over to me and whispered, "If you can get me Jennifer Aniston's socks, I'll give you a percentage."

"A percentage of what?" I asked, not so much to be snarky, but out of genuine curiosity. Gerry had generated some local press but had yet to make a dime off his collection.

"You're doing it again," Veronica yelled.

"I am not!" I banged my fist on the table in frustration. My fork was clutched in my fist, and perched on its end was one of Aunt Kuki's gloriously golden marinated meatballs. The impact of my fist against the table sent the meatball sailing. It hit Veronica squarely in the sternum.

Everyone at the table gasped.

"I'm sorry," I choked. "It was an acc—"

Before I could finish, Ronnie plucked a meatball from her own plate and lobbed it across the table. It bounced off my forehead and fell onto Monica Broccoli's lap.

"My skirt!" Monica screeched, picking up the meatball and regarding Ronnie and me with the same sneer of contempt. After a moment's indecision, she retaliated at both of us, hurling the meatball at Ronnie—its speed and velocity evident by the swiftness with which it became lodged in her cleavage—and pitching a forkful of mashed potatoes in my hair.

I acted on instinct, grabbing my water glass and flinging it in Monica's face. She stumbled and backed into the wall phone, sending the receiver flying off the hook.

By now, Betty, Bernie, and Leo had backed away from the table, trying to get out of the line of flying food. Betty and Bernie, who had no children of their own, looked completely bewildered, while Leo was wagging a finger ineffectually and saying, "Now see here. Stop that—"

Gerry was trying to pry a bowl of creamed corn out of Monica's hands, and Ronnie had me in a headlock, my face inches above Kuki's candied yams. Gerry was no match for Monica, who knocked him over and came at me with the creamed corn just as Ronnie overturned a bowl of mashed potatoes au gratin on my head. I was blindly groping for something to use as ammunition. Finding nothing, I grabbed a fistful of her hair and yanked.

"Ow," Ronnie yelled. "Daddy, make her stop!"

"Ooh, baby," I teased. "You want your daddy to save you?"

"At least I *have* one," she spat.

That did it. With all the force I could muster, I flipped her over on her back, flat into the carcass of the turkey that had given its life in her honor.

At that moment, Kuki reentered the room bearing a large sheet cake, dotted with twenty-six flickering candle flames. She opened her mouth to sing but didn't get past "Hap—" before her mouth fell open and all the color drained from her face.

Ronnie and I froze. In seconds, Kuki had set the cake down and yanked me off the table by my ponytail. The color had rushed back into her face with a vengeance. If her face had grown any redder, I feared she'd sunburn from the inside out. I stopped struggling and went limp, like a kitten dangling by the scruff of its neck.

I looked around at the stage-four disaster area that was formerly Kuki's formal dining room. I was overcome with remorse. There was nothing I could say or do that could make up for turning Veronica's birthday dinner into a food-flinging free-for-all. Not that it was all my doing, of course, but I knew from experience that Ronnie would spin things in such a way that she emerged unblemished in her mother's eyes.

I looked over at Ronnie, who had sunk into a chair and was woefully watching the candles on her birthday cake burn to nubs.

"Sorry," I whispered hoarsely to no one in particular.

The silence was deafening. All eyes were on Kuki. Everyone was waiting for her to speak. Leo, Betty, and Bernie cowered in a corner, while Gerry picked pickled pigs' feet out of Monica's hair.

I thought I heard a faint, tinny rendition of "Copacabana," but I couldn't be certain since I had an earful of creamed corn.

Then I realized the rings were emanating from somewhere in the vicinity of Aunt Betty's groin. Betty lifted up her shirt and gaped at the cell phone clipped onto the waistband of her skirt. Realization dawned. "Oh, goodness! No one's ever called this phone before. I didn't know what it sounded like."

She opened the phone and put it to her ear. "Hello?" Then she brought the phone to her mouth and spoke into it like a microphone. "Who's speaking?" Clearly confused by the phone's diminutive size, she shifted it swiftly from mouth to ear and back again. Shout, shift, repeat. "Who? . . . What? . . . I can't hear . . ." She looked up helplessly. "How does this thing work?"

Ronnie reached over and took the phone from her hands. "Hello?" She listened for a moment and then thrust the phone in my face. "It's for you."

I raised both eyebrows in disbelief but reached for the phone. Kuki relaxed her grip on my ponytail and I brought the phone to my ear.

"Hello?"

"Holly, thank God," Danny shouted. "I've been trying to reach you all over."

"Danny? How did you get this number?"

"I left a message at your apartment, and Gerry's, and then I tried your aunt Kuki's but the line was busy. I called your aunt Betty and her answering machine said in case of emergency to call this number."

"Well you found me. What's the emergency?"

"Carter's in the hospital. The baby's coming. You gotta come quick."

"But she's not due for another month."

"Yeah, I know," Danny was panting. "I guess Max didn't get the memo."

"Max?"

"The baby. We decided last night."

Max? I wasn't sure if this was another of Danny's jokes, but I kinda liked it.

"You gotta get on the next plane," Danny was saying. "Carter needs you." He paused, then his voice got all squeaky. "*I* need you."

I was momentarily speechless. The demise of our act and subsequent rise of his solo career had put a bit of a strain on our friendship. I'd told myself it didn't bother me, but in truth I missed having Danny around to bounce ideas and jokes off.

Betty was tugging on my sleeve, and Ronnie was giving me a death glare. I inched away from the table, lowering my voice. "I can't leave yet. I have to make arrangements for all my animals, reschedule my clients, and I haven't even gotten my ticket—" Not to mention the fact that I wasn't going anywhere without a shower. My hair was matted with mashed potatoes, and I was pretty sure creamed corn had trickled into my bra.

"I called the airline," Danny cut in. "There's a prepaid ticket waiting for you at JFK. You just need to show up. Bring two forms of ID and leave your blowtorch at home."

"I don't . . . I can't . . ." I stuttered. As much as I wanted to be there for Carter, I'd vowed to take charge of my finances. Leaving town, missing work, and becoming indebted to Carter and Danny would be a terrible way to start my new era of fiscal responsibility.

"It's not a loan," Danny said as if reading my mind. "We owe you, Holly. At least I do. I wouldn't be here if it wasn't for you. You were always the one pushing to get us booked, to improve the act, to get us publicity. And you introduced me to Carter. If I hadn't met you, I'd still be waiting tables at the Broadway Bistro. And I wouldn't be about to become a father." He cleared his throat. "Now get your ass out here."

He rattled off airline and flight information and disconnected. I stood in stunned silence for a moment, a million questions racing through my mind: who would take care of my pets? How would I get to the airport? What would I tell my clients? What about Tom?

I turned back to the table. Everyone was staring at me expectantly. "Carter's in labor!" I shouted. "I'm flying to Los Angeles in two hours."

There was an explosion of activity at the table as everyone started clearing dishes, uprighting chairs, and carrying plates into the kitchen. Ronnie blew out what was left of her candles and cut a big chunk out of her cake.

"You'd better be back in time for my wedding," Monica said.

I was touched that, despite our differences, she wanted me to attend her big day. "I'll try."

She put her hands on her hips and said, "You have to be there. For Gerry. And I want you to bring Rocky."

"You want a snake at your wedding? Won't he be a little . . . disruptive?"

"He's a sweetheart. People will love him. They can have their picture taken with him, as a souvenir."

"Why don't you just do Jordan almonds like everyone else?" I didn't have time to argue the point, and besides, odds were still against Monica and Gerry actually making it down the aisle. So I said, "Fine."

Betty slapped my back with enough force to loosen a molar and wished me good luck.

"Sorry we won't be finishing Lamaze," I told her. "I know you enjoyed it."

"If you don't mind, I think I'll stick with the class," she told me. "I like talking to the ladies, and I want to learn the rest of those techniques."

"You'll need a partner."

Betty shrugged. "Maybe Monica will come with me."

The thought of Monica Broccoli and Maya the Militant Lamaze Instructor in the same room made me smile.

"Here," I said, handing Betty her cell phone.

"You keep it," she said. "In case of emergency." She gave me a hug and an affectionate bite on the cheek. "Besides, the darn thing confuses me."

I squeezed her tight and whispered in her ear, "Stay dry."

She nodded and said, "I'll try."

Everyone had cleared out of the dining room except me and

Kuki. I didn't know what to say to her. I had probably sunk as low as I could in her estimation. Well, I reasoned, if there was one good thing to come of the evening, it was that she would most likely rescind her invitation for me to move in.

I glanced at the wall clock, wincing when I saw mashed potatoes splattered across its face. It was nearly eight and Danny had booked me on a ten-fifteen flight. I had no time to spare, but as I was partly responsible for the mess, I had to stay to pitch in with the cleanup.

I bent and picked remains off the floor, just as Gerry swung through the door and reached for a casserole dish.

Kuki retrieved a set of keys from a drawer in the sideboard and handed them to Gerry. "Holly needs a ride to the airport," she told him. "Take the wagon." She turned to me. "You should be going."

I nodded numbly, not sure whether I should approach her for a good-bye hug or just slink away with my head hung low. She made the decision for me, turning on her heels and walking briskly into the kitchen without another word.

7

Hee Hee Hoo

My mashed-potato-spiked hair barely elicited a raised eyebrow from airport security. I guess they see stranger things every day.

A stern-faced guard confiscated the laser pointer from my purse, and if he doubted my story that I use it to coax a monkey to perform tasks, he didn't give any indication.

I made it to my gate mere minutes before takeoff. Gerry had driven like a Manhattan cabbie, which he had been, briefly, after high school. Despite his mother's insistence that he take me directly to JFK Airport, Gerry understood my pressing need for a pit stop at my apartment. I could get by without a shower, but I'd never endure a six-hour flight with creamed corn oozing out of my bra.

Gerry circled the block while I ran the six flights up to my apartment and let myself in, breathing a heavy sigh of relief when the key turned in the lock without hesitation. I quickly traded my food-splattered clothes for a clean pair of sweats and a pink sweetheart tee. Not exactly the outfit I'd envisioned for my Los Angeles debut, but it was comfy and didn't smell like pickled pigs' feet.

Grouch was rubbing against my leg as I shoved random garments into an oversized duffel bag, not keeping track of what matched what.

"Sorry, buddy," I said, sidestepping the cat on my way to the bathroom, where I grabbed my toothbrush, makeup bag, and curling iron and dumped them into the bag.

Grouch followed me to the kitchen, where I refilled his food and water bowls before moving on to the other nonhuman members of my household. I provisioned Felix the Rat, Whoopi the Goldfish, and Jack the Bunny with bigger-than-usual portions of food pellets, fish flakes, and leafy greens. I knew Brian would take good care of them—as we'd previously arranged—but I couldn't be certain when he'd get the message I'd left about my premature departure.

I'd just fed Rocky the Boa his weekly ratsicle the day before—as evidenced by the golf ball–sized lump in his midsection—so I just blew him a perfunctory kiss, surprising myself when I felt a little lump in my own throat and realized I might actually miss the darn snake.

My buzzer rang, three long blasts, Gerry's signal that I was taking too long to wrap things up. I grabbed my DayPlanner and check-book, took a last look around my apartment, and locked the door.

I tore down the stairs, stopping when I hit the first floor. Lean-ing against Pete's door, I wrote out my rent check for the full amount, even though my bank balance was still forty-three dollars short. I was still hoping for a miracle—that some way, somehow, I'd get the money in the bank by the time the property management company cashed the check. In any case, this would buy me some time, I thought, sliding the check into the slot on the metal lockbox mounted beside Pete's door.

Gerry was double-parked, honking and hollering at me to get my rear in gear. I slung the duffel bag over my shoulder and dashed out the door.

Los Angeles was shrouded by a sea of fog. My plane circled for two hours waiting for clearance to land. Normally I wouldn't mind, but my best friend was in labor, and I was afraid I'd miss the blessed event because I was stuck in the sky.

Though I hadn't been keen on the idea of being a labor coach in the beginning, I had to admit that—except for the blood—I'd been secretly looking forward to witnessing the birth of Carter's baby. And for all I knew, she'd already given birth. I had no idea how long these things typically took. Kuki said she'd been in labor with Gerry for two days, but that Ronnie flew out like a torpedo on the first push. I hated to wish a protracted labor on my dearest friend, but I hoped Carter could at least hold out until I made it to the hospital.

I took a series of shallow breaths, trying to calm my nerves. I looked out the window and saw lights twinkling through the dense fog. I kept breathing, two rapid bursts followed by a longer exhale. It took me a moment to realize I was doing a Lamaze technique.

I squinted through the fog and wondered which little dot of light represented the hospital where Carter was either cradling her newborn son in her arms, or screaming in the throes of natural childbirth.

"Thank you for your patience, everyone." The pilot's voice boomed over the speakers. "We've been cleared for landing." There was a smattering of applause and a few shouted hoorahs, but most of the weary travelers just started packing up their reading material and laptops and returning their seatbacks to the upright position in preparation for descent.

Even though I knew chances were slim Danny would be waiting when I reached the arrivals area outside baggage claim, my heart still sank a little to see my fellow passengers being rushed by waiting loved ones, wrapped in big bear hugs, and pulled out of the queue. No one rushed forward to greet me.

There were a half dozen drivers holding placards bearing the names of the passengers they'd been dispatched to pick up. Though I knew it was equally unlikely there'd be a limo out front waiting for me, I read the names on the signs anyway: Lightfoot, Ashbrook, Daltry, Repond, Young. No Heckerling. I was on my own.

I powered up Betty's cell phone, hoping there was a message from Danny, with an update on Carter and instructions on how to get to the hospital. My head was pounding from the long flight. While I waited for the cell phone to come to life, I unzipped my duffel bag and reached inside for some aspirin.

I didn't find pain relievers of any kind, but I came up with a tube of lipstick. It would take a lot more than Mango Madness to make me presentable, but it was the best I could do for now. I uncapped the tube, gave it a twist, and puckered up.

I had just put stick to lips when I was slammed from behind by something I could only assume—from the force and velocity of the blow—was a jet aircraft that had missed its gate and crashed into the terminal.

I looked up as a walking refrigerator dressed all in black, from his Ray-Bans to his wing tips, barreled past me, barely breaking stride. He was accompanied by several other black-clad musclemen—a veritable army of appliances surrounding a much smaller man, who was punching buttons on his BlackBerry. He wore a gray suit jacket over a tight-fitting Polo shirt and a pair of jeans. His jet-black hair had that intentionally tousled look that probably took forty minutes and a half bottle of hair gel to achieve.

He gave me the briefest of glances, as though curious, but wholly unconcerned about what lower life-form had dared to impede his posse's progress through the terminal. None of the men stopped to offer assistance or an apology.

And they say New Yorkers are rude.

I had belly flopped onto the floor and slid to a stop at the feet of the Lightfoot driver, who glanced down only long enough to confirm that I wasn't his intended passenger, then moved a few feet away.

The testosterone tanks pushed through the crowd, clearing a path for their leader, until they reached the Daltry driver. Presumably the hair-gel guy was Daltry and the tanks were his bodyguards. The driver led them to a motorized cart, its flatbed already piled high with luggage.

I was still sprawled on the terminal floor. A few people stopped to gawk; then everyone resumed their mad rush to baggage claim, ground transportation, or waiting relatives.

I spit out the remains of the tube of lipstick I'd nearly swallowed when I was flung to the floor, scrambled to my knees, and began gathering up my belongings, which had gone flying upon impact. As I picked up my duffel bag, some of its contents spilled out from the unzipped side. I quickly gathered them up and shoved them back in the bag—curling iron, mascara, deodorant, sports bra.

I heard a crunch and saw my Mango Madness lipstick being crushed under the wheels of a passing luggage cart. Damn. I had little time to mourn the lost lipstick when I realized Betty's cell phone had also gone missing. I was on my hands and knees, scooting around, looking between legs and behind trash cans, trying to avoid being further trampled, and breaking into a cold sweat because the phone was my lifeline to Carter and Danny. I'd never been to LA, didn't know my way around, and didn't even know the name of the hospital Carter was at.

Then I heard it . . . a zippy, digitized version of "Copacabana." Sports bra still in hand, I slung my duffel bag over my shoulder and hurried in the direction of the sound, which led me to the back of the Daltry cart. The phone must have landed amid the baggage. I couldn't see it, but I could hear the digital ditty emanating from the pile.

The cart began moving.

I called to the driver. "Excuse me."

No one turned. Perhaps they hadn't heard me over the terminal noise. I pursued the cart, shouting at the top of my lungs.

The cart didn't slow. It was nearing a hallway marked AUTHORIZED ENTRY ONLY. A guard stood at the side of the entrance.

I was out of breath, gasping for air, ready to collapse in a heap and call it a day. But my best friend was in labor and she needed me. I couldn't let some rich punk make off with my cell phone. I sucked in air and ran with full force toward the restricted-access sign.

The driver was probably going only ten miles per hour, but I felt like I was doing sixty as I edged past the cart, cutting it off just before it exited the main terminal.

"Stop!" I screamed, holding one hand out in front of me. Unfortunately, it was the hand in which I was still clutching the sports bra.

The cart came to a halt. Now I had everyone's attention. Refrigerator One lifted his Ray-Bans and shot me an icy glare. Hair Gel guy stopped talking into his mouthpiece. Several mouths went slack-jawed.

"Thank you." I shoved the sports bra into my pocket. "Now if one of you will give me my cell phone—"

"What the hell?" Hair Gel guy cut me off. "What are you talking about?"

"Step aside," the driver said to me.

The airport security guard approached. "What's the problem?"

"Prob'ly a fan," Refrigerator One said, hopping off the cart and walking toward me with a big, beefy arm outstretched. "Don't worry, Mr. Daltry. I'll take care of her."

"I'm a lawyer," I shouted.

I don't know why I said that. Everything I know about the law I learned from watching *Matlock* reruns with Aunt Betty. But somehow I sensed shouting, "I'm a comedienne," wouldn't have sounded as foreboding.

The security guard stopped in his tracks and Refrigerator One's arm dropped to his side. Everybody's afraid of a lawsuit these days. Now I just had to throw some legalese around to sound convincing. "One of your . . . associates . . . knocked me over back there. With malice aforethought. I could have sustained bodily injury. I could sue him for physical assault and reckless endangerment. And you"—I pointed at Daltry—"as an accessory after the fact, you could be liable for punitive damages, pain and suffering, negligence, restitution . . ." I trailed off, having exhausted my legal vocabulary.

"Restitution?" Daltry repeated with a smirk. "For what?"

Okay, so restitution had been a bad choice, since I hadn't lost any money. But I couldn't back down now. What would Matlock do? "My lipstick was crushed," I said. "And my cell phone, which I was holding when I was struck from behind, is missing."

Daltry pulled a pen out of his pocket, scribbled some numbers on the back of a business card, and handed it to the compact appliance sitting next to him. If the big dude was a refrigerator, this guy was a dorm fridge.

Dorm Fridge climbed out of the cart and handed me the card.

"My attorneys," Daltry said. "They'll handle your complaint. Now step aside. I'm late for a fitting."

The driver started the cart and the bodyguards climbed aboard, satisfied that everything had been settled.

I stood my ground as the cart inched forward. "Get outta the way," someone shouted.

I put hands to hips and let loose a string of obscenities. Jaws went slack and looks were exchanged. Clearly everyone thought they were dealing with a lunatic. For the first time, I considered what I must look like—wild eyes, mashed-potato hair, sports bra dangling from my front pocket. I was guessing they didn't buy my story about being an attorney. "Just give me my phone and I'll drop everything."

"What phone?" Daltry looked impatient.

"It flew onto your cart"—I hooked my thumb in the direction of Refrigerator One—"when Magilla Gorilla body-slammed me back in baggage claim."

Dorm Fridge walked around to the back and gave a cursory glance at the luggage piled up on the flatbed. "No phone."

"It's there. I heard it," I said.

"I didn't hear anything," Daltry said.

"She's crazy," the bodyguard said. "She just wants to start something, get her picture in the paper or something."

Oh, yeah. That would be the icing on this particular cake from hell.

Refrigerator One hopped back out of the cart. He approached me from behind and lifted me off the ground. My feet were dangling a good six inches off the floor as he carried me out of the cart's path and set me down. The cart began rolling forward.

Refrigerator One nodded at Daltry as he passed. I regretted never mastering the playground art of projectile spitting. I'd have loved to hock a loogie into his smug face.

Then the unmistakable strains of "Copacabana" came beeping from somewhere on the cart. I saw Daltry flinch. He was going to pretend he hadn't heard anything. But Dorm Fridge began bobbing his head to the tune. "Da-da-da-Lola . . . dee-dee-dee-showgirl . . ."

Daltry remained stone-faced as the driver stopped the cart and Refrigerator One walked to the back. He tossed aside bag after bag until my cell phone was unearthed.

He handed it to me wordlessly. I flipped it open and shouted hello. "Danny? How's Carter?"

"She's fine," Danny said. "Still in labor. Did you get my messages? Where are you?"

"I'm at the airport," I said. "I've been . . . unavoidably detained."

I cut a glance at Daltry, who reached into his breast pocket and handed something to Fridge the First.

"For your inconvenience," Fridge said, handing me a crisply folded hundred-dollar bill. He climbed onto the cart.

I wanted to scream something about not being able to be bought off that easily, but I couldn't take my eyes off the bill. It had been a long time since I'd seen a bill higher than a twenty.

It was so pretty.

I was reminded of Tallulah, who could be fully engrossed in a task but if she spied a shiny object, she'd drop everything to follow it.

Danny was shouting rapid-fire instructions into the phone, something about a rental-car counter and a reservation number.

I tucked the hundred-dollar bill into my pocket and hissed at Daltry. "You'll be hearing from my lawyer."

He raised an eyebrow. "I thought you *were* a lawyer, darlin'."

Oh, yeah. I tried to think of a response, but the cart had driven away.

Compared to Manhattan, Los Angeles is enormous. LAX is practically a city unto itself. It took me fifteen minutes to navigate my way out of the loop that encircles the airport's many terminals.

I'd told the rental-car clerk that I'd never been to LA and was an infrequent driver. As a result, he'd strongly suggested I take the optional extra insurance and upgrade to a vehicle with a navigation system. Normally I'd balk at such strong-arm sales tactics, but given my rusty driving skills, I decided to pay a little extra for peace of mind.

Since I live in Manhattan, driving isn't a necessity. It's not even a luxury. It's more like a death wish. An expensive, impractical death wish.

But I grew up in Brooklyn, where driving is more of a personal choice. Carter chose not to learn, relying on mass transit to get her wherever she needed to go. But at Kuki's insistence, I took driving lessons in high school. I renew my license every time I have to, whether or not I have any intention of getting behind the wheel.

Not that Kuki ever lets me drive the station wagon. She rarely lets her own children drive the gas-guzzling behemoth. I recalled once driving her home after an optometrist appointment when they'd given her eye drops that dilated her pupils. She had no option but to let me drive. The entire way home she gripped the door handle with one hand and the dashboard with the other—as though that would protect her from the head-on collision she clearly anticipated. When she wasn't bracing herself for impact, she was grumbling that I was driving too fast and calling me names like Speed Racer and Leadfoot.

"I'm going thirty-eight miles per hour," I said, glancing at the speedometer.

"Eyes on the road!" she screamed, causing my heart to jump into my throat. "It's a thirty-five zone. You want to get us arrested?"

"Three miles above the limit is not speeding." I signaled for a turn and noticed my hands were shaking. My driver-ed teacher, Mrs. Graziano, looked like the Wicked Witch of the West, smelled like curdled milk, and sprayed spittle when she talked. But driving with Kuki always made me miss Mrs. Graziano. "Besides, they don't arrest you for speeding. They give you a ticket."

She turned toward me, and though she was wearing dark sunglasses, I could tell she was giving me one of her "gotcha" looks— the one you'd get if she spied you snatching a gherkin off the pickle tray before the guests arrived or using the fancy hand towels in the downstairs bathroom. "How do *you* know?"

Now that I was in Los Angeles, I was secretly grateful she'd forced me to drive. From what I'd heard, LA's subway system leaves much to be desired. Few stations, long waits, and at the end of the line, you're still miles from your ultimate destination. I was better off in the air-conditioned comfort of my rental car, with its nifty navigation system, which, according to the rental clerk, would guide me to any address I input into the computer. It could also direct me to the nearest location of any business establishment—banks, restaurants, dry cleaners, and so on. Even Starbucks.

I was dying to test that particular trick, but I'd have to wait until after I'd fulfilled my duties as labor coach. In this case, friendship trumps Frappuccinos.

I punched in the address of Cedars-Sinai Hospital and a feminine mechanized voice filled the car's interior. It was an authoritative yet soothing voice. It sounded like one of our neighbors in Brooklyn, Nancy Barraschino, a bank teller who also did voice-overs for commercials.

"Please proceed to the highlighted route," the voice intoned. I did as I was told and found myself moving east, away from the airport. After a few blocks, the voice instructed me to turn left.

I immediately signaled and moved into the turn lane, wrinkling my forehead in confusion when I saw that I was turning into a hotel's valet-parking entrance. A man in a red jacket approached my car and reached for the door handle, but I shook my head and proceeded to make a three-point turn.

This threw Navigation Nancy into a tizzy. "Turn left. . . . Turn right. . . . Turn left. . . ." If I didn't know better, I'd have sworn the computerized voice was getting a little snarky. It was bad enough I was driving in the fog, in Los Angeles, on unfamiliar streets, in an unfamiliar car. Now the navigation system was giving me attitude.

"Please return to the highlighted route."

"I'm trying."

"Please return to the highlighted route," it repeated.

"Hold your horses," I told the disembodied voice. "Here we go."

I pulled back onto Century Boulevard and eased into the left-turn lane. As I waited for the light to turn green, the voice in the dashboard told me to proceed north for 1.4 miles.

"Before or after I make this left turn?" I asked.

Silence.

The green arrow was lit, so I turned left, driving north. According to the navigational display, I was on Airport Avenue. But I couldn't read a single street sign through the fog.

"Turn right," the voice said. I signaled and turned onto a small gravelly road.

"Wrong turn," the voice intoned as the little street dead-ended in front of an auto body shop.

"No shit, Nancy," I said, resisting the urge to bitch-slap the dashboard.

Twenty minutes later, I was wondering whether the optional insurance premium would cover the damage I'd inflict if I ripped the navigation system out of the car.

When it said, "Turn right," I assumed it meant to turn right at the next possible opportunity—whether it was a major thorough-fare, a side street, a freeway on-ramp, or a McDonald's drive-through. But two McDonald's drive-throughs and one shopping mall parking lot later, I learned that turning right is open to interpretation. I also learned that the dashboard diva was immune to threats of litigation.

Giving it the finger was also wholly ineffective, though it made me feel a little better.

The cell phone rang as I was pulling into Cedars-Sinai's guest parking lot. I flipped it open with one hand while maneuvering into a parking spot with the other. "I'm here. I'm here," I told Danny. I pocketed the car keys, slammed the car door shut, and ran toward the hospital.

Danny met me in the lobby. He looked pale and his eyes were bloodshot. Beads of sweat dotted his forehead and upper lip. He gave me an update in the elevator. "Contractions are two minutes apart, and she's fully dilated—"

Too much information, I thought, not wanting to envision my best friend's fully dilated hoo-hah. Then it hit me that, like it or not, I was about to get a live view of said hoo-hah and it would be bad form to freak out. "Great," I said. "Can't wait to get in there and see for myself." Gulp.

"Good." The elevator doors opened and Danny pulled me down the hallway by my elbow. "She's been asking for you."

We rounded a corner and Danny nodded to a security guard at a desk just outside a set of double doors marked MATERNITY.

A nurse appeared from nowhere. "This is her?" she asked Danny. From her expression and inflection, I could tell she was hoping the answer was no. Danny nodded his head.

"You'd better get back in there," she told Danny. Danny disappeared and the nurse whisked me into a large, cold room. She led me to a sink and told me to scrub up. I washed my hands up to my elbows as instructed, then turned to face her.

She was eyeing me with a look bordering on disgust. "What's in your hair?"

Sensing that mashed potatoes au gratin—especially eight-hour-old mashed potatoes au gratin—might not be welcome in the sterile environment of a hospital delivery room, I lied.

"Hair gel." I raised one hand to my hair and tried to flip a section over one shoulder. But my hair was one big food-encrusted helmet. I let out a nervous giggle. "It's the newest thing in New York."

Not amused, she reached into a drawer and pulled out a crinkly blue shower cap. "Put this on and follow me."

She'd obviously led me into the wrong room.

The moment the door opened, my ears were assaulted by a screeching-wailing-howling sound that couldn't possibly have human origins. It was like nails on a chalkboard in the Seventh Circle of Hell. I didn't know what had made that sound. Hell, I didn't *want* to know what had made that sound. I just wanted to get out of there before it devoured me whole.

That couldn't have been Carter's birthing room.

Carter was a certified prenatal yoga instructor and meditation guide. She'd carefully planned the soundtrack to her birth experience—including Mozart's concertos for harpsichord, Yanni, and an entire track filled with the sound of raindrops falling gently on a field of sunflowers. She'd chosen several poems to recite during her labor, to soothe the baby and focus her mental energies. Exposing the baby to poetry from the moment it entered the world, she had explained to me over the phone, would imprint him with a love of the majestic beauty and cadence of the English language. Or some such nonsense.

Hearing neither poetry nor raindrops, I turned to leave. As I reached for the door, Danny appeared, tugging my sleeve and pulling me toward the infernal noise.

The sound came to a sudden stop just as I reached Carter's bedside. A nurse mopped her forehead.

"That was a big one," the doctor said. "It won't be long now."

Carter was whimpering. At least I thought it was Carter behind the wild eyes and beneath the cavewoman hair.

I put a hand on her shoulder. "Hey, Carter, it's me."

"Holly!" She grabbed my hand and squeezed. "I thought you'd never get here."

"How are you doing?" I asked.

Her eyes bulged from their sockets. "I'm in a fuckful of pain and they won't give me any damn drugs. They say I missed the window for an epidural. Nobody told me about any freaking window."

She grabbed my paper gown, pulled me close, and whispered, "You got any drugs on you?"

I'd clearly stepped off the plane and into an alternate universe. My best friend, who I'd known since I was twelve, had just asked me for drugs even though I'd never taken anything stronger than Excedrin Migraine. And did she just say "fuckful"? What happened to rhymed verse and mellow melodies?

I shook my head no to the drugs. "Sorry."

"Fuck it." She bit down on her bottom lip. "Let's just try this Lamaze shit."

Danny had picked up a handheld video camera and was pointing it in my direction. "This is Holly, Carter's best friend and Lamaze coach," he said, presumably for the benefit of the home-viewing audience.

No one had told me about a video camera. I tried to force my lips into a smile but failed miserably.

A nurse whose name tag read PHYLLIS DEMING, RN, handed me a wet cloth. "Okay, Holly, she's a little tense. Keep her focused on her breathing." Then she stepped aside.

Carter looked at me expectantly. Danny pointed the camera at me and mouthed, "Action." Even the doctor looked up from whatever it was he was doing between Carter's legs. All eyes were on me.

"Um, well . . ." I said, straining to remember something—anything—from Lamaze class. Aside from the image of Betty watering the linoleum, I was drawing a blank. And it's not as if I could fake it, there, surrounded by Zen Master Carter and a bunch of bona fide medical personnel.

"Okay, Coach," Phyllis prompted, "coach."

Carter wiped her nose on the sleeve of her hospital gown. Her lips were dry and cracked. I took a moment to observe that next to her, I looked pretty darn pulled together.

I breathed in deeply and Carter followed suit. Then I exhaled, slowly, blowing through pursed lips. I repeated this rhythm a few times. I had no idea what I was doing, but it seemed to have a calming effect on Carter. I varied the pattern a little, improvising, alternating short breaths with long, inhales with exhales.

"I don't know this one," Carter said, after mimicking a "ha-ha-ho-ho" routine.

I shrugged. "It's a New York thing."

Phyllis looked at me askance. "A 'New York thing'? There is no regional variation in Lamaze."

Carter eyed me uncertainly. "You did take Lamaze, didn't you?"

I nodded my head vigorously. "But I had to drop out after one class 'cause *someone* went into premature labor—"

"Yeah, but you took one class, right? What did you learn?"

"Not to bring Aunt Betty anywhere without a tarp."

Phyllis rolled her eyes and pulled me toward her. "Just keep her breathing like this," she said, demonstrating. "Hee-hee-hoo, hee-hee-hoo. That's all you gotta do."

The shallow breathing was starting to get to me. The room was stuffy. I felt light-headed. My knees buckled and I would have zonked out completely but Carter suddenly dug her fingernails into my wrist.

And we were back in the Seventh Circle of Hell.

"Ahhhh-eeee-owwww-fuckfuckfuckityfuck," Carter yowled as she writhed in unanesthetized agony.

"Remind me never to get pregnant," I said to no one in particular.

The maternity staff came to life, manning the monitors and doing whatever it is they do. Carter's legs were lifted into the stirrups, and the doctor rolled his wheeled chair closer. "You're in the home stretch," the doctor said. "One really big push."

Danny had stopped filming me; his movie camera was now zooming in on Carter's hoo-hah. "I see his head," he said.

Everyone was shouting at Carter to push. Her teeth were clenched and steam seemed to be coming from her ears. I hoped it would be over soon. I hated seeing my best friend in pain, and besides, if she squeezed any harder, I feared I would lose the use of my right hand.

It was hardly the idyllic birthing experience Carter had planned. She was howling and spewing profanities. I hoped whatever she'd read about babies being imprinted by the sounds they hear at birth was bunk. Otherwise "fuckity-fuck-fuck-fuck" would be indelibly impressed on Max's wee soul.

"Want me to put on the Mozart CD?" I asked, partly out of concern for the baby's tender ears, but mostly out of self-preservation. If she said yes, she'd have to let go of my hand.

"There's no time," Danny screamed. "His head's out. Holly, you gotta see this!"

I shook my head. "No, no, Carter needs me."

She let go of my hand and shoved me in Danny's direction. I made my way to the foot of the bed, standing just behind and to the left of the doctor, whispering, "Don't faint, don't faint, don't faint," the whole way.

"Recite a poem," Carter commanded. "Something happy!"

"I don't know any poems," I objected. I looked at Danny. "Do you know any poems?"

"He just knows dirty limericks," Carter said. "You work with kids. You telling me you don't know a single fucking poem?"

I racked my brain. I'd never been big on poetry. The only thing that came to mind was an Emily Dickinson piece I memorized in the sixth grade: "Because I could not stop for death, he kindly stopped for me. . . ." That wouldn't do. And I knew the same dirty limericks as Danny, who'd taught them to me in the first place. But real, honest-to-God poetry? I was clueless.

Then, from out of nowhere, I could hear my father's voice. Reciting a poem. Or maybe it was a song. It used to make me laugh. Not so much the words, but the funny honey bear voice he used. I closed my eyes, trying to remember. Then I began:

> *Fuzzy Wuzzy was a bear.*
> *Fuzzy Wuzzy had no hair.*
> *Fuzzy Wuzzy wasn't fuzzy,*
> *Was he?*

I repeated the same stanza over and over, since it was all I knew. Then I opened my eyes and watched as Carter's little boy came into the world.

8

Postpartum Impressions

"Go home and shower," Carter said, giving me the once-over. "You're scaring the baby."

While it was true that the baby had been crying nonstop for the past ten minutes, I suspected that had more to do with the trauma of being born than with my disheveled appearance.

His tiny face was beet red and scrunched up tight. As his sobs finally subsided, I marveled that through it all he hadn't shed a single tear. Nurse Phyllis informed me that newborns' tear ducts don't kick in until after a week or two.

I desperately needed a shower. My hair was an immovable mass, and the headache I'd had when stepping off the plane had blossomed into a full-fledged migraine. My ears were ringing, and Carter's voice echoed inside my head: *fuckity-fuck-fuck-fuck.*

And I needed to make some phone calls. I had to check in with my family, and Tom, and there were several clients I needed to reschedule.

But I couldn't take my eyes off the baby. Maximillian Montgomery Crane had captured my heart from the moment of his birth.

Well, maybe not the very first moment. But once they washed the blood off him and clipped the umbilical cord, then he had me—hook, line, and umbilical stump.

His fingers were so tiny and perfectly formed, and they gripped my finger the minute I put it in the palm of his hand. The nurse said it was the grasping reflex—an instinct all newborns share— but I knew it was because he recognized me as one of the good guys.

"He's got no hair," Danny commented.

It was true. Little Max had no hair. I bent over and kissed his little bald head. "Good night, Fuzzy Wuzzy."

I continued to watch Max long after he drifted off to sleep, in a little incubator on wheels that had been positioned next to Carter's hospital bed. Carter had finally fallen asleep a few moments before. Now I was nodding off, too.

Danny nudged me. "Come on, I'll take you back to our place and get you settled in."

"No, you stay," I said. "Just give me the address. My rental car has a navigation system."

"Sweet."

"Actually, she's a bitch," I said. "She kept yelling at me."

Danny grinned. "Navigation systems don't yell at people."

"This one did."

"Come on," he said, scribbling a note for Carter. "The nurse said they'll both sleep for hours. You can follow me in your car. I need to go shower and shave. Then I'll come back."

I nodded and yawned. The wall clock read ten thirty, but my body clock was at half-past comatose. Other than a brief catnap on the plane, I hadn't slept in two days. I was exhilarated and ex- hausted. I stole a last look at baby Max and tiptoed from the room.

Carter and Danny lived in a two-story apartment building a few blocks south of Hollywood Boulevard.

Danny led me to a tiny rectangular room that was empty except for a futon on the floor. "Guest quarters," he said, with an exaggerated flourish of his hand. "Decorated by yours truly."

"Going for the minimalist look?"

He progressed down a narrow hallway. "Bathroom's at the end of the hall. Closet here. Bath towels, soap, and so on." The closet he opened was so tiny I couldn't imagine it held much "and so on."

"Where's the nursery?" I asked.

"The what?"

"Nursery," I repeated. "You know, for the baby? Bald-headed, bowlegged kid we just left at the hospital?"

"Oh, him. Yes, I suppose he'll want to live with us." He stroked an imaginary goatee as though pondering some abstract philosophical principle instead of a six-pound human being.

Danny pushed open the door to another bedroom, this one twice the size of the guest room. It, too, was sparsely furnished, but at least it had the basics—queen-sized bed, dresser, nightstands. And in one corner, a bassinet swathed in blue fabric, with Winnie-the-Pooh bedsheets and matching mobile.

"It's got wheels." Danny said, pushing the bassinet next to the bed to demonstrate. "So Max can sleep right next to our bed for now. And eventually, he'll get *your* room." He lowered his eyes. "We're hoping you'll have moved out on your own by then."

"Just visiting," I snorted. "In fact, as Lamaze coach, my work here is done. I can be on the next plane."

"Aw, come on, Holly," Danny said, grabbing my hand and pulling me down so I was sitting next to him on the bed. "Don't'cha want to see him grow up? Say his first words? Take his first steps? Go on his first date?"

"We've been through this before," I said. "I'm not moving to Los Angeles."

Danny slapped my leg and stood, making his way toward the bathroom. "We'll see."

★　★　★

While Danny was showering, I got out my date book and started making calls. First I dialed my own number. I bypassed the outgoing message and punched in the code to retrieve my messages.

After a series of beeps, Brian's voice came through the line. "Hey, Holly, I sure hope you get this. I got your message about having to leave town early. The thing is, I can't watch Grouch and the gang this week. I'm flying to London tomorrow to film a commercial. And my agent set me up with a couple go-sees while I'm there, so I'll be gone a week. Sure wish I could help you out."

There was a long beep. Then the next message began. "Brian again. I popped in on the guys. Filled food bowls and tickled bellies and that sort of thing. Gotta run now. My flight's at nine. Hope you find someone to fill in for me. I'll call you."

There were a few hang-ups and then Tom's voice. "Hey there. Sorry I missed your call. I wish I could have seen you before you left. . . ." He paused and my stomach lurched. "I need to talk to you." Another pause. Then he said, "Bye," dragging it out over two syllables.

I need to talk to you. What did *that* mean? I took a deep breath and told myself not to read anything into it. It could be a perfectly benign statement.

Then why were my hands shaking as I dialed his number?

The phone rang once, twice, three times. I glanced at the clock and tried to calculate what time it would be in New York. Three hours' difference. Add three, or subtract three? I couldn't remember. I was too tired to think straight.

His voice mail picked up. He was probably teaching, I told myself. Unless he was out on a date with his ex-wife. *At least he can't bring me the leftovers this time,* I thought, remembering the take-out bag from Hong Kong Palace. And his utter cluelessness as to why I was upset. The symbolism should have smacked him in the face.

Then I had one of those D-oh! moments as I realized that Tom had not only dined with his ex on the night of our six-month anniversary, but he had taken her to *my favorite Chinese restaurant.*

There was dead space on the phone and I realized the machine had already beeped and I was just sitting there, stewing over symbolic leftovers.

"Um . . . hi . . . it's Holly." Since my voice was shaking, I kept the message brief—the flight arrived safely, the baby is healthy, everyone's fine. Then I rattled off the number for Betty's cell phone and added, "I need to talk to you, too." Two can play that game.

I dialed Aunt Kuki's number and was relieved when Gerry answered the phone.

I relayed the information about my flight and Max's birth.

"Carter had the baby!" he shouted to whoever was sitting around the dining room table. I heard voices erupt with questions and congratulations. Then he spoke back into the phone. "Monica and I are here going over the invitation list with Ma and Aunt Bet. They say to give the baby a kiss. And Ma says she's knitting him a baby blanket."

I smiled, relieved that last night's melee hadn't completely destroyed my relationship with my aunt Kuki. Or at least if it had, she wasn't taking it out on the baby.

"And Monica wants to know if you're bringing a date to the wedding," Gerry added. "Besides Rocky, of course."

I rolled my eyes. "She's serious about the snake?"

"Don't get me started. You know how I feel about that snake, but it's her big day and I want it to be perfect for her."

I felt a lump in my throat. Hard to believe, but I was actually jealous of Monica Broccoli. She had found a man who was willing to turn his wedding into a freak show just to make her happy. Then I heard her voice in the background, grumbling something about keeping the guest list down.

"So what is it?" Gerry said. "Do we put Tom's name on the invitation, too?"

"It's on a Saturday, huh? Tom's never free on Saturdays, so—"

Monica had snatched the phone away from Gerry and was screeching into the mouthpiece. "Great. I'll put you down as 'Holly Heckerling and Rocky Broccoli.' "

"Swell."

"Don't forget, you promised to come back in time for the wedding."

How could I miss it? My cousin was getting married. All of our relatives would be there. And I had a date with a snake.

But before I could answer, Monica hung up the phone.

I hit redial. This time Aunt Betty answered. "Holly, dear," she said, sounding surprised. "Gerry was just talking to you."

"I know. I need to talk to him again."

"Okay," she said. "You be sure to give that baby boy a little nip on the cheek from me."

"Sure," I said, hoping Max didn't make Betty's acquaintance until he was old enough to bite back.

"Oh, and ask Carter about hemorrhoids."

"What about them?"

"I'm getting terrible hemorrhoids, and I want to know how she managed them. I hear they're a common symptom of pregnancy."

"You're not pregnant," I reminded her.

"I know that," she huffed. "But a hemorrhoid is a hemorrhoid." She handed the phone off to Gerry.

"What's up?" he asked. "Change your mind about Tom?"

"No. I need a favor. A big, big favor."

"Name it." That's what I love about Gerry. When it comes to family, he's a no-questions-asked kind of guy.

"My neighbor Brian was supposed to take care of my animals while I'm gone, but he left town, too. Could you . . . ?"

"Sure, no prob. What, like once a week?"

I suddenly remembered why Gerry had never been able to keep a pet alive—little things like food and water kept slipping his mind. "Once a day. Never mind. I'll try to find someone else."

"Once a *day*?" he balked. "Are you sure?"

I exhaled. "I'll ask Tom to do it. It's just . . . you have a key to my place, so I thought it would be easier."

"No, no, I'll do it. It's just, you know, you live all the way in the city."

"I know. Forget it. Can you ask Monica to take care of Rocky? I can probably find someone to take care of Grouch and Felix and Jack and Whoopi. But I can't ask anyone to babysit a boa constrictor."

"Don't worry, Holly. I'll take care of all of them. I won't let you down."

I turned my attention to my appointment book. It would have been a good week for Holly's Hobbies—one of those increasingly rare instances where income exceeds expenses. Too bad I had to cancel all my bookings.

I called David first. Margie answered and told me that David was resting but she'd relay the message that I was canceling our engagement at PS 11 on Wednesday morning.

"That's too bad," Margie said. "He really looks forward to those visits with the kids. It's given him new purpose in life." She lowered her voice. "Tell the truth, I think he gets more out of it than the kids."

Margie's comments gave me an idea. "He should go without me," I said.

"Oh, no, that's not possible—"

"Sure it is. You do the driving anyway. And David and Tallulah are the stars of the show. Me and my guys are just the warm-up act. You've seen the faces on those kids when David rolls in the classroom with Tallulah on his shoulder."

Margie protested, "He'll never agree to go without you."

She was right. David would be too timid to give a presentation by himself. He had a very narrow comfort zone. It took a lot of prodding to get him to try new things. Tallulah was the adventurous one. Without her, David would most likely never venture from his apartment except for medical appointments. Tallulah loved getting out and mingling with people—most of whom were so captivated by the capuchin that they got past their own self-consciousness about David's handicap.

"Don't tell him," I said. "At least not until the last minute. Then tell him I can't make it and he has to do it without me. For the kids."

"I don't know. . . ."

It hit me that I was asking her to lie to David—the very person whose well-being she was paid to protect. He was not only her patient, but her boss and her friend. I couldn't put her in that position. "Don't tell him anything. Just forget I called. On Wednesday morning, get him ready to go, and at the last minute, I'll call to say I can't make it."

"I don't know. . . . Are you sure he'll go for it?"

"I'll give him the whole show-must-go-on speech. He'll do it."

"For the kids," Margie and I said in unison.

By the time I worked through the list of clients whose appointments I needed to reschedule, Danny was out of the shower.

"All yours," he called over his shoulder as he scooped his keys off the kitchen counter and headed for the door. "You remember how to get back to the hospital?"

"Not really . . . I wasn't paying attention on the drive over. I just focused on your back bumper."

"Kinky," he said. "Watch out. I'm practically married."

"And that's practically funny." Danny and I used to enjoy an easy banter, bouncing jokes back and forth whether onstage or off-. But things had changed. There was dead air as he exited the apartment and locked the door behind him.

Moments later, he returned. He popped his head inside the door and called, "I'm leaving you a map of LA. Just in case."

I heard papers shuffling and keys jangling; then he was gone again.

In the shower, I found creamed corn in crevices that defied logical explanation. I had been fully clothed during the food fight, after all. Best not to ponder how everything wound up where it did, I told myself, letting the shower spray linger in my nooks and crannies.

I allowed extra time for the shampoo and conditioner to work their magic on my hair. My torso was still dotted with yellow-brown bruises, but I no longer cared.

When I was squeaky clean and dressed in fresh clothes, I stretched out on the sofa. I wanted to get back to the hospital to see Max and Carter, but needed to rest my eyes for a few minutes before I'd be fit to drive.

A few minutes stretched into two hours.

I woke with a start. I had dreamed I returned to my apartment building to find all my belongings stacked in boxes on the sidewalk. I'd been evicted. Even my pets were out on the street, their cages and carriers lined up in a neat row.

My heart was racing. Disoriented, I stared around the room bug-eyed for a few moments before I realized where I was.

And what day it was.

Monday.

Late afternoon in New York. My building owner could have already attempted to cash my rent check, which would have bounced. My bank charged steep fees for returned checks. Of course bank fees would be the least of my problems if the owner got his court order to evict me.

I dashed to the bathroom and grabbed my discarded jeans off the floor. The crisp hundred-dollar bill that arrogant Daltry dude had given me the night before was still in the pocket. I'd wanted to shove it back in his smug face. But now I was glad I'd kept it.

Clutching it tight, I raced back through the apartment, gathering up my purse and rental car keys and stooping to pick up the map Danny had left for me.

The "map" was a spiral-bound book the size of an encyclopedia. Its sheer mass was intimidating. The entire map of Manhattan can fit on a pocket-sized laminated card, after all. As I flipped through page after multicolored page—all divided into grids and dominated by squiggly lines that presumably correlated to squiggly streets—I began to rethink my decision to dismiss Navigation Nancy. Perhaps I'd judged her too harshly.

"Welcome to LA," I told myself, tucking the encyclo-map under my arm and locking the door behind me.

"Let's try again," I said, turning the key in the ignition and waiting for the navigation system to boot up.

The rental-car clerk had helpfully pointed out the system's ability to lead me to the nearest location of any restaurant, bank, or coffeehouse. Once Nancy was awake, I keyed in the name of my bank and waited while it searched for local branches.

"Please proceed to the highlighted route," Nancy said. I looked at the display and tried to orient myself. Then I put the car in gear and drove in the direction indicated.

Nancy's instructions were no less vague than they had been the night before, but now that I was somewhat rested, I had a higher tolerance level for her imprecision. Having learned that "turn right" doesn't necessarily mean "turn right *now*," I took longer to evaluate my route and the options ahead of me before acting.

We were doing well, Nancy and I, until we turned onto Sunset Boulevard. Traffic was heavy and cars were darting between lanes. I felt like I was in a NASCAR arcade game. My shoulders were tense, and I had a death grip on the steering wheel. The little screen seemed to indicate I was approaching the bank, but Nancy hadn't chimed in yet.

I was in the far-right lane when I spotted my bank on the left side of the street. I signaled to change lanes but no one was giving me an opening. I wondered why Nancy hadn't warned me to get into the left lane. Half a block after I had passed the bank, she finally came to life. "Turn left." I could see the bank in my rearview mirror.

"You have passed your destination," Nancy intoned. "Please return to the highlighted route."

Twenty minutes later I was circling Cedars-Sinai, looking for a place to park. I'd deposited eighty of Daltry's dollars into my account, keeping twenty bucks spending money, and I didn't want to waste any of it on parking fees. I found a spot several blocks south of the hospital and locked the car.

As I walked north, I reflected on my brief conversation with the bank teller. My account was still in the black, she informed me, confirming that my new balance was just enough to cover the check I'd left for Pete. A close call, but I'd avoided eviction. My belongings wouldn't be thrown into the street, and I wouldn't have to room with Ronnie in Kuki's house.

When I got to Carter's room, she and Danny were arguing. I paused in the doorway, not wanting to intrude.

"You said you didn't want any anesthesia, under any circumstances," Danny was saying. "You said you could handle the pain—"

"You don't know diddly-fucking-squat about *pain*," she hissed. "You were cracking jokes the whole time."

"I was trying to help. I didn't know what else to do." I believed it. Humor was pretty much Danny's only defense mechanism.

"You should have insisted they give me something."

"Shhh, you'll wake the baby."

Max was cradled in the nook of Carter's arms, sleeping peacefully despite the storm brewing around him.

I crept forward, and Carter looked up, all smiles. "There you are. I thought maybe you were lost."

"Or comatose," Danny added.

"A little of both," I said, leaning over to get a closer look at the new arrival.

We were all silent for a while, watching Max sleep. Then Danny's cell phone sang out the *Tonight* show theme. He darted out into the hallway to take the call.

Carter rolled her eyes. "They're probably calling him back to the set. I was surprised he stayed this long. He even turned his cell phone off during the delivery."

"Of course he did."

"You'd be surprised. That thing rings, he jumps. He's on set day and night, and he has a small part. He says they just have him sitting around on the set all day, waiting."

"I think that's normal."

"I think it's suspicious. Sitting around all day. Probably in Jennifer Aniston's trailer. You know, she broke up with what's-his-name."

"You're paranoid," I said. "He loves you."

The door swung opened and Danny entered. He looked contrite as he told Carter he'd been summoned to the set.

He punched my arm. "Why don't you come with me?"

I shook my head. "No way. No one's gonna pry me from this little guy's side. I haven't even had a chance to hold him yet."

"The nurse said he'll sleep most of the day," Danny said. "And Carter should, too."

Carter nodded her head in agreement, but I remained steadfast. "Sorry, Danny. This is what having a solo career means. You're on your own."

A nurse entered the room with a food tray, which she set on the rolling table next to Carter's bed.

Danny pulled me aside. "You gotta come with me, Holly. There's a monkey in the movie. Just like Tallulah. And a bunch of other animals, too. Right up your alley."

I'd never been on a movie set, and I was curious about the critters. More important, I wouldn't have minded catching a glimpse of Hugh Jackman. But my first obligation was to Carter.

The nurse returned Max to his incubator. Carter was picking at the tray in front of her, making a sour face at a mound of macaroni and cheese.

Danny gave her a peck on the cheek and said he'd break away from filming as soon as he could. "I'll bring you back some real food," he promised, heading for the door.

"Wait," she called. "Holly's going with you."

"No, I'm not."

She looked at me with raised eyebrows and mouthed something I couldn't understand.

I shrugged. "I want to stay."

"Don't you want to meet Hugh Jackman?" she said, nodding her head as though answering for me. "And Jennifer Aniston? Hmm?"

Aha. Earth to Holly. Now I got it. She wanted me to keep an eye on Danny and make sure he wasn't becoming too friendly with a certain former Friend.

"Jackman dropped out," Danny said. "Scheduling conflict or something. That's why they want me back. I gotta reshoot the one scene I did with him."

"Hugh's out?" Carter asked. "When? Why didn't you tell me?"

"Yesterday," Danny said. "It slipped my mind, what with all the screaming and swearing." He turned to me. "You coming, or what?"

I turned to Carter, who was making shooing motions with her hand. "As soon as I finish my craparoni and cheese, I'm going to sleep."

"I'm a little concerned about the foul language," I said, when Danny and I were in the corridor. "Aren't you?"

Danny snorted. "Why? She's always talked like that."

"Yeah, back in her chain-smoking, club-hopping days. But since she got pregnant, she's been Miss Purity Sunshine, always talking about embracing harmony, purging her soul of negativity, filling her mind with poetry, and—"

"And all that crap?" Danny finished for me.

"Yeah. What happened to that?"

He shrugged. "I guess childbirth shocked her back to her old self. Don't worry. I'm sure she'll tone it down by the time Max is old enough to understand." He punched the elevator button. "Otherwise, I'll call social services on her ass."

Holly Does Hollywood

Vets in the City was filming at a hospital in West LA. Since going bankrupt in the early nineties, the once-genuine medical facility now served as a setting for numerous film and television productions. Apparently there was more money to be made in location rental fees than in hospital bills.

"Turn right." Even though I hadn't entered a destination into the computer, Nancy was still trying to tell me where to go. But I ignored her, keeping Danny's Volkswagen in my sights. We'd decided to take two cars so that if he got held up for hours, I could get back to the hospital on my own.

I followed Danny into the lot, pulled into a parking space, and turned off the ignition.

I appraised my appearance in the rearview mirror and decided I looked pretty darn good. I'd spent less than two minutes on my hair at Danny's, but it looked fabulous—full-bodied, glossy, and flipping up subtly where it met my shoulders. Normally it would take two hours with hot rollers and a curling iron to achieve this look. But today . . . ? Perhaps the California atmosphere agreed with me. Or maybe mashed potatoes made a damn good conditioner.

Danny was standing at my window, tapping his watch. I climbed out of the car and followed him in through the lobby.

We took a cramped elevator to the second floor. The doors opened onto a small waiting room and an abandoned nurses' station.

We rounded a corner and walked down a corridor. At the far end, I could see camera equipment set up and people milling about, sipping coffee or talking on walkie-talkies.

As we walked, Danny filled me in about the hospital's history and rattled off a list of shows and movies it had been used in. Everywhere I looked, medical supplies were scattered about. A stethoscope dangled from a ceiling fan. Someone had painted a smiley face on a bedpan and affixed it to the wall, where it had become a repository for crushed coffee cups and other trash.

We walked past a room filled with banks of monitors and film equipment. Another had been converted into hair and makeup quarters, with three barber chairs aligned in front of a wall of mirrors.

When we reached the crew, a short, stocky man wearing a headset slapped Danny on the back. "Congratulations, Papa."

Danny pulled a Polaroid out of his pocket. It was the baby's first "official" photo, taken by the hospital staff just after his birth. Though Danny had taken hundreds of his own photos with his digital camera, not to mention video footage, he still bought the $21.99 hospital photo package, including six wallet-sized and two laminated photo–key chains.

"Nice." The man with the headset nodded. "Now get to makeup." He handed Danny some papers and was pushing him toward the makeup room when he spotted me.

"Who's this?" he said, looking at me but addressing Danny.

"My friend Holly. From New York." Danny turned to me. "Hol, this is Giovanni, the AD." He added as an aside, "Assistant director."

"Closed set," Giovanni announced. "She can't be here."

"Someone doing a nude scene?" Danny asked, a bead of drool forming at the corner of his mouth.

Giovanni looked over his shoulder. I followed his gaze to a far corner of the set, where a juvenile chimpanzee was seated on a director's chair. Next to the chimp stood a brawny man wearing a bright red shirt. He had a finger pointed at the chimp as though he was scolding it.

"Monkey's on set," Giovanni said, apparently oblivious to the fact that chimpanzees are apes, not monkeys.

"So?" Danny said, arching one eyebrow. "Is the monkey gonna be naked?"

"Set has to be cleared of all nonessential personnel whenever working animals are, you know, working," Giovanni explained.

"Really?" Danny looked downcast. "I dragged her all this way. Can't we say she's my dialogue coach or something?"

"Why do you need a dialogue coach?" Giovanni asked. "You only have one line in this scene."

One line? I thought this was Danny's big break.

"I understand," I said. "They don't want the animals to be stressed. I can go."

Danny stopped me before I could turn away. "But Holly works with animals," he told Giovanni. "She's got a degree in . . . what's it called . . . monkeyology."

"Primatology," I corrected. "But I'll leave—"

"She babysits this monkey, Tallulah. And she's got a boa constrictor."

"You got a boa?" Giovanni asked me. This had his attention. Not every day you meet a chick with a boa constrictor. "What is it, a red-tail?"

I shook my head. "Are you kidding? Red-tails grow to be ten feet. Rocky's a rosy."

"You feed it live prey?"

I grimaced. "I tried, but I couldn't go through with it. Ended up with a pet rat."

He let out a burst of laughter that turned into a raspy cough. When he could speak again, he said, "My wife and kids won't let me feed Nemo anything with a pulse."

"Nemo?" Danny asked.

"My four-year-old named him. We order online from Frozen Rodent.com."

"Me, too," I squealed. "Small world. Do you thaw overnight or nuke 'em?"

He let out another cough-chuckle combo. "I nuked one and my wife nearly had a coronary when she went to pop some popcorn and found little beady eyes staring back at her."

I made a face. "I'm afraid of dead-rat particles floating loose and ending up on whatever food I microwave next."

"Isn't this sweet?" Danny said, patting both our backs. "Strangers bonding over zapped rats. Now what's it gonna be? Does she stay or go?"

Giovanni scanned the room. "Trainer won't care. I don't see the Humane Association rep." He put one hand on my shoulder. "Lay low. Monkey's off-limits. If the Humane lady sees ya, I'll act like we've never met."

So much for our newfound friendship.

"Thanks," I said. "By the way, it's not a monkey—it's a chimp."

He shook his head. "I know, I know. Monkey's its name." He circled one finger in the air, the universal sign for crazy. "Monkey the Chimp."

"Is it a boy or girl?" I asked, curious about the little ape on the far side of the room.

"Probably a girl. They use females so they don't have to worry about their little, you know, wangdoodles showing up on film."

Hmm. We never learned the term "wangdoodle" in primate anatomy class.

"Thanks, Gio," Danny said as the AD left in pursuit of an errant extra who'd just strolled in, cigarette dangling from his lips.

"Put it out, Chet," Giovanni barked.

I followed Danny to the hair and makeup room. He hopped into a chair and a tall, rail-thin woman who looked like a movie star herself started applying foundation to his skin with a sponge. He introduced me as his personal assistant, and she gave me a nod by way of greeting.

"Xiana," she said. "With an X."

"Nice to meet you."

"Hey, Zee, wanna see my kid?" Danny pulled the Polaroid out of his pocket and waved it in her direction.

She glanced at it and made an appropriate googly noise.

Danny leaned back, closed his eyes, and folded his hands across his chest.

The chair next to Danny was empty, so I climbed into it. With nothing better to do, I began eyeing the rows of cosmetics and hair products arrayed on the counter in front of me. High-end stuff: some brands I'd never heard of before; others I was familiar with but couldn't afford. A few of my hairstyling clients insisted on particular brands. For them I'd make special trips to Sephora or Frédéric Fekkai. But for the others, and my own needs, I usually stalked the bargain bin at Duane Reade.

"Nice hair," Xiana said. "What product do you use?"

I glanced at myself in the mirror. I truly was having a good-hair day. But I knew it wasn't the result of any bargain-basement conditioner or gel. "Idaho Spuds."

She nodded uncertainly before returning her attention to whatever it was she had to do to make Danny camera-ready.

I was reading the fine print on a bottle of spritzer when I heard heavy footsteps approach from behind and someone tapped my shoulder. "Outta the chair," a husky-voiced woman said.

"Sorry," I said, scooting off the chair and squeezing through the space that separated it from Danny's.

"Hey, Shauna," Danny said, opening one eye. "This is Holly."

Shauna was an Amazon—tall, big-boned, and strikingly beautiful, with bone-straight, jet-black hair that went halfway down her back. A cell phone and a two-way radio were clipped to the waistband of her cargo pants. She eyed me critically. "Actor?"

"Nah, she's nonpro," Danny said. "We used to do stand-up together, back in New York, but she left me to go work with animals instead."

"What's the difference?" Shauna said, wiping down the chair with a towel as though to rid it of my nonpro cooties.

"What's the story with Jackman?" Danny asked the Amazon.

"Scheduling conflict," Shauna said.

"That's the official line, anyway," Xiana added.

Danny sat up. "And unofficially?"

Xiana said, "I hear he didn't like the monkey."

"It's a *chimp*," I said.

I was shushed by Shauna, who grabbed her two-way, pressed a button, and spoke into it. "Tell Colin I'm ready for him."

"Colin?" I mouthed to Danny.

"New guy," Danny said sotto voce. "Colin Daltry."

"Never heard of him," I said. But even as I said it, a sinking feeling was sneaking over me that not only had I heard the name Daltry, but I'd already made the new star's acquaintance.

"What rock have you been living under?" Shauna asked me.

Xiana smiled solicitously. "Colin Daltry is, like, so hot. He's on the cover of this month's *Vanity Fair*. He was in *Total Meltdown II*, *Annihilation Nation*, and, like, a bunch of other movies. I can't believe you haven't heard of him."

I shrugged my shoulders, registering a blank. I tended to avoid death-and-destruction films in favor of flirty romantic comedies. "What's a guy like that doing in a chick flick?"

"He wants to branch out," Shauna said authoritatively. "Reach a different demo."

"Demo*graphic*," Danny whispered in my ear.

"Yeah," I said. "I got it."

Just then Daltry himself filled the doorway of the makeup room. He leaned one arm against the doorframe and smiled. It was the same self-serving, condescending grin he'd flashed me in the airport, when bribing me with the hundred bucks. The five Frigidaires were nowhere in sight, but I would have recognized him anywhere, even without his supersized sidekicks. Same chiseled cheekbones, same deliberately windswept hair.

He looked much taller than he had at the airport, perhaps because he wasn't surrounded by a bunch of Mr. T wannabes.

The sinking feeling turned into full-fledged nausea. I slunk behind Danny's chair, taking solace in the fact that while Daltry looked much the same as he had in our earlier encounter, I looked entirely different. No way would he recognize me—with my clean clothes and fabulous hair—as the Mrs. Potato Head who'd chased him down in the airport, sports bra in hand.

I just had to play it cool.

Daltry shrugged out of a black blazer and slid into Shauna's chair. "Hello, doll."

Shauna wrapped a cloth towel around Daltry's neck and began applying his makeup.

Xiana reached around her to stick her hand out to Daltry. "I'm Xiana. With an X."

"With an X," Daltry repeated, shaking her hand. "Sexy."

Xiana giggled. Danny leaned forward in his chair. "Danny Crane. I play Tobey."

"Tobey." Daltry tipped an imaginary hat in Danny's direction. "Pleasure."

I held my breath, hoping Danny wouldn't feel the need to introduce me. Just then Giovanni stuck his head in the room and pointed a stubby finger in Danny's direction. "They're waiting for you in wardrobe."

Saved by the AD.

Danny darted out the door and I followed on tiptoe. I needn't have worried about Daltry recognizing me with Xiana and Shauna fawning over him. He didn't even bat an eyelash in my direction.

* ★ ★

I found an unobtrusive spot on the set to sit and watch the action. We were in a large area that had once obviously been two small rooms. A wall had been knocked down to allow one side to be used by the crew. The other side, formerly an actual examining room, had been made over to resemble a veterinary exam room. On one wall hung a poster diagramming the musculosketetal system of a dog. Another sign urged owners to spay or neuter their pets.

A property master worked his way across the room, methodically checking supplies and equipment. Other crew members bustled around, positioning cameras and unfurling cables. Giovanni called for stand-ins to take their places, and a waiflike blond woman approached the exam room. She kicked off her clogs and stood in her bare feet on the spot indicated by the AD.

Two men followed suit, strolling to their marks without enthusiasm. The first was short, slender, and looked all of twelve. I surmised he was supposed to be Danny's stand-in. The other was tall and broad-shouldered, and he looked enough like Hugh Jackman to cause me to do a double-take. I guess the double hadn't been replaced when Jackman dropped out.

The trio struck uninterested poses as lights were positioned. Giovanni approached the examining room and set a two-foot-tall brown object on the metal table. It looked like a dead Christmas tree with feet and a beak. It took me a moment to figure out that it was a stuffed Big Bird doll that had been spray-painted brown.

Giovanni positioned the doll so that it was facing the tall stand-in.

He passed me on his way to the corridor, and I couldn't help asking about the spray-painted Muppet.

"Stand-in for the chimp," he answered. He cracked a smile. "We call him Big Turd."

Sensing I was about to ask a dumb question, I opened my mouth anyway. "If the real chimp's on set, why not use him?"

"Humane Association rules," Giovanni said. "Primates can only be on set for the action. We can't use them as stand-ins."

"Oh." I was beginning to sense that Giovanni wasn't thrilled with the Humane Association's myriad rules.

Someone called, "Places," and the stand-ins scurried off the set. Colin Daltry assumed the spot vacated by the Jackman look-alike. I shrunk down a little farther in my chair just in case he should cast his gaze my way.

Danny had emerged from wardrobe having apparently traded his own distressed jeans and navy pullover for a costume consisting of professionally distressed jeans and an emerald green pullover. He walked through the exam room and exited through a door.

Kelly Ripa bounced onto the set wearing a white lab coat over a scoop-necked burgundy dress. A stethoscope dangled around her neck. She looked pretty and perky and impossibly petite. I wouldn't have believed anyone could appear smaller in person than she did on my teensy-tiny TV set, but she did.

She was smiling and waving and shouting hellos as she came onto the set. A hair stylist came forward and made sure every blond strand was in place, then backed away slowly so as not to stir up a breeze.

When the three humans were in position, Giovanni retrieved Big Turd and radioed for the animal handler. Moments later the brawny man I'd seen earlier strode onto the set carrying the chimpanzee. He pointed to the metal table. The chimp leapt onto the precise spot and reached a hand out for a reward.

I craned my neck for a closer look at the chimpanzee. Not a wangdoodle in sight. Giovanni was right. Monkey was a girl.

The trainer reached into a pouch at his waist and handed the chimp a treat. Then he leaned closer, presumably giving the animal instructions, but I couldn't hear anything. He pointed at the chimp, stiff-fingered, the whole time. It made me vaguely uncomfortable. The chimp was small, probably less than three years old. It was dwarfed by the trainer, and probably terrified.

The trainer backed away, stepping to one side of the action. A woman in a khaki uniform stood next to him. Probably the fearsome Humane Association representative Giovanni had warned me to avoid.

Someone ran forward with a clapper, shouting the scene and take number. Then the director called, "Action."

I felt a surge of excitement as I realized that I was on a bona fide movie set. Living in Manhattan, I'd seen my share of celebrities going about their daily lives—hailing cabs, sipping lattes, dining out. I'd also stumbled onto several location shots for film or TV series set in New York. Just last week, I'd had to detour around a *Law & Order* shoot that had taken over a street in my neighborhood.

But I'd never been an invited guest on a set before. Danny and I had once dreamed of working together in showbiz, and while the dream had only half come true, it was thrilling nonetheless.

In the scene being filmed, Daltry brings his pet chimpanzee to the veterinarian—played by Kelly—for a checkup, claiming the chimp has been acting strangely. It soon becomes obvious that there's nothing wrong with the chimp—her owner just wanted to chat up the pretty vet he'd met earlier in some implausibly cute way. While Daltry and Ripa flirt, the chimp raids a supply cabinet and wraps itself in gauze bandages. As Daltry bends to retrieve his pet, the chimp throws a box of tongue depressors in his face. Meanwhile, Danny, playing Kelly's brother and veterinary assistant, has entered the room, and the chimp escapes through his legs, a trail of gauze in his wake.

Kelly and Daltry rush out of the room in pursuit of the mischievous ape, while Danny stands there looking flummoxed. After a beat, he quips, "Was it something I said?"

All that waiting for one line? Danny's delivery was dead-on, but I hoped there was more to his part than the occasional wise-crack.

The scene was filmed three times in quick succession. After each take, crew members rushed forward to replace the gauze and tongue depressors, and stylists primped and spritzed the stars. The red-shirted animal trainer proffered treats to the chimpanzee and led her off to a quiet corner of the set.

From where I was sitting, I could hear the director talking to the cinematographer. Neither seemed satisfied with the way the scene was going. I thought it was cute in an entirely unrealistic way. It was obvious Daltry was green when it came to romantic comedy. He was trying too hard. His expression at the end of the scene looked more like he was about to burst into a burning building to rescue a dozen orphans than chase a mischievous chimp around a veterinary hospital. He wasn't having fun.

Someone asked Hal, the director, if they were moving on, and after a long pause, he sighed heavily and said, "Let's do one more." Then he called Daltry over and they had a brief conversation. I could only make out the tail end, in which the director told Daltry to "lighten up."

Good call, I thought. *Maybe I have a knack for this movie business.*

Someone called, "Places," then, "Action," and the scene was repeated once more.

This time, I paid closer attention to Daltry, willing him to dial down the *Die Hard.* Not that I cared about Daltry, but this was Danny's movie, too, and I'd hate to see it tank because no one told Daltry he was in a comedy.

Daltry's performance was a little less wooden on the fourth take, but something was still off. Midway through the scene, I finally put my finger on the problem. While Daltry had palpable chemistry with Kelly, he was obviously uncomfortable with the chimp. With Kelly, he was slick and—dare I say—sexy, but when interacting with the chimp that was supposed to be his pet, he seemed stiff and—dare I say—scared.

I was congratulating myself on this astute observation when I heard a 1970s pop song chirping from the deepest recesses of my purse.

Damn. I had forgotten to turn off the cell phone.

I reached into my purse, rummaging around, as the "Copacabana" grew louder. I fumbled for the phone and hit the button to silence the song, praying that no one else had heard it.

No such luck.

"Cut!" someone yelled. "Whose phone is that?"

I looked up to see all eyes on me, glaring.

"Sorry," I yelped, shrinking even farther into my seat.

"Who is that?" the voice repeated. "What moron didn't turn off his cell phone?"

I raised a hand in the air sheepishly. "Sorry. I said I'm sorry." I gathered up my purse and began backing out of the room. I'd just go find some hole to crawl into.

Everyone was looking in my direction, including the Humane Association officer I'd been instructed to avoid.

"I'm leaving," I said, continuing my backward trajectory.

Now the director was standing. "Who the hell are you? You ruined the take."

"I'm nobody. Just visiting."

"Visiting *whom*?"

My stomach lurched. I didn't want to get Danny in trouble. But I also didn't want everyone to think I was some freak who'd crashed a movie set. I looked up at the exam-room set. Danny hadn't made his entrance yet, so he was still in the hallway. I could see his shadow through the door. I'd give him three seconds to come forward and claim me as his guest before I blew his cover.

Two seconds.

One second.

"She's with me," a male voice called from the set. It wasn't Danny. "I forgot to tell her to turn off her bleeping phone," Daltry said, adding, "Sorry, Hal."

I was too stunned to say anything.

"What's she doing here?" the director asked. "It's a closed set."

The Humane Association rep stepped forward. "Filming cannot proceed if nonessential personnel are present—"

"She is essential," Daltry said. He was walking toward me. I had nowhere to run, nowhere to hide. I wasn't sure if he recognized me, or if he was just trying to be nice. "She's absolutely essential."

He stopped a foot short of me, flashed a fiendish smile, and said, "Hello, Lola."

Daltry grabbed me by the hand and pulled me forward. "This is Lola," he said to the director. "My attorney."

Okay, so he recognized me. I felt my face flush, recalling my lame attempts to pass myself off as a lawyer at the airport.

The Human Association rep had closed in. She was shaking her head. "Lawyers are not essential personnel. I hate to do this, but I'm gonna hafta close down this shoot if the set isn't cleared."

The director swore. Shutting down without the scene in the can would be costly.

Daltry just smiled. "Excuse me. I didn't catch your name." He held out his hand, and she shook it.

"Angela Ambrosino, American Humane Association. It's my duty to ensure the welfare of all the animals on this set, and—"

"Angela, doll." Daltry cut in. "I understand the rules. I got the briefing from Giovanni about the set being closed. But Lola's not just my lawyer—she's more like my manager. She advises me in all avenues of my career."

"She may be essential to *you*," Angela said, clearly unimpressed. "But she's not essential to this scene."

"You're wrong," Daltry said, still smiling. "She's here to help me whenever I need it. And I need help with this scene."

"You can say that again," I muttered.

Daltry shot me a wide-eyed look. I couldn't tell if he was annoyed or amused.

Angela turned to the director and gave a palms-up.

"What kind of game are you playin', Colin?" the director asked. "You never mentioned needing a lawyer on set."

"No game, Hal." He cocked his head to one side. "Lola's not here in a legal capacity," he said, his voice dripping with innuendo. "She's got great . . . insights." Wink-wink, nudge-nudge.

There was a moment of silence as everyone on set gave my insights the once-over. I found myself in the rare position of being flattered and revolted at the same time. I was being treated like a plaything, true, but I was being treated like the plaything of an A-list movie star.

I allowed myself a moment to bask in the lecherous attention of the crew before indignation took over. "As a matter of fact, I do have some insights," I said, "that concern this scene."

The director let out an indulgent chuckle. "All right, Lola, let's hear your insights."

I sucked in my stomach and proceeded with my amateur assessment of what was wrong with the scene. "He's supposed to be the chimp's owner," I said, pointing at Daltry. "But he acts like he's afraid of her."

"Damn right," Daltry said. "I know how vicious chimpanzees can be. A few years back, a chimp mauled a guy. Bit his nuts off."

The trainer stepped forward to defend his charge. "She's never bit anyone!"

"Monkey here is less than three," I said, "and obviously docile." I approached the exam table, where the little chimp was sitting, obediently waiting for her cue. Angela followed sharply on my heels.

I ignored her, addressing Daltry instead. "When you reach out to her, your arm is stiff. You wouldn't do that if she was your pet."

I approached Monkey with my head lowered and one arm outstretched, palm down, back of my hand facing her. It was something I'd learned while volunteering at a primate sanctuary during college. My supervisor, Dotty, had taught me to always approach an ape submissively, to seek their permission before touching them.

I crouched down so I was closer to her level. "Hi, sweet girl," I said in a low voice.

I looked over my shoulder at Daltry. "You treat her like she's got a communicable disease. You keep her at arm's length when she's on the exam table. If she was really your pet, you'd lean closer, act like you give a damn."

Monkey leaned forward and examined my hand. She seemed especially interested in my wristwatch, raising one finger and tapping its surface. "It's okay," I said. She scratched the watch with her thick fingernail. Then she put her hand on mine.

I leaned closer and whispered. "Actors, huh? I bet you could tell me some stories."

Then she leapt on my body and threw her arms around me.

A smattering of applause broke out.

"The monkey likes her," Kelly said. "He really likes her."

Angela threw her arms up in the air. "This is highly inappropriate. No one without proper training can handle an animal on the set."

Now Giovanni stepped forward. "It's okay. She has a degree in monkeyology."

"Primatology," I corrected.

"You do?" Daltry said.

"You have a very interesting attorney, Mr. Daltry," the director said. "I'll give you five minutes to sort this out, and then we'll do another take."

"Take five, everybody," Giovanni shouted. Cast and crew

dispersed, most heading toward craft services—a cafeteria-length table in the hallway that was covered with enough food to feed an army. Food and cigarettes trump movie star and Monkey. Even Danny had dematerialized.

The director bent in conference with the DP. The trainer snapped his fingers and Monkey loosened her grip on me and climbed onto his back.

"Can I have a minute with the chimp?" Daltry asked.

Both the trainer and Angela shook their heads, Angela citing the regulation that mandates regular breaks for performing primates. The trainer disappeared through the doorway with Monkey on his back. I watched them go, waving when Monkey turned back to look at me.

Daltry turned to Angela, putting his roguish charm into overdrive. He placed his hand on her elbow as he assured her that the well-being of the chimpanzee was of the utmost importance to him, and that it was his deep and abiding concern for the animal that led him to hire me as a consultant. By better relating to the chimp, he theorized, he could give a better performance, and therefore improve the public's understanding and appreciation for all primates.

I could tell Angela was buying it. Maybe not hook, line, and sinker, but she was at least a little bit hooked.

Heck, by the end of his soliloquy, even I was nearly convinced that barring me from the set would do a disservice to animals everywhere.

She agreed to let me stay on set for the remainder of this scene, but said she'd have to write up an incident report. She shot me a look that said she'd be watching me. And she gave Daltry a look that said she'd be watching him, too, but in an entirely different manner.

Then she was gone, and it was just Daltry and me on the set. I willed myself invisible. When that didn't work, I bit my lip and gave a little finger wave.

"We meet again, Lola," he said. "I almost didn't recognize you."

"What gave me away?"

"Your ring tone." He raised one eyebrow. "Manilow fan?"

"It's my aunt's phone."

"You didn't answer my question."

I gave an indifferent shrug. I wasn't about to let him know that "Mandy" always makes me a little melancholy. I deflected his question. "Where's your posse?"

He laughed. "Yeah, I was rolling deep last night."

"Rolling deep?"

"My publicist insists I have bodyguards whenever I'm in public."

"You got a stalker?" I asked.

He shook his head. "Just part of the game."

Eager to leave, I started to back away, careful not to trip over the many cables that were snaked across the room.

"You're not really an attorney, are you?" Daltry said.

"Figured that out, did you?" I said, tapping my forefinger to my temple.

"What do you do?"

The question hung in the air for a moment. It was one I always had difficulty answering. Even when I was doing stand-up, I didn't earn enough income from comedy to confidently claim it as a career. Ditto for hairstyling, tax preparing, pet-sitting, word processing, and animal presentations. I'd give Daltry my stock answer about doing anything for money, but I was afraid he'd take it literally. I finally said, "This 'n' that."

Daltry was being hailed by the director, who was standing in the doorway with a couple of guys in suits. He walked toward them, calling back to me over his shoulder, "Stick around, Lola."

10

Whatever Lola Wants

I tiptoed up and down the corridor, looking for Danny. He wasn't in the makeup room or by craft services. Not in any of the unoccupied patient rooms.

I took the elevator to the lobby and went out to the parking lot. Danny wasn't among the clusters of people who were hanging around, smoking and chatting. There were several motor homes parked next to the building. I presumed they were the stars' trailers. Danny didn't have his own trailer, so I tromped over to his car, which was sitting unattended in the lot.

Fine. He wants to hide, let him hide. I needed to get back to Cedars-Sinai, anyway.

I scanned the lot, looking for my rental car, which was parked a row away, next to a large van with a familiar-looking logo painted on the side: MIKE'S MONKEYS over a cartoonish rendering of what was obviously a chimpanzee. It was the same logo on the red shirt the chimp's trainer was wearing.

As I approached my rental car, I saw that the back of the red van was open. "Mike" was standing by the cargo doors.

"Sorry if I was in the way back there," I said to him. "I didn't mean to interfere."

He was securing something in the back of the van. He looked up from his task. "No worries. It's the Humane Association you gotta watch out for."

I nodded. "Well, it's their job to look out for the animals, right?"

He muttered something under his breath, and I surmised that his relationship with the AHA had been a rocky one. "Anyway, she likes you."

"Angela?" I said, surprised.

"No," he cackled. "Monkey." Then he leaned forward. "Don't you, girl?"

I craned my neck so I could see around the cargo doors. The interior of the van had been converted for animal transport. Several small cages lined one side. The left side was dominated by one large steel-barred cage. Inside the cage, two juvenile chimpanzees were seated next to each other, eating grapes from a bowl.

One looked up at me and vocalized, "Woo-hoo-hoo," a greeting known as a pant-hoot. Monkey, I presumed.

"Told you," he said.

"Who's her friend?" I asked.

"That's Morty."

"Is he in the movie, too?"

Mike shrugged. "Only if Monkey here acts up. Otherwise he's just here to keep her company."

I took a closer look at the van. "When she's filming, he's just . . . locked up in here alone?"

"Not that it's any of your business, but no. When we work with large animals, there's two of us. Suzanne—who just went to fetch me some Mickey D's—she stays in the van with Morty. It's air-conditioned, and it's got tunes." He pointed to a portable DVD player that had been mounted to one side of the van's interior. "Movies, too."

The enclosure was clean, and while not especially spacious, it was large enough for both chimps to move around freely. Several plastic toddler toys were piled in one corner. Morty was sitting with his legs wrapped around a basketball.

I'd heard stories about animals being beaten to perform in the movies. Supposedly their teeth were removed, they were electro-shocked or beaten with sticks, and they were kept in a perpetual state of starvation so they'd perform for food. Maybe those things happened, but it didn't seem like that was the case with Monkey and Morty.

"Are you Mike?" I said, gesturing at the logo on his shirt.

He shook his head. "No, Mike's the owner. I'm one of the train-ers." He wiped his hand on his pants, then held it out for me to shake. "Lenny."

He reached into a cooler and pulled out a bottle of water. He loosened the cap and passed the bottle through an opening in the cage. Monkey took the bottle, uncapped it, and began drinking. Lenny repeated the process with Morty, then retrieved a third bot-tle and offered it to me.

"Thanks." I gestured at the logo once more. "You might want to tell Mike that's not a monkey—it's a chimp."

"He knows. He's got monkeys, too, up on his ranch. And a bunch of other animals. But the chimp looked better on the logo."

A tall blonde with her hair pulled into a ponytail approached the van, carrying two bulging bags of fast food. She eyed me suspi-ciously. "Who's she?"

Lenny said, "She's Daltry's girl."

"No, I'm not—" I cut in, but it was clear Suzanne didn't care who I was. She just didn't want me around. She barreled past me with the food, handed one bag to Lenny, and opened the van's pas-senger door.

"Anyway, she was just leaving."

I nodded. "Nice meeting you," I said to Suzanne's back as she hopped in the van and slammed the door shut. Lenny followed suit, only he gave me a wave before turning his back.

★ ★ ★

I sat in my rental car and pondered whether I should stay on set or return to the hospital to see Carter. I powered up Betty's cell phone. After a few false starts, I figured out how to retrieve messages.

There was one message, from Gerry. "Hey, Hol, I've got everything taken care of. You don't need to worry about a thing. Your pets, your place—everything is fine. Just enjoy LA."

I breathed a sigh of relief and hit the DISCONNECT button. Then I placed a call to Carter's hospital room.

"How's Max?" I asked.

"Sleeping," she whispered. "What's going on? Where's Danny?"

"I don't know."

"You don't *know*? You were supposed to keep an eye on him. Where's Aniston?"

"She's not even on set. He's doing a scene with Kelly Ripa."

"Watch out for her, too."

"She's married," I pointed out. "And Danny's not cheating. He loves you."

"You know how many actors dump their wives or girlfriends once they become successful? Usually for their leading lady."

I sighed. Pregnancy hormones had turned my best friend into a jealous, foulmouthed lunatic. "Chill out. I can see Danny now," I lied. "He's talking to some guys from the crew, showing them the Polaroid of Max."

"Really? Awww . . ." And she burst into tears.

"Why don't I come back to the hospital and keep you and Max company? I'm kind of in the way here, anyway."

"No, I'm okay." She sniffled one last time. "You stay and have fun. Besides, the lactation counselor should be here any minute—"

"The what?"

"Lactation counselor. You know, to teach me how to breast-feed. She came around this morning and tried to help me, you know, position the baby. But Max wasn't latching on—"

"Latching on?"

"To my boob." She sounded exasperated. "She said she'd come back to try again. I hope she gets here soon because he's making hungry noises."

"Can't you give him a bottle," I asked, "until he gets the whole boob thing figured out?"

"No bottles!" she shouted with more conviction than Joan Crawford on an anti–wire hanger crusade.

"Sheesh. It was just a question."

"I'm sorry. I'm worried about nipple confusion."

"Oh-kaaay." I took small comfort in the fact that even if the rest of my life was falling apart, at least my nipples were not the least bit confused.

I watched through the windshield as the clusters of crew members broke up and everyone headed back inside the building.

"I gotta go," I said. "I think they're starting up again."

"Okay," she said. "Keep an eye on Danny, will ya?"

I returned to the second floor and bumped into Danny in the lobby.

"Hey, thanks for hanging me out to dry," I told him. "Why didn't you say something?"

"I panicked," he said, pulling me aside, out of earshot of the passing crew. "I was gonna say something, but I froze. This is my first film, Holly. I don't want to blow it. If they got rid of Jackman, they won't think twice about canning me."

"I thought Jackman had scheduling difficulties."

"Whatever. Everyone's expendable. Especially me. I only have one line in this scene."

I nodded in agreement. "And it's not even a good line. 'Was it something I said?' Could they get more clichéd?"

He shot me a wounded look. "I didn't write the script."

"I know," I said. "And you did great. I just think you'd get a bigger laugh if it wasn't such a trite punch line."

He started down the hallway and I followed. He stopped short. "You're not going back in, are you?"

"Well . . . yeah. Daltry told me to stick around. And the animal advocate said it's okay with her. I checked in with Carter. She has an appointment with a lactating counselor."

"The counselor is lactating?"

"Whatever." I exhaled loudly. "She wants me to stay here."

"Fine," Danny said. "Just turn off your cell phone."

Giovanni's voice boomed down the hallway. "Back in five."

Danny stopped in front of the craft services table. He picked a pastry off a tray. My stomach was grumbling, but I didn't dare take anything from the spread intended for the cast and crew.

"Go ahead," Danny said.

"You sure?"

He picked up a napkin, plopped a pastry on top, and handed it to me. "How would you write the punch line?"

"Me? I'm not a screenwriter. I haven't even read the script. How would I know?"

"Just play with me."

I rolled my eyes. He was pulling me back into our old routine, when we'd brainstorm bits for our stand-up act. One of us would be going down a route the other thought held no promise, and we'd say, "Play with me," meaning, "Indulge me. Let's see where this goes."

"Okay," I said. "Tobey works at the clinic. Why? Does he love animals, or is it the only job he could get?"

"I dunno," Danny said. "Not in the script."

"Are there any scenes where you interact with the animals? How do you act with them? What do you say about them?"

"Hol, all my lines fit on one side of an index card. Nobody cares how Tobey gets along with the animals."

"Well, shouldn't you?" I took a bite of my bear claw. "Even if it's not in the script, shouldn't it register on your face? When you see the chimp covered in bandages, what do you think? Does Tobey go gaga over the cute little chimpy-wimpy?"

He considered for a moment. "I'm annoyed. I'm the one that's gotta restock the supplies. I've always gotta clean up after them." He was bouncing on his feet, ideas percolating in his brain. "This is good. It's never expressed, but I think Tobey really hates his job and feels dumped on by his sister." He took a last swig of his coffee. "So how would you rewrite the line?"

I nearly choked on my bear claw. "I wouldn't! I don't know much about moviemaking, but I do know you don't just go changing punch lines."

"No shit," Danny said. "I want to hold on to my job, remember? Just for fun." He smiled. "Play with me."

"Okay . . . Tobey comes in. His sister's flirting with some hunk. There's a mess everywhere. Chimp escapes, sister and the hunk go in pursuit, and Tobey knows he's gonna be the only one cleaning up the mess." My eyes scanned the ceiling. Then I said, "I don't know. Maybe something like, 'I should have gone into real estate.' "

"That's better," he admitted. "Still feels overdone."

"Best I could do on short notice."

Giovanni called places. Danny tossed his coffee cup into a trash bin. I followed him to the edge of the exam room set, still turning the punch line around in my brain. Guy hates animals, has to clean up after them—what kind of career would he fantasize about?

"Taxidermy," I whispered into Danny's ear just before he dashed to his station outside the exam room door.

Crouching behind a filing cabinet, well out of everyone's way, I watched as the other stars resumed their positions and Lenny carried Monkey onto the set. He situated her on the examination table, gave her a hand signal, and stepped off to the right, outside of the camera's range. Angela from the AHA was standing nearby, arms folded across her chest.

I confirmed for the fourth time that my cell phone was turned off.

After what seemed like an interminable wait, someone shouted, "Action."

The scene replayed as before, but this time there was an appreciable change in Daltry's demeanor. He was more relaxed, especially around the chimpanzee. In earlier takes, he had focused his attention entirely on Kelly, and he had treated Monkey as little more than a prop. This time, he interacted with the chimp on a different level. He stood close to her, patted her gently, and even winked at her behind Kelly's back, as though letting her in on his intentions toward the pretty vet.

Finally, Daltry's interest in Ripa won out and the chimp scampered away, on cue, to raid the medical supplies. As before, she wrapped herself in gauze and purloined a box of tongue depressors. But this time, when Daltry bent to pick her up, the box didn't pop open. Monkey shook the box, but there was no explosion of tongue depressors. The lid was stuck.

The director yelled, "Cut!" and the prop master ran forward to check the box and restock the supply cabinet.

Monkey scurried off the set in response to a cue from Lenny, awaiting the scene to be reset. The trainer peeled layers of gauze off the chimpanzee.

"Great work, Colin and Kelly," the director said. He stood and turned around. "Where's Lola?"

He couldn't be talking about me, could he?

I slowly crept out from behind the filing cabinet I'd been using as a shield. I wiggled my fingers.

"Whatever you did to him," the director said, waving me closer, "do it again."

"Excuse me?"

"Whatever you said to him," he said, nodding his head in Daltry's direction, "to get him to loosen up with the chimp, it worked. Keep it up."

Angela raised a stiff arm in protest. "Sir, she's not registered as an animal trainer on this production."

"I'm not an animal trainer," I objected. "Besides, sometimes it's not the animals that need to be trained. It's the actors."

I heard some titters and chuckles and one wheeze-laugh that I recognized as belonging to Giovanni.

Someone handed me a rolled-up newspaper and told me to whack Daltry's nose with it if he got out of line.

Daltry said, "You can train me anytime, Lola," and there was another round of laughter.

"All right, settle down," Hal said. "Let's take it from the top."

Someone gestured to an empty chair and I sat, grateful to be closer to the action.

Daltry was even more agreeable in the next take, displaying an almost paternal affection toward the chimp. It was hard to believe he was the same guy who earlier this morning had feared the little ape would chomp off his cho-chos.

I could almost recite the dialogue verbatim by this point. But still, with each take, I grew more excited to see how it would all come together. I knew I would someday buy the film on DVD and sit home in my living room, pausing the scene and reliving this moment.

I watched intently as Daltry wooed Kelly, and Monkey expertly repeated her mischief-making performance, wrapping herself up like a mummy and sending tongue depressors flying skyward. Then Danny entered the exam room and the chimpanzee darted for the door to make her escape.

Danny's attitude was discernibly different this time around, though I doubted anyone else picked up on it, given his brief screen time. It was evident to me that he now regarded the marauding chimp as a nuisance and his sister as his oppressor.

Instead of tossing his line out carelessly the moment the chimp scampered through his legs, Danny took a beat, letting his gaze sweep the exam room. Then he deadpanned, "Was it something I said?"

The camera held on Danny's close-up for a few moments before the director yelled, "Cut!"

"Crane," Hal beckoned to Danny. "Over here."

Danny trundled over toward the director. I had a feeling Hal was telling Danny his new take on the character was too heavy-handed and he should revert to the happy-go-lucky guy who didn't have a care in the world or a thought in his head. I was going to catch hell from Danny for even suggesting he examine his character's inner life.

A third person was called into their confab and I saw Danny speaking but couldn't make out his words. The director was nodding and considering.

I saw Danny look in my direction and I shrank down in my seat, praying he'd keep me out of it. I'd already interfered enough in the production. I certainly didn't need Danny blaming me for influencing his performance.

Then Hal shouted, "Let's take it from the chimp's exit."

The cast resumed their places. Lenny returned Monkey to the set, and repositioned the gauze bandages. Then he retreated and the director yelled, "Action."

The exam room door swung open and Danny entered, his gaze taking in the topsy-turvy exam room. Monkey scooted through his legs and out the door. Daltry and Kelly gave each other a worried look, then ran in pursuit of the fleeing ape.

A beat passed before Danny sneered and said, "I coulda been a taxidermist."

★ ★ ★

"That's a print," Hal shouted. There was a burst of applause.

The set was suddenly bustling with activity. Camera dollies were rolled away, cables were disconnected, and props were removed from the set. Lenny swept Monkey up and carried her out of the room and down the hallway.

I was shell-shocked. Had Danny really used my line?

Danny bounced toward me, slapping me on the leg. "Good call, Lola."

"Don't call me Lola," I said. "What happened?"

He shrugged. "Hal called me over, said my performance was 'edgier.' I apologized, but he said to go with it. He thinks edgy is better than sad-sack. I told him my thoughts about the line being trite, and he asked what I would suggest—"

"*Your* thoughts?"

"Yeah. I told him the taxidermy line, and the rationale behind it, and he said to try it out. They've got enough takes in the can with the old line. They'll probably use one of those. But who knows? I think I nailed it this time."

He seemed all pumped up, so I decided not to belabor the point of who came up with the line. Besides, I didn't want anyone involved with the production to know I had anything to do with changing the script.

I nodded in agreement. "You nailed it."

I replayed the day in my head as I drove east on Olympic Boulevard, heading in the direction of Cedars-Sinai. I had abandoned Nancy in favor of the ginormous map Danny had given me, finding it just as confusing, but refreshingly mute. I only made a few wrong turns before making my way back to Cedars-Sinai.

Once I oriented myself to the neighborhood, I drove around until I found a Starbucks. It had been more than twenty-four hours since I'd had a Frappuccino, and I was in full-fledged withdrawal. Carter and the baby could wait—I was a girl with priorities.

I lucked out and found a parking space right in front of the store. There were still fifteen minutes on the meter. Serendipity was on my side.

While waiting for my 'cino to be frapped, I pulled out the cell phone and dialed Gerry's number.

He answered on the first ring. "Yo."

"Hey, Gerry. It's Holly."

"How's the baby?" he asked. "Put Carter on. I wanna say hi."

"I'm not at the hospital right now. I'm on my way back. I just wanted to check in about my animals."

"Yeah, isn't it great? Ronnie rocks."

I heard my name being called and saw my grande Mocha Frappuccino slide onto the bar.

"What?" I shouted over the whir of blenders. "Did you say Ronnie?"

"Yeah. Didn't you get my message?"

I retrieved my Frappuccino and unwrapped a straw. "You said everything was taken care of."

"It is. Ronnie agreed to house-sit for you."

I choked on my Frappuccino. "She *what*?" I sputtered as blended beverage shot up my nostrils.

Gerry ran on. "It's perfect. She's been butting heads with Ma, so she's totally psyched to have a place in the city for a while. And she'll take care of your pets and your apartment, so you can forget about everything. Win-win."

"Ronnie hates me! I don't want her staying in my apartment. She's gonna be drawing faces on the pictures in my photo albums, poisoning my pets—"

Gerry snorted. "Don't be ridiculous. We're family. She doesn't hate you."

"Oh, yeah?" I asked. "Weren't you there for the food fight smack down?"

"How could I forget? Just this morning Mom found a baby gherkin in the chandelier."

I sucked Frappuccino through my straw, suddenly needing my caffeine fix more than ever. "I don't want Ronnie to house-sit," I told Gerry. "I'll find someone else."

"Too late," Gerry chirped. "I just dropped her off at your place and gave her the key."

11

Long-Forgotten Lullaby

It could be worse, I told myself, as I circled the block behind Cedars-Sinai looking for a parking spot. We are family, like Gerry said, so Ronnie couldn't despise me completely. And even if she did, she wouldn't take it out on my pets. Would she?

I tried to recall if I'd ever seen Ronnie displaying any kindness toward animals. She'd never had pets—Kuki wouldn't allow animals of any kind in the house. When we were kids, Ronnie taught me how to pull the flasher off a firefly and stick it on my shirt like an illuminated sequin. That was the only image I could conjure of Ronnie interacting with a nonhuman creature, and it didn't bode well for my animals.

I sucked up the last remaining whipped cream residue from the bottom of my Frappuccino cup and tossed it into a trash can in the hospital lobby. Carter had kicked caffeine cold turkey when she got pregnant—a Herculean effort on her part—so I figured it was best not to wave my Frappuccino in her face.

I took the elevator to the floor housing the maternity wing, nodded at the security guard, and made my way to Carter's room. She looked up when I entered. She was cradling Max against her chest and she looked radiant.

She smiled. "He figured it out."

As I stepped into the room, I realized Carter was in the process of breast-feeding the baby. "Oops, sorry. You want me to come back later?"

"Don't be silly." She leaned forward and stroked the top of Max's tiny head. "He doesn't mind."

Actually, Max wasn't the one I was worried about. I tiptoed closer to the bed. "Your nipples aren't confused anymore?"

Carter scrunched up her nose. "What's that smell?"

I sniffed the air. Other than the usual hospital odors, I didn't detect anything.

"You had coffee!" She pointed an accusing finger in my direction. She sniffed again. "Mocha Frappuccino. Extra shot."

"Got me." I raised both hands in a show of mock surrender. "Sorry I didn't bring you one—I figured you were still off caffeine."

"I *am*," she said. "How could you do this to me? How could you come in here smelling like Starbucks?"

"Have we met?" She was beginning to scare me. She was the one who'd introduced me to Starbucks, after all. I didn't even *like* coffee when a new franchise opened on my block and she got a job as a barista. I started hanging out there to be around her. Once I learned to tolerate the taste of coffee, it was a slippery slope to full-fledged addiction—made all the more easy by the fact that she regularly slipped me free Frappuccinos when the other baristas weren't looking. "Remember? Me, addict. You, supplier."

"Get away!" She brought one hand up to cover her face. "I can't stand the smell of it. I'm going to vomit."

She was shooing me away with one arm, while supporting Max with the other. I backed out of her room and into the hallway, where I stumbled into Danny. He was carrying a take-out bag from a submarine shop.

"Watch it, pardner," he said to me.

I pointed at Carter's room and whispered. "She's crazy. She just threw me out because I have Frappuccino breath."

Danny nodded. "The last few months, she can't stand the smell of coffee. It's one of those pregnancy-aversion things. First she wouldn't let me make it at home anymore. Then she made me promise not to drink it at all. Said she could smell it on my breath and in my clothes."

"But I saw you drinking coffee on the set."

"Shhh." He yanked me farther from Carter's doorway. Then he reached into his breast pocket and gave me a quick peek of a tin of Altoids with the stealth of a drug dealer flashing his stash to a kid on a playground. He pulled me closer and spoke into my ear. I felt like I was being briefed for a CIA mission. "Go to the gift store. Buy mouthwash. Gargle, spit, repeat. While you're there, load up on breath mints and gum. Especially if you're going to be staying for a while. If you do go to Starbucks, pay cash and throw away the receipts. Don't leave any evidence."

"She honestly expects me to stop drinking coffee altogether?"

Danny nodded emphatically. "Not just you and me. Anyone who comes in contact with Max. Eventually, she'll try to rid the entire world of caffeine's evil influence."

I rolled my eyes. "Isn't that a bit hypocritical, considering she works at Starbucks?"

"She quit a few months ago. Took a job at Jamba Juice."

Jamba Juice? What was this world coming to? "What about her Starbucks' stock options?"

"Cashed 'em in."

I was tempted to laugh, but the absurdity of the situation was eclipsed by its more serious implications. How would I endure the rest of my stay without Starbucks? "Why didn't you warn me about the new anti-Starbucks regime?"

Danny shrugged. "I didn't think you'd come."

He had a point.

★ ★ ★

My breath was minty fresh. Indeed, it had never been mintier or fresher than when I emerged from the restroom adjacent to the gift shop, where I had purchased a toothbrush, dental floss, trial-sized mouthwash, wintergreen breath mints, and gum.

I'd spent more money ridding my mouth of all traces of Frappuccino than I had on the Frap itself. I said a silent prayer that Carter's aversion to coffee would pass quickly now that she was no longer pregnant.

When I returned to her room, she and Danny were finishing up their subs. Danny handed me a bag. "Turkey or tuna?"

I grabbed a turkey sandwich and gobbled it down greedily. While I ate, Carter filled me in on her breast-feeding session, which apparently was a great success, and reenacted every gurgle and coo Max had made since we'd left that morning. Danny told her about his character's evolution and the script change—giving me credit for coming up with the new punch line. Carter laughed, and we all hoped the last take would make it into the final film.

Then I filled her in on my conversations with Daltry and my interactions with Monkey the Chimp.

"Colin Daltry?" Carter gasped. "He took over for Hugh Jackman?"

I nodded.

Carter fanned herself. "Ohmigod. He's so yummy."

Was I the only person who hadn't heard of this guy? "I'll admit he's attractive, but he's definitely a step down in terms of box office. Right?" I turned to Danny. "So why does everyone on set act like he's their savior?"

Carter was picking at a small side salad. "I dunno. I love Hugh, but he's been around for a while. Colin Daltry is red-hot right now. He's the guy of the moment."

"I can't believe you've never heard of him," Danny said. "I bet even those aunts of yours know who Colin Daltry is."

"I'll take that bet," I said. "How much?"

"Five bucks," Danny said.

"Easy money." I reached into my purse, pulled out the cell phone, and dialed Betty's home number.

She sounded out of breath when she answered. "Holly, honey, how is Carter? How's the baby?"

"They're both great. Are you okay? You sound breathless."

"I'm fine. Just a little winded, that's all. How are things in Hollywood? Have you met any movie stars?"

"As a matter of fact, I have. I went to the set of Danny's movie, and I met Colin Daltry."

There was silence on the line and I flashed a victory smirk in Danny's direction. Then, before I could mentally envision Danny's five dollars fraternizing with the spare change in my pocket, Betty wheezed, "Colin Daltry! I gotta sit down for this."

"Hold on. . . . You know who Colin Daltry is?"

"Of course. I watch the news shows. He just broke up with his girlfriend, a supermodel. Name like a horse. Destiny or Chestnut or some such. It was on *Entertainment Tonight*." She wheezed. "Wait till I tell everybody you met Colin Daltry. The girls at Lamaze will get a big kick out of it."

Danny was grinning and reaching out his hand, palm up. "Pay up."

I waved him away. "You're really going back to Lamaze?" I asked Betty.

"Of course. I found a new partner."

"Who?"

"Veronica."

"Ronnie?" I was beginning to sense a disturbing pattern. "Ronnie's going to take Lamaze?" Ronnie was never much of a joiner; it was hard to get her to participate in anything that didn't involve picking up guys. And since Lamaze is generally not a good place to meet single men, I couldn't believe she'd agreed to go along. "How did you talk her into it?"

"She volunteered. Saved me from having to ask Monica Broccoli." She lowered her voice. "Don't tell Gerry, but that Monica can be a pain in the patooty."

No kidding. My patooty hurt every time I thought about Monica. But now Ronnie was inflicting her own special brand of pain on my patooty.

After bidding bye-bye to Betty, I forked over my last five spot to Danny. He tried to let me off the hook, but I insisted he take the cash. "A bet's a bet."

Maybe it was a good thing Carter had developed a caffeine aversion, I told myself, wondering how long it would be before I could afford another Frappuccino.

Max was awake, and not attached to Carter's breast, so I finally got to hold him. He looked frighteningly fragile. I didn't want to take the chance of tripping over anything while I carried him, so I settled in a chair and let Danny lower him into my arms.

He was seventeen inches long, from his tiny hairless head to his perfectly formed toes. I couldn't see much of him; he was swaddled in a hospital blanket like a baby burrito. But what I saw had me completely and utterly enthralled. I was dumbstruck. Literally struck dumb by his tiny presence.

"Talk to him," Carter nudged me. "Let him hear the sound of your voice."

I didn't know what to say. I knew that it didn't really matter, that it would be months before Max would begin making sense out of the English language, but I felt I should say something profound to welcome this little guy to the world. *Hi, I'm Holly* didn't seem to cut it.

I closed my eyes and sang. I wasn't sure where the words were coming from. A dream, or a long-ago memory perhaps.

> *Prancing in the sky,*
> *My little monkey star,*
> *You brighten my life*
> *Just the way you are.*
>
> *The sun is no match,*
> *The moon not by far,*
> *You have no equal,*
> *My little monkey star.*

There was a blinding flash of light and I looked up to see Danny hovering above me with his digital camera. "Say cheese."

"Where did you learn that?" Carter asked me.

I shrugged. "It's from when I was little. I think my dad used to sing it to me. Or maybe it was my mom. I don't know." I furrowed my forehead. "Yesterday, I couldn't have dredged up those lyrics if you'd paid me, but today . . . holding Max . . . they suddenly came to me."

Danny took another picture. "Did you ever hear from your dad again, after you found out he was your mystery client?"

"Not really." When I first discovered his identity, I thought we'd lay the groundwork to rebuilding some kind of a father-daughter relationship. But aside from a terse greeting card he left in my milk cubby on my birthday, I'd heard nothing from him. And though I told myself I didn't care, I still found myself thinking of him at odd times. Like now.

As though reading my mind, Danny asked, "You ever think about him?"

Carter answered for me: "Yes."

My thoughts were interrupted by "Copacabana," this time

emanating from my back pocket, where I'd stuck the phone after speaking to Aunt Betty. I didn't move a muscle out of fear of disturbing the baby, who was nestled peacefully on my lap.

Max started to whimper, so I bounced my knee slightly and whispered, "Shhhhh."

But by the time Lola met Rico, Max's whimpers had escalated into full-fledged screams. Danny leaned over and picked Max up. It was almost magical how quickly Max's sobs subsided.

I pulled the cell phone out of my pocket and flipped it open. I could hear Gerry's voice booming before the phone even reached my ear. "When were you going to tell me you met Colin Daltry?"

I groaned, belatedly realizing my mistake in telling Aunt Betty about Daltry. I should have known she'd immediately spread the news to the rest of the family. And that it wouldn't be long before Gerry came a-calling.

"Did you get me his socks?"

I sighed. "Sorry. I didn't have a chance to ask."

"You didn't even *ask* him?" Gerry let out a disappointed sigh. "Where did you meet him? Did you talk to him?"

"On the set of Danny's movie. He took over Hugh Jackman's part."

"What kind of socks was he wearing?"

"How should I know?"

Gerry groaned. Clearly I wasn't cut out for the sock business.

"It was chaotic on the set. The director was there, and all the crew. I couldn't just interrupt to ask for his socks. I was trying to stay out of the way." *Trying* and failing miserably.

"Okay, okay, I get it," Gerry conceded. "When are you going back?"

"I'm not. It was a once-in-a-lifetime thing."

I saw Carter and Danny exchange glances and knew they were hoping to persuade me to return to the set, each for different reasons.

"Please, Holly," Gerry said, bordering on a whine. "You gotta do this for me. I helped you out with your animals."

I huffed. "You gave a key to my apartment to your sister, who has considered me her sworn enemy ever since we were kids."

"That's not true—"

"It *is* true. And if anything happens to my animals, I'll hold you both responsible."

"Don't worry. I'll check up on her."

"I'd appreciate that." I was more nervous with Ronnie having unrestricted access to my apartment than I was when Tallullah was on the loose. At least I knew the monkey liked me. "Make sure she doesn't go through my things. Or use my computer. Or make long-distance phone calls. Or—"

"Can she eat what's in the fridge?"

"Sure," I said, wondering if I should warn her about the freezer full of frozen rats and deciding against it. "If she can find anything edible, she's welcome to it."

"Got it."

I gave him a rundown of what to feed each of my animals, making him take notes and read them back to me. When I finished, Gerry said, "No prob. Everything's under control. Now back to business. I'll give you fifty bucks for a pair of Daltry's socks. Sixty if they're still dirty."

I let out a heavy sigh. He wasn't going to give up. Though I hated to let him down, I felt I'd already embarrassed myself enough. Even if I did set foot on the set again—which I didn't plan on—I couldn't ask Colin Daltry for a pair of his socks. "Danny's in the movie, too. I'll send you his socks."

"No offense, Hol, but he's not exactly on par with Daltry."

"So you don't want Danny's socks?"

Danny made an exaggerated frown as though offended.

"I'll take 'em," Gerry said. "I'm just sayin' it's not the same thing."

"Consider it an investment. He's gonna be a big star one of these days. You should have seen him today, in this scene with Colin and Kelly Ripa—"

I regretted the words the moment they left my lips. But it was too late. I wished I had Daltry's socks so I could stuff them into my mouth.

"You met *Kelly Ripa*!" Gerry shouted. "Did you get me her socks?"

"I didn't even talk to her," I said. "I just saw her."

By the time I talked Gerry down to reality, explaining that it would be poor form for a visitor to a film set to accost the actors and ask for their socks, he'd rattled off a wish list of stars whose footwear he coveted—everyone from Tom Hanks to Britney Spears to Tom Cruise and Katie Holmes and their daughter. "I'd kill to have some A-list booties," he'd said, not the least bit in jest.

I said I'd do my best, crossing my fingers as I made the promise, and making a silent vow that if I encountered any more movie stars, I'd keep my big mouth shut.

Danny was called back to the set a short while later. He and Carter both urged me to tag along, but I refused. I'd done enough damage for one day. Besides, I desperately needed to catch up on my sleep.

After Danny left, Carter and I caught up on everything that had happened in recent weeks. It felt good being in her company again. I realized just how much I missed having her to share every little detail with. We still talked by phone, but it wasn't the same.

Visiting hours ended at nine. I stole one last lingering look at Max, hugged Carter, and said good-bye.

I punched Carter's address into the navigation system—not so much because I needed directions, but because I knew Nancy's annoying voice would keep me awake at the wheel.

I was stopped at a red light on Beverly Boulevard when my cell phone rang. I pulled it from my pocket and glanced at the display, my heart racing when I recognized Tom's number. Part of me wanted to talk to him, to tell him all about my crazy day, but I was already uncomfortable driving in LA. Trying to simultaneously talk on the cell phone could spell disaster.

The light changed and I stepped on the gas, letting the call go to voice mail.

Traffic was heavy, and by the time I reached Carter's, I was barely conscious. I bid Nancy good night and trudged to the apartment, letting myself in with the key Danny had given me.

After showering I felt somewhat refreshed, and I was tempted to go out exploring. It didn't seem right to spend my first night in Hollywood sitting in an empty apartment. Danny would likely be out all night—when he was finished filming, he'd return to the hospital, where a cot had been set up for him in Carter's room.

I was on my own, smack-dab in the middle of Hollywood. I contemplated cruising down the Boulevard, putting my feet in the footprints at Grauman's Chinese Theater, stopping for a bite at Musso & Frank's Grill—a Hollywood landmark rumored to still be a popular spot among showbiz old-timers—maybe even driving to the beach and getting my first glimpse of the Pacific Ocean. Or I could hike up to the Hollywood sign and touch a true show business icon.

But I was tired, broke, and still a little wary of driving in Hollywood. With no one but Nancy to guide me, I'd probably get lost and end up in South Central. I'd seen enough movies to know I'd be out of my element in the hood.

Instead, I puttered around the apartment, feeling restless. It was after one in New York, too late to return Tom's call, I told myself. I peered into the refrigerator and was surprised to find it well-stocked. But based on the multiple jars of olives and pickles and two tubs of ice cream in the freezer, I surmised the fridge's contents had been mainly dictated by Carter's cravings.

I made myself a peanut butter sandwich and ate it while flipping through the 217 channels on the cable system.

There was a thick script on the coffee table. Danny's copy of *Vets in the City*. I picked it up and thumbed through it, noting the pages on which Danny had highlighted his lines. He was right about them all fitting on one side of an index card. But before I could feel sorry for him, I reminded myself that he was in a big-budget movie, after all. He was living his dream.

I turned off the TV and took the script into the guest bedroom, planning to read a few pages before falling asleep. Instead I read it straight through, surprising myself by laughing out loud a few times. While the plot stretched the limits of plausibility, it was quirky and funny and just oddball enough to set it apart from run-of-the-mill romantic comedies.

As I read, I found myself paying attention to the scenes featuring animals—which was most of them—and wondering how they would achieve some of the shots. Most seemed simple enough—dogs barking on cue, a parrot making prank calls when left alone at the clinic after hours—but others would surely prove trickier. In one, Colin unwittingly loosens the lid on an aquarium, freeing a snake, which slithers up his back and over his shoulder as he flirts with Jennifer Aniston. In another, Danny is cleaning cages when a rodent climbs up his pant leg, sending him into a frenzied dance around the clinic, knocking over cages and freeing a half dozen animals, including a capuchin monkey.

I tried to imagine Tallulah on a movie set, surrounded by lights, cameras, people, and several other animal species. Aside from Rocky, whom she feared, Tallulah held my pets in low esteem—lower life-forms barely worthy of her notice. The script called for the monkey to interact with a cat, a dog, and a rabbit. That would be something to see, I thought, finally setting the script aside and drifting off to sleep.

Get a Grip

Though Max had been born a month prematurely, his lungs were fully developed, his reflexes were normal, and he was given a clean bill of health. He and Carter were ready to go home.

I was waiting in front of the apartment when Danny pulled up. He leaned over and waved through the open passenger-side window and I climbed in. A grande Mocha Frappuccino was sitting in the cup holder. It's good to have friends.

Danny was drinking his coffee straight.

"You're not worried she'll smell it in the car?" I asked.

"Nah." He gestured to the open windows. He accelerated and my hair blew every which way. A small price to pay for my morning jolt of caffeine.

I craned my head around. The vehicle's already tiny backseat was almost entirely consumed by the baby's car seat. "Are we all gonna fit in here? Maybe we should have taken my rental car."

"You kidding? It took me two hours to install that car seat. The instructions were written in Sanskrit. You can't just pop it out and put it in another car."

"I hate to tell you this, but I think it's facing the wrong way."

Danny laughed. "Has to be rear-facing. Until he's one. It's the law."

"Oh." Nipple confusion, rear-facing car seats, crying without tears. I had a lot to learn about babies. Not that I was in any hurry

to have one. So far I'd never had the urge to mother anything without fur. And seeing what pregnancy and childbirth had done to
Carter had not made me eager to follow suit.

"Not exactly a family car," I pointed out.

"It was affordable."

Danny pulled into the patient pickup lane at the hospital and
parked. I dumped the evidence of our coffee consumption in the
trash while Danny sprayed pine-scented air freshener in the car and
locked up. In the lobby, we went to our respective restrooms to
brush, floss, and sanitize.

Danny was waiting for me when I exited the ladies' room.
"Breath check," he said, stepping closer and blowing a puff of hot
air in my face.

"You're good," I said, then followed suit.

"Ditto."

We took the elevator to the maternity floor and found Carter
dressed in her street clothes, fitting a tiny cap onto Max's hairless
head. Danny whipped out his camera and started taking pictures.
"Max's first outfit," he said, clicking away. "Max and Mommy getting ready to go home."

"Here, let me," I said, reaching out for the camera. While I took
over as photographer, Danny helped Carter finish readying Max for
the trip home. By the way he was bundled up, you'd have thought
he was going mushing in Alaska.

A nurse came in with some paperwork for Carter to sign. Then
an orderly brought a wheelchair and helped her into it. Danny
placed Max on her lap, then gathered up Carter's bags. He kept
pace as the orderly pushed Carter out of the room and down the
corridor. I followed them, snapping pictures the whole way.

Caring for a newborn is much like babysitting a monkey, I told
myself as I changed my shirt for the third time in as many hours. I

seemed to have an uncanny knack for picking Max up just as he was about to burp. And if I had a towel in place on my shoulder, Max managed to spray a geyser that drenched everything in sight—except the towel.

Diapering was much easier. Carter, having struggled through the first few diaper changes alone, was amazed at my Pampering prowess until I reminded her of what a challenge it had been to wrangle Tallullah into her little diapers while she swatted at me with her arms, legs, and tail. I'd eventually mastered the task—one of many accomplishments in my life that had little application outside its original context. It's not like listing "monkey diapering" on my résumé would get me anywhere.

As with the monkey, we quickly realized that Max wasn't going to conform to our schedules—we had to adjust to *his*. At least until he figured out the whole day-night thing, which could take weeks, according to one of Carter's many baby care books. The books, with titles ranging from *Raising a Healthy Baby in a Toxic World* to *Mothering Without Smothering*, were piled on every available surface in the house, with the exception of Danny's nightstand, which held just one: *Babies for Boneheads*.

It had been three days since we'd brought Max home from the hospital, but it felt like weeks. I'd wanted to help as much as possible, so each time I'd heard Max cry in the night, I'd gotten up, too. I couldn't assist with the breast-feeding, but I could change a diaper, fetch a clean blankie, or just keep Carter company while she fed Max. Danny tended to sleep through most of these nightly interruptions, claiming the need to get his beauty sleep so he'd look good on camera.

During the day, I'd run errands as needed. The first day, Carter had sent me to Target to pick up some preemie diapers and a few other items she hadn't anticipated. I'd scanned the list, scrunching up my forehead at the last item. "Nipple conditioner? I don't suppose that's in the hair-products aisle."

She shook her head. "Probably in with the baby supplies. Or maybe lotions. I don't know—I've never bought it before."

"That makes two of us."

"Sorry to ask you to do this, but my nipples are really cracked and—"

I raised my hands to my ears and shouted, "Stop!" While I'd gotten past my initial discomfort at seeing Carter breast-feed, I was reticent to get into discussions about sore nipples. Danny, on the other hand, had initiated a ten-minute dinner table debate over whether Carter's boobs should be christened Max's "snack bags" or "happy sacks."

By Day Three, Carter was feeling a little stir-crazy, so we loaded Max into his stroller and took him for a walk around the neighborhood. Carter had covered him from head to toe so as to protect him from the balmy seventy-degree weather, and the stroller was draped with mosquito netting. As I watched her slip a pink bottle of SPF-50 sunscreen into the diaper bag, I wondered how long it would be before Max actually saw the sun, let alone suffered the damaging effects of its rays.

Provisioned with spare clothes, bibs, booties, receiving blankets, lotions, creams, medicines, rattles, and toys, Max's diaper bag held more than I had packed for my entire stay in Los Angeles. Carter loaded the bulging bag onto the stroller and we made our way out of the building, heading in the direction of Jamba Juice. Carter wanted to show off the baby to her coworkers and introduce me to the joys of Jamba.

When we neared the intersection of Hollywood and Western, I saw the Jamba Juice storefront—*right next to a Starbucks.* Cruel and unusual punishment.

I held the door open so she could maneuver the stroller inside the citrus-scented store.

While the juice shop's staff fawned over the baby, I scrutinized the menu board, finding nothing appealing. The description of one frothy fruit concoction promised it would put pep in my step, so I asked the girl behind the counter if it contained caffeine.

"Absolutely not," she chirped. "The blend of antioxidants and carbohydrates will give you a natural energy boost with no *caffeine* whatsoever." From her intonation it was clear she ranked caffeine lower than strychnine as a dietary additive.

"Do you have anything that *is* caffeinated?"

She crinkled up her nose. "Well, our Matcha Green Tea Blast has seventy-five milligrams of naturally occurring caffeine."

"Naturally occurring?" I asked, in defense mode. Was she suggesting that my Frappuccinos were *unnatural*?

"Yepper. All natural for a totally natural high."

My eyes rolled skyward as I tried to calculate how many Green Tea Blasts I'd have to drink to get the same jolt as one of my Frappuccinos. Since a grande Mocha Frap had roughly five hundred milligrams of caffeine, I'd have to drink seven Blasts to reach my customary caffeine quota for the day. Even I wasn't that desperate.

Carter had convinced me to try a Mango Mantra instead, which I drank while plotting a surreptitious Starbucks run.

After changing into a clean T-shirt, I carried a load of clothes down to the building's laundry room. I was amazed at how quickly the baby could go through his entire wardrobe. Ditto for anyone who came in contact with him.

I returned to find Carter zonked out on the rocking chair in front of the television. Max was sleeping in his bassinet at her side.

It was late, so Danny helped Carter into bed while I gently rolled Max's bassinet into the room next to her and turned on the baby monitor.

Carrying the handheld receiver, I followed Danny into the dining room. He picked his script off the table. "Wanna run lines?" he asked me.

I smirked. "Don't you mean 'run line'?"

"Very funny. Actually I have two lines in the scene I'm filming tomorrow."

Danny handed me the script, which was turned to the appropriate page. It was a scene with Colin and Jennifer Aniston in which Danny walks in on the two in a this-isn't-what-it-looks-like clinch and makes a suitably snide remark. Will he tell his sister? Or will he use it as leverage to get Jen to finally agree to a date?

"Whose lines do I read?"

"All of them except mine."

I was about to read Jen's first line when my cell phone rang. I hauled it out of my pocket and glanced at the readout.

It was a 212 number I didn't recognize.

"Hello?"

"Holly? Where are you?" It was David's sister, Paula, and she was whispering. I heard screams in the background.

"What's going on? Is David okay?"

"He's in a state," Paula said. "He called your apartment and some woman answered and said you left town and might not be back for weeks. She gave him this number."

Ronnie. I'm sure she put the worst possible spin on my absence.

Paula continued. "How could you go away without telling him?"

"It was unexpected," I said. "But I was planning to call him first thing tomorrow." Indeed, I'd already set both my cell phone alarm and bedside alarm clock to wake me in time to place the call. "We have an elementary school gig planned, and I was going to try to convince him to go without me."

"Without you?" she said, surprised. "He couldn't go without you."

"Sure he could. With Margie's help."

"Margie's involved with this, too?"

"No, no," I answered quickly, not wanting to implicate Margie in what Paula was making sound like the crime of the century. "I just thought, since she drives the van, and he brings the monkey, that they don't really need me. And he gets so much out of the classroom visits, I thought he should do it without me. For the kids. And for him."

Paula exhaled deeply. "He feels betrayed, Holly. He thought he was your friend."

"He *is* my friend." I rubbed my eyes and groaned. I'd clearly made an error in judgment, thinking I could spring it on David at the last minute. "My best friend went into premature labor and I was her labor coach. But I should have been the one to tell him. I didn't count on him calling my apartment."

"He wanted to ask you to come early tomorrow. He needs a haircut. He was hoping you'd give him a trim so he'd look respectable for the kids. He was so looking forward to it. . . ."

I was silent for a moment, my stomach twisted in knots. "Can I talk to him?"

"Hold on." She covered the phone and I could hear mumbled voices, one well-modulated and the other clearly distraught. Then she was back on the line. "He doesn't want to talk to you."

I sighed. "Please. Let me say I'm sorry."

After another brief silence, she said, "Okay. I'll put him on."

While waiting for Paula to bring the phone to David, I tried to compose my thoughts. I wanted to convey how sorry I was for not calling sooner, but also confirm my belief that he could—and should—do the show without me. I didn't know if he'd listen, but I had to try.

But the moment David said a hesitant hello and I opened my mouth to speak, an eerie silence came over the phone. At first I thought he'd hung up, but then I looked at my cell phone. The screen was dark. "It died," I yelled, banging the phone against the dining room table.

Danny took the phone from me, then pressed some buttons. "Battery's dead," he announced. "Where's your charger?"

Charger? Why hadn't I thought of that?

"I don't have a charger. Betty didn't give me a charger."

"You've been using it for days without charging it? I'm surprised it lasted this long."

"Well, quick, give me your charger. I have to call David back. He probably thinks I hung up on him."

Danny shook his head. "I have a different provider. My charger won't work with that phone." He handed me a cordless phone. "Time to go low-tech."

I raced to my guest room, found my DayPlanner and looked up David's number. Paula picked up the phone. But this time, David refused to speak.

Paula sounded exhausted. "I'm sorry, Holly. He's really worked himself up. He hasn't been like this in a long time." She lowered her voice. "I know you meant well, but I think it was a mistake getting him involved in these animal shows. It was only a matter of time before you moved on and he got his hopes dashed."

"What? No, it wasn't a mistake. He loves visiting the classrooms. And I haven't 'moved on.' I just took a trip."

"When will you be back?"

"I don't know." Truthfully, I hadn't even begun thinking about a return date. I hadn't yet come down from the high of witnessing Max's birth and altering Hollywood history. Okay, so maybe the tiny role I'd played in the making of *Vets in the City* wouldn't actually change the course of history, but it was thrilling nonetheless. And it had taken my mind off my recent disasters in New York.

"Well, when you figure it out, let me know," Paula said. "Until then, you'd better cancel all your school visits."

"I'll reschedule them for later in the month," I said, not wanting to let Paula bully me into backing down.

"We'll talk when you get back," Paula said before hanging up.

"One more call," I told Danny, punching in my home number.

"Hello?" Ronnie said sleepily.

"Are you trying to ruin my life?" I asked.

"Who is this?" she grumbled.

I wondered how many lives she was in the process of ruining that she had to ask the question. "Holly."

"Holly's not here. She's in LA."

"Wake up, Ronnie!" I yelled into the receiver. "It's me, Holly."

"Oh. Why didn't you say so? How's it goin'?"

Any remorse I'd had about the food fight instantly evaporated. "Not good. My friend David is distraught because he called there and you told him I left town."

"Big whoop," she said. "You did leave town. Nobody said it was supposed to be a secret."

"It's not a secret. But I hadn't told him yet. We were supposed to do a classroom gig tomorrow morning, and I was going to try to talk him into going alone. But he called to ask me to come early to give him a haircut so he'd look nice for the kids. And you told him I took off, and he feels betrayed, and now—"

"Wait," she interrupted. "Is this the guy in the wheelchair? The one with the monkey?"

"Yes," I said. "His name's David. And he's a great guy who—" I stopped myself, realizing I was on the verge of tears and not wanting to expose any vulnerabilities to Ronnie. I pulled myself together. "Just don't answer my phone."

"You want me to live here and take care of your animals, but I'm not allowed to answer the phone?"

Actually, I didn't want her to live there, but I decided not to argue the point while the fate of my animals was in her hands. "I appreciate you taking care of my pets. But I get a lot of business calls, and I don't want to cause any further confusion. David won't even talk to me. What did you say to him?"

"I dunno. He sounded upset. I think I told him to get a grip."

"Get a grip?" My eyes filled with tears, envisioning David's reaction to such a brusque comment from my cousin. I took a deep breath before speaking. "You told a man who is a quadriplegic, whose life is spent in a wheelchair—mostly in his apartment—who has trouble making friends, whose highlight of his life is going into elementary school classrooms and seeing kids' faces light up when he comes in the room, who keeps a scrapbook of all the thank-you cards and drawings the kids have made for him—you told him to 'get a grip'?" She was lucky she was three thousand miles away.

"I'm sorry. You want me to call him and explain?"

"No. You've done enough."

Danny was yawning. His need for sleep now outweighing his desire to run his lines, he decided to turn in.

Good idea, I thought. Max's sleep cycles were so unpredictable I knew I should grab some sleep whenever the opportunity presented itself. But the situation with David had shaken me. I couldn't blame Ronnie entirely, but I knew it wouldn't have happened if anyone else had been watching my apartment.

But who else? I wondered when Brian would return. I found my DayPlanner and flipped through it until I found Brian's listing.

I dialed his cell number and was immediately switched to voice mail. "Hey, Brian, it's Holly. I'm wondering if you're still in London and, more important, when you're going back home. I have a situation . . . a house sitter from hell. Anyway—" It suddenly occurred to me that I didn't know who was watching Brian's cat, Kramer, a task that would usually fall to me. "Hey, who's watching Kramer?

You think they'd mind stopping in on my guys, too?" I rattled off my numbers and hung up.

Next I dialed Tom. I'd been putting off calling him back. Ever since our anniversary-date debacle, I'd been feeling unsure about the state of our relationship. I hated to impose on him to feed my animals, but I knew if I asked him, he would do it despite having a daughter to care for and a full course load at NYU. And I could tell Ronnie to take a hike.

It was past midnight in New York, but Nicole would be at her mother's, so I didn't have to worry about waking her.

He answered on the first ring.

"Holly?" His voice registered surprise.

"Sorry we keep missing each other," I said. "It's been crazy out here."

"I want to hear all about it. I've missed you." His voice took on a tender tone and I felt myself melting.

"I've missed you, too."

"How's the baby?" Tom asked.

"Perfect. He smiled at me today, which totally made my day until Carter told me it was just—"

"Gas," Tom said with authority. "Real smiles won't come for a few months."

"Right."

I'd forgotten that while infants were alien creatures to me, Tom had already raised one of his own. What was strange and wondrous to me was old hat to him.

"Is he colicky?"

"No." At least I didn't think so. Truth is, I didn't know what colic was, only that babies who suffered from it became insufferably grumpy, which didn't describe Max at all.

"How's he sleeping?"

"He wakes up every two hours or so. I've been helping Carter change him and sometimes I get to rock him back to sleep."

"Nicole was a terrible sleeper," Tom said. "Nothing worked except taking her for long walks in the stroller. Some nights we'd be out at three a.m., circling the block, over and over again, waiting for her to fall asleep."

The image of Tom and Bianca taking their newborn on a midnight stroll struck me like a blow to the chest. He said it so casually, as though he was telling me about the weather in New York or what I'd missed on *Letterman*.

I should have been glad that Tom felt comfortable enough to share his past with me, I thought. But instead, I was just filled with a profound sadness, knowing that if he and I ever had a child of our own, we wouldn't be fumbling through it together. He'd have long-established opinions about all manner of child-rearing issues, from the best brand of diapers to the pros and cons of pacifiers, and he'd inevitably compare everything—"Bianca only used *cloth* diapers"; "Nicole liked to be rocked *this* way. . . ."

While I hadn't spent much time fantasizing about having kids, I had always assumed that when the time came, I'd stumble through it with someone as clueless as I was.

Tom was still talking about his and Bianca's efforts to get Nicole to sleep through the night. Desperate to change the subject, I said, "What did you want to talk to me about?"

"Huh?"

"Your message the other day. You said you needed to talk to me."

"Oh, yes. I wanted to tell you that I'm not going through with the family counseling. Bianca tried to talk me into it, but I said no."

"You're not?" I said, my spirits lifting slightly.

"No. It feels like a step backward. I'll do anything to help Nicole, but I don't think this is it."

I breathed a sigh of relief. "I have to admit, I didn't like the idea of the three of you seeing a family counselor together."

"I know. But Bianca and I did agree to do more things together with Nicole. So she won't feel like she's leading two separate lives."

"Such as . . . ?"

"Tomorrow her school is having a family fun festival. She wants us all to go together—"

"As a family," I finished for him. A single tear slid down my cheek. I squinted hard, in hopes of cutting the others off at the pass. It didn't work; the lone tear soon had a bucketful of friends. I envied little Max his ability to cry without tears.

"You don't mind, do you?" Tom said. "Nicole begged. If it means anything to you, she wanted you to be there, too, but I told her you were out of town."

It did mean something to me. Nicole was a sweet and sensitive girl who had captured my heart the moment I met her. She reminded me of myself at her age, a few years before I lost both my parents. I couldn't blame her for fighting to keep her family intact. The fact that she'd give anything to have her parents reunite didn't diminish my affection for her; it might even have endeared her to me more, because I knew that in her simple world, I would be part of the equation, too.

I choked on my tears. "Bianca would have loved that. Family fun plus one."

"Maybe not," he admitted. "You said you needed to talk to me, too. What did you want to talk about?"

Oh, yeah. At the time, I didn't really have anything particular in mind. Now there were a dozen things I wanted to talk to Tom about. But I feared none of them would end well. "I was going to ask you if you could feed my animals. But it's taken care of. Ronnie's gonna do it."

"Your cousin? That reminds me, how was the birthday dinner?"

"It was great."

I sniffled into my sleeve. I had never felt so disconnected to Tom.

"What is it? Are you crying?"

I brushed tears from my eyes. "I can't do this."

"Do what?"

"This," I said. "Us."

Tom's tone grew serious. "Don't say that."

I spoke quickly, knowing that if I paused to take a breath I might lose it altogether. "I know Nicole comes first with you. And she should. But I'm tired of coming second. And I certainly won't stand for coming third."

"You don't—"

I pressed on. "Don't get me wrong. I love that you drop everything the minute Nicole needs you. But I don't want to spend my life waiting home in a slinky red dress while you have family fun time with your ex-wife and daughter."

There was a protracted silence while we both absorbed my words. Finally, he said, "Let's not do this over the phone. When will you be back?"

"I don't know." Truth is, at that moment I wasn't entirely sure I wanted to go back.

"It's late," Tom said on a heavy sigh. "Why don't I call you in the morning?"

I knew a good night's sleep wasn't going to change anything. "Don't," I said. "I need some time to think. I'll call you when I get back in town."

Then I hung up before I could change my mind.

13

When Opportunity Knocks

The digital alarm clock woke me the next morning. I'd forgotten to turn it off after Paula's call had rendered the early-morning wake-up unnecessary. My eyes were puffy from crying. All night long I'd fought the urge to call Tom and tell him to forget everything I'd said. We'd make it work somehow. The important thing was that we loved each other.

Then I'd remind myself that he'd never actually said he loved me, and would cry myself back to sleep.

Once awake, I decided to get an early start to my day. The apartment was quiet—even Max was sleeping soundly—so I dressed quickly and snuck out the door.

I drove down Hollywood Boulevard, finding it oddly uninhabited at the early hour. There were knots of people here and there, probably engaged in activities I was better off not knowing about.

I found a parking spot on Sycamore and walked east along Hollywood Boulevard, reading the names in the stars in the sidewalk—Johnny Depp, Meryl Streep, Tom Hanks, Bill Cosby—until I reached the forecourt of Grauman's Chinese Theater, where I tried my hands in several stars' prints until I found the best fit: Doris Day.

My next stop was Hollywood and Highland, home of the Kodak Theatre, where the Academy Awards had been held for the past several years. A multilevel complex with ornate archways and pillars topped with huge elephant sculptures, it was basically a glorified shopping mall. It seemed much less glamorous in person than on television. I tried to figure out where the red carpet was placed and which steps the stars walked up to make their entrance on Oscar night.

As I climbed the main stairway to the second-level courtyard, I was feeling deflated. My little predawn foray had removed some of the glamour and mystery of Hollywood. It was just a bunch of streets filled with strip malls, burger joints, and tourist attractions.

I stopped and leaned over the second-floor balcony, looking out at the Hollywood hills. The sky was hazy and a light mist filled the air. Dawn was breaking, and in the distance, I saw the Hollywood sign. The sun was just poking above the horizon, illuminating the sign from behind with an orange-yellow glow, and the hazy mist made the letters almost pulse with life. The effect of the haze-shine on the Hollywood sign took my breath away.

Maybe there was still a little bit of magic left in Hollywood after all.

When I let myself back in the apartment, Danny was up and moving around. "My call time's at nine. Come with me. We'll grab a bite on the way."

"Baby duty," I said, shaking my head.

"Carter's capable of handling Max alone for a few hours. Besides, she wants you to go with me."

"She told you that?"

"Yes. She wants some time alone with the baby." He pocketed his keys and cell phone. "Plus I made the mistake of telling her I'm doing a scene with Jennifer Aniston. She thinks I need a chaperone."

As much as I loved taking care of Max, a few hours on the set would be a welcome diversion. This time, I'd stay out of the way. At least I could rest assured that my cell phone wouldn't go off at an inopportune time, since the battery had conked out.

"You sure it's okay? Is it a closed set?"

He shrugged. "Just to nonessential personnel. But you're essential," he said, adding with a wink, "aren't you, Lola?"

I was never going to live down the Lola label. I made a mental note to change the ring tone on the cell phone, if and when I figured out how to charge the darn thing.

"Let's go," I said, grabbing my purse and following Danny out the door.

While waiting in the drive-through lane at McDonald's, I used Danny's cell phone to call David. I couldn't stand knowing I'd hurt him.

After four rings, his nurse, Margie, answered. She sounded breathless. "We were just leaving," she said. "I ran back to get the phone."

"Leaving? Where are you going?"

"PS Eleven," she said, as though the answer was obvious. "They're expecting us at ten, right?"

I heard David's voice booming in the background. "The show must go on!"

David always said Margie was a miracle worker, and I was beginning to believe it was true. She'd brought him back from the brink of depression, and now he'd consented to do the show alone.

Danny pulled up to the window and handed the clerk a twenty.

"Wow," I said into the phone. "How did you talk him into it?"

"It wasn't me," Margie said. "It was your cousin Veronica."

"What? How? When?" And most important, why?

"I can't talk now, Holly. We don't want to be late. I'll have David call you later with a report. We have your cell phone number."

"It's dead—" I protested, but she had already disconnected.

The car inched forward, finally reaching the pickup window. The clerk handed Danny a bag of food, which he passed off to me while he maneuvered the car back out onto the busy street.

Margie had disconnected but I still had the phone pressed to my ear as though waiting for an explanation. How, and why, had Veronica talked to David? I'd told her to stay out of it; she'd done enough harm. My outrage at her interference was tempered by my relief over David's improved mood. His voice had sounded cheery, almost boisterous. If Ronnie was responsible for that, maybe she wasn't as self-obsessed and immature as I'd always believed. Maybe I'd misjudged her. Maybe she'd grown beyond the girl who'd turned a Pippi Longstocking puppet into a Holly voodoo doll, constantly raiding her mother's sewing kit for more needles to jab into my surrogate self.

Maybe it was my turn to get a grip.

My musings over what had motivated Ronnie to call David were interrupted by a strange and wondrous sight—a Starbucks with a drive-through window. *Los Angeles is the city of angels, after all,* I mused as Danny turned into the lane.

Danny's scene was being filmed on a studio soundstage in Burbank. When we reached the gate, Danny rolled down his window. The guard checked his name against a list on his clipboard, and let us enter.

We parked the Beetle and Danny led me through the lot, past a series of large, numbered warehouses. As we approached stage fourteen, I saw the red Mike's Monkeys van parked outside, alongside the stars' trailers. I wondered whether Monkey was inside. She wasn't in the scene Danny was filming this morning, but I didn't know what else was on the day's agenda.

"Stay out of trouble, okay?" Danny teased.

"Don't worry. I plan on flying under the radar today."

Giovanni was consulting a clipboard and barking orders into

his two-way. He waved Danny over. "Crane." He coughed after clipping his radio onto his back pocket. "You're late."

"Holly's fault," he said, crooking a finger in my direction. "She saw a drive-through Starbucks and nearly had an orgasm."

Giovanni smiled at me. "Welcome back, Lola."

"It's Holly," I said. "Sorry we're late."

"No problem. I was just gonna call. Your scene's been pushed back. We haven't even done the snake scene yet. Problem with the trainer."

"What's the problem?" Danny asked.

Gio leaned closer and lowered his voice. "He was arrested last night."

"Lenny?"

Gio nodded.

"Why was he arrested?" My stomach clenched. "Is Monkey okay?"

Gio shrugged. "I dunno. Mike's Monkeys couldn't find another trainer to fill in on such short notice, so Mike had to come out himself." He pointed over at the van, where a silver-haired man with a handlebar mustache was unloading crates from the back. "He just got here."

"What about the other trainer, Suzanne?"

"She's Lenny's girlfriend. I suspect she's out trying to raise bail money right now."

Giovanni's two-way crackled and he was off in the direction of the stage door. Danny headed for the hair and makeup trailer, but I wanted to stick around and find out what had happened to the trainer. I was worried about Monkey. What if Lenny had been arrested for animal cruelty? I replayed stories I'd heard about trainers beating animal performers into submission, and I remembered my initial reaction to seeing Lenny on set with the little chimp. He didn't harm her, or even yell at her, but she nonetheless seemed intimidated by the stiff finger he pointed in warning.

I walked around the back of the Mike's Monkeys van. The large cage that had formerly housed Monkey and Morty was empty. "No chimps today?" I asked.

Mike eyed me suspiciously and slammed the cargo doors shut. "You see any chimps?"

"Are you Mike?"

"Who's askin'?"

"Holly Heckerling," I said, holding out my hand.

He glanced up but didn't shake my hand. I watched as he secured two large carriers onto a dolly. He slung a large knapsack over one shoulder, tilted the dolly, and pushed it toward stage fourteen.

I fell into step beside him. "I'm just curious about the chimps. I heard something happened to Lenny, and I—"

He shot me a sidelong glance. "You a friend of Lenny's?"

"No. I just met him the other day. But I heard he was arrested and I was worried—"

"Don't worry about Lenny. He'll survive. Cockroaches always do."

Yeesh. "I'm not worried about Lenny. I'm worried about Monkey and Morty. Are they okay?"

We arrived at the soundstage and I reached around Mike to open the door, holding it open as he rolled the dolly through. "You with the crew?" he asked.

I shrugged noncommittally.

"Then you probably know you're not supposed to be around the animals."

"Yes." I nodded. "I'll leave you alone. Just tell me if Monkey and Morty are okay."

"Why wouldn't they be?"

Mike had an aggravating way of answering every question with a question. I wasn't going to get any information out of him.

"What are you trying to hide?" I asked.

"Who says I'm trying to hide anything?"

I heard heavy footsteps and saw Angela Ambrosino striding in our direction. Not wanting to butt heads with her again, I quickly changed course, heading toward the craft services table.

Daltry was spreading cream cheese on a bagel. "Lola, doll. Where've you been?" He flashed me a cocky grin and added, "I've missed you."

I knew he was toying with me. I wasn't sure why, but I amused him. I knew he'd had a string of supermodel girlfriends—I'd skimmed the *Vanity Fair* article in the checkout aisle on my diaper run—and half the women on the set were drooling over him. Surely, he couldn't be seriously making a play for me.

Not that I'd be interested if he was. I had a boyfriend, after all. Who, at this very moment, was at a family fun festival with his ex-wife and daughter. Ugh.

I tossed my hair over one shoulder. It wasn't as lustrous now that the potatoes had been thoroughly washed out, but it was still reacting well to the California climate. "Been busy."

"Busy with what?"

"This 'n' that."

He took a bite of his bagel and washed it down with some coffee.

"You hear what happened to the trainer?" I asked.

He nodded. "Guy had a python in his pants." He tossed his empty cup into a trash can. "Can't keep something like that a secret."

My lip curled at the image of Lenny's "python." While I felt palpable relief that it wasn't an animal-cruelty charge that resulted in Lenny's arrest, it disturbed me that I'd come face-to-face with a python-packing pervert. "So it was some kind of sex scandal?"

Daltry tipped his head back and laughed loud enough to attract the attention of a half dozen crew members. "Nothing that salacious. Just a little smuggling."

I wrinkled up my nose. "He didn't look like a drug dealer to me."

"Not drugs. Reptiles. Tried to smuggle them through customs in his pants."

I raised both eyebrows in disbelief. Surely Daltry was pulling my leg. I glanced around to see who else was in on the joke, but no one was paying any attention to us. "He just popped a python in his pants and tried to leave the country?"

"He wasn't smuggling them *out* of the country. He was smuggling them in. He flew to Brazil Wednesday night, picked up a shipment of black-market reptiles, and flew back. I heard he had a baby crocodile strapped to one leg and a python strapped to the other. Plus some kind of rare rodents in his pocket, worth about fifty grand each."

My mouth was agape. I knew there was a lot of money to be made in illegal wildlife trafficking. But I couldn't picture someone like Lenny hopping on a plane, loading up his pants with endangered species, and flying back to the States. And a python of all things. "Wasn't he afraid the python would bite?"

"Guy's got balls. You gotta give him that," Daltry said. "I hear the baby croc's mouth was held shut with a rubberband and it was stuffed inside a paper towel tube strapped to his leg, but still, I wouldn't let something with teeth that sharp anywhere near my 'nads."

I felt color creeping into my cheeks and turned away, feigning interest in a Hostess snack cake. I didn't want to give Daltry the satisfaction of seeing me blush over the mention of his 'nads.

"How do you know all this?" I asked him, ripping open the plastic pastry package. "Giovanni didn't know what happened to Lenny, and he's the one coordinating the schedules."

"Angela," Daltry said. "She told me the whole lurid story. She wasn't too keen on Lenny."

I could believe that. "She's not too keen on anybody."

"Oh, I don't know," Daltry said, tugging on his shirtsleeves. "She seems rather fond of me."

He looked over his shoulder at where Angela was standing, hands on hips, talking to Mike. She was scowling, and I wondered if he was being as evasive with her as he had been with me. She looked up at Daltry and her face immediately softened.

"See what I mean?" he said, giving me a nudge.

I rolled my eyes. The guy was so full of himself.

Angela broke away from the trainer and headed in our direction. "Gotta run," I said, tossing my snack wrapper in the trash.

"Stick around," Daltry said, grabbing my elbow. "I need you."

"For what?"

"To do like you did the other day. Train me."

"Sorry." I shook my head. "I left my newspaper at home."

"I'm serious. I'm doing a love scene with Jen and a snake, and I'm a bit nervous."

"Why?" I said, smiling. "I'm sure Jen won't bite."

Angela was now walking toward us. Daltry leaned closer and whispered conspiratorially, "You ever handle a snake?"

"A few," I said. In truth Rocky was the only snake I'd ever touched, and he still gave me the willies. But I was playing it cool. "If it's the one in the script, it's a little milk snake. Nonvenomous. Nothing to be afraid of."

"Good." He nodded. "Got any tips?"

"Yeah," I said, turning on my heels to walk away. "Don't put it in your pants."

I wandered aimlessly, trying to stay out of the way. I wanted to find Danny, but I'd lost all sense of direction inside the soundstage, which was filled with mini-sets—an apartment here, a classroom or pub or flower shop there—each of which appeared amazingly authentic despite the fact that they were open on one side, as though the contractor forgot to install the fourth wall.

From well-worn furnishings to rumpled bedsheets and bookshelves filled with hollow books, the faux rooms looked as though they were truly inhabited by the characters. Since reading the script, I felt I'd come to know these characters, and it felt almost like trespassing to be tiptoeing through their world.

I was trying to find my way back to the soundstage entrance when I turned a corner and nearly collided with Mike. He had a cell phone pressed to his ear and a dark look in his eyes.

"Sorry," I said, ducking aside to let him pass.

"Bitch," he said, snapping his cell phone shut.

I spun around. "Excuse me? I said I'm sorry. You don't have to be rude."

"What?" He looked me over as if noticing me for the first time. "Not you. The other bitch. Suzanne."

"Oh." The *other* bitch? Was that supposed to make me feel better?

He rubbed one hand over his face. He had dark circles under his eyes and was sporting a stubbly two-day growth. He was obviously exhausted. I could continue to pick a fight, or I could try another tactic.

"Suzanne's a real piece of work," I said.

He blew air through his nostrils, like a bull about to charge. "I know she's got a thing with Lenny, but we have a job to do here. I say let his sorry ass rot in jail for a while. Serves him right for getting greedy."

"Cockroach," I said, nodding in sympathy.

"You said it."

"Is it true he had a python in his pants?" I asked.

Mike shook his head. "Pit viper. Bunch of other endangered species from Brazil. A black caiman hatchling—that's a Brazilian crocodile—and a couple newborn pacaranas he picked up from a dealer for a few thou and was fixin' to sell for a hundred grand."

"Pacaranas?"

"It's a rodent. They get up to twenty pounds."

The mind boggles. "Who would pay a hundred thousand dollars for a giant rodent?"

He let out a harrumph, which for him was probably the equivalent of a belly laugh. "Lots of people. Especially in this town. People like to brag about their exotic pets. You know how many Beverly Hills broads have traded in their poodles for pet monkeys? Tiny tamarins they carry around in their Louis Vuitton handbags."

"How'd he get caught?" I asked. But what I really wanted to know was how he had boarded the plane to begin with. The security guards at LAX had managed to find my little laser pointer, which I'd forgotten was buried in my purse. How could Lenny have boarded an international flight with live cargo on his person?

"They only do spot checks. Can't pat down everybody. If they keep their cool and don't get flagged, smugglers can scoot right on by." He rubbed his face again. "But I'm guessing someone noticed Lenny was walkin' funny and pulled him out of the line. Dumb bastard."

I imagined the inspector's surprise at seeing Lenny's pants bulging in all the wrong places. "I don't get it. Why would he risk something like that when he has a great job?"

Now Mike let loose an actual belly laugh. "It's the money, honey. Even after paying off his partners, he'd still come away with a sweet payday. Beats the five hundred a day he'd make here."

"Five hundred? Dollars? A day?"

Mike shrugged. "Give or take. Less for domestics—dogs and cats. Chimps and monkeys and snakes—yeah, five hundred and up."

My mind was spinning. Even on my most manic multitasking workday, I'd never pulled in five hundred dollars.

"They're fine, by the way," he said.

"Who?"

"Monkey and Morty. Didn't mean to give you a hard time back there, but I got three trainers out of town on a location shoot and my wife, who doesn't like to get her hands dirty, back at the ranch taking care of the chimps. I'm trying to juggle this project and another one way out in Valencia—and that one's got twenty-seven different animals. If I don't scare up another hand soon, I'm gonna lose one of these gigs."

Bells were going off in my head. I'd never been much of a believer in fate, but it seemed like cosmic forces were conspiring to put this opportunity in my lap. I needed money. I loved animals. And Mike clearly needed another trainer to fill in for Lenny. I had no idea how to train animals, of course, and no real concept of what a trainer did on the set. I'd seen Lenny work with Monkey, but she was clearly repeating things they'd already rehearsed. And chimps were only part of the story in this film. How did you train a snake? I didn't even think such a thing was possible.

Five hundred dollars a day. Even a day's work would help me out of my financial slump.

Even as I knew it was the craziest thing I'd ever get myself into, I decided to go for it and offer myself up as an animal trainer. I opened my mouth to speak, but was interrupted by Mike's cell phone.

He looked at the number and pressed the phone to his ear. "Hey, Manny, thanks for getting back to me. I got a gig for you."

My heart sank. Even though I'd only entertained the idea of being a trainer for a few seconds, it hurt to have the dream snatched away. Mike turned and tramped across the soundstage without even a backward glance in my direction.

I found Danny outside, near the hair and makeup trailer. "Where were you?" he asked me.

"I went to get a Twinkie, and I ended up talking to Daltry and the trainer, Mike."

"I've got something for you," Danny said, reaching into his pocket. "Xiana, the makeup artist has a Nokia phone, too. I borrowed her charger for you."

"Great," I said, reaching out to take the charger. I'd been trying not to dwell on my dead cell phone. I was determined not to become a phone drone, a slave to my cell phone, like so many of my friends. But I was dying to find out what had happened with David's classroom talk and Margie had said they'd call my cell with an update. I pulled the phone out of my back pocket and clicked one end of the charger into place. I regarded the other end curiously. "Where do I plug this in?"

He tossed me his car keys. "It's a car charger, so you've got to go plug it into the cigarette lighter and start the engine."

I looked in the direction of the parking lot. It was a long way from the soundstage. As if reading my mind, Danny said, "You're not gonna be missing anything. I just heard we've been pushed back another half hour."

My spirits were low as I trudged across the lot to the parking garage, kicking myself mentally the whole way. The moment I sensed Mike had a staffing shortage, I should have seized on the opportunity. Surely there were people working with animals in Hollywood with far less experience than I had.

By the time I reached the car, I'd convinced myself I had never had a chance to begin with. There were probably licensing requirements, specialized training, reams of paperwork. It was foolhardy to think that someone could step in off the street and be hired as a trainer. By not speaking sooner, I might have saved myself the embarrassment of having Mike laugh in my face.

I unlocked the Beetle and slid behind the wheel. I plugged the charger, phone attached, into the receptacle for the cigarette lighter. I turned the key in the ignition and a light on Betty's cell phone glowed green.

I didn't know how long it would take to get a charge, so I waited a few minutes before trying to make a call. There was no answer at David's, so I left a message.

Then I called my apartment. No answer. Either Ronnie had heeded my warning about answering my phone, or she was too busy interfering with my life to pick up. Either way, I was in no mood to leave a message.

I hit redial, this time bypassing my outgoing message and entering the code to retrieve my messages. There was one, from Pete, my building's superintendent. "I got good news and bad news. Your rent check didn't bounce, so you're safe for now. Bad news is the owners want you out. They got eviction papers ready and are just lookin' for an excuse to fill in the blanks. I talked them out of charging you for the damage to the wall, but I can't do no more. You're on your own, kid."

Here we go again, I thought, snapping the phone shut and banging my head against the steering wheel. The unpredictability of my life was almost predictable. I'd squeaked by for another month, but rent would be due again in a few short weeks, along with the rest of my bills. Maybe I should move home after all. Get a regular job. Listen to Kuki say, "I told you so," for the rest of my life.

I thumped my head against the steering wheel a few more times in frustration. My head-banging reverie was interrupted by the sound of someone knocking. I looked up to see Danny standing next to the car. He motioned for me to roll down the window.

"They're looking for you," he said.

"Who's looking for me?"

"Gio, Colin, the animal dude. And the Humane Association chick."

I coughed. "Yeah. Right."

"Seriously. What were you doing when I was in makeup?"

"Nothing."

"Well, you'd better hurry. Colin's holding up filming. Gio's having a conniption. And everyone's lookin' for Lola."

So much for flying under the radar.

When we reached the soundstage, I saw Daltry in a huddle with Gio and Angela. Gio's jaw was clenched and Angela wore her customary disapproving scowl. But Daltry had a giddy schoolboy expression. I knew he was up to no good, but had no idea how it involved me. Mike was a few feet away, pacing and taking puffs on a cigarette.

Giovanni looked up as I approached. "Colin's demanding you prep him for the snake scene," he barked.

All eyes were on me. I didn't know what to say. "Prep him? How?"

We all turned to Daltry.

"I'm not comfortable shooting with a live snake," he said. "I need her to talk me through it, like she did with the chimp."

"It's customary for the actors to have some time to warm up to the animals they're working with," Angela offered. "And vice versa."

"Why didn't that happen this time?" I asked.

"It did," Gio said, coughing and kicking at a spot on the ground. "Jackman—and the rest of the cast—spent a day with Lenny reviewing the animal stunts."

"I'm not Jackman," Daltry said pointedly, "in case you haven't noticed."

"You want him to freak out when the camera's rolling?" Angela said to Giovanni. "A little prep work now could save you some time in the end."

Gio turned to me. "Mike offered to teach him how to handle the snake. But he's demanding you do it. Says he needs an hour."

Mike looked at his watch and cursed. "An hour? I was supposed to be out of here by noon." He crooked a finger at Daltry. "Come with me. I'll have you playing kissy-face with the snake in two minutes. Hell, it ain't even venomous."

"That wouldn't work." Daltry shook his head. "My character's *supposed* to be afraid." His expression was hard, but I thought I detected a mischievous glint in his eye. "Mike, no offense, man, but it's not the snake I'm worried about—it's my performance. Sometimes it's not about training the animals—it's about training the actors."

My eyebrows shot up at hearing my words come out of his mouth.

Daltry pointed at me. "She knows snakes. Knows me. Knows the script." He winked at me before adding, "And she's a darn sight prettier than you."

Mike threw his cigarette to the ground and stamped it out with his boot. "Then why doesn't she just take over as damn trainer?"

14

In the Wings

When I was in the seventh grade, my school put on a production of *Annie.* I auditioned for the title role, along with every other girl in school. But unlike the other girls, I had an edge. Not only was my hair naturally red, but I was practically an orphan myself. Who better to convey Annie's hard-knock life than someone who'd suffered a similar fate?

My natural affinity for the role was lost on the school's drama coach, who flatly informed my grandmother, "She can't sing." The role went to Cecily Christian, a girl with bone-straight blond hair, two living parents, and a spectacular singing voice. I'd cried for days, taking no solace in the fact that I did land a role in the production—a nonsinging, nonspeaking part identified in the program as "Unnamed Orphan." A pity part.

My job was to blend into the background in the orphanage scenes. I was allowed to dance during the musical numbers—years of ballet lessons finally paid off—though I was instructed not to sing but rather to mouth the words to the songs.

The day of the final dress rehearsal, Cecily Christian was caught smoking in the girls' bathroom. She was banned from the play. The rest of us were onstage, in our costumes, when the director informed us of Cecily's wayward behavior, adding that if a replacement couldn't be found immediately, the show would be canceled.

I'd been to every rehearsal. I knew every song. I'd memorized every one of Annie's lines—not intentionally, but through osmosis. Aunt Betty had bought me a cassette tape of the original Broadway cast recording, and I'd listened to it every night before going to sleep, using headphones so I wouldn't disturb Ronnie. When I was alone, I'd sing along.

While "Tomorrow" was Annie's signature song, I was partial to "Maybe," in which the orphans wonder what their parents are like and what they are doing in that moment—straightening a tie, paying a bill. For parentless girls, these seemingly mundane tasks are the stuff of fantasy. It had been four months since I'd seen my father, and while I never would have guessed that nearly twenty years would pass before I saw him again, I'd begun to suspect he wasn't coming back. I, too, spent a great deal of time imagining what he was up to.

In truth, when I'd fantasized about landing the lead in *Annie,* part of the dream involved looking out at the audience on opening night to see my father in the front row.

This is my chance, I thought as the director asked if anyone present felt they could take over the role. Leeza Kiefer, who played Tessie, was the official understudy for Annie, but she admitted she hadn't memorized the character's lines or paid any attention to the blocking. No one else stepped forward right away. It was now or never. I willed myself to speak, but my lips wouldn't cooperate.

What if everyone laughed at me? After all, I was the girl who couldn't sing. They didn't know I'd been practicing. They didn't know that my connection to the character would transcend any deficiency in my musical abilities. They didn't know, *period.*

The director looked us over, in our ragtag clothes, shoe polish smudged on our faces to resemble dirt. I held my breath, waiting, hoping that, when she looked at me and our eyes met, she'd know that I was meant to play Annie.

But she barely glanced at me before moving down the line. "Janelle," she said to the girl standing next to me. "You're Annie."

Janelle beamed. "But who will play my part?"

Now the director looked at me. "Do you think you can play July?"

My eyes stung. July, the shy orphan, had few lines. The director looked less certain that I could fill the minor part than she was of Janelle stepping into the lead. I nodded, unable to speak.

"Good." The director nodded.

"But she'd have to sing," Leeza objected.

"That's okay," the director said to me. "Just try to blend in."

My aunts and grandmother made a big deal about me being upgraded to a speaking role, even though it represented a personal tragedy in my mind. It was too late for the programs to be reprinted, so I would go down in history as "Unnamed Orphan." Janelle was a good singer, but she acted as though she was in a Colgate commercial, smiling broadly throughout every number, even the bittersweet "Maybe," in which Annie's longing to be reunited with her parents is underscored by the knowledge that her dream will probably never be realized.

While waiting in the wings on opening night, I scanned the faces in the audience, picking out my aunts, uncles, cousins, and grandmother. My father wasn't there.

With all eyes on Janelle, no one noticed me in the background, singing along, softly but sincerely, rivulets of tears streaming down my face.

As I stood on the back lot with Daltry, Gio, Angela, Mike, and Danny all staring at me, I felt like I was in the seventh grade all over again. I was filled with the same fears of being laughed at, dismissed, or overlooked altogether.

But if there was one thing I'd learned since junior high, it was never to make the same mistake twice. My life was filled with missed opportunities, derailed relationships, social gaffes, and flat-out disasters, but I'd learned something from each one. Since mistaking Binaca for Visine and nearly blinding myself before a stand-up gig, I was always careful to check the label before use. I'd learned not to talk and chop vegetables at the same time after stabbing myself in the nose when gesturing—butcher's knife in hand—as I told Kuki about a classmate's new nasal piercing. A humiliating drunk-dialing incident led to my dual policy of limiting my alcohol intake and, if that failed, disconnecting my phone before I could make maudlin calls to old boyfriends or classmates.

And I was fairly certain I'd never again attempt to enter an apartment through a diminutive hole in the wall.

So when Mike challenged, "Why doesn't she take over as damn trainer?" I knew I had to squelch my fears and insecurities and just go for it. I was well aware that Mike's challenge hadn't been serious, but in his sarcasm, he'd opened the door—and I was going to shove my foot into it.

"Okay," I said. "I'll do it."

Everyone turned and stared at me. Danny and Daltry were grinning, while the others wore expressions ranging from astonishment to abject terror. At least I knew who was on my side.

Angela stammered something about impropriety, while Mike, shouting over her, questioned my qualifications.

Daltry and Danny both defended my honor, Danny listing my primatology degree and pet-sitting experience, and Daltry blathering about my singular ability to finesse his performance.

I cut through the cross-talk, addressing Mike directly. "Let's face it. You need me. I can take over here, while you go take care of things on the other set."

"You're an animal trainer?"

It depended on how you defined the term, I supposed, but I said, "Yes."

"What films have you done?" he asked.

"None," I admitted. "I do a live show. Monkeys, snakes—that sort of thing. It's very popular." Popular with first graders, that is. "And weddings."

"Weddings?" Giovanni coughed.

"Yeah," I said, leveling my gaze at Mike. "You know how many Beverly Hills broads would kill to have a boa constrictor at their wedding reception—let guests take home a souvenir photo instead of a sack of candy-covered almonds? It's an untapped market that I'm just beginning to exploit."

Mike frowned. "You got no film experience? Or training?"

"She has training." Danny stepped forward. "She went to monkey school." I'd gotten a bachelor's degree in primatology from Columbia University, which my aunts had always referred to as "monkey school."

"Moorpark?" Mike asked. I presumed that was some kind of animal trainers' academy.

I shook my head. Normally I'd boast about my Ivy League education, but since my studies at Columbia centered around primate natural history, behavior, and ecology—and not how to get them to perform stunts—I figured it was best to be vague. "Back in New York. I'm from Manhattan."

"We can't afford more delays," Gio said. "You say you already know the script?"

I nodded emphatically.

Gio looked at Mike. "She's got a boa constrictor."

Mike nodded. His expression was beginning to soften. It was time for my final gambit. I sucked in my stomach and spoke forcefully. "I'll finish the day out here, for half the going rate. Two-fifty. If I do a good job, you'll let me finish the film and pay me five hundred a day."

Mike scuffed his boot on the pavement, considering. He glanced at his watch again. I knew if his back wasn't up against the wall, he'd never give me the time of day. But he was a desperate man. "I dunno. . . ."

"Crissakes," Daltry said. He turned to Gio. "His operation isn't the only game in town, is it? I bet you can find an outfit with twice the animals and half the attitude."

Gio adjusted a knob on his two-way. "I'll get Brandon to make some calls."

"All right," Mike grumbled. "She's got the job."

"This here's Lucinda," Mike said, lifting a plump boa constrictor out of one of the plastic crates I'd watched him haul inside earlier that morning. "She's a sweetie. Loves to be handled." He handed Lucinda to me while he reached into the next crate.

I forced myself to smile as Lucinda wound around my arms and explored my upper body. A red-tail boa, she was bigger than Rocky and more muscular. I reminded myself to breathe. It wouldn't do to pass out in my first few minutes as an animal trainer.

As Lucinda and I got acquainted, Mike dropped names of shows she'd been in and actors she'd worked with, from a photo shoot with Madonna to an appearance on the *Tonight* show. An impressive résumé for an ectotherm.

Then he held up a sleek snake, just over a foot long, with bold red, black, and white stripes. "Reba's a little skittish at first, but she'll warm up to you right quick. Won't you, darlin'?" Reba's forked tongue darted in and out of her mouth rapidly, seemingly tasting the air, but really trying to sniff me out and determine if I was predator or prey.

After introducing me to three more snakes and giving me a quick rundown of filming procedures and safety regulations, he returned them to their compartments inside the crates. "When they're not filming, keep 'em back here, where it's quiet and cool. Call me when you wrap."

We exchanged cell phone numbers and he had me sign an impromptu waiver he wrote in longhand on the back of a discarded call sheet. Though I questioned the legality of a document that stated that if anything happened to the snakes my "ass would be grass," I signed at the X, adding my own stipulation that my first day's fee would be payable in cash at the end of the workday.

Mike folded the paper and stuffed it into his back pocket, along with his keys. "I'll take the van and come back at the end of the day to pick up the snakes." He looked me up and down, still clearly uncertain about my suitability for the job. "If it works out, tomorrow you'll come to the ranch first and take one of the vans. You got a driver's license, don't you?"

I nodded. "Of course." He didn't have to know about my infrequent use of said license, or the fact that I'd never driven anything as big as the Mike's Monkeys van.

He raised one eyebrow. "And you can handle a van?"

"You think I get the animals in my act around Manhattan on the subway?" Two could play the answer-a-question-with-a-question game.

He stomped away, grumbling under his breath.

I glanced around the small room that served as the animal holding area for this shoot. I resisted the temptation to burst into song—the triumphant final stanza of "Tomorrow" came to mind—but I couldn't suppress the huge grin that spread across my face. Sometimes dreams do come true.

I couldn't contain my excitement. I had to share my news with someone. But who? Betty would be thrilled, but she'd spread the news to the rest of the family. Kuki would add this latest adventure to her mental list of "Holly's follies" and command me to return home to a life of boredom in the barbershop, while Gerry would be on the phone pleading with me to procure socks from the entire cast.

I thought of Tom, who would ordinarily be the first person I called with potentially life-changing news. But I didn't know where things stood with him at the moment.

I pulled my cell phone out of my pocket and dialed Carter's number. She answered on the first ring.

"Congratulations," she squealed. "Danny just called to tell me about your new job. I can't believe it. It's too perfect! Does this mean you'll move here for good?"

"Whoa, slow down," I said. "It's just a one-day trial run. By tomorrow I'm sure a dozen trainers will have come out of the woodwork, and I'll be out of a gig."

"Don't think like that," Carter said. "You'll do great and they'll keep you on. And you'll move in with us. Of course we'll have to find a bigger place, but—"

"It's one day, on one movie," I interjected. "I never said anything about moving here."

"This is only the beginning. I can feel it."

"We'll see." I changed the subject, suddenly afraid of jinxing my good fortune by speculating where it would lead. "What are you doing?"

"Not much I can do with the milkmeister attached to my breast, except watch TV." She let out a laugh. "Maybe that's why they call it the boob tube."

"How is Max?"

"Hungry." She made some gurgling noises at Max, then returned to the line. "Hey, I almost forgot. Your aunt Betty called me today."

"Yeah? What'd she want?"

"It was weird. She asked me about morning sickness. And heartburn. And hemorrhoids."

I groaned inwardly. "Ever since Lamaze class, she thinks she has pregnancy symptoms. At first she was just trying to fit in. Now I don't know. Maybe she's talked herself into a hysterical pregnancy."

"Aunt Betty, pregnant?" Carter snorted. "That would be hysterical."

"What did you tell her?"

"I told her to try saltines for the morning sickness, Pepto for the heartburn, and good old Preparation H for the hemorrhoids."

"Do me a favor," I said. "Don't ever tell her about nipple confusion."

The snakes were snug inside their crates, and I was perusing the script, looking for the scene in which Colin visits Jennifer's apartment and discovers her impressive collection of reptiles.

"I figured you as the pussycat type," he says, to which she purrs, "I have one of those, too."

He inadvertently loosens the lid on one terrarium, and a red snake—played by Reba—escapes. That would be easy enough to accomplish, I decided. Snakes have a natural tendency to climb. The few times I'd left Rocky's aquarium unsecured, he'd immediately gotten loose.

The next part, in which the snake slithers up Daltry's back and around his shoulder would be trickier. If Daltry stood close enough to the terrarium, the snake just might see him as an escape route and try to climb up his back. But it was just as likely that she'd lower herself to the floor, where she'd quickly dart away, under a bed or into any number of hiding places on the set.

Why couldn't my first day as a trainer involve a species that was actually trainable? I wondered. A monkey or an ape or even a dog. Intelligent and eager to please, primates and canines can be coaxed to perform in exchange for treats or verbal praise. Tempting a snake with food, on the other hand, can be dangerous—you don't want a snake to equate your hand with its next meal.

I wished I had more time to familiarize myself with the snakes and read up on their behavior. But the schedule had already been delayed, and I knew I'd be called to the set any minute.

I was surprised Daltry wasn't here, breathing down my neck. Despite all his demands for "prep time," once I'd been given the green light to take over as trainer, he'd disappeared.

A racking cough accompanied by heavy footsteps signaled Giovanni's approach. The door opened and he entered, followed by Angela. They both carried sheaths of paper. Giovanni walked over to a small table that occupied one corner of the room.

"Here's a call sheet," he said, setting it on the table. "From now on, you'll get one of these every day from Brandon—he's the second AD. It'll tell you where you need to be and when you need to be there. If you got a problem, I don't want to hear about it." His two-way cackled and he shouted, "Hold on," and dialed down the volume. "Once you check in, you don't go anywhere without clearing it with me or Brandon."

He continued with a litany of instructions and I did my best to absorb them all. Then he said, "We've juggled the schedule to give you time to work with Daltry. I pushed the snake scene back till the afternoon. We're gonna start with the kickboxing class instead."

I'd laughed aloud while reading that section of the script. After a break-in at the clinic, Jennifer, Kelly, and Danny sign up for kickboxing lessons. During their first class, Danny lets slip that Jennifer has been seeing Daltry behind Kelly's back. The two women are teamed for a sparring exercise, which turns into a full-fledged boxing match. Danny steps between them to break it up and gets cold-cocked by Kelly.

I thanked Gio, knowing it hadn't been easy to rearrange the day's shooting schedule and wanting to kiss him on the cheek for giving me more time to prepare. I wondered how long it would take them to film the kickboxing scene.

As if reading my mind, Gio said, "Including lunch, it'll be four, five hours by the time we're ready for the snakes."

He walked away. Now it was Angela's turn to dump documents on the table. She began with a spiral-bound book with the Humane Association logo on the cover. It contained detailed guidelines for the use of animals in film and television. I thumbed through it, surprised to see separate chapters for various types of animals, including primates, reptiles, amphibians, even insects.

"You guys even look out for the ants?"

"Ants, spiders, cockroaches," Angela said, nodding. "I've even done maggots for *CSI.*"

"*Maggots?*" I frowned. "You have to make sure that no maggots are harmed in the making of the show?"

She nodded. "Every living creature is worthy of protection."

Protecting maggots. There really is no business like show business.

I thanked my lucky stars I'd seen no mention of maggots in the *Vets in the City* script. Snakes make me squirmy enough. No way would I work with maggots—not even for a half grand a day.

Angela gave me a quick history of the use of animals in film, starting with a 1939 Western in which a stunt rider on horseback had gone over a cliff and into a raging river. The horse had lost its life, while the stuntman just lost his hat.

I understood the outrage the incident inspired and was glad that such stunts were a thing of the past. But perhaps they'd gone a little overboard if they felt compelled to monitor the health and well-being of maggots.

After wrapping up her spiel, Angela made it clear that she was in charge. "If I don't think the animals are safe, comfortable, and healthy, I can shut down filming. That doesn't make me popular, but it's my job and I take it seriously."

She handed me photocopies of her notes on the *Vets* script, indicating potential areas of concern. I promised to look them over. I was feeling a bit overwhelmed, but determined not to show any anxiety to Angela. She started toward the door, then stopped and turned around. "I know we got off to a bad start, but we're really on the same side. We both want what's best for the animals."

"Of course."

She leaned against the table. "You know, I started out as a trainer." She proceeded to tell me her background, which ranged from zoos to circuses to film sets on several continents. I was duly impressed.

She finished speaking and stared at me, probably waiting for a similar recitation of qualifications from me. Instead I said, "You must think I'm completely obnoxious, trying to jump into this job with no training or license."

"You don't need a license to train the animals, just to own or exhibit them. And you'd be surprised how many people get into training with no experience. They see it on TV and it looks easy. And the owners will bring in their friends, cousins, and neighbors, many of them less qualified than you."

I wasn't sure if I should take that as a compliment. Then she added, "At least you've handled snakes before."

I let out a sigh. "About that . . ."

"You do know how to handle a snake, don't you?"

"Yes, I know how to handle snakes. But I don't know how to *train* them."

She tipped her head back and laughed. "That's because you can't train a snake."

I'd read through all the papers Gio and Angela had left behind. I'd taken all five of my charges out of their crates, handled them, and put them back without incident. I'd reviewed the afternoon's scene and thought about how to prepare Daltry.

But Daltry still hadn't appeared.

Eventually I decided if the star wouldn't come to me, I'd have to go to the star.

A small knot of people was gathered outside the soundstage. A tall guy in a flannel shirt held a clipboard in one hand and a two-way radio in the other. Having learned from my brief showbiz experience that guys with clipboards and two-ways tend to know what's going on, I targeted him with my question. "You know where I can find Colin?"

The tall guy introduced himself as Brandon, the second assistant director, and pointed to a large motor home. "That's his trailer. I saw him go in there a while back."

I thanked him and walked to the trailer, noticing for the first time a placard reading DALTRY taped to the door. I rapped on the door and waited.

The door opened and all I saw were legs. Long legs, attached to a toothpick-sized midsection and a mass of flowing chestnut hair. She leaned down, poking her head through the door. "Yes?"

"Um, sorry," I stammered. "I'm looking for Colin."

"Yes?"

"Oh. Um. We're supposed to rehearse. I'm Holly."

"Hold on." She closed the door, leaving me to wait outside while she went to speak to Colin. I was guessing she wasn't his personal assistant. And she definitely didn't look like one of the five Frigidaires. Probably not there in a professional capacity. Perhaps she was the supermodel ex-girlfriend Betty had told me about. The one with a name like a horse.

Or maybe she was the new mare in his stable.

Either way, she was stunning. I felt foolish for thinking, even for a second, that Daltry might have been flirting with me.

The door opened again and the legs were back. This time she didn't even lean through the opening. "He's busy," she said before clicking the door shut.

Fueled by indignation, I stamped back to the soundstage. He was the one who'd insisted on prep time, and now he was too busy with his supermodel of the moment to even talk to me. *Fine,* I thought. Let him have his fun.

But by the time I reached the soundstage entrance, my indignation had turned to anger. No way would I let Daltry ruin my big break. Gio had rearranged the entire schedule to accommodate us, and damn it, we were going to rehearse.

I spun around and marched back to Daltry's trailer. This time I knocked louder. The door opened and the chestnut-haired beauty looked down at me with undisguised disdain. "Ye-e-e-s?"

"Tell Colin that Lola needs him. Now."

She clicked the door shut again, and I waited, tapping my foot on the pavement. Then the door swung open and Colin stood there, naked except for a towel around his waist. His hair was wet, and the beads of moisture on his chest glistened in the midmorning sun. I shielded my eyes with my hand so he wouldn't be misled by my temporary sun blindness and think I was gawking at his nearly naked body.

"Lola, why didn't you say it was you?" He grabbed my hand and pulled me inside the trailer. "When I heard about the schedule change, I figured I'd have time to catch a quick shower."

I blinked, trying to adjust my eyes to the dim light of the trailer's interior. "If we're going to work together, you should probably call me by my real name. It's Holly."

He put one hand on his heart. "You'll always be Lola to me."

"A-hem." Daltry's leggy friend cleared her throat.

"Sorry, doll. Did I forget my manners?" He gestured to me and said, "This here's Lola, who apparently also answers to Holly." He put a proprietary hand on the supermodel's shoulder. "This is Velvetina."

Velvetina? Betty had said she had a name like a horse. I thought she had a name like a brick of processed cheese.

"She likes to be called Velvet," Daltry added.

I forced my lips into a smile, trying not to sneer. It wasn't that I had anything against supermodels—or horses—but Velvet wasn't making it easy. She pursed her lips together and tilted her head slightly in my direction.

I tried not to drool as I let my gaze wander around the motor home. It was big—probably bigger than my apartment in Manhattan—and luxuriously appointed. The main room had separate sitting and dining areas and a fully equipped kitchen. A narrow hallway led to the bathroom—or so I assumed, from the steam pouring through the open door—and bedroom, the door of which was also ajar. A pile of clothing had been discarded at the foot of the bed, and the sheets were rumpled.

"Wait while I towel off," Daltry said to me before heading in the direction of the bathroom. He leaned in as he passed and whispered in my ear, "Then we'll go handle the snake."

I bit my lip, refusing to be rattled by Daltry's snake innuendo.

Velvet regarded me with an icy glare. Not the friendliest filly in the stable. I wasn't going to sit by and be snarled at, so I made my way toward the door. "Tell him to come find me when he's ready."

My stomach was grumbling, so I made a pit stop at craft services. I snarfed down a bear claw, washed up in the restroom, and returned to snake central.

When I opened the door, I was stunned to see Daltry standing in the middle of the room, his back turned to me. His hair was still damp, but he was dressed in jeans, a white T-shirt, and cowboy boots. One of the crates was open and Lucinda, the boa constrictor, was twisted around Daltry's arm. With the other hand, he stroked her body. He was talking to her in a low, steady voice, utterly devoid of anxiety.

I'd been had.

"Looks like you've gotten over your fears," I said.

He turned his head at the sound of my voice, and his face broke into a grin. "Lola, doll," he said, winking, "would you like to pet my python?"

15

Lights, Camera, Action

"You played me," I said, taking Lucinda from Daltry and lowering her back into the crate. I snapped the lid closed and turned to face Daltry, both hands on my hips. "What's going on here?"

He was still grinning. "What do you mean?"

"You may not know the difference between a python and a boa constrictor, but you obviously know something about snakes."

"I had older sisters. They tortured me when I was little—liked to dress me up in their dolls' clothes, that kind of thing. When I got a little bigger I learned that the occasional snake in the bed kept 'em in line."

"If you're not afraid of snakes, then what are you really up to?"

He shrugged. "Who says I'm up to anything?"

I threw my hands in the air. "You held up filming for hours, demanding time to be prepped, to get over your fears."

He cocked an eyebrow at me. "Worked out well for you, didn't it?" He fingered the crew badge that Giovanni had hung around my neck an hour earlier. He tugged on it, pulling my face closer to his. "You got a job."

I stepped back and snatched my badge away from him. "Don't toy with me. I'm not here for your amusement."

"That's too bad." He grinned. "Because you definitely amuse me, Lola."

I opened Reba's crate and lifted her out. I turned to face Daltry. "Your hands clean?"

He nodded. "Just came from the shower, remember?"

"Have you eaten anything since then? You don't want to handle reptiles if your fingers smell like food."

"No food."

"Good," I said, handing him the red, white, and black snake. "Say hello to your costar."

Ten minutes later, Daltry knew as much about snakes as I did. Which wasn't much. But he was comfortable with Reba slithering up his arm and around his shoulders. Now the trick was figuring out how to get her to perform on cue.

"Isn't there some kind of scent they're attracted to?" Daltry asked. "Something to lure her to hit a certain mark."

"That's it!" I gave an exaggerated head bob. "We'll spritz your neck with rat pheromones, then wait for Reba to climb up and sink her fangs into your jugular."

"Very funny."

Drawing on my own limited experience and the few tips Angela had imparted after affirming my fear that serpents are untrainable, I explained to Daltry that we had to try to set up the scene to take advantage of the snake's natural behavior. "They like to climb," I pointed out, "and they're naturally drawn to dark, enclosed spaces. So if you put a paper bag on the floor and plop the snake on the ground, she'll head for the bag and curl up inside."

I lifted Reba's crate onto the table and removed the lid. Then I motioned for Daltry to stand against the table with his back to the crate.

"Now don't panic," I said, tugging the back of his T-shirt out of his jeans and lifting it out a few inches to create a welcome opening.

It didn't take long for Reba to lift her head out of the crate and investigate the gap. She flicked her tongue back and forth, testing the air, and then ascended.

Daltry sucked in air as the snake slipped inside his shirt and glided up his back. When she reached the top, she poked her head out the opening, then quickly retreated inside. I watched the shifting outline her body made against his cotton T-shirt as she traveled around to the front, finally settling into a ball just above his waist.

Daltry gave an involuntary shudder. His expression registered fascination tinged with fear. "That was . . . oddly sensual," he said, his voice raspy. "The snake . . . against my bare skin . . ." He looked up at me. "That's not in the script, is it?"

"No. I just wanted to illustrate that you can predict certain behaviors. I knew Reba would be attracted to the dark, enclosed space inside your shirt. And your body heat." I tried not to think about what it would feel like to crawl inside his shirt, feeling his bare skin against mine and curling up in the warmth of his body.

"The trouble is," I continued, "the script calls for her to slide up on the outside of your shirt, and I can't figure out how to persuade her to do that."

Even a charmer like Lucinda would naturally shy away from people. So why would a skittish snake like Reba choose to climb up Daltry's back, exposed? Perhaps her skittishness was the key. If she was nervous on the set, under the lights, with people and equipment and bright lights, she might seek out a warm, friendly body for comfort.

"I want you and Reba to be friends."

"Darlin'," he said, gesturing to the coiled lump under his shirt, "she and I are bosom buddies."

His BlackBerry rang. In one fluid movement, he pulled it out of his back pocket, clicked a button, and held it to his ear. "Talk to me." He nodded, grumbled, "Yeah," a few times, then disconnected without saying good-bye. "My agent," he said, though I hadn't asked. He slid the phone back into his pocket before carefully extracting Reba from his shirt and returning her to the crate.

"Let's do it again," I said.

I watched as Daltry backed up against the crate and allowed Reba to slither inside his shirt. She followed the same path up his back, around his shoulders, and down to his waist, then settled in. We repeated the process several times, twice interrupted by his ringing cell phone and monosyllabic conversations with his agent.

After her sixth circuit, Daltry carried Reba back to the crate. "No," I said. "I want you to keep contact with her up until the moment we film. Don't put her down."

"Might make it hard to take a piss."

I rolled my eyes. "Aside from lunch and restroom breaks, I want you to hold her. Keep her close. Let her feel your heat." I gestured to the blazer he'd draped over a chair. "Does that have a pocket?"

He nodded. I picked up the blazer, Daltry slipped Reba into one of the pockets, and he put it on. She explored the pocket for a moment before settling down.

"You want me to walk around with her in my pocket the rest of the morning? You don't mind letting her go off with me?"

"No, no, no. I'm not letting her out of my sight. Which means I'm not letting *you* out of my sight."

He rubbed his hands together and cackled. "My evil plan is working."

I rolled my eyes, ignoring the implication that he'd faked a snake phobia in order to spend more time with me. "Let's go get her used to the sounds on the set."

I followed Daltry across the soundstage. In the distance I heard an eighties pop tune, punctuated by grunts and shouts. Either filming had begun on the kickboxing scene or someone on the crew was dancing to the oldies.

As we walked, I said, "Say something. I want her to get to know your voice."

"What should I talk about?"

"Doesn't matter. Tell me your life story. Your theories on the role of hydrofluorocarbons in global warming. Recite nursery rhymes. Just keep talking."

He launched into a Shakespearean soliloquy—*Hamlet*, I think, but I'd never been big on the Bard. He was bemoaning the frailty of women when we reached the apartment set. He stopped mid-monologue to ask, "How do snakes hear without ears?"

"I don't actually think they *can* hear."

"You had me recite *Hamlet* for your own personal amusement?"

I suppressed a smile. Now who felt toyed with? "Snakes may not hear like we do, but they can pick up vibrations." I'd seen something on cable TV about how snakes might be able to interpret low-frequency sound waves through internal auditory structures. "I think."

He arched one eyebrow. "You think?"

"I know it's a long shot," I admitted, "but if you stand close enough and she hears you talking, can sense your vibrations and pick up your body heat, I think she'll want to get closer to you."

"But she won't be able to go inside my shirt when I'm in costume."

I nodded. "I'm hoping that when she can't find an opening, she'll choose the next best route." Or she'll drop onto the floor and slither away, along with my newfound career.

There were several aquariums on a shelf along one wall of the faux apartment. Only Reba would "perform" in the scene; the other four snakes would serve as atmosphere. Daltry lifted the lid on the terrarium that would house Reba.

"Should we give it a go?" he asked.

I shook my head. "Not till cameras are rolling." I had a feeling we'd only have one chance to get it right, and I didn't want to blow it.

We went our separate ways for lunch, alternating snake-sitting duties. I'd decided not to handle Reba again until after filming so she'd only have the chance to bond to one person. Plus, I still hadn't completely gotten over the whole "snakes are icky" thing.

She was snug in her crate when Daltry returned from lunch with a smile on his face and a faint flowery fragrance I could only assume he'd picked up from the supermodel.

"Good lunch?" I said.

He licked his lips in response.

Daltry lifted Reba from her crate and let her wind around his arms. I couldn't believe this was the same guy who'd convinced me—and everyone else on the production—that he was terrified of snakes. Maybe he was a better actor than I thought.

During my downtime, I'd figured out how to reprogram Betty's cell phone, replacing "Copacabana" with a sedate, run-of-the-mill *brinnng-brinnng* sound. So when it rang, Daltry gave me a wounded look.

"Lola," he said on a sigh.

My pulse raced when I saw David's number on the readout. I flipped the phone open. "David?" *Please, please don't let him be mad,* I thought.

"You should have told me you were leaving," he said. The lilt in his voice lifted my spirits.

"I know. I screwed up."

Colin regarded me quizzically. I turned my back to him and pressed the phone closer to my ear.

"It's okay. I forgive you," David was saying. "Veronica explained everything."

My relief over his forgiveness almost eclipsed my curiosity about Ronnie's involvement. But not quite. "What exactly did Veronica say?"

"She said Carter's baby came early and you had to leave. And you wanted me to do the show without you. But I couldn't do it alone. So she went with me."

"She *did*?"

"She gave me a haircut, too. Did you know she graduated from Flushing Beauty Academy?"

"Yes." Ronnie frequently pointed out that her cosmetology certificate was not only more practical than my "monkey school" degree, but it had also been less of a financial burden to my aunt and uncle. "She showed up at your place, gave you a haircut, and went with you to the school?"

"Yes," he said, as though there was nothing out of the ordinary about this freakish chain of events.

"And how was the show?"

"I was nervous, but Veronica told me to just be myself and talk to the kids." He laughed. "Of course, Tallulah stole the show."

"Of course she did." I smiled. "And Veronica?"

"She was a big help, making sure the kids stayed in line and came up one at a time to pet Tallulah."

"Uh-huh." Something did not compute. Ronnie didn't have an altruistic bone in her body. She must have had some ulterior motive in helping David. But I couldn't figure out what it was. And the important thing was, David wasn't mad at me.

I heard a kiss-squeak come through the line and David laughed. "Tally says hi."

I smiled. "Tell her I miss her."

"I will," he said. "And, Holly?"

"Yeah?"

"I'm sorry I got so mad at you. I was afraid you were gone for good, and that would be the end of our act." His voice started to crack. "And next to Tallulah . . . you're my best friend."

Tears sprung to my eyes. "You . . . too . . ." I rasped, struggling to get the words past the giant lump in my throat.

"I know," he said, his voice once again chirpy. "So what have you been up to in Hollywood? Met any big movie stars?"

"As a matter of fact," I said, moving farther away from where Daltry stood stroking the snake. "I know this is gonna sound crazy, but—"

David interrupted, laughing. "You know how many of your stories start that way?"

Now I was laughing, too. "I lost count."

"Boyfriend?" Daltry asked after I'd hung up the phone.

I shook my head, but declined to elaborate. Let him wonder.

"But you do have one?"

"One what?"

"Boyfriend."

I looked up at the ceiling as though searching for an answer. Was Tom still my boyfriend? Yesterday I'd have responded yes without a moment's hesitation. Today I wasn't so sure.

Before I could answer, the cell rang again. "Hello?"

"Hey, neighbor," Brian's voiced boomed over the phone. "Got your message."

"Brian!" I remembered my frantic phone call, asking when he'd be back in New York and ready to resume cat-sitting duties. "I guess you're still in England," I said.

"London. West End. I'm heading home on Monday."

Three more days. I wondered if my animals—and my sanity—would survive that long. "Who's watching Kramer?"

"Since you weren't available, I boarded him at the Pampered Pussy. Probably the pissed-off pussy by now."

I groaned. "Poor guy."

"Poor *me*. It's setting me back a pretty penny putting him up in that posh place. You should raise your rates." There was crackling on the line and he said, "Hey, did you get your rent thing straightened out?"

"For now," I said.

"Good. 'Cause the eviction notice on your ass? So last season."

"I'm losing you."

The static increased and Brian shouted, "Kisses," before disconnecting.

I repocketed the cell. Daltry was watching me, one eyebrow raised. "Boyfriend?" he asked.

I shook my head.

"But you do have one?" he asked again.

Again I didn't know how—or if—I should answer. As the question hung in the air, Gio popped his head in the room. He pointed at Daltry. "You're due in wardrobe in five."

Daltry saluted and followed Gio to the door. He turned and looked at me. "Coming?"

I snapped up my cell phone, and because I presumed hair and makeup would be our next stop after wardrobe, I also grabbed the charger I'd borrowed from Xiana.

I held Daltry's blazer—Reba nestled in the pocket—while Daltry changed into his wardrobe for the scene, charcoal gray dress slacks with a cream-colored long-sleeved shirt. I nodded approvingly. Reba's bold colors would stand out against the light shirt, and its long sleeves and high collar would prevent her from getting inside.

He slipped the blazer on and led the way to the hair and makeup trailer. Just before we entered, he said, "Can you imagine the look on Shauna's face if she finds out I have a snake in my pocket?"

Shauna didn't seem the type to be afraid of a little snake, but I could be wrong. "Just be sure to keep her under wraps," I said.

As Shauna worked her magic on Daltry, I sat in an adjacent chair. I kept my eyes glued to his blazer pocket, ready to mobilize if Reba stirred. I knew I looked like a starstruck idiot, staring at Daltry's lap, but I couldn't risk having my star snake on the loose minutes before filming.

We had only a momentary scare, when we were leaving the trailer and Xiana asked me about her cell phone charger. While Daltry had been in wardrobe and I'd held his blazer, I'd slipped the charger into the blazer's other pocket.

"I almost forgot," I said to Xiana. "It's in his pocket."

Spying the coiled shape stretched against the fabric, she began to stick her hand inside his pocket. Daltry and I both reacted at once, shouting, "No!" and spooking both Xiana and Reba. The snake squirmed around, probably trying to dig deeper into the pocket. Daltry and I exchanged worried glances but neither Shauna nor Xiana seemed to notice the snake's gyrations.

"Wrong one," Daltry said, reaching into the other pocket and pulling out the charger.

Xiana looked puzzled as she took the charger. "Touchy."

With one hand guarding his left pocket, he reached out with the other hand and cupped her chin. "I'm sorry, doll. I'm a bit jumpy."

She bit her lip. "You didn't have to yell."

"In a few minutes, this one here"—he tilted his head in my direction—"is going to make me handle a snake. My 'nads are in a knot just thinking about it."

She flushed crimson. Daltry had a habit of mentioning his 'nads in casual conversation, probably just to see what effect it had on the opposite sex.

"I'd totally spaz if I touched a snake," Xiana said, clueless as to how close she'd come to having done just that.

We emerged from the makeup trailer and were shepherded

back to the soundstage. When we reached the animal holding room, Daltry handed me his blazer. "Take care of this, will ya?" As he was being escorted away, he called over his shoulder, "See you on set, Lola."

I extracted Reba from the blazer pocket, returned her to the crate, and loaded all the snakes onto the dolly. Mike had also given me a golf bag–sized carrying case filled with snake-handling equipment—heavy gloves, a snake hook, and a couple of metal sticks with bags on the end for scooping up escapees. I strapped it to the dolly and took a deep breath before heading out the door.

"It's showtime."

A production assistant directed me back to the apartment set, which was now filled with people. Giovanni pointed out the five terrariums along one wall and confirmed which one would house Reba. He offered to help position the snakes, but I demurred, not wanting to be thought of as needing any special assistance. I was a professional snake wrangler now.

There were three camera dollies nearby. Gio explained that all three cameras would be rolling during the scene, to maximize the amount of usable footage in the event the snake actually cooperated.

Daltry's double was standing on the apartment set, next to a statuesque brunette. They were chatting amiably while lights were adjusted and props were checked.

The real Daltry was off to one side of the set, in a huddle with Jennifer Aniston. She was laughing at something he'd said. She blew a wayward strand of hair from her face, and a stylist materialized from nowhere and began spritzing. She looked extraordinary despite having just filmed a kickboxing scuffle.

I went to work positioning the snakes in their terrariums, leaving Reba for last. Angela was already on set. Despite our earlier

antagonistic encounters, I now viewed her as more of an ally than
an enemy. Even so, it made me nervous to be scrutinized by someone who'd spent her life working with animals.

Hal, the director, strode onto the set, joining Jennifer and Daltry in their huddle for a moment before taking his seat behind the
monitors. I had rolled the dolly and empty crates out of the way and
stood near Reba's terrarium ready to lower her into place.

Gio signaled me that it was time to position Reba. I retrieved
her from her crate and lowered her into the terrarium. A prop master came forward to secure the lid. The first part of the scene—up
until Daltry backs into the terrarium—would be filmed first. Then
the lid would be loosened and the snake's action would be filmed.

Suddenly Daltry was behind me, shaking his head. "You don't
expect me to touch that thing, do you?" he was saying.

I turned to face him, confused. Then he shouted at Gio. "Is
there a snakebite kit on set? Where's the medic?"

Gio shot me a pleading look. "Tell me he's joking."

"No joke." Daltry shook his head. Now everyone was staring at
him. "How close are we to the nearest hospital? What if I have to
be airlifted? Where will the Medevac land?" He stuck his arms in
front of him. His fingers were trembling. "I don't know if I can go
through with it."

Hal stood and said, "What's going on?"

Daltry said, "I need a minute with the trainer." He turned and
looked at Gio. "You mind, man?"

Gio walked away, shaking his head and grinding his teeth.

I whispered to Daltry, "You're laying it on thick."

He winked. "Just play along."

"How'd you get your hands to tremble like that?"

"I played a drug addict once. Got real good at the shakes." He
leaned closer to me. "Put your hand on my shoulder. Like you're
giving me a pep talk."

I did as he asked. "Okay. Now what?"

"Now lean in close."

I complied.

"Closer."

I was so close I could feel the warmth of his breath on my neck. I felt all eyes on me. "I don't think this looks like a pep talk," I said under my breath.

"I know," he whispered into my ear. "But it feels nice."

If I didn't think it would have cost me my job, I'd have kneed him in his precious 'nads. Instead I hissed a well-worded warning into his ear and backed away.

I resumed my spot next to Angela and waited.

I felt a tap on my shoulder and turned to see Danny smiling and giving me a thumbs-up sign. He whispered, "Break a leg," into my ear.

Gio called to Daltry, "Ready?" The star responded with a nod. Someone shouted, "Quiet on the set," and a loud horn sounded in the distance. A series of commands followed—I wondered if all the terminology would ever make sense to me—before Hal called, "Action."

This was it.

Tension buzzed through every inch of my body, from my scalp to the soles of my feet. My finger jitters made Daltry's DTs pale by comparison. I shoved my hands into my pockets to steady them.

With cameras rolling, I knew I should have been watching the snakes. But I couldn't take my eyes off Daltry. While I was a jumble of nerves, he was completely at ease being the center of attention. I'd mistaken his self-assurance for arrogance when I'd encountered him at the airport. He'd been in a hurry to get to a fitting—for this role, I presumed—and some crazy-talking girl was holding him up. It was only natural he'd come off as brusque and dismissive.

Now that I'd had a chance to get close to him—to witness his playful manner and good humor—I questioned my hasty first impression. Perhaps his confidence wasn't driven by conceit, but rather an appreciation of life and his good fortune.

The exchange between Daltry and Aniston was becoming more heated, and I snapped to attention. With each step she took forward, he inched back, closer to the aquarium-lined shelves. They were playing a cat-and-mouse game in which it seemed Aniston was the cat, and Daltry was the not completely uninterested mouse. By this point in the script, he was head over heels for Kelly Ripa's character, but he wasn't immune to the charms of her ultracompetitive colleague.

Now Daltry backed into the terrarium, causing the shelf to rattle. The director yelled, "Cut!" and the scene was repeated from the top. I was on the points of my toes, straining to see how Reba was reacting to the sounds and lights on the set. She'd been restless during the first take, but she seemed to have settled down. I wondered whether her background actions would make editing the scene difficult, since they surely wouldn't match from one take to the next.

There was one more take before the director announced we were moving on. The camera dollies shifted position.

"Holly?"

I was watching the snake so intently I didn't hear my name being called. Angela nudged me. "That's you."

Giovanni was staring at me. "You good to go, Holly?"

"Oh, uh, yeah." I nodded my head. "Good to go."

I noticed Angela was holding a snake hook. *Good idea,* I thought, reaching for one of the snake-bagging contraptions.

Gio called for quiet. Then the prop master rushed forward, made some adjustments to the lid, and scurried aside.

A few more shouted commands, and cameras were rolling. The scene picked up at the line before Daltry backed into the terrarium. The lid already loosened, Daltry's nudge opened the gap wider. He stood with his back pressed against the glass as he said his next line. I hoped that the combination of his voice and body heat would make Reba perform.

But she was completely still, coiled into a colorful knot.

Jennifer said her next line. Reba didn't move a muscle. She was probably sleeping. I wished I could get behind the set and jostle the terrarium from behind.

I was wondering whether I should slink off set now or wait to get fired when Daltry launched into his next line, and I thought I detected a slight flicker of movement in the terrarium behind him. He kept talking but began edging slightly forward. I sucked in my breath, hoping Reba wouldn't lose his scent.

And then it happened. Reba lifted her head up, paused for a moment, then began her ascent. From where I was standing, I could see her exploring with her tongue, tasting the air and seeking an opening in the back of Daltry's shirt. Finding none, she began to glide up his back.

I noticed cameras gliding closer, tightening the shot. Reba peered over Daltry's shoulder. There was dead silence on the set as she hung in the air, flicking her tongue back and forth, her face an inch from Daltry's.

Daltry froze, his eyes darting left and right, his upper lip trembling.

"Don't move," Jennifer said, stepping closer.

"D-d-d-d-don't worry," Daltry stammered.

Reba paused for a moment longer as though deciding whether to retreat or continue. Then she plunged forward, gliding across his chest with her body draped just below his neck.

I heard someone gasp, then realized it was me. I held my breath and watched as Reba disappeared around his back, reappearing a moment later on the other side. She slithered around some more before circling his waist and sliding into the pocket of his pants.

He looked down, then back at the camera, in alarm. I knew that the last part wasn't in the script. In fact, after Reba's initial exploration, we would cut and replace her with a rubber stunt double. Daltry would lose his cool, jerking around and tossing the fake snake into the air.

Jennifer had her hands over her mouth. She broke into a wide smile and laughed. She pointed at his pants pocket, where Reba's shifting shape was making for an odd bulge.

"Is that a python in your pants or are you just glad to see me?" she improvised.

"Cut!" Hal shouted. "That's a print."

The set erupted in applause. I dashed toward Daltry, who was removing Reba from his pocket. I could have kissed them both. He gave me a wink and handed me the snake. I lowered her into the terrarium, then secured the lid under the watchful eyes of Angela and the prop master.

I turned back to see Daltry high fiving Aniston and basking in the congratulations of the crew. Someone asked how he'd managed to keep his cool despite his inner terror.

He shrugged, displaying a practiced nonchalance, and said, "I guess I had a breakthrough."

Never Fade Away

"The snake whisperer?" Carter said, spearing a pot sticker with a toothpick and bringing it to her mouth. "They really called you that?"

I smiled sheepishly, trying to play it cool while inside I was bursting with pride. "A few people on the crew."

We were dining on take-out Chinese, my treat from my day's earnings. Even after splurging on dinner, I still had a nice wad of cash in my pocket.

"It was awesome," Danny said, "especially since Daltry was so squeamish about snakes. Jen told me she didn't think he'd go through with it."

Carter's nostrils flared. "Jen?"

Danny continued. "Then he just stands there, frozen, as the snake crawls all over his body." He made an S-shaped motion with his arm, mimicking Reba's performance, gliding his hand up Carter's body and around her neck.

Carter squirmed. "Eeeek."

"Made my balls shrivel to see it," he finished. Did all men measure the shock value of an event by the effect it had on their genitals?

Carter reached for an egg roll. "And they got it all in one take?"

"They filmed a few more, for safety," I said. Reba hadn't been as charismatic on the second take, and by the third, she refused to climb out of her enclosure at all. But the director seemed certain we'd gotten enough footage the first time around.

Once I'd returned Reba to her crate, the prop master brought out a rubber replica. It was close in size and had a similar red, black, and white pattern, but it wouldn't stand up under close scrutiny. I'd hoped it wouldn't be onscreen for long.

Several takes were filmed of Colin jumping and jerking around, the rubber snake being tossed about wildly. They filmed close-ups and reaction shots of both stars from several angles before the director announced we were moving on.

Though hours had passed, I could still feel the congratulatory backslaps and high fives. People I didn't even know seemed to be singing my praises. All except Daltry, who'd disappeared the moment the scene was in the can.

Giovanni and Angela had both given glowing reports to Mike, who'd inspected each snake and made sure every piece of equipment was accounted for before handing over my pay. Gio had handed us all the next day's call sheet and asked whether I'd be back. Mike had given me a long, critical look before telling me if I wanted a job, it was mine.

A high-pitched cry carried over the baby monitor. Max was waking from his nap. Carter pushed her chair back. "He hasn't let me finish a meal yet."

"Let me go," I said, standing. "I'm too excited to eat anyway."

Carter nodded gratefully and spooned more moo goo gai pan onto her plate.

Max's fists were clenched into tight little balls. I leaned over the crib and smiled at him. "Hey, Fuzzy Wuzzy."

He wailed louder. I lifted him out of his bassinet and sat down on the rocking chair positioned nearby. It surprised me how quickly I'd gotten used to holding him. I no longer feared he'd break when I picked him up.

He continued to whimper as I rocked him. I whispered into his ear, "I know you want your mama, but she's had you all day while I've been stuck with a snake."

Sometime in the last day or two, Max had begun to cry real tears. I brushed them away with my thumb. As I rocked him, I began to sing:

> *Prancing in the sky,*
> *My little monkey star,*
> *You brighten my life*
> *Just the way you are.*

> *The sun is no match,*
> *The moon not by far,*
> *You have no equal,*
> *My little monkey star.*

> *When morning's upon us,*
> *And sun lights the day,*
> *Promise me, monkey,*
> *You'll never fade away.*

By the time I finished the last verse, Max was asleep in the crook of my arm. I stood and lowered him gingerly into his bassinet. I blew him a kiss, tiptoed out of the bedroom, and eased the door shut.

When I reached the dining room, Carter and Danny were polishing off the pot stickers. "I didn't know there was another verse," Carter said.

I raised both eyebrows. Danny pointed to the baby monitor. "Big Brother is listening."

"Oh," I said. "I guess so. It just came to me."

"Well, Max certainly likes it," Carter said. "I don't know what we're gonna do when you leave."

Danny shrugged. "It's probably available on CD somewhere."

Carter gave him a less-than-surreptitious kick under the table. Danny yelped and said, "Not that we want you to leave." He stood and began clearing plates. "In fact, now that you've got a career in showbiz, you hafta stick around."

Carter nodded wordlessly.

I was speechless myself. In all my excitement about my day's work as an animal trainer, I'd never stopped to consider what it would mean if I signed on for full-time employment. Even when Mike agreed to take me on as a Mike's Monkeys trainer, instructing me to show up at his ranch at seven the next morning to fill out paperwork and meet Mrs. Mike, I'd been thinking of the job as extending at best through the end of the *Vets in the City* shoot. I hadn't considered the possibility of making it a career.

A career. I had to admit, I liked the sound of that. No more scrimping by one odd job to another. No more red eviction notices plastered to my ass. No more deer-in-the-headlights look when people asked me what I did for a living. I knew the film industry wasn't known for stability, but at five hundred dollars a day, I could afford the occasional dry spell. And if I lived with Carter and Danny for a few months, I could save up money for my own place. . . .

I shook my head, cutting off my thoughts before I could get carried away. "Today was great, but what if it was a fluke? What if I can't cut it as a trainer?"

Danny snorted. "Don't be ridiculous." Still, he agreed that moving across country based on one day's work might be a bit premature. He and Carter promised not to pressure me further until I had survived a full week in Hollywood.

By Day Four of my animal-training career, I'd been kicked, bitten, scratched, and clawed. All minor injuries, and all par for the course according to Mike, who'd laughed when I asked whether any of his staff had ever been seriously hurt.

"Every trainer pays his dues," he'd said, showing off a grisly ten-inch-long scar on his calf that had been made by a tiger. "Lenny was nearly mauled by emus a while back," Mike said, adding, "Beware all flightless birds. Being grounded makes 'em mean."

I'd nodded and filed that little nugget away for future reference, along with Mike's frequent admonition to keep my fingers to myself if I wanted to keep them at all.

I was fond of my fingers and did, in fact, want to keep all of them, so Mike's helpful tidbits made me question my decision to take the job. But at least I knew my limits. No way was I going to try to tame a tiger. Even snakes were beyond my comfort zone, though Reba had earned a special place in my heart.

Thankfully, since the snake scene, I'd been dealing with small, easy-to-manage animals—rabbits, cats, dogs, and birds.

Each morning I'd don a pair of jeans and my red Mike's Monkeys T-shirt, drive my rental car to Mike's ranch in the San Fernando Valley, and load a van with whatever animals the day's shooting schedule called for. Then I'd drive to the studio, flash my crew badge to the guard, and pull the red van right up to the soundstage.

Today's cargo was light—a pair of ferrets named Jango and Boba—so I'd taken them in my rental car rather than maneuvering the big red van through the mountains. I was unloading their crates from the backseat when my cell phone rang. I knew at once it was Aunt Betty. A few days earlier I'd found a wireless store where I'd picked up a charger and a user's manual for my cell phone model. I now knew how to personalize ring tones, as well as how to delete the seventy-three photos of the inside of Betty's pocketbook that were filling the phone's memory card.

I hesitated only a moment before flipping open the phone. I'd been avoiding all communication with my family for the past few days, but I knew I couldn't put it off forever. Besides, I was dying to hear about Betty's latest Lamaze lesson.

"Hello?"

There was an asthmatic wheeze and then my uncle's voice filled the line. "You've got to talk some sense into her, Holly."

"Uncle Bernie?"

"I found a pregnancy test in the bathroom wastebasket," he rasped. "A pregnancy test, for Crissakes. Ever since she started taking that class, she's been crazy."

I locked the car, loaded my supplies and the animal crates onto a dolly, and headed toward the soundstage, cradling the cell phone against one ear. "I think being around the pregnant ladies has made her feel like she missed out on something. Maybe you two should get a puppy."

"A puppy? That's all I need. It's bad enough she started having little accidents around the house. A puppy. Hmph."

I waved at Brandon, who noted my arrival on his clipboard before opening the soundstage door for me. "Have you tried talking to her about it?" I said into the phone.

"That's why I'm calling you. So you can talk to her. I'm no good at these kinds of things."

As though discussing reproduction with my elderly aunt would come naturally to me. I groaned. "Okay, I'll talk to her. I guess it's kinda my fault for taking her to Lamaze in the first place."

"Darn tootin'."

I let myself into the room I'd been using for animal holding. I rolled the dolly inside, set my purse on the table, and plunked down into a chair. "How is everything else? Everyone okay?"

"Let's see." He clucked his tongue, considering the question. "Ronnie moved out."

"I heard."

"Kuki's in a rage. She thought she was gonna get both her girls home again, and now you're in LA and Ronnie's in the city."

And surely she'd blame both events on me, even though I hadn't invited Ronnie to invade my apartment. Perhaps I'd been right to avoid calling Kuki.

"And how are you?"

"Me? Fit as a fiddle on a Tuesday. Pregnancy test gave me a bit of a scare, though. Thank goodness it was negative."

Could there have possibly been any doubt in his mind?

"You looked?" I asked, trying not to imagine him hunched over the wastebasket, fumbling for his reading glasses, and holding the test stick up to the light.

"Of course I looked," he groused. "A man finds a pregnancy test in his wastebasket, he's gonna check to see how it turned out."

The day's schedule was light, animalwise. The ferrets were featured only briefly in a scene with Kelly and Jennifer. They didn't have to perform any special stunts.

According to Brandon, the previous shot was running long, so I had time to grab a bite. I left the ferrets in their crates and walked over to the craft services table. I was beginning to get used to the convenience of having a huge spread of goodies available at any time during filming. Too bad real life doesn't come with craft services.

I grabbed a breakfast burrito and a container of orange juice and went outside. I found a ledge to sit on. While I ate, I tried to mentally prepare myself for the phone call I had to make. How did you explain the facts of life to an eighty-year-old?

The breakfast burrito was messy. Its contents dripped down my fingers and arms with each bite. I was licking red sauce off my forearm when I heard Daltry's voice.

"Stop. You're killing me," he said.

I looked up, embarrassed, still chewing the final bite of my burrito. He was walking toward me, a sleepy smile on his face. I hadn't seen him in a few days—most of my scenes had been with Jennifer and Kelly, both of whom were comfortable around animals and needed no extra coaching from me.

I tried not to be alarmed at the way the sound of Daltry's voice had sent my stomach into spasms. Could have been the burrito, after all. I wiped my face with a napkin and tried to surreptitiously run my tongue around my teeth to remove embedded food particles. I smiled without parting my lips, just in case I'd missed anything.

"I love you just the way you are," he said, coming closer.

It was hard to hear over the churning of my stomach, but did he just say "I love you"? Three little words I'd been longing to hear. From someone else. Was it possible that the words Tom had held back for so long had just come casually tripping off Daltry's tongue? I didn't know what to say.

"I . . . I'm . . . I'm flattered, but—"

I stopped short as Daltry flashed me a quick finger wave and walked on by. It wasn't until he passed that I noticed the tiny earpiece clipped to one ear.

He'd been talking on the phone. Not to me.

My face was red with embarrassment. Did he hear me say I was flattered? Did he know I'd assumed he was talking to me? Telling me he loved me? I was suddenly back at the eighth grade homecoming dance, reliving the moment when Robby Francomano had pointed at me during the initial beats of Madonna's "Crazy for You," and I'd taken a few hesitant steps in his direction before realizing he'd been gesturing to pep squad leader Lisa Correa, who'd been standing next to me.

I sat for a while, the breakfast burrito a burning lump in my stomach, waiting for my pulse to return to normal.

Suddenly my birds-and-bees talk with Betty didn't seem so embarrassing. Might as well get it over with. I pulled out my phone and punched in Betty's number.

"Holly, honey, how are you? I've been so worried."

"I'm fine. Sorry I haven't called. How's Lamaze?"

"Maya was surprised to see me back. Nearly choked on her whistle when I walked through the door. But I told her we'd paid good money and I intended to finish the class."

"Good for you."

"And the ladies send their regards. They want to know if Colin Daltry is as hunkabootylicious in person as he is onscreen."

Never having seen him on the big screen, and having no idea what "hunkabootylicious" meant, I declined to offer an opinion. But I did drop the bombshell that I'd met his equine ex.

"You met the supermodel?" Betty gasped.

"Yes."

"Nobody's just a model anymore," Betty said. "They all call themselves supermodels. If they're all supermodels, then what's so super?"

I couldn't argue on that point. "Her name's Velvet."

"That's it. I knew she was named after a horse," Betty said. "Just like in that Elizabeth Taylor movie."

"National Velvet," I said. "And Velvet wasn't the horse. Elizabeth Taylor played Velvet."

"Are you sure?" Betty asked.

I'd seen the movie a dozen times as a pony-obsessed preteen. "Positive."

"Oh. What was the horse's name?"

I thought for a moment. "Pie."

"That's a dumb name for a horse."

I couldn't argue on that point either.

"Where did you meet her?"

This was it. I couldn't dance around the subject of my employment any longer. Best to spit it out, quickly, then sit back and wait for the questions to roll in. I took a deep breath and said, "I got a job as an animal trainer on the set of Danny's movie."

"That's nice, dear. Do me a favor. Ask her how she stays so thin. I've put on a few pounds around the middle lately."

I'd just announced that I had taken a job in Hollywood, and my aunt wanted weight-loss tips. Probably she hadn't absorbed the news, which was a good thing. Best to stick with the pregnancy talk. "Maybe you've been eating too many snickerdoodles."

She considered for a moment. "No more than usual."

"Maybe the senior spread is finally hitting you."

"No, that's not it either."

"Well," I said, "there's only one other thing it could be."

Her voice grew serious. "I'm listening."

"Are you sitting down?"

"No, but I have a low center of gravity."

"You might want to sit down anyway."

"Okay." I heard a dining room chair scrape against the linoleum. Then she said, "Hit me."

I took a deep breath. It was now or never. "Have you ever heard of a hysterical pregnancy?"

"Sure, like Mary Todd Lincoln, Martha Washington, the Virgin Mary . . ."

"Not a *historical* pregnancy," I sighed. "A hysterical one. Having pregnancy symptoms without actually being pregnant." I decided to try another approach. "You know how when you're around someone who's yawning, you yawn yourself. Or if they're British, you talk with an English accent. Or if they limp, you find yourself limping in sympathy?"

"That's why I never got a poodle," Betty said.

Huh? "Huh?"

"Haven't you seen those pictures of dogs and their owners who start to look alike after so many years? That's why I always said, if you're gonna have a dog, pick one you wouldn't mind seeing staring back at you in the mirror in ten years. Remember Archie, the bloodhound we had when you kids were little? We picked him 'cause he already looked just like your uncle. Droopy jowls, long face, watery eyes, big nose."

Now that I thought about it, Uncle Bernie did bear a striking resemblance to a bloodhound.

"My hair is frizzy enough on its own," Betty was saying. "Can you imagine if we'd gotten a poodle?"

"What I'm trying to say is, I think that Lamaze class, and being around the pregnant ladies, may have made you think you're pregnant."

"I may be old, but I'm not stupid," she said, clearly offended. "I went through the change years ago. How could I possibly be pregnant?"

"Maybe it's subconscious. Your body might be mimicking the symptoms without you realizing it."

She hmphed and then fell quiet. Finally she said, "You really think that's what it is?"

I nodded. "Yes."

"That's a relief." She let out a big sigh. "I was getting worried," she admitted. "The cravings, the foot swelling, the dizziness, the shortness of breath—it all seemed so real. I even took a pregnancy test and made an appointment with an ob-gyn."

"Maybe you should cancel it," I suggested. "And stop taking Lamaze. I think you'll feel better."

"Maybe you're right," she said. "And I guess I can stop practicing those Kegel exercises, too."

"I don't know about that." Carter had told me that Kegels, the pelvic-floor exercises recommended for post-pregnancy reconditioning, were also good for maintaining bladder control later in life. "I think you can keep doing those."

"Oh, good," she said. "Bernie will be glad to hear that."

Eeeks. I really didn't need to know that Bernie still took an interest in my aunt's pelvic floor muscles. Time to change the subject. "Did you and Uncle Bernie want kids?" I asked offhandedly.

She didn't answer. I mentally smacked myself for not realizing it was probably a sensitive subject. Why didn't I just ask about the weather? "If you'd rather not talk about it—"

"It was never the right time," she said finally. "When I was young, there was so much I wanted to do. I didn't want to settle down at first. I was your age by the time I finally married your uncle."

She said "your age" as though it was synonymous with old maidenhood.

"We wanted to wait until the time was right before having kids," she continued. "Save money. Buy our own home. Bernie wanted a job that would support a family so I wouldn't have to work when the kids were young. Then he got laid off from the factory he was at. We used up our savings waiting for him to find another job. I liked working at the library, but the pay was patooey."

She whistled through her teeth. "It seemed like every time we brought up the idea of having kids, something happened to set us back. Bernie needed a hernia operation. Then I had my appendix out. Bernie's sister's house burned down and we took in her family. All of us living in our tiny apartment. She was a single mother on welfare, four kids. It wasn't like she could afford to chip in. The bills piled up. Kids got sick a lot. The little one, Bucky, broke the same arm twice roughhousing in the backyard. They didn't have insurance, so we paid for everything. They stayed with us three, four years. She had a drinking problem, not that I could blame her, but she was always taking off for weeks at a time, saying she needed to find herself. Leaving me all these kids to take care of. Kids that weren't even mine. I always wondered, when do I get to go off and find myself?"

I knew I was only getting snippets of my aunt's life story, and I felt bad that most of it was stuff I'd never known. I'd always assumed my aunt had been childless by choice, too free-spirited to want to settle down. It was hard to imagine her drowning in debt and bogged down with a houseful of kids belonging to an alcoholic sister-in-law.

"By the time they got on their feet," she continued, "I felt like I'd been raising the world. I wasn't ready to raise a baby of my own. Then my mother started getting sick, and Kuki and I took turns caring for her. Then it was too late." She exhaled loudly. "I always thought when the time was right, I'd know it. But I never did. Not like your mother. She was born ready."

I bit my lip at the mention of my mother. I'd been thinking about her a lot lately. Being around baby Max made me wonder about my own early years. But I was always hesitant to discuss my mother with my aunts. I sometimes wondered, since they'd known her for so much longer than I had, if they felt the loss more acutely than I did.

"She always wanted kids?"

"Oh, yes. I knew from the time she was little, the way she always had baby dolls that she'd dress up and feed and change, that she would be a good mother. She and your dad had nothing when you came along. No savings. No house. He was working as a fry cook and trying to be a songwriter. He was a bit of a dreamer, if you ask me. Never stayed in one job for long. Your mother was the practical one. She was a secretary for an insurance company, and on the weekends, she helped out at the barbershop. They lived in a room over the bar and grill where he worked. One room, with a bathroom down the hall that they shared with two other families.

"But she didn't care. She wanted a baby. Your grandmother and your aunt Kuki gave her a hard time when she announced she was pregnant. They were worried about her, having nothing. But she was happier than all get out."

I leaned back, letting my head rest against the side of the building. I closed my eyes, and images of my childhood came flooding back. I could vaguely recall playing pinball in the bar and grill, waiting for my father to pick up his pay. "I thought we lived in a house?"

"Just before you were born they got an FHA loan and bought a little house over in Red Hook."

"There was a swing set in the backyard."

"Your dad put that up for you."

We were both silent for a while. I was puzzling together pieces of my past, trying to figure out where certain pieces fit. Brandon's voice snapped me out of my reverie. "Five minutes."

"I hafta go to work," I croaked into the phone.

"Work?" Betty chirped. "But you're on vacation."

"I got a job, remember? I'm an animal trainer on the set of Danny's movie. But don't worry. It'll probably just be for another week or two."

"Heavens to Betsy!" my aunt exclaimed. "Holly has a job in Hollywood," she was shouting, probably trying to get Bernie to look up from a ball game on TV. "Why didn't you tell me, dear?"

"I *did* tell you," I said. "But they say pregnancy makes you forgetful." I couldn't resist the joke.

"Don't make me laugh," she tittered. "I'm not wearing my granny nappy, and Bernie hates it when I tinkle in the dining room."

I snorted. "Granny nappy?"

"That's what Ronnie calls them. She says it sounds way cooler than adult undergarment."

She laughed again, and I smiled, grateful that despite a life filled with heartache, Betty could still find humor in memory loss and incontinence.

"An animal trainer," Betty marveled. "Wait till I tell the girls at Lamaze."

"I thought you were going to drop out of Lamaze."

"Oh, yeah," she giggled. "I forgot."

Shifting Gears

After filming the ferret scene, I slunk back to my car, still embarrassed by my encounter with Daltry. How could I have thought, even for a millisecond, that he was talking to me and using words like "love"?

He must have been talking to Velveeta, his processed cheese spread of the month. And he sounded rather flip. Probably wasn't seriously professing his love to anyone. And why did I care, anyway?

I didn't, I told myself, even while I knew that on some strange level, I did. Maybe it was just morbid curiosity. Our society's obsession with celebrity made us all a teeny bit intrigued by the romantic exploits of movie stars. It wasn't my fault that I was susceptible to the salacious instincts instilled in me by my own culture. Inquiring minds want to know, damn it.

I clicked my keypad and the car alarm chirped off. I reached for the door and felt a tap on my shoulder. I turned to see Danny standing next to me. "You heading back home?"

I shook my head. "I have to get Jango and Boba back to the ranch first."

He held out a set of keys. "Whaddya say we swap cars? I've been dying to check out the navigation system."

I shrugged. I supposed it couldn't hurt. The insurance policy the rental car clerk had talked me into was so comprehensive I was probably covered even if I let Monkey the Chimp drive the car.

We traded keys and he hopped into the driver's seat. He put the key in the ignition and the dashboard came to life. "Meet Nancy," I said, gesturing to the navigational display screen. "I hope you two hit it off."

I gave him a quick tutorial, then climbed out of the car and watched him drive off. I rolled the dolly over to Danny's Beetle.

It was a tight squeeze, fitting the two ferret crates in the back along with Max's infant seat, but I managed to cram everything inside and slip behind the steering wheel. I stuck the key in the ignition, turned it, and winced as Nickelback blared from the stereo speakers.

I lowered the volume, adjusted the rearview mirror, and reached for the gear shift.

The what?

To confirm my suspicions that I'd made a major blunder in trading cars with Danny, I looked down at my feet. Sure enough, to the left of the brake pedal, there it was: a clutch.

Why hadn't I remembered that Danny's Beetle had a stick shift? I hadn't really paid attention when he was driving. I felt a stab of panic. Despite Kuki's urging, I'd never learned to drive stick. The station wagon was an automatic, and I'd never spent enough time in any other car to make learning to drive a manual worth the trouble.

My terror abated when I realized that I'd joined the technology age and was in possession of a cell phone. I simply had to call Danny and ask him to turn around.

I pulled Betty's phone out of my pocket, congratulated myself on it being fully charged, and dialed Danny's number. The call was immediately dumped into voice mail, which meant his phone was turned off. He probably forgot to turn it back on after he finished filming.

Now it was time to panic.

I banged my fist against the steering wheel and let loose a string of profanities. The ferrets scrambled in their crates, probably seeking out escape routes to flee the verbal barrage.

"Sorry," I said. They continued burrowing, unimpressed by my apology.

I got out of the car and looked around the lot. Danny was long gone, and I didn't see anyone else I recognized. I dialed Danny's cell phone again. Again I was sent straight to voice mail. This time I left a message, explaining my predicament and urging him to call me immediately.

I sat back in the driver's seat, leaving the door open to cool off the car's interior. I'd learned from Mike that ferrets have poorly developed sweat glands, and I didn't want them to overheat. Heat stroke was apparently a leading cause of ferret fatalities—another of Mike's helpful nuggets.

Don't panic, I told myself. Eventually Danny would turn on his cell and get my message. I just had to wait. And if I got tired, I could always go back inside the soundstage. It wasn't like I'd been stranded in Siberia, after all. Being stuck at a movie studio was a far cry from being wedged in a hole in my apartment back in Manhattan, to put my recent calamities in perspective.

When my heartbeat slowed to a normal rhythm, I dialed Danny's home number. Carter answered on the first ring. I heard Max crying in the background. "I was just about to call you," Carter said, sounding relieved. "I have an emergency."

My pulse shot up again. "The baby?"

"I can't quiet him down. I've done everything. He's dry. He's been fed and burped. He doesn't have a fever. He just won't stop screaming. I've been singing to him and it's not working. When will you be back?"

"Good question," I said. "Danny took my car, and I can't drive his because it's a stick. So I'm stuck."

"What?" Carter was shouting. Between the baby's cries and the weak signal my cell got in the parking lot, we could barely hear each other. "Did you say you're sick or you suck?"

"I'm *stuck* with his *stick*," I yelled.

"Stuck on whose stick?" she asked. "Never mind. I can't wait for you to get here. Just sing the song over the phone. I'll hold it up to his ear."

"What song?"

"The freakin' monkey song. I don't know all the words. I searched online, hoping to find a downloadable track, but nada. I called three music stores and they've never even heard of it. I've tried every lullaby I know, and he still—"

"Maybe it's gas," I offered.

"Just sing the freakin' song," she yelled.

I was beginning to think that the only thing wrong with Max was his mother's short temper. But I sang.

By the end of the first verse, Max's cries had died down to a whimper. By the end of the second, Carter was humming along softly. By the end of the third, I realized I had an audience. Colin Daltry was leaning against a lamppost a few feet from the Beetle. He applauded.

"He's asleep," Carter whispered. "I'm hanging up."

"Wait!" I said, "Tell Danny I'm stranded—"

But she was gone.

Daltry approached the car, his eyes wide with amusement. "I always knew you were a showgirl, Lola. You just need some feathers in your hair and a dress cut down to—"

"Stop." I buried my face in my hands. "I'm not in the mood."

"Are you ever?"

I looked up at him slanty-eyed. "Not lately."

He rolled back on his heels and smiled. "Come with me."

He turned and strode purposefully away from the Beetle. I shouted after him, "Why? Where?"

He didn't stop walking but called over his shoulder, "Didn't I hear you say you're stranded?"

★   ★   ★

We were sitting in the back of a Town Car as it headed north on the I-5 freeway. The two ferret crates were aligned on the backseat between us. Daltry had wanted to put them up front with the driver, but I insisted that my professional integrity depended upon my keeping them within arm's reach. Besides, they provided a welcome buffer zone.

I eyed Daltry suspiciously. "If you have a driver, what were you doing in the parking lot?"

"You caught me." He raised both hands in the air. "I went for a walk to have a smoke. I wasn't headed for the lot. But then I heard the siren song and felt compelled to come closer. Even though I knew it would lead to my destruction."

He might be charming if he wasn't so smarmy, I thought. "You can't smoke in your trailer?"

"Don't want the place to stink of tobacco. Then people would know that I like to light up now and again. It's my dirty little secret." He wiggled his eyebrows suggestively.

I watched the traffic for a while before turning back toward him. "Don't you drive?"

"Of course." He nodded. "But I prefer to be driven. This way, I can study my script, make a few calls, catch some z's."

I nodded and returned my attention to the passing cars. We exited the freeway and headed down the twisting road leading to Mike's ranch.

"This where they keep my monkey?" Daltry asked.

"If you mean the chimpanzee that plays your pet in the movie, yes."

"Think I can see her?"

I shrugged. "Probably." As a matter of fact, since tomorrow's schedule included a scene with Daltry and the chimp, it was probably a good idea to let the two get reacquainted. I had already called Mrs. Mike to let her know I was en route with the ferrets. I hit the redial button and waited for her to pick up.

"I have Colin Daltry in the car with me," I told her when she answered. Her sharp intake of breath told me that she knew who Daltry was and was suitably impressed. "He wants to see Monkey the Chimp. Is that all right?"

"Sure," she squealed. "Just pull on up in front."

"Okeydoke." I'd always been instructed to pull my car around back. I guess there was a different protocol when transporting movie stars than ferrets.

As we pulled into the drive, Mrs. Mike, whose first name I'd yet to learn, bounced over to the car and pulled open the back door.

"Mr. Daltry, I'm so pleased to meet you," she said, sticking out her hand and pumping his up and down vigorously.

I unloaded the crates and followed Daltry into the main house. Mrs. Mike scrunched up her nose upon seeing me with the ferret carriers. "Why don't you take them out back where they belong?"

She took Daltry's arm and led him toward a hallway, pointing at a life-sized painting of a rhinoceros that ran the length of one wall. I'd never been inside the main house and was curious to see the artwork and artifacts Mike had gathered on his intercontinental travels. But this was clearly a private tour, and I'd been dismissed.

I cleared my throat. "We came to see Monkey. Colin's doing a scene with her tomorrow."

"Don't worry, dear," she said, dismissing me with a wave of her hand. "I'll bring him to you when we're done."

Behind the main house were several other structures, including a barn, two stables, and a warehouse-sized building filled with cages of varying sizes. I went inside the warehouse and was greeted by the smell of fresh hay, which was used as bedding for many of the animals. A small room off to one side held separate hutches for rabbits and ferrets.

I retrieved Boba and Jango from their carriers and returned them to their enclosure, where they were met by high-pitched squeaks and titters emanating from their cage mates, probably the ferret equivalent of "Where have you been, and why do you smell like perfume?"

The other side of the warehouse held primate cages. Monkey and Morty shared a large enclosure adjacent to one occupied by her mother, Mona, and a new infant, Migas. A third enclosure, beyond Mona's, lay empty. All three chimp cages had been outfitted with tire swings, climbing apparatus, den boxes, and plenty of durable toys. Doors between them could be opened to allow the various groups to interact. But since Migas's birth, he and Mona had been kept separate from the rowdy youngsters out of concern for the infant's safety.

The chimps hooted when I approached. Monkey and Morty reached their hands through the chain-link fencing. I lowered my head and reached a downturned hand toward them. Morty was the first to reach out and touch the top of my hand. Monkey followed suit. After a minute or so, I reached into my pocket and pulled out the keys.

The cage was equipped with a double set of steel doors to prevent escape. I unlocked the outer door, stepped inside a vestibule-like area, locked the first door behind me, then unlocked the inner door. The moment the door swung open, Monkey swooshed up to me and threw her arms around my leg, nearly knocking me off balance.

"Hey, you," I said, still not comfortable calling a chimp "Monkey," even if it was her official name. It offended my primatological sensibilities.

I heard a lip-smacking sound and turned to see Mona reaching her fingers through the steel bars of her enclosure. I hadn't been formally introduced to this matriarch of the M family. Mike had told me she hadn't been profitable as a performer, but had proven invaluable as a breeder. Migas would be the sixth of her offspring to join the family business.

Mona made a raspberry sound and smacked the steel bars, trying to get my attention. She was not a pretty chimp. Her face was long and thin; her lower lip drooped. Her skin was mottled and flaky, and she had bald patches on her upper arms. Her patchy skin and stooped posture reminded me somewhat of Aunt Betty.

I said hello, crouching down to get a closer look at the baby who was clinging to her torso. Migas's big, floppy ears stood out from a wrinkled pink face with a faint white beard. He was the kind of cute that sold greeting cards and posters. I had no doubt he'd be a star like his sister, Monkey.

My cell phone rang. Morty watched intently as I pulled the phone from my pocket and answered it.

"Why didn't you tell me you can't drive a stick?" Danny said.

"I didn't realize the Beetle was a stick. Hell, I didn't think *anyone* drove stick anymore."

"Where are you now?" he asked.

"At the ranch. Colin gave me a lift."

"He did?" Danny said with a level of incredulity in his tone that would have been appropriate if I'd said I'd given birth to a two-headed chicken.

"Why is that so hard to believe?"

"It's not," he protested. "Colin Daltry is your personal chauffeur."

"Actually his driver did the chauffeuring. Colin just came along for the ride."

"Oh-kay," he drawled. "Can he ride you back to the studio?"

I rolled my eyes at the implication. "Yes. He has to be back there by four."

"Great. I'll have Nancy back before then."

He disconnected and I snapped the phone shut. Before I could react, Morty had reached out and swiped the phone out of my hands. He scampered into a corner and climbed up onto a plywood platform that was positioned about six feet off the floor.

I held one hand out toward him. "Give that to me."

He opened the phone and pecked at the numbers with one gnarled finger. Then he held the phone to one ear and opened his mouth wide, showing both rows of teeth. He flapped his jaws and nodded his head, as though carrying on a conversation. I wondered whether he'd been taught the routine for a film or television show. Maybe he'd starred in a cell phone commercial. Or perhaps he was just mimicking me or the other trainers, yapping away on cell phones.

After a moment, he tossed the phone back to me. I didn't know whether to applaud or check my outgoing call log to make sure the chimp hadn't phoned his relatives in Africa.

Daltry still hadn't appeared, so I decided to check in with my own relatives. I figured I should call Gerry before he'd heard about my new job from Betty. First I dialed my home number and punched in the code to retrieve my messages. After a series of beeps, I heard a male voice I didn't immediately recognize. "Hey . . . um . . . I hope you don't mind, but I got your number from your aunt. Well, I got my uncle Angelo to ask your aunt for the number."

Eddie, I thought, my face flushing at the memory of my ball-handling comment. I'd been trying to banish thoughts of Eddie and his balls out of respect for Tom. But now that Tom and I were in limbo, I had to admit I was intrigued by the strong, silent paramedic.

"I've been thinking about you," he continued, "ever since we met."

The heat in my face began spreading to the rest of my body. I remembered the sensation of his rough fingertips against my skin as he palpated my pelvis. I guess I wasn't the only one feeling a little tingly during the encounter.

"I'd really . . . I mean . . . I'd like to—" he faltered, and I found myself biting my lip, waiting for him to finish the sentence. After spending so much time with the cocksure Daltry, I found Eddie's hesitance refreshing. "I'd love to take you out sometime," he finally finished.

He recited his home and cell phone numbers and added that he hoped I'd call soon. I glanced at my watch. Before I had a chance to calculate the time difference and decide how long to wait before calling back so as not to appear desperate, he added, in a tender tone, "Good night, Veronica."

Of all the loops I'd been thrown for in my life, this was the loopiest. Had I heard right? I pressed my mental rewind button and replayed the call in my mind. Yep, there it was: "Good night, Veronica." Of course, I could call back, retrieve the message again, and confirm that my ears hadn't deceived me, and Eddie had indeed uttered Ronnie's name instead of mine. Better yet, I could delete the message and prevent Ronnie from getting it if she hadn't already heard it.

It had been two days since I'd called in to pick up my messages. For all I knew, she'd already called Eddie back and they were having hot, steamy sex. In my bed.

What was it with Ronnie? She'd moved into my apartment, replaced me as Betty's Lamaze partner, filled in for me at PS 11. And now she was dating my EMT.

It was like she was living my life, only better.

I emitted a strangled scream and snapped the cell phone shut. *Forget about erasing the message,* I told myself. *If Eddie's dumb enough to fall for Ronnie, then he deserves her. At the rate she chews up and spits out men, their fling will be over before I get back to town.*

"Boyfriend?" The sound of Daltry's voice startled me. I looked up to see him leaning against the wall opposite the chimps' enclosure. I wondered how long he'd been standing there.

"I've known you for less than a week, and your jokes are already sounding stale," I said, unlocking the first of the enclosure's double doors.

"You never answer the question," he remarked.

I closed the first door behind me and unlocked the outer door, letting Daltry in to the cramped space. "What makes you think I was talking to my boyfriend?"

He gestured to my face. "Your cheeks are flushed. Your pupils are dilated. Your breathing is rapid." He shrugged one shoulder. "Looks like *somebody* flipped your switch."

"It was a wrong number."

I pushed open the inner door, and Daltry followed me into the cage. He stood, stiff limbed and stone faced, and looked around the enclosure. The chimpanzees were cowering in a corner of the cage.

I reminded him to bow down to their level, making himself appear smaller. "It may be hard for an alpha male like you," I said, "but try being submissive."

It didn't take long for him to loosen up and for the chimps to make tentative steps toward him.

"Which one is Monkey?" Daltry asked.

"The one without a wangdoodle."

He looked both chimps up and down. "Oh." He lowered himself to the ground, sitting cross-legged on some hay. Since he'd already settled in, I decided not to point out that the floor of a chimpanzee enclosure wasn't the most sanitary place to sit. He gestured to Monkey, who shyly approached, head lowered, swaying from side to side.

He reached out one hand and she sniffed it. Then she began grooming the hair on his arms.

"She looking for bugs to eat?" he asked me.

I shook my head. "Grooming is an important social activity for chimps. She's bonding with you."

Mona was watching through the bars of the adjoining cage. Daltry cocked his head in her direction. "What's with him?"

"Her," I corrected. "She's Monkey's mother. Probably doesn't think you're good enough for her daughter."

"She looks sad."

Mona's sagging lip made her look perpetually depressed, but it was true she looked even more anguished than usual, perhaps the result of seeing her daughter consort with a movie star.

After a while, Mike appeared at the side of the enclosure. He nodded at Daltry. "The missus said you were out here."

Daltry said, "Thought I'd come by to rehearse."

I was grateful he didn't mention my mix-up with the cars and need for a ride. I didn't want my new employer to think I was a total screwup.

Mike looked over at me. "Suzanne's been working with her on the scene. She'll take the lead tomorrow."

My eyes bugged. "Suzanne? She's back?"

Mike nodded. "Yeah. Came back to work this morning. Spent the day here training Monkey."

"What about Lenny?" I asked.

"Released on bond," Mike said. "Pending trial."

"He's out?" If Lenny was out of jail, then he'd probably come back to work, too, which meant I'd be out of a job.

"Don't worry," Mike said. "I won't take him back on. He's too risky. After he was arrested, Fish and Wildlife Service inspectors spent two days here at the ranch, checking my permits and turning the place upside down. I acquired all my animals legally. Got the paperwork to prove it. But Lenny has a rep now, and I don't want anyone thinking I'm mixed up in wildlife trafficking."

I breathed an audible sigh of relief. I was disappointed that

Suzanne would be calling the shots on the next day's shoot, but at least I still had a job. "You're not worried about Suzanne? That she might have been involved in the smuggling?"

"She says her hands are clean." Mike shrugged. "And I got no proof otherwise. Can't fault her for having bad taste in men."

Daltry stood and approached the fence. "What did you mean about Suzanne taking the lead?"

"We always have at least two people when working with certain animals," Mike explained. "Chimps included."

"But Lola—I mean, Holly—she's been working with me all week. I don't know this Suzanne person."

"She's one of our top trainers," Mike said. "Graduated from the animal academy at Moorpark College, and worked at the Playboy Mansion."

"The Playboy Mansion?" I asked. Suzanne didn't seem the bunny type. And anyway, I didn't see how being a Playmate spoke to her abilities as an animal trainer.

"Hefner has a zoo on his property," Mike explained. "Birds, monkeys, reptiles. Suzanne was a keeper there. She knows her stuff. Don't worry. You'll be in good hands."

"But I want to be in Holly's hands," Daltry said.

18

Little Bitty Lies

The next morning when I pulled into the ranch, Suzanne was already loading one of the big red vans. I parked my rental car and walked around to the back of the van. Monkey and Morty were huddled in one corner of the large steel cage. Suzanne was passing some fruit into the cage through a chute.

Her eyes darkened when she saw me approach, but she said nothing. *Probably not a morning person,* I thought. Or maybe she was just grumpy because her boyfriend was a crook. I decided to make the best of the situation.

"Morning," I said, smiling and waving.

She grunted, slammed the van's cargo doors shut, and disappeared around the side of the van. I heard the driver's-side door open and close and the engine roll over. "Guess I'm riding shotgun," I said to myself before coming around to the passenger side.

I'd barely closed the door before she revved the engine and sped down the drive. "Nice day," I said, trying to make small talk.

Suzanne's jaw was clenched. I had a feeling she and I were not going to be friends. After a few miles, she finally said, "If you go over my head again, I'll see to it you never work another day in this business."

Yeah, I thought, *ix-nay on the ends-fray.*

"Go over your head?" I said, trying to figure out what she meant.

"Mike told me you demanded lead on today's shoot. I have seniority. I'm lead trainer here."

I turned in my seat. "It wasn't me. It was Colin. And no one demanded. He just said he'd feel more comfortable working with me."

She pulled onto the freeway on-ramp and cursed when she saw how slowly traffic was moving. "Just 'cause you're sleeping with the star doesn't mean you can push people around."

"I'm not—"

"I've paid my dues," she seethed. "People spend years scooping poop and scrubbing cages before ever getting a break in this business. And you think you can just hop out of Colin Daltry's bed and into a career?"

I'd never been in Daltry's bed to begin with, but that was beside the point. "Lenny was in jail. You were bailing him out. The other trainers were busy. And Mike was desperate."

"Well, I'm back now. And Lenny will be, too, once he's cleared in court."

"You really think he'll be cleared?"

"Of course." She nodded. "He's innocent."

Her conviction might have been more convincing had the circumstances not been so damning. "But they found the reptiles in his pants."

"It was a misunderstanding. He thought he was transporting them legally."

"He thought he was legally transporting them in his *pants*?"

"He was set up," she huffed.

Sure he was.

We inched along in traffic, all eyes ahead. This was going to be a long day. We were shooting at the hospital location again. I'd learned from Angela that using the real hospital facility was better for the scenes with chimps and monkeys because of its smaller, more enclosed rooms. It's tough to secure a soundstage against a monkey, she'd explained. They can find escape routes anywhere, including up. She'd shared a few stories of monkeys swinging in rafters while crew and trainers tried everything to lure them down. With the hospital building, doors could be locked, hallways secured, and the number of potential getaway routes limited.

When Suzanne exited the freeway she became chatty again. "You'll stay in the van. But be careful. Chimps, even the little ones, are very strong. You don't know how dangerous they can be—"

I was getting tired of her dismissive attitude. "I do know. I have a degree in primatology, and—"

"So you studied chimps in a textbook. You ever been bitten by one?" She held up her right hand and I noticed for the first time that her index finger was a little shorter than it should be. The tip was a nailless nub. "Monkey's older brother, Macho, did that."

Why did trainers regard their battle scars as badges of honor? I wondered. It seemed to me that missing a body part would be a sign that you'd done something wrong. But nearly everyone I'd met on the ranch had introduced themselves by stating their name, dropping a few film credits, then playing show-and-tell with missing digits or other disfigurements. One of the ranch hands told me he'd gotten his nickname, Chewy, because he'd been bitten so many times the other trainers started calling him Chew Toy.

"I have more experience in this finger than you have in your whole body." Suzanne pointed the nub in my direction as she maneuvered the van with her left hand.

"Eyes on the road. Both hands on the wheel," I said, channeling Aunt Kuki. "We have live animals in back," I added, since I doubted she cared about *my* safety.

"Don't tell me how to drive," she said, taking the steering wheel in both hands and turning into the lot of the abandoned hospital.

Suzanne parked the van and we both hopped out. She walked around to the back and paused with her hand on the cargo door handle. "I'll handle it from here. Hope you brought a book to read."

I hadn't brought a book, and aside from a few dog-eared issues of *Car and Driver*, I found no reading materials in the van. I'd already read the AHA rule book and relevant passages of my cell phone manual—the only documents I carried with me.

Since it was warm, I left the cargo doors open so Morty and I could watch the activity of people coming and going. I sat on the back of the van with my legs dangling outside. Morty was playing with a big bucket of wooden blocks.

"So tell me about your life," I said to the little chimp. He looked up briefly and then went back to stacking the blocks.

"Hurry up and wait" was a refrain I'd heard often in my week on set. Between quick bursts of activity, movie productions were notorious for prolonged periods of waiting. I'd thought these lulls were tedious on the set, but that was nothing compared to waiting outside in the van, not even being able to watch what was going on inside.

After a few more abortive attempts to engage Morty in conversation, I pulled my cell phone out of my pocket. That got the chimp's attention. Mike had confirmed my suspicion that Morty had performed in a series of cell phone commercials, dressed in a business suit and carrying a briefcase. The behavior was now so ingrained in him that for the rest of his life, he'd probably be swiping cell phones and reenacting the scene, expecting to be compensated with a treat.

I scooted farther from the cage to ensure I was out of his reach and flipped the phone open. The screen said I'd missed a call, though I'd never heard it ring. That wasn't unusual, with reception being spotty in the mountains around Mike's ranch.

I hit a few buttons and the message began playing. It was Aunt

Kuki. Her voice was snappish. "I'm not going to say I blame you. But I do. Veronica's always been a good girl, but since she moved into your place, she's gone wild. Throwing herself at the bingo boy and pimping people on the Internet. Your aunt Betty's acting like a pregnant teenager. And now Gerry's talking about moving to Hollywood with you."

My aunt was talking at a brisk clip, and my brain wasn't keeping up. What was this about Ronnie pimping people? And what did it have to do with me? And did she say Gerry was thinking of moving out here? I pressed the phone closer to my ear.

Now Kuki was invoking the name of my "dear departed mother" and chastising me for not calling sooner. "I thought I raised you to have some common courtesy," she said. "When were you going to tell me about this new job of yours? You should have told me you weren't planning on moving back home. I've been busy packing up Leo's army bric-a-brac and converting that room so you wouldn't have to share with Ronnie. Now I guess I don't have to worry about either one of you girls."

She sighed, a long-suffering sigh I'd heard repeatedly throughout my life, a sigh that allowed her to express all her disappointment and disdain without actually uttering a word. Then she added, "I saw on the news there's a cold front headed for Los Angeles. Don't forget to wear a sweater." Another pause and she said, "It's Aunt Kuki." As though there were any number of people who called to tell me I'd been a perpetual disappointment and to remind me to wear my sweater.

I banged the phone against my forehead. I was bristling at the suggestion that I was responsible for Ronnie's behavior, and panicked by the possibility of Gerry moving to LA, but there was enough truth in what she'd said that I couldn't escape the heavy weight of guilt descending upon my shoulders. I should have been up front with her about the fact that I'd never really planned to move back in with her. And I should have told her about my job.

I took a deep breath and dialed her number. After four rings, the answering machine picked up. "I'm sorry for not telling you about my job. I didn't know how long it would last and didn't want anyone jumping to conclusions. It'll probably be over in a week or two. So tell Gerry not to bother thinking about moving out here."

I knew the longer I rambled, the deeper the hole I'd dug for myself would become. So I promised to wear a sweater, take my vitamins, and call soon. Then I hung up.

I dialed my home number. As I prepared to punch in the code to retrieve my messages, I heard Ronnie's voice shouting, "Hello?"

I grunted and put the phone to my ear. "Why do you keep answering my phone?"

"Holly," she said flatly. "I wasn't gonna. But Aunt Betty's been giving this number out as mine, so I've been getting calls here. Don't worry. I've been nice to people who call for you. Not that there's many of them."

I rubbed my temples, hoping to stave off the headache I felt coming on.

"And I straightened things out with David," she added.

"He said you showed up at his apartment?" I said, still disbelieving. "How did you even know where he lives?"

"I looked him up in your records."

This didn't make sense, since I'd brought my client book with me. "What records?"

"On your computer."

She said it without any hint of apology. She seemed utterly unaware that raiding my computer files might be considered immoral if not downright criminal.

"Didn't Gerry tell you not to use my computer?"

She snorted. "Yeah, right. I can't live without a computer. Get over it."

Get over it. This from the same girl who'd had a conniption when I'd played with her Easy-Bake Oven without permission when we were kids. Maybe I should have had Gerry affix labels bearing my name to all my belongings. Speak to Ronnie in her own language.

"Just tell me about David."

She exhaled dramatically, as though I had no right to question her about her meddling in my life. "You said he needed a haircut. I figured, I'll do it, get you off my back and maybe he'll give me a good tip. Plus I was curious to see the monkey."

I should have known. It's always about the monkey.

Ronnie continued. "While I was cutting his hair, he kept complaining to his nurse about not wanting to do the show without you, and I told him he was being totally lame."

A stabbing pain shot through my temple. "You told a quadriplegic he was being 'totally lame'?" My cousin had never been known for her tact, but I was surprised that even she could demonstrate such a low level of sensitivity.

"Yeah," she snorted. "He nailed my ass for that one. Then when he kept whining, I told him to stand up and be a man."

The migraine had arrived full force. It felt like a thick rusty nail had pierced my skull. "How did he take that?"

"He laughed. Says most people are too PC and censor everything they say around him. He liked that I speak my mind, without thinking first. He's a pretty cool guy when he's not blubbering like an idiot."

I shook my head in disbelief. But I reminded myself that David had not only survived the encounter with Ronnie—he'd sounded chipper when I spoke to him later that day.

"I'm going over there later. Want me to say hi?"

My temples throbbed. "You're not going back," I said. It was not a question.

"I have to," she said. "I promised to help him with his MySpace page."

David was on MySpace? That was news to me. I knew he had

a computer, which was totally tripped out with the latest voice-recognition software and assistive devices, including a mouthpiece that functioned in place of a keyboard and mouse. But aside from watching webcasts and webisodes of his favorite shows, he mainly used it for sending and receiving e-mail. I couldn't imagine him hanging out on the teen-dominated networking site. "Since when does David have a MySpace page?"

"Since I set it up for him. His ID is CapDaddy2. You should check it out."

"When did you do this?"

"After the school thing the other day. He was moaning about being lonely and I told him he could hook up with lots of people online, maybe even get a girlfriend."

So *that* was what Kuki had meant by Ronnie pimping people on the Internet.

"I'm going back today with my digital camera to take some pix of him with Tallulah."

The misgivings I'd had about Ronnie watching my pets were now compounded by fears that she'd infiltrate and sabotage every corner of my life, hurting innocent people in the process. I had to put a stop to it. "Don't mess with David. You're having fun now, but it's only a matter of time before you lose interest, and he'll end up with his feelings hurt." I gasped when I realized I was parroting the lecture David's sister, Paula, had given to me. "Just don't hurt him, okay?"

Ronnie grumbled something about me not being her mother and said she had to go.

"Wait," I shouted into the phone. "I wanna know what's going on with you and Eddie."

She inhaled sharply. "How do you know Eddie?"

"How do *you* know Eddie?" I shot back. "I heard the message he left for you."

"You listened to my messages?" she hissed.

I blinked. "You mean the messages on *my* answering machine?"

She blew out air. "I went to bingo with Aunt Betty."

"You did?" First Lamaze, now bingo. Was I completely replaceable?

"She didn't want to go alone, and Bernie didn't want to go without my dad. Dad didn't want to go without Ma. And Ma wasn't in the mood for bingo. So I went. And when I won the jackpot—"

"You won a jackpot?" I asked. *Of course she did.*

"Six hundred and fifty bucks," she cackled. "I was so excited, I ran up to the guy who was pulling the numbers and I kissed him."

That must have shocked the staid look off Eddie's face. "What did he do?"

"Duh. He kissed me back," she said. "Tongue and everything."

I could imagine the scene—Eddie struggling for breath, half the seniors staring in wide-eyed shock, the other half yelling at him to hurry up and start the next game. "Was there a riot?" I asked.

"No. But when Mrs. Mannisto won the next game, she shuffled up to Eddie and told him to pucker up."

A chuckle erupted from my throat, catching me off guard. Mrs. Mannisto, who'd been widowed ten years earlier, had a ribald sense of humor. I could imagine her chasing after Eddie and asking for her turn. I coughed to cover up my laughter so Ronnie wouldn't think she was off the hook.

But Ronnie hadn't noticed my momentary lapse. She was blathering on about Eddie's broad shoulders and big heart. "We went out last night and he gave me a necklace," she said. "It's the bingo ball from my jackpot. He had it laminated and mounted on a gold chain."

I took a deep breath and reminded myself that I had no claim to Eddie or his bingo balls.

"B-ten," she said on a sigh. "He says it's our number."

I'd been watching cast and crew come and go from the hospital.

Colin Daltry had exited the building a few minutes ago and walked to the far side of the lot, where he stood under a tree and lit up a cigarette.

"What do you care about Eddie, anyway?" she asked. "You have a thing for him?"

"Of course not. I have Tom," I said, though I'd never felt less secure in that statement than I did now.

"Oh, yeah," she snarked. "Your phantom boyfriend. The one who never comes to the house. He's not even coming to Gerry's wedding. I saw the guest list. 'Holly Heckerling and Rocky Broccoli.' What's the matter, Hol? Couldn't get a human date?"

I watched Daltry take a drag on his cigarette. "You're right," I said into the phone. "Tom and I are through. There's someone new in my life."

She snorted. "Yeah? Who?"

"Colin Daltry," I said. I knew the lie would one day come back to bite me in the ass, but for just one moment, I wanted to triumph against Ronnie. She might have gotten Eddie the hunky paramedic, but she couldn't top a movie star.

"You're dating Colin Daltry?" she said, indicating by her tone that she didn't for an instant believe it was true. "Isn't he engaged to Velvet Montana?"

"They broke up," I said. "Don't you watch *Entertainment Tonight*?"

Daltry stamped out his cigarette and turned back toward the hospital building. But then he veered off course, turning and heading directly for the van. *Uh-oh.* This was why I rarely told a lie. My bad luck and horrible timing always conspired against me, revealing my deception in the most embarrassing way possible.

"I hafta go," I said into the phone, just as Daltry reached the van and leaned against the cargo door.

"Lola," he said, smiling. He pointed at the phone and whispered, "Boyfriend?"

I shook my head. "Cousin."

"Who is that?" Ronnie shouted in my ear.

"It's Colin Daltry," I said. "He's waiting for me to get off the phone so we can go have a quickie in his trailer before he has to go back to the set." I rolled my eyes for Daltry's benefit, hoping to convey that nothing I said was to be taken seriously. Still, he wiggled his eyebrows and hitched a thumb in the direction of his trailer.

Ronnie clucked her tongue. "Yeah, right. The phantom professor was bad enough. Now you've got a phantom movie star?"

Before I could reconsider the wisdom of my next move, I thrust my phone out toward Daltry. "Mind saying hello to my cousin Veronica? She doesn't believe that I know you." If I was going to be exposed as a liar, I might as well go down in flames.

Daltry's face broke into a huge grin. He put the phone to his ear. "Veronica, doll? Yes, it's me." He winked at me as he listened. "Well, if you're any bit as cute as your cousin is, I'd love to meet you one day, too."

Knowing he was intentionally laying it on thick didn't prevent color from creeping into my cheeks.

"Yes, that's right," Daltry said. I could only imagine what Ronnie was asking. I held my hand out for my phone, hoping to cut their conversation short, but Daltry was having too much fun and waved me away.

I saw Gio stomping toward the van, waving his arms. I nudged Daltry. "I think you're needed on set."

Daltry turned and said, "Whoa, gotta go," into the phone and tossed it to me. He trotted off toward Gio and they both disappeared into the building.

"Hey," I said, putting the phone to my ear.

Ronnie was hyperventilating. "Oh. My. God," she panted. "He. Is. So. Hot."

"Take a breath," I ordered. "He's a person. Not a god."

She sucked in air. "I'm sorry I didn't believe you. It's just . . . Wow!"

"That's okay." After her breathing was back to normal, I asked about my pets and she reported that all were doing fine. I repeated my pleas that she be careful with David and that she not answer my phone or use my computer.

"I hafta run," she said. "I'm meeting Eddie at Starbucks. I want him to see my picture on the bulletin board."

"Why is your picture on the bulletin board?" I asked.

" 'Cause I'm the Customer of the Month."

Morty and I lunched on bananas and trail mix. I popped a DVD into the player for Morty, closed the back of the van, and climbed into the passenger seat to call Carter.

The minute she answered, I started ranting about Ronnie. "She's been staying in my place just over a week, and she's already Customer of the Month at *my* Starbucks. I've been going there every day for years and they never made *me* Customer of the Month. Not even when my best friend was the manager. Why didn't you ever make me the Customer of the Month?"

"You never paid for your drinks," she said. "So technically, you weren't a customer at all. More like a squatter."

"She took over as Betty's Lamaze coach," I continued. "She did a Critter Comedy presentation with David, and now she's setting up a MySpace page for him. She's using my computer, answering my phone, and dating my bingo caller."

"Your what?"

"I go to bingo with Betty, split an eleven-dollar win three ways, and embarrass myself talking about Eddie's balls. Ronnie goes to bingo, wins six hundred and fifty bucks, and ends up making out with him." I exhaled loudly. "It's like she's living my life, only better."

"Maybe it's not your life anymore," Carter said.

"What?"

"Maybe it's time for you to start a new life. If Ronnie wants the old one so bad, let her have it."

Carter's words were still echoing in my ears hours later, as I drove my rental car down the winding road leading away from Mike's ranch. The dirt road was unmarked, so I turned the navigation system on to see how Nancy would handle it. The display screen showed the car plowing its own course through an unmarked gray blob north of the freeway. Nancy commanded, "You are not traveling on a recognized roadway. Please proceed to the highlighted route."

When I reached the freeway on-ramp, Nancy seemed to sigh with relief. She was back on familiar territory. "Proceed south on Interstate Five for 7.2 miles." By now I knew the route back to Carter and Danny's by heart, but Nancy's nagging was oddly comforting after the day I'd spent with Suzanne.

On the drive back to the ranch, she hadn't spoken to me at all, aside from a few grunts in response to my questions about the shoot. The rest of the ride, I watched as she clenched and un-clenched her jaw. After we unloaded Monkey and Morty, she'd stormed into Mike's office and complained that I'd made the set a hostile work environment. Quite an accomplishment, I thought, considering I hadn't set foot inside the building all day, except for bathroom breaks.

Mike had twisted the ends of his handlebar mustache through-out her rant, then informed her that he'd heard nothing but glow-ing reports about me from the AHA and the production. Not to mention Daltry. Now I was the one with a hand on my hip and a smirk on my face.

Eventually Mike told us we'd have to work out our differences amongst ourselves if either of us wanted to continue working for him. "Can't have trainers feuding," he said. "Takes away focus from the animals. Leads to mistakes."

Faced with possible unemployment, Suzanne and I had both agreed to keep the peace. To my relief, Mike informed me that I'd be with someone else for the next day's shoot. Suzanne was starting a new project, involving horses, her favorite animal. My shoot involved a capuchin monkey, Jane.

Before I headed out, Mike introduced me to Jane and showed me the commands she had been taught. All the training at Mike's revolved around positive reinforcement. Negative reinforcement—shocking, striking, or even yelling—was a thing of the past. Some trainers still used fear and intimidation, he told me, but he wouldn't tolerate such tactics from anyone on his staff.

Jane was a sweetheart, Mike said. She liked her treats, but she'd perform just as eagerly in exchange for a kind word and a scratch on the head.

Mike stepped aside as Jane and I sized each other up. She was roughly the same size as Tallulah, with similar coloration. But Tallulah's face was slightly narrower, her hair a little fuzzier on top.

Jane reached a slender hand through the cage bars to take the treat I held out for her. She popped it in her mouth and sat back with both hands folded close to her body. Tallulah would be sticking a greedy hand out for another treat, and if none was forthcoming, she'd reach into my pockets or tug on my sleeve impatiently. Jane just waited, no trace of Tallulah's mischievous glint in her eyes.

I thought of the two monkeys as I drove home, still contemplating Carter's statement. *"Maybe it's time for you to start a new life. If Ronnie wants the old one so bad, let her have it."*

Perhaps Tallulah represented my old life, and Jane the new?

My cell phone rang as I was exiting the freeway. I picked it up and glanced at the display. *Tom.*

Old habits die hard. At the end of the day, I still longed to hear his voice. I flipped the phone open with one hand, gripping the steering wheel with the other. "Hey," I said.

"Hey, yourself." Though my brain had decided Tom and I were never going to work, my heart apparently hadn't gotten the memo. It still did a little back flip at the sound of his voice.

There was a momentary silence, while I mentally scrolled through options of Things to Talk About. Should I ask about family fun day? Tell him that the bruises that had inspired him to utter "Ugh" on our anniversary date had nearly disappeared? Or just admit that I missed him and couldn't wait to see him again and sink into his warm embrace.

Before I could decide, he said, "I talked to Ronnie."

My hands jerked and the car swerved, barely avoiding oncoming traffic. My head was spinning and my life was flashing before my eyes. Well, maybe not my whole life, but the last several hours, in which I'd made the monumental mistake of telling Ronnie I was having a fling with Colin Daltry. "Hold on a second," I shouted before dropping the phone onto the passenger seat.

I maneuvered the car into the right lane and turned into the lot of a Ralphs grocery store. I pulled into a parking space, turned off the ignition, and picked up the phone.

Tom was shouting, "Holly? Are you okay?"

"Sorry," I said, trying to affect a nonchalant tone. "I'm back."

His tone was steady. Unreadable. "Where are you?"

"At Ralphs."

"Who's Ralph?" He sounded jealous.

I stifled a chuckle. "It's a supermarket."

"Oh."

Silence stretched between us. I sucked in my stomach, bracing myself for the worst, and said, "What did Ronnie tell you?"

"That you took a job in Hollywood and you're in love with a movie star."

I felt a pain in my backside as the lie I'd told to Ronnie offi-cially came back to bite me in the ass, just as predicted. "That's only half true."

"Which half?"

"The job," I said. "The movie star thing was just something I said to get her goat. You know she and I have been at each other's throats since I was eleven. And when I talk to her, I still act like an eleven-year-old. I can't help it. It was stupid. And it's not true."

"She said she talked to him."

"He's a big flirt," I said. "He was walking by and I handed him my phone and asked him to say hi to her. I wanted to make her jealous."

"Why?"

Good question. "She's living in my apartment. Using my com-puter. Answering my phone. Probably torturing my pets. She's Cus-tomer of the Month at my Starbucks. *My* Starbucks," I repeated to underscore the seriousness of this particular infringement. "She's Betty's bingo buddy and Lamaze partner. And now she's dating my EMT."

"Your . . . what?" he asked.

"The paramedic who treated me after my wall-wedging inci-dent," I explained.

"So? Why do you care about that?"

Another good question. "I don't know. It's just weird."

"I see." His tone was measured. The professor probing for an-swers.

I reclined the car seat, settling in. "When did you talk to Ron-nie?" I asked, feeling a flash of indignation.

"I called her. I knew she was staying at your place and I wanted to know if she'd heard anything about when you were coming home."

"Why didn't you just call me?"

"You told me not to. You wanted to wait until you got home. I respected that." He paused, then added, "But I was getting worried that maybe you'd never come home."

"Of course I'm coming home," I said without conviction.

"But you took a job in Hollywood. That's a helluva commute."

I let out a long sigh. I didn't know what to say.

He broke the silence. "So you're really working as an animal trainer?"

"Yes," I answered without hesitation. "Tomorrow I'm doing a scene with a monkey named Jane who's like Tallulah on Ritalin. Don't tell David I said that. And there's this chimp, Morty, who acts like he's talking on a cell phone, yapping away. And you wouldn't have believed it if you knew how many snakes I've handled this week. And ferrets. Oh, Nicole would love these little ferrets."

"I guess that's my answer."

"Answer?"

"You *are* in love," Tom said. "I can hear it in your voice."

"I am not," I insisted. "Colin Daltry is an arrogant actor who won't remember my name once he moves on to his next film."

Tom cleared his throat. "I wasn't talking about Colin Daltry, whoever he is." The fact that Tom was perhaps the only other person on the planet besides me who'd never heard of Daltry made me smile. "I was talking about the job. You love what you're doing."

"Yeah. I do."

The words hung in the air while we both anticipated his next question. But when it came, it wasn't a question at all. "You're staying out there."

I took a deep breath. "Maybe." It was the first time I'd copped to the possibility of making a permanent move. I felt giddy and light-headed.

"I see."

"Why don't you move out here to be with me?" I asked. My mind was racing, imagining the possibilities. "You're a professor.

You can teach *anywhere.* I hear UCLA has a fabulous English program—"

"What about Nicole?"

"She can come, too," I said earnestly. "She'd love it."

"And Bianca?"

I rolled my eyes. It always came back to Bianca. "She's not invited."

His words were so predictable I could have said them myself. "I can't leave New York. Bianca and I share custody. If I leave, I'll lose my daughter. I won't be one of those dads who only see their kids twice a year."

"But I—" I stopped short, not able to get the words "love you" past the giant frog that had lodged itself in my throat.

"If she was older, it might be different," he said. "But for now . . ."

"I know," I croaked. "Nicole comes first."

I stayed in the car, staring at the large illuminated Ralphs sign long after we disconnected. Tears streamed down my face. I didn't know what to do or where to go. Part of me wanted to start the car and drive all the way back to New York. To see Tom face-to-face.

But when I closed my eyes, the face that came into view wasn't Tom's, but Colin's.

What was it about Daltry? Was he truly interested in me, or was it just a game? Maybe it was time to find out.

On the dashboard, I spied the business card Daltry's goon had given me in the airport. There was a number scribbled on the back. His attorney's number, he'd said. I stared at the number for a moment, contemplating dialing it. Though I'd seen him several times since, I didn't have any other way to reach him. I didn't have his cell number. Didn't know where he lived.

I could drive back to the hospital and knock on his trailer door.

If he was gone, I could head over to the studio. But I didn't want to run into anyone else. They'd wonder why I was there when there were no animals on set. People would talk. They'd quickly figure out I was there to throw myself at Colin. And if he shot me down, I'd be humiliated.

After concocting a cover story to give the lawyer, I punched in the number. It was just after four o'clock, so the law firm would still be open. The phone rang once, twice, three times. Then someone answered, *"¿En que puedo servile?"* I could barely hear over the clanging of dishes in the background, but I was pretty sure it wasn't English.

"Hello? *Hola?* I'm looking for Colin Daltry's lawyer?"

"¿Qué?" The phone was muffled but I heard the speaker shouting to someone. *"La chica esta buscando un abogado."*

I had no idea what he said, but I presumed I was the chica and he thought I wanted an avocado.

"What? Hello? Are you a lawyer?"

Another voice came on the line. This one spoke English. "Can I help you?"

"This isn't a law firm, is it?" I said, realization dawning. Daltry hadn't given me his attorney's number at the airport. He'd made up a phony number, to get rid of me.

"No, it's Chico's. Best Mexican food in LA."

19

No Visitors Allowed

"Have you ever noticed that a chimpanzee's testicles are like, humongous, compared to a man's?" Robyn, my partner for the day, asked as I navigated the van to the hospital set. Unlike the torturous silence of my drive with Suzanne, Robyn and I had chatted amiably the whole way. Robyn had done most of the chatting, actually, which was fine with me as I just wanted to focus on little things, like driving and sulking over the state of my life. "With balls that big, you'd think they'd have a big penis, too. But it's tiny."

It had been a long time since I'd actually seen a man's penis, but I knew she was right about chimps. "It's all about sperm competition," I said, repeating what I'd learned in primate anatomy class. "Species in which females mate with multiple males have larger testicles so they can manufacture more sperm and increase their chances of fathering her offspring."

"That explains why their balls are big, but not why their weenies are small," Robyn noted.

Distracted by all the testicle talk, I missed my turn. I slowed down, looking for a place to turn around. "They aren't, compared to other primates. Just next to humans."

"So why are human men so lucky?"

I'd have argued that it was human *women* who were the lucky ones, but I'd gotten flustered and missed the turn again.

Visions of wangdoodles danced in my head. I found myself wondering about Tom and Colin and even Eddie. Though the way things were going, I'd probably never satisfy my curiosity about any one of them. Tom had made it clear he'd never move to Los Angeles, even if I decided to stay. Colin had brushed me off with a fake number. Okay, so I was looking a little deranged at the time, with mashed potato–matted hair and a sports bra in my pocket, but still, it struck me as a low move that probably spoke volumes about the kind of man he really was. And Eddie's balls—bingo and otherwise— were now bouncing in Veronica's court.

I blinked a few times, trying to get rid of the mental image and failing. "Can we change the subject, please?" I asked Robyn. "I haven't had breakfast yet." Not that I'd be any more inclined to discuss primate genitalia on a full stomach.

She shrugged and resumed an earlier discussion thread she'd abandoned: whether she should pursue a career in animal training or go back to school to get her degree in veterinary medicine. She'd admitted to me that she'd taken the job at Mike's to test the waters. Her lifelong dream of being a vet had been sidetracked during col- lege when she took a job at Universal Studios in Florida and ended up working on their live animal show.

"So I don't know. I need, like, three more years of school to get my DVM, and that's not even counting the time I'd have to spend as an intern or a resident."

"But if that's what you really want to do . . ."

She nodded. "I thought so. But I can make good money now if I do this." She gestured at the back of the van, where Jane and several other animal stars were awaiting their day's work. "And it would save my parents from paying my tuition for three more years. You know what my stepmother calls vet school? Kitty col- lege."

I snorted and shared my aunts' designation of Columbia Univer- sity as "monkey school."

As I finally pulled into the hospital lot and came to a smooth stop, I felt my gloom lifting. Today was going to be a good day. At least it couldn't be worse than yesterday.

I left Robyn in the van while I checked in with Giovanni. Today was the big day—the scene in which I had to wrangle several animals simultaneously. The one I'd known would be the most challenging since I first read the script—though at the time I had no idea I'd be the one coordinating the animal action.

Gio gave me a sideways hug. I marveled at how quickly I'd gone from nonpro intruder to one of the gang. "You look like shit," he said affectionately.

My eyes were red and puffy from crying. Between helping with Max and studying the script, I'd only gotten a few hours' sleep. Making matters worse, I'd tried mixing some mashed potato flakes in with my hair conditioner, hoping to achieve the same look I'd had the previous week, but instead of lustrous and shiny I'd ended up with limp and starchy. "Just tryin' to fit in," I said, gesturing at his well-worn sweatshirt and ripped jeans.

His chuckle erupted into the hacking cough that I'd come to think of as his signature song.

"You ever think of seeing a doctor?" I asked.

"He seems to think it has something to do with the three packs of smokes I go through in a day." He shook his head and added, "Quack," sounding like a duck with tonsillitis.

Gio said we were on schedule and could start moving the animals inside. "Do me a favor," he said, catching my sleeve as I turned back toward the van. "Tell Danny it's a closed set. His friends can hang for now, but they can't watch filming."

"What friends?" I asked, forehead scrunched. Danny hadn't mentioned bringing any friends to work today.

Gio shrugged. "Tall chick in stilettos. Dude looks like a pound puppy." He wheeled on his heels and was gone.

I stood there a moment, trying to squash a growing sense of dread. Carter and Danny hadn't lived in Los Angeles long. They had made few friends, and none I could think of that matched Gio's description.

Tall chick in stilettos. Dude looks like a pound puppy.

Though I doubted Danny's "friends" could be any other than Monica Broccoli and my cousin Gerry, I said a silent prayer that I was wrong.

As I strode into the hospital lobby, Kuki's message began replaying in my head. "And now Gerry's talking about moving to Hollywood with you." Gerry had undoubtedly heard about my job from Betty. The moment I'd told Betty the news, I'd figured he'd begin a barrage of phone calls begging me to snag the stars' socks for his collection. When he hadn't called, I'd naively assumed I was off the hook. Maybe he'd just decided to take matters into his own hands.

I took the elevator to the second floor and started down the hallway. I stopped abruptly when I saw Danny, Gerry, and Monica halfway down the corridor. What had started out as a good day was about to turn bad.

Danny was pointing out various rooms and pieces of equipment, and introducing crew members who happened to pass by. Gerry was eagle-eyed, peering into every room and around every corner, obviously hoping to catch a glimpse of someone famous.

Monica Broccoli was indeed wearing stilettos, not the best footwear for a movie set, with cables snaked along the floors and multimillion-dollar equipment propped in corners and doorways. I watched her saunter down the hallway—with no trace of a limp—and noted several turned heads among the crew.

Though my stomach was grumbling, I didn't pause at the craft services table. I strode up to where Danny was showing a camera dolly to Gerry and Monica.

Gerry saw me first. He held his arms out wide and shouted,

"Surprise!" Then he squeezed me tight and whispered in my ear, "Don't be mad at Monica. It was my idea to surprise you."

"You surprised me, all right," I said through a plastered-on smile. "When did you get here?" I turned to Monica, arms slightly open in case she expected a hug, too. But her arms were folded across her chest, so I just nodded and said, "Hey."

"Late last night. We checked in to our hotel—we figured with the new baby, we shouldn't ask to bunk with you guys—and then showed up early this morning at your place. Danny said you'd already left to pick up the critters."

"A hotel?" I asked. "Can you afford that?"

"We dipped into our honeymoon fund." Gerry's smile widened. "I figure since I'm here in a professional capacity, the whole trip is tax deductible, so I'll get some of it back at tax time."

I groaned. "It's not tax deductible."

"Why not?" Gerry asked. "You told me that everything you buy for Holly's Hobbies is deductible, right down to the paper clips."

"That's because it's a business."

He puffed his chest out. "So is Celebrity Socks."

"I make a profit," I said. Although "profit" might have been a strong word to define this year's earnings from my business. "It's my livelihood."

"I quit being a cater-waiter so I could focus on building my sock empire."

"Have you made any money?"

"Not yet." He shook his head. "I'm still in start-up mode. Gotta build up my inventory. Hence this trip."

Monica stuck her stiletto between us. "I heard you don't have to make a profit for the first few years."

"True," I said. "But in order to claim a loss, you have to prove that what you're doing is a business and not a hobby."

Gerry wrinkled his nose. "How would I prove that?"

"By conducting it in a professional manner," I said.

"I had business cards printed." He reached into his back pocket and pulled out a card. I took it from him and held it up to the light. Illustrated socks in neon pink and green stood out against a background of glittery gold stars. I had to blink a few times to focus on the text, which read *Celebrity Socks, Gerald Corelli, Proprietor*, in a curlicue font. His Web site address was printed in block letters along the bottom.

"What do you think?" Gerry asked.

"Cute," I said, squinting as the letters swam in and out of focus.

Danny was looking over my shoulder. His expression was unreadable. "Cute," he echoed.

"Monica picked out the colors and graphics," Gerry boasted. "We did it at the same place we got our wedding invitations."

I nodded, unsurprised by that revelation.

"Check out the back," Gerry said.

I turned the card over to see Gerry's slogan emblazoned on the back in a bold purple script: *Because famous people have feet, too.*

I held the card out to him, but he waved it away. "Keep it," he said. "I had ten thousand printed."

Monica nudged me. "Those are tax deductible, aren't they? They're business cards, so they're a business expense."

"Printing business cards isn't enough to constitute a legitimate business. You have to demonstrate that you are attempting to generate revenue. And there has to be a reasonable expectation that you *will* generate revenue. You should develop a business plan, one that clearly spells out your profit potential."

"I see," Gerry said, nodding.

Monica was tapping one stiletto impatiently. "Where are the stars' trailers?"

Deliberately ignoring her question, I said, "This is a bad day. It's a closed set. You can't be here."

"Closed set?" Gerry asked. "Someone doing a nude scene?"

Monica elbowed Gerry in the ribs.

I shook my head. "Animals on set. No visitors allowed."

Monica barked, "But you're in charge of the animals. So you can let us watch."

I shook my head again. "It's not my call. The American Humane Association oversees all the action with animals. They won't let anyone on set. Even crew members aren't allowed unless they are essential to that particular scene."

"I tried to tell them," Danny piped in.

"Really?" Gerry looked forlorn. "We came all this way."

"Can't you say we're your assistants or something?" Monica asked.

"I'm sorry. You could come back another time, when there are no animals on set. And the AD—that's the assistant director—said you can hang out for now, but you'll have to clear out when we start filming. And you can't go near the animals."

"It's not the animals we're interested in," Monica stated.

Danny was backing away, obviously feeling his responsibilities as tour guide had been nullified by my arrival. "I'm due in makeup."

"Great," I said. "Take them with you."

He was shaking his head no, but I pushed on. "I have to go unload the animals." I turned to Monica. "Don't you wanna see where Colin Daltry gets his hair styled? See what kind of spritz they use on him?"

Danny flared his nostrils at me, but pointed them in the direction of the hair and makeup room.

I grabbed his sleeve and whispered, "Why did you bring them here? Are you crazy?"

"They stormed the apartment this morning. Carter was flipping out. She said Monica was scaring the baby." He shrugged. "Anyway, how much harm can they cause?"

I cocked my head in Monica's direction. The exaggerated limp was back. Step, drag, step, drag. Stilettos and all. "I bet she crashes into something before the day is out. She's so tall and lanky, she could take out a whole bank of monitors with one false step." I tossed my hair over one shoulder. "Sure glad *I'm* not the one who brought them here."

Danny quickened his pace, catching up to Gerry and Monica and ushering them into hair and makeup.

Gerry and Monica's arrival on the set did not necessarily portend disaster, I told myself as I took the elevator back to the ground floor and exited the building. It was possible their visit would pass without incident.

But as I walked toward the red van, I mentally replayed every Broccoli-borne disaster I'd endured in the last few years, my anxiety mounting with each step.

I was so lost in thought that I didn't see the pair of denim-clad legs leaning against the red van until I nearly tripped over them. " 'Scuse me," I said, looking up and into the blue eyes and chiseled jaw of Colin Daltry.

"Hello, doll," he said.

"Don't 'doll' me," I snapped. "Do you even know my name?"

"You'll always be my Lola."

I put one hand on my hip. "My *real* name."

"Holly," he said without hesitation. "What is this, a quiz?"

"Yes," I said, my eyes narrowing. "Ready for round two? What's your attorney's phone number?"

He looked confused for a moment, then his eyes widened in surprise. "You called the number I gave you in the airport?"

I nodded. "Chico says hi."

Daltry rolled back on his heels and laughed.

"What's so funny?" I asked, my hand still firmly planted on my hip.

"Just remembering what you looked like in the airport. I'd never have guessed you'd clean up so well."

"Your bodyguard knocked me to the ground and hijacked my cell phone and you were going to brush me off with a phony phone number. What kind of a person does that?"

"The kind of person who has to fend off fans every time they go out in public. Most are perfectly nice, but more than a few have asked me to pose for a picture, then turned around and sold it to a rag sheet—along with a story that I groped them in an elevator or offered them drugs at a party. So when someone chases me down in the airport, I have to be careful." He winked at me. "Especially if they're waving a brassiere in my face."

"Well, I wasn't after anything except my cell phone," I said. "I didn't even know who you were."

"And now that you know," he said, cocking his head to one side, "what are you after?"

"Nothing." I stepped around him and unlocked the back of the van. "What makes you think I'm after anything?"

"You called my attorney."

"You mean Chico?" I grunted.

"You wanted something. Did you miss me?"

I shook my head. "It was a momentary delusion. It passed."

Robyn had exited the van and come around to the back to help unload. I introduced her to Colin and they shook hands.

Robyn gave him a long head-to-toe appraisal before letting go. "We were just talking about you."

Colin raised one eyebrow. "Really?"

"Well, not you, per se. Male primates in general."

He gave her his trademark smile-wink combo and leaned against the open cargo door. "What about us?"

She returned his smile sans wink. "We were discussing evolutionary influences on male reproductive anatomy."

His eyebrows shot up a notch. Clearly not the answer he expected, and one for which he had no snappy comeback. "Oh."

I unloaded the dolly, then climbed into the van and began handing Robyn the small animal crates, still trying not to dwell on Daltry's reproductive anatomy.

"You ladies need help?" he asked.

Robyn looked up. "With the anatomy lesson?"

He shook his head and took a step back. "With the animals."

Robyn and I answered, "No," simultaneously.

"You shouldn't really be here," Angela Ambrosino said to Daltry, quoting the appropriate regulation from the rule book. She'd just arrived, looking as stylish as possible in her khaki uniform and hair pulled into a ponytail.

Daltry nodded and took a few steps back. "Just needed to ask Holly for a favor."

He tugged my sleeve and I followed him to the side of the van. "Can I borrow your cell?" he asked. "I dropped mine and it broke."

"That's the favor?" I asked. "Send someone to fetch you a new one." I'd seen assistants coming and going from his trailer, all paid to keep his life running smoothly.

"Already did. But I need to make a quick call. It'll just take a minute."

I shrugged and handed him the phone. He punched in a number, pressed it to his ear, and waited. A moment later, he handed it back to me. "Line's busy."

He turned and headed toward his trailer, tossing an offhanded "Thanks" over his shoulder. As I watched him walk away, I could have sworn I heard a ring emanating from a bulge in his back pocket.

Under Angela's watchful eye, Robyn and I carted the animals into a small room on the second floor of the hospital. It had most likely been an exam room at one time, but it had been stripped of everything but a counter and sink and a few chairs. We got all the animals settled, filled water bowls, and settled in to wait.

In addition to Jane, the scene included a guinea pig, a bunny rabbit, a Persian cat, and a Pomeranian dog. We also had a number of additional animals that would fill the cages in the background—an Indian star tortoise, a Mexican red-kneed tarantula, and a pair of chinchillas. They wouldn't be part of the action but would serve as atmosphere.

There was a knock on the door and Danny popped his head inside. "What do you want me to do with Tweedle-Dee and Tweedle-Dum? They're getting restless."

I bit my lip. "Did you show them wardrobe?"

He nodded. "They've seen every inch of the building."

"Where are they now?"

"Filling their faces at craft services."

I left Robyn with the animals and followed Danny down the corridor. Gerry was surveying the buffet with a critical eye, probably noting how none of it stacked up to his mother's cooking. He looked up and shook his head. "I still can't believe we're here. An actual movie set." He punched my biceps. "And you're actually working here."

"Pretty wild, huh?" I said. "I wish you could stay longer, but—"

He gave me an imploring look. "You're not kicking us out already, are you?"

"I don't have a choice. It's the rules."

Monica plucked a grape off a fruit platter and plopped it in her mouth. "Where are we supposed to go? Danny drove us here, and he can't leave, can he? He's in the scene."

I turned to face Danny. "Can they borrow your car? You can ride back with me."

Danny shot me a look that was equal parts fear and loathing. "Why don't you lend them the van?"

"I can't. I need to load the animals back into it after the scene.

Besides, it's not mine. I could lose my job." I looked at Gerry. "You can drive a stick shift, can't you?"

"I dunno," he said. "It's been a while. And I don't know my way around LA." Too bad my rental car was back at the ranch. I would have loved to see Monica Broccoli take on Nancy the Navigator.

Gerry asked, "Is there a subway stop around here?"

"No," I answered. "And if we call a cab, it'll take an hour to get here and cost a small fortune." I fished the van keys out of my pocket and handed them to Gerry. "There's a big red van in the parking lot. You can wait there, but don't drive it. It has a TV and DVD player, in case you get bored." I looked at Monica, pointing a stern finger in warning. "Do not step foot outside the van until Danny or I come get you."

She pouted, but took the keys and flounced down the corridor, Gerry following behind her like a well-trained puppy. Danny and I exchanged nervous glances before going our separate ways.

The scene we were filming looked complicated on paper, but when broken up into several smaller segments, it wasn't nearly as daunting. Robyn and I had placed the "atmosphere" animals into their cages, which would remain locked throughout the scene. Then we loaded the critters whose cage doors had been rigged by the prop department to open on cue.

In the scene, Tobey is cleaning cages when a hamster gets loose and crawls up his pant leg, sending him on a herky-jerky dance around the room. He crashes into cages and frees a half dozen additional pets. The actual cage crashing would be filmed later, with replicas in place of the live animals. This morning, we filmed the individual escapes and Danny's reaction shots.

While the magic of editing would make it appear that all the animals were running loose at once, we never had more than two out at one time. One being Jane, the unflappable capuchin who'd been trained to remain calm and composed despite the controlled chaos around her. Jane would eagerly abandon her cage, but instead of getting caught up in the melee, find a spot atop a filing cabinet to watch the other creatures run amok.

For one shot, Robyn and I stood just out of view on either side of the cabinet, each taking turns getting Jane's attention with a clicker. The result was that Jane would appear to be watching animals dart back and forth as though she was observing a tennis match. Jane performed expertly, once even appearing to roll her eyes at the antics of the smaller animals as though she found them droll.

We filmed several takes with the "atmosphere" critters in their cages and the other doors swinging wide, while Danny ran around the room chasing invisible animals, trying to trap them with a wastebasket or scoop them up with a dust pan. Eventually he would grab a broom and just start swinging. The imperative to never put an animal in harm's way meant that footage of Danny swatting at thin air would later be intercut with footage of the fleeing animals, to make it appear they barely evaded being squashed by the broom.

We worked our way through the long list of needed shots in rapid succession. Most were done in a few takes. A few—such as the hamster climbing up Danny's pant leg—required several attempts before the director was satisfied. All in all, the animals behaved as expected and were duly rewarded. The "escapes" were controlled, with either Robyn or me standing just outside camera range, ready to scoop up the runaway once Hal shouted, "Cut."

I shuddered to think of how the day would have gone if I'd been paired with Suzanne instead of Robyn. Mike was right. Tension between trainers would take attention away from the animals. Knowing that Robyn had my back, I could focus fully on doing my job. Even the constant fear of Monica Broccoli bursting onto the set didn't distract from the task at hand.

I felt a surge of confidence when I caught a glimpse of Angela nodding approval from the sidelines. By the time we broke for lunch, I was euphoric. Landing this job might have been a total fluke, but keeping it wouldn't be.

It wasn't long before my euphoria came to a crashing halt. Robyn and I had returned all the animals to the holding room and flipped a coin over who got to grab lunch first.

I won the coin toss and was making my way toward the cafeteria when I saw Daltry emerge from hair and makeup, yawning widely.

"Lola, doll, you should get in line," he said.

"In line for what?"

"Foot massage." He smiled serenely. "Production sprung for a couple of masseurs. While we're being made up, they do our feet."

Did the perks of stardom never end? While one artist styles your hair and another applies your makeup, someone rubs your feet, and an entire army of people runs your errands. "I'm sure it's just for the cast."

Daltry shrugged. "I can pull some strings with the gal who did me. I think she likes me." He winked. "She worked wonders on my pressure points." He gestured down to his bare feet, which shimmered with oil.

"No, thanks." I shook my head. "I only have a few minutes to eat." Besides, I wanted to load up a couple plates to bring down to Gerry and Monica.

"Suit yourself," he said, padding back toward the hair and makeup room.

My progress down the hallway was arrested by the sound of Daltry's voice. "Anybody seen my socks?"

A chill went down my spine. I froze in place, straining to hear. "My socks," he repeated. "They were here a minute ago."

Daltry's socks were missing. My cousin the celebrity sock hound was somewhere in the vicinity. I knew the odds of those two facts being unrelated were less than infinitesimal. My ire at Gerry and

Monica for disregarding my orders and thus jeopardizing my job was almost surpassed by my shock that they'd managed to concoct such a scheme. I'd have expected them to try something obvious, like sneaking into the stars' trailers. But giving complimentary foot massages in order to get the stars to shed their socks—it was almost inspired.

Time for damage control, I told myself, turning back toward hair and makeup. A few crew members had gathered outside the door, probably drawn there by the moans that were now emanating from the room. "Oh, oh, yes, right there, harder."

Kelly wasn't due on set today, so Jennifer Aniston was probably the moaner. Which would explain the growing knot of people craning their necks to see into the room. I was trying to squeeze through the crowd when Daltry emerged, carrying his shoes.

"Change your mind?" he asked.

"Just curious," I said. "Sounds like Jen's enjoying herself."

He shook his head. "That's not Jen. It's, um, a friend of mine."

The hesitation in his voice told me who it was. "Velveeta?" I asked, deliberately mispronouncing her name.

He didn't correct me. "She came by to drop something off, and—"

"Whatever," I snapped. I mentally smacked myself for sounding like a jealous girlfriend. "Find your socks?" I asked, trying to affect a casual tone.

He shook his head. "They vanished. Crazy, isn't it?"

"Totally," I agreed.

"I'll have to go fetch a clean pair from my trailer." He slipped his feet into his shoes. "Come with me?"

I shook my head. "Not on an empty stomach."

If Jennifer Aniston had been the unwitting victim of my sock-thieving cousin, I'd have marched in and put an end to the charade.

But the cheesy supermodel could fend for herself—at least until after I'd had lunch.

I was scarfing down my lunch—a delectable chicken and penne in pesto prepared by the catering crew—when Danny sidled up to me. "I heard something about free foot massages and missing socks. Doesn't take a brain surgeon to figure out who's behind it."

"You are," I said.

His eyebrows shot up. "Excuse me?"

"They passed themselves off as being hired by 'the production.' Won't take long before word gets to Gio. He's gonna know something's fishy. Since they came as your guests, you should say they're professional massage therapists and you hired them for the day."

"Think he'll buy that?" Danny asked.

"Probably not. But it's better than telling the truth."

"What's wrong with my feet?" Jennifer Aniston was saying. She'd kicked off her sandals and was twirling her toes in Gerry's direction. "Colin said he got a foot massage that was out of this world."

I paused in the doorway to hair and makeup, stifling a snicker at what I saw—Gerry crouched on the floor, Aniston's feet dangling in his face, Monica tossing a bottle of gel into her purse and looking up at me like she'd been caught with her hand in the cookie jar.

"I, um, well—" Gerry stuttered. He looked utterly dejected. To have come so far, and gotten so close, only to have Aniston show up sockless.

"They were only hired for an hour," Danny interrupted, pushing his way into the room. "Time's up."

Monica and Gerry exchanged guilty glances as they edged toward the door, Monica slinging her purse over her shoulder. "Sorry," she grumbled.

"I'll pay them to stay another hour," Aniston said.

This got Monica's attention, but before she could agree, I shepherded her out of the room. "They have clients waiting across town."

"I'll do your feet," Danny offered.

I didn't stick around to hear her response, my primary goal being to escort Gerry and Monica as far away from Aniston's feet as my lunch break would allow.

Starry Starry Night

"Colin Daltry's socks," Gerry was crowing, waving the aforementioned footwear in Carter's face.

She waved them away. "Yuck. I'm eating."

We were crowded into a booth at Jerry's Deli, a few blocks from the hospital where Max was born—Gerry and Monica and I on one side, Carter and Danny on the other, Max asleep in his car seat between them. After arguing for twenty minutes about what kind of food to eat, we'd settled on Jerry's because its billboard-sized menu offered something for every taste bud.

Gerry tucked the socks into the breast pocket of his sports jacket. "Not bad for my first day in Hollywood, huh?" He looked at me. "This'll show the IRS I'm serious, won't it?"

I didn't see how the acquisition of Daltry's socks would legitimize Gerry's business in the eyes of the federal government, but I didn't want to revisit that argument, since it was my urging to take his business seriously that prompted Gerry's "free foot massage" ruse to begin with.

He'd told me that he and Monica had sat in the van for ten minutes trying to formulate a business plan. After brainstorming ideas of how to expand their inventory to the point where they could interest investors or online advertisers, they'd spied Daltry walking across the parking lot. They decided that serious businesspeople wouldn't just sit and watch Daltry's socks walk on by.

"We thought about walking up to him and asking for his socks," Gerry was telling Carter. "But in my experience, that's not usually effective. Stars will give you the shirt off their back if it's for charity, but if you just want to collect or exhibit it, they think you're crazy or something."

"You don't say." She took a sip of her smoothie.

"So I got to thinking," Gerry said, "my first few specimens were acquired, how shall I say, surreptitiously."

"You stole them," Danny said.

"In a manner of speaking," Gerry agreed. "So I decided to go back to my roots."

Monica piped in, "The foot massage was my idea. He wanted to break into Daltry's trailer."

Gerry nodded. "I would have, too, only I saw his girlfriend go inside."

"She's not his girlfriend," I said with a tad too much fervor. "They broke up."

"Then Monica found some gel in the van," Gerry said.

I stopped with fork poised in midair. "What gel?"

She fished a small plastic bottle out of her purse and handed it to me. " 'Bitter Apple Gel,' " I read. "This is a chew deterrent for dogs. Colin Daltry let you put this on his feet?"

"I didn't let him see the bottle," Monica purred. "I kept him focused on other things." She arched her back so that her "other things" jutted over the top of her low-cut blouse.

Carter leaned over the baby as though to shield the buxom Broccoli from his view.

I was scrutinizing the gel's active ingredients. "I hope this doesn't have any adverse effects on human skin."

"I hope he doesn't have dogs," Danny added with a smirk. "It'll drive them insane."

Gerry waved his arms in the air to get Carter's attention, as she was the only one who hadn't yet heard his latest sock-stealing adventure. "So while Monica was doing his feet, and the makeup girl was doing his face, I snuck his socks into my pocket. He didn't see a thing."

He bit into a knish, and Monica took over. "Then he asks us if we wouldn't mind doing Velvet Montana's feet. You know, the model."

"*Super*model," Gerry interjected. "She's his girlfriend."

"They broke up," I murmured into my napkin.

Gerry reached for a French fry. "She has surprisingly large feet."

"This time, Gerry did the massage, and I snitched her socks." Monica reached into her purse and pulled out a pair of pink knee socks that looked like they could be hung as Christmas stockings.

"Wow," Carter gaped. "I didn't know Colin Daltry was dating Sasquatch."

"They broke up," I repeated.

Prompted by Carter, who made no attempt to disguise her dislike of Monica Broccoli, conversation turned to their intended departure date. "Day after tomorrow," Gerry said, adding, "unless we decide to move here for good."

I choked on a potato wedge.

"Just kidding," Gerry said, nudging me with his elbow. "We have to get back to meet with the florist on Sunday. There's so much to do with the wedding less than a month away."

Danny leaned forward, braving the question that was foremost in both our minds. "What's on your agenda for tomorrow?"

"Since Holly says we're not allowed back on the set," Monica said, snarling in my direction, "we're gonna cruise Beverly Hills. Check out some of those upscale stores on Rodeo Drive. Maybe buy a map of the stars' homes."

Gerry nodded. "Tonight we thought we'd go to some of the nightclubs we heard the stars hang out in—Hyde, SkyBar, the Viper Room. Maybe if they're drunk enough, they won't mind giving us their socks." He looked at me. "You'll come with us, won't you?"

If anyone could charm the socks off of drunken celebrities, it was my cousin Gerry. But I couldn't bring myself to tag along. I drained my soda glass, crunching the ice between my teeth. "Sorry. I have an early call tomorrow."

Danny looked across the table at Gerry. "So your business plan is to stalk celebrities and steal their socks?"

Gerry nodded. "In a nutshell."

Carter glanced at me and deadpanned. "They're sockerazzi."

Over dessert, Gerry described his anguish at seeing Jennifer Aniston's sandal-clad feet stroll into hair and makeup and his decision to forgo her foot massage on moral grounds. "It just didn't seem right. I was only doing it for the socks, and she wasn't wearing any."

I opened my mouth to speak, but decided against it. If Gerry could understand his code of ethics—a code in which giving foot massages under false pretenses was acceptable only if it led to the theft of the recipient's socks—then who was I to question it?

"We would have figured out a way to get into Aniston's trailer," Monica said, "but Holly Go-Rightly had someone babysit us the rest of the afternoon so we wouldn't get into any trouble."

Since the afternoon's session had been lighter—involving Danny, Jennifer, and the monkey, Jane—I left Robyn in charge of the rest of the animals. I also asked her to rein in Gerry and Monica, using brute force if necessary. The AHA regulates fair treatment of animals and children—gate-crashing adults were not subject to its protections.

Max became fussy, prompting Carter and Danny to gather up their diaper bag, bottles, and innumerable other props of parenthood and climb out of the booth.

"My treat," Danny said, slipping several twenties in with the bill.

We exchanged thanks and good nights, and I told Carter I'd

be home after dropping Gerry and Monica at their hotel. I kissed Max's forehead, which didn't diminish his crying but gave me a rush of gooey emotion. *He still has that new-baby smell,* I marveled, wishing I could bottle it up and keep it with me forever.

"You mind dropping us on the Sunset Strip?" Gerry asked as I unlocked my rental car and climbed into the driver's seat.

"You guys were serious?" I asked.

"We're only here one more day," Monica said from the backseat. "We have to make the most of every minute."

"You could do some shopping," I offered. "See the sights. Catch a show."

"There's no time for any of that," Monica said.

"We have work to do," Gerry announced, strapping on his seat belt. "We're the sockerazzi."

Monica dictated an address on Sunset Boulevard, and I entered it onto Nancy's touch screen. Her instructions led me to a small establishment about two miles northeast of Jerry's Deli. Even before Nancy announced that I had reached my destination, it was obvious from the valet-only parking and the long line of people held back by velvet ropes that I'd found the right place. Neon letters on the building's facade identified it as Hyde Lounge.

Traffic was bottlenecked in front of the lounge. A limo angled to the curb in front of me, discharging its passengers—obviously A-listers as evidenced by the photographers who emerged from the ether, bulbs on their massive cameras flashing rapid-fire, and the swift manner in which the club's gatekeepers parted the velvet ropes and ushered them inside the club.

"Was that Britney?" Gerry said, sounding breathless.

"I only saw an elbow," Monica answered. "But it looked like hers."

"I smell definite potential here," Gerry said, leaning over to kiss my cheek and thanking me for the ride.

"Good luck," I shouted as they hopped out of the car, their

arrival accompanied by none of the fanfare of the previous guests.

I'd agreed to drive them to their first destination, but for the rest of their sock-snagging adventure, they'd be on their own. They were above the legal drinking age and had cash for cab fare and two working cell phones. So why was I so worried?

I was inching forward in traffic when I felt my cell phone buzz against my backside. I'd recently learned it was easier to leave it on vibrate than to remember to turn it off and on during filming.

I pulled it out of my pocket and glanced at the screen. The caller's number was blocked. I opened the phone and said a tentative hello.

"Lola." Colin's disembodied voice threw me for a loop.

"How'd you get this number?" I asked. Then I remembered how he'd borrowed my phone earlier in the day, made a call, and hung up quickly moments before I heard his supposedly broken phone ring. He'd dialed his own number so that his phone would have a record of the incoming call. "Never mind. Your phone was never busted. You played me. Again."

"A game I'll never tire of," Daltry chuckled. "What are you up to?"

"This 'n' that," I said, rolling the car to a stop at a red light. "Why?"

"How'd you like to go out?"

I paused for a moment, absorbing the question. I still hadn't recovered from my earlier blunder in thinking he was professing his love to me when he was really talking on the phone. "What do you mean?"

"Go out. With me."

The light changed and I eased up on the brake. A car was pulling away from the curb in front of me, so I signaled and pulled into the space it had abandoned. Driving in LA was enough of a challenge for me without the distraction Daltry inevitably provided. "What do you mean? Like a . . . a . . ." I don't know why I stumbled over the word "date," except that it was something normal people did. Colin and his crowd probably considered dating passé.

"A date?" he prompted. "You want to know if I'm asking you on a date?"

Before I could answer, Nancy intoned, "You have passed your intended destination. Please return to the highlighted route."

"You have company," Daltry said. "Sounds like neither boyfriend nor beast."

"Navigation system," I grunted.

"Lost?"

"No. I just dropped friends off at a club and I'm heading home."

"Which club?"

"The Hyde Lounge," I said. "It's on Sunset."

He chuckled. "I know where it is. Who are your friends?"

"My cousin and his fianceé. They're visiting from New York."

"I mean *who* are they? Are they anybody?"

I grunted annoyance at the Hollywood attitude that divided people into somebodies and nobodies. "They're nobody. Like me."

"Don't take offense, doll," he said. "What I meant was, if your friends aren't major players, they're not going to get into Hyde."

"Oh." I assumed their entry wouldn't be as swift or spectacular as Britney's—or whomever the famous elbow was attached to—but that after a long and ego-deflating wait outside they'd eventually be admitted. "Not at all?"

"Not unless they know someone." I wondered if having massaged the feet of Colin Daltry and Velvet Montana qualified as "knowing someone."

I blew out air. "I guess I'd better go back and get them."

"They really want in?" he asked.

"Desperately."

"What about you? You weren't up for a night at Hyde?"

I didn't want to admit I'd never even heard of the place before. "Not really. I had a long day. Besides, it's not really my scene."

"What is your scene, Lola?"

I chewed on my lower lip, considering. A few scenarios came to mind, which were surely too pedestrian for Daltry. A bowl of popcorn, a hand to hold, and a black-and-white screwball comedy on the tube. Or a comfy chair, a warm fire, and a good book.

"Maybe no one's ever shown you a good time before," Daltry added.

"That's not true," I insisted. "But my idea of a good time doesn't involve loud music and flashing lights."

"Meet me in front of the club," he said. "We'll get your friends inside, and then, if you're not impressed, I'll take you somewhere else. Something more your speed."

There were many reasons why I should have turned down the invitation. Topping the list was the fact that Colin would instantly recognize Gerry and Monica as the marauding masseurs he'd met earlier, which would lead to embarrassing questions and even more embarrassing answers. Also, Carter was expecting me home soon. Since my job kept me so busy during the day, late nights with her and Max were the only time we had to catch up. And I truly was tired. It had been a long day, and I had an early call in the morning. Mixed in there somewhere was the nagging feeling that even though we'd broken up, saying yes would be disloyal to Tom.

I couldn't think of any reason to accept the invitation, aside from the way the sound of his voice was making my limbs quiver and my palms sweat.

"Well?" Daltry said. "Is it a date?"

"A date." The reception on my phone was crisp and clear; I hadn't misheard or misunderstood. Colin Daltry, a somebody, was asking me—Holly Heckerling, a nobody—on a date. One by one, my objections melted away and I heard myself saying yes, almost as though I was an observer witnessing the exchange from outside my body. I watched the cars cruising by me on Sunset Boulevard and felt slightly dizzy. I had a feeling that after tonight, nothing would be the same.

"Don't act starstruck," I warned. I'd pulled Gerry and Monica out of the queue and we waited curbside for Daltry's Town Car. "Don't gawk at Colin or anyone else. Pretend you fit in."

"Are you two having a fling?" Gerry asked. "If so, you know, you could have saved us a lot of trouble in getting his socks. You could have just grabbed a pair from his house."

I shook my head. "We're not having a fling, and I've never been to his house. This is the first time I've seen him in a social setting," I said, mentally adding that it would probably be the last. A double date with Gerry and Monica Broccoli. What was I thinking? I prayed that the music inside the club would be loud enough to drown out anything Monica said.

She pulled a compact from her purse and checked her lipstick for the third time in as many minutes. "You think he'd come to our wedding?"

"Ooh, yeah," Gerry shouted. "That'd be awesome. Let's ask him."

"No, no, no." I shook my head. "He's not coming to your wedding."

Gerry craned his neck to see who was stepping out of a just-arrived BMW. "Does this mean Tom's out of the picture?"

Before I could answer, a silver Town Car slid to a stop at the curb and Daltry stepped out. Someone shouted his name, and it echoed through the crowd. Cameras flashed and someone thrust paper and a pen toward him, asking for his signature.

He strode purposefully toward us, brushing past the paparazzi and the crunch of autograph seekers. He put one arm around me and another around Monica, nodding a greeting to Gerry. If he recognized them, he said nothing.

I hadn't noticed the second car that pulled up behind Daltry, but instantly recognized the black-clad behemoths who emerged from it. Daltry's bodyguards, otherwise known as the Five Frigidaires. When they had all piled out, I realized there were only four this time. The compact model was missing. Perhaps Dorm Fridge wasn't allowed out on a school night. The Frigidaires enveloped us, paving the way toward the club's entrance.

I felt ridiculously miscast in the role of Daltry's date. Monica was dressed for a night on the town, while my last-minute preparations for the evening had consisted of a dab of lipstick and a quick finger comb in the rearview mirror. Onlookers would surely assume Monica was Daltry's diva du jour.

One of the gatekeepers addressed Daltry by name and we were all whooshed inside. The club consisted of a small room aglow in candlelight. Candles lined the walls; their light reflected off copper-plated vaulted ceilings. The place was wall-to-wall people, most of whom probably earned more in a day than I had all year. We weaved through the crowd and slid onto a cushy ottoman upholstered in faux crocodile skin.

The Frigidaires dispersed, but all remained within striking distance. I made a mental note to keep a grip on my cell phone, for fear of repeating the airport incident.

Colin disappeared briefly and returned with drinks for everyone—some kind of imported beer for himself and Gerry, apple martinis for me and Monica. Normally I'd bristle at someone being presumptuous enough to order for me, but in this case, I was relieved. I had no idea what to order in a place like this.

The room thrummed with music, the noise level overruling any possibility of conversation. I shouted introductions over the noise. Colin shook Gerry's hand, then Monica's. Finally, recognition hit. He leaned closer to me. "Your cousin's the masseur?"

I nodded.

"Why didn't you tell me?"

I shrugged.

"What happened to my socks?" he asked.

I shrugged again. I didn't feel like screaming over the noise, and besides, I felt it was best to leave it a mystery.

Two appletinis later, mystery seemed like an overrated concept. I'd gotten giggly; the image of Daltry being swindled out of his socks now struck me as ridiculously funny. "They played you," I said, pointing at Daltry and laughing.

He cupped one hand to his ear. "What?"

"Show him your card," I urged Gerry, who eagerly complied.

Daltry held the business card up to the light and squinted. After a while he flipped the card over, squinted some more, then tucked it into his pocket.

He pointed an accusing finger at Gerry. "You stole my socks."

Gerry averted his eyes and nodded.

Colin drained his beer and slammed the empty mug down on the wooden table. "You'll be hearing from my attorneys."

The color drained from Gerry's face. Monica was slack-jawed, rendered speechless for perhaps the first time in her life.

I bit my lip. Colin's jaw was tight, the ever-present playful glint absent from his eyes. As I flirted with the idea that he could actually be serious about pressing legal charges, he turned toward me and winked. "Lola, doll, give me Chico's number."

Their fears of prosecution allayed, Monica and Gerry took to the dance floor, where they were more focused on the famous feet around them than on actually busting a move.

While it was good to see my cousin happy, I couldn't share his enthusiasm for the club. The heavy beat of the music and the shouts of people competing to be heard over the din had combined to give me a headache. While Gerry and Monica were abuzz with excitement every time another star entered the room, there was only one celebrity I was interested in. And I had to admit, I'd found him much more interesting when it was just me and him and the snake.

I was contemplating a fourth appletini when I felt my cell phone vibrate. I pressed the phone to my ear and shouted hello.

"Where are you?" Carter asked. "I thought you were coming home right away."

"I went out with Gerry and Monica," I yelled. "A club called Hyde."

"How'd *you* get in to Hyde?"

I blew a strand of hair out of my eyes. "Colin got us in."

"You're out with Colin Daltry?" she asked, the disbelief in her voice cutting through the noise.

Colin tapped my leg and pointed toward the bar. I nodded and he slid off the ottoman. Refrigerators One and Two mobilized instantly, shadowing him as he made his way across the crowded club.

"Is Max okay?" I shouted into the phone.

"He won't stop crying," she said. I couldn't make out most of what she said, but my pulse spiked at the word "hospital."

"Hospital? What's wrong? Does he have a fever?"

"No fever, no rash." There was a brief pause between songs and I heard her clearly. "Maybe I'm just overreacting. Can you sing the song again?"

I rolled my eyes. I was beginning to wish I'd never remembered the damn song. Daltry was still at the bar. A leggy blonde in red leather had sidled up to him and they were chatting and smiling. The refrigerators maintained a respectable distance, obviously not considering her a threat.

I turned away from the crowd, crouching as low in my seat as I could go, until my head was parallel to the tabletop.

"PRANCING IN THE SKY, MY LITTLE MONKEY STAR—"

A scream pierced through the phone line. I abruptly stopped singing. "Was that Max?"

"No, it was me," Carter said, "begging you to stop."

"You asked me to sing."

" 'Sing,' not screech," she said. "You're making it worse."

I straightened in my seat and saw that another appletini had appeared on the table. Colin stood in front of me, head cocked to one side, regarding me quizzically.

"Sorry," I told Carter. "I'll be home as soon as I can." I hung up and returned the phone to my pocket.

Colin slid onto the seat next to me. "Boyfriend?"

"I gotta go." I pulled myself off the ottoman. "My best friend needs me."

Daltry reached out and grabbed my elbow. "Don't go, doll," he said. "The party's just getting started."

The room was spinning. I knew I'd had too much to drink, but it wasn't until I tried to walk that I realized just how intoxicated I was. Colors and faces and noises swirled around, making me dizzy.

"I'm gonna faint," I said to Daltry. I reached out to steady myself against the table but somehow misjudged its height and landed heavily on my elbow. The table wobbled under my weight.

Daltry had stood and was mouthing something to me but I couldn't hear his words. It seemed like someone had turned down the volume in the club. Now they were dimming the lights. I felt Daltry's hands encircle my waist and then his face faded from view.

I woke in the back of Colin's Town Car, with no memory of how I'd gotten there. I had a vague sense I'd floated through the sky, carried by clouds and surrounded by shooting stars.

Daltry's voice rose above the echoes in my head. "You still with me, Lola?" He was stroking my hair. I was stretched out on the backseat, my head on his lap.

"I think so." I saw the world whizzing by the window. Or maybe we were whizzing by the world. The movement disoriented me. "Where are we?"

"Just driving. I wanted to get you out of there. Away from the crowds and the paparazzi."

I groaned. The photographers must have had a field day. Colin Daltry's date passes out at Hyde. I could imagine my aunts' reaction if my picture ended up in the tabloids—Kuki would be mortified, while Betty would buy copies for all her bingo buddies. "How did I get out of there? I don't remember walking."

"My guys got you out. They lifted you over everyone's head." He cocked his head and smiled. "Photographers were knocking each other over to get a shot." I presumed the shooting stars I'd imagined were the flashing bulbs of the paparazzi. "Can't wait to see the spin they put on this one."

Colin pressed a button on his arm rest and the moon roof slid open. The cool air felt nice. I took a deep breath. My head was still pounding, but my vision was starting to come into focus. I looked around the roomy backseat. "Where's Gerry and Monica?"

"They're still inside. I told them I'd get you home."

I struggled to sit up. "No, I need to get my car. It's parked a few blocks from the club."

"Darlin', you're in no condition to drive."

I put my head in my hands and held on tight, hoping to still the spinning sensation in my brain. Daltry was right. There was no way I could drive myself home. "Gerry will drive me," I said. "I can't leave my rental car on Sunset overnight. It'll get towed."

"All right," he said, leaning forward and talking to the driver.

I leaned back and closed my eyes. A few minutes later, we passed the club again. I directed Daltry to where my rental car was parked. The driver pulled up alongside it. It took me a while to get my footing and longer to fish my car keys out of my purse. Daltry took them from me and unlocked the passenger door. "Wait for me here," he instructed. "Don't you dare try to drive."

I nodded and slipped into the passenger seat. Through the haze in my brain, I knew I needed to get home to baby Max.

The numbers on my cell phone's keypad kept shifting around, rendering it nearly impossible for me to dial Carter's number. After several attempts, I got through.

Carter was whispering. "He's asleep."

I breathed a heavy, apple-scented sigh of relief.

"How was Hyde?" she asked.

"Great," I said. "I passed out and was carried out of the club by Colin's bodyguards."

"I guess that means you'll be home soon."

It was cold in the car, so I turned the key in the ignition and got the heater going. Just for kicks, I punched a few of Nancy's buttons.

"Please input your destination," Nancy droned.

"Can I ask you something, Nance?" I took her silence for assent. "What am I doing here?"

"Please input your destination," she repeated.

"I don't *know* my destination." I'd told Carter and Danny I couldn't consider moving until I'd survived a week working in Hollywood. It was past midnight of the seventh day and I was no closer to knowing whether I should stay in LA or return to New York. I'd been composing a mental list of the pros of living in each city. Topping the New York column were Tom, Aunt Betty, David and Tallulah, and Gerry. The LA list had Carter and Danny, financial stability, and exploring whatever was going on between me and Daltry. Kuki made both lists. While escaping her constant criticism was a point in favor of moving to California, she was the closest thing I had to a mother, and despite her barbs I'd miss her. "What would you do?" I asked Nancy, only to be met by silence.

There was a knock on the driver's-side window. Daltry was back. I unlocked the door and he slid behind the wheel.

"Where's Gerry?" I asked.

"Still at the club," he said. "I told them my driver will take them anywhere they want to go. They can drop my name, say they're meeting up with me. The bodyguards will stick with them, make sure they don't get in any trouble. They should have no problem getting in wherever they want."

I nodded appreciation. Gerry and Monica would have the night of their lives. And I could go home and sleep off my appletinis in the comfort of my own bed. Or, rather, in the relative comfort of a futon on the floor of my best friend's guest room.

Daltry gestured to Nancy's illuminated display screen. "You weren't planning to drive anywhere, were you?"

"We were just having some girl talk."

Nancy repeated her request for destination data. I leaned my head back and closed my eyes as Daltry drove. My stomach still hadn't settled; it felt like we were driving on hairpin turns when I knew full well the route back to Danny's was nearly a straight line. Then I realized I hadn't told Daltry where I was staying.

I opened one eye, then the other. We were on a steep, twisting road, somewhere in the Hollywood Hills. "Where are we going?"

"You'll see."

After a while, the twisting ceased. Daltry turned onto a dirt overlook that jutted off the main road.

"You are not traveling on a recognized roadway," Nancy scolded.

The car rolled to a stop. I rubbed my eyes and looked out through the windshield. The Los Angeles skyline was spread out below us, a dazzling tableau of twinkling lights. The night was clear, the moon bright and full. The sky was filled with stars. "Wow."

Daltry put the car in park and tilted his seat back slightly. We sat in silence for a while, staring into the night.

After a while, he reached over and took my hand in his. My stomach did a flip-flop, and I wasn't entirely sure whether it was reacting to Daltry's touch or the lingering effects of the liquor.

He traced a circle on my palm with his thumb. "Feeling better?"

"Yes," I lied. I didn't want to admit that I was such a light-weight that three apple martinis made my head spin. Or that I'd been completely out of my element in the überhip nightclub, a square peg in a sea of suntanned and sophisticated round holes.

He reached over to brush hair from my face, and a spark of static electricity zapped my cheek. He laughed an apology and withdrew his hand. He touched the leather seatback first, then tried again. This time, the electricity that surged through my body wasn't the static kind.

My brain was buzzing, and I was fairly certain his touch, and not the alcohol, was responsible. I was no longer seeing double. In fact, my vision was supersharp. Adding to the heightened visual acuity was the sensation that the nerve cells in my skin had multiplied a thousandfold.

He pulled me closer, his warmth a welcome buffer against the cold night air. In contrast to the cool outside temperature, the atmosphere inside the car was pulsing with energy. Since Nancy was cold as ice, I presumed Daltry was the source. When his fingers brushed my lips, they tingled with heat. I hypothesized that if he kissed me I'd spontaneously combust.

A moment later I had a chance to test my theory.

When Lips Collide

I'd never worried about my kissing technique before. Well, not since junior high, when I'd surreptitiously practiced on my pillow, envisioning Robby Francomano's face as I pressed my parted lips against the pillowcase and squirmed around, ending up with a mouthful of cotton and no clue whether I was doing it correctly. When I finally kissed a real, live boy, I realized all the angst had been unnecessary. Once my lips met his, the rest came naturally.

From those first fumbling kisses to my more recent marathon smooch sessions with Tom, I'd felt fairly confident that kissing was something even I couldn't screw up. But now I was kissing Colin Daltry, whose lips had been linked to some of the world's most beautiful women—including recent onscreen conquests Jennifer Aniston and Kelly Ripa. Those kisses might have been scripted, but a kiss in character is still a kiss.

As Colin's lips moved against mine, his tongue playfully darting in and out of my mouth, my fears that I wouldn't stack up to Aniston or Ripa or even Velvet Montana made me feel clunky and awkward, almost as clueless as I was back in my pillow-puckering days. Instead of getting lost in the moment, I premeditated every move, thinking about what goes where and for how long.

Colin pulled away. "What's wrong?"

I looked at the blinking lights beyond the windshield. "You could have any woman you want. Why me?"

"Why not?" He threaded his fingers through mine. "I like you."

I sighed. If I'd harbored even the faintest glimmer of hope that he'd declare real feelings for me, I'd have been sorely disappointed. "Thanks."

He brought my hand to his lips and kissed it. "You're not like the women I'm used to."

If the long-legged, lush-lipped Velvet Montana was any indication, he was right about that.

"When I saw you in the airport, you looked . . ." He paused, searching for the right word.

"Deranged?" I offered.

He shook his head. "Delectable."

I rolled my eyes. Did he really think he could con me into thinking he'd been smitten with me at first sight? The image was still fresh in my memory. Me, with my hastily assembled thrift-store outfit, spud-spiked hair, and lipstick-smeared face. Him, smartly attired, perfectly coifed, and surrounded by musclemen paid to prevent people like me from coming into contact with him in the first place. I know he found me amusing, perhaps even attractive, but "delectable" was stretching things beyond the bounds of believability.

"You looked a little deranged," he admitted, "but you stood your ground." His face broke into a grin at the memory. "Going nose-to-nose with guys five times your size, threatening legal action, waving a brassiere in the air. I was impressed."

"Mm-hmm." I raised one eyebrow. "So impressed that you gave me a phony number."

He shrugged one shoulder. "I blew it. But then you turned up on the set, and I had a second chance. Why do you think I finagled to keep you around? Macho guy like me pretending to be afraid of a little snake?"

"I've been wondering about that."

He kissed my wrist, then started working his way up my arm. "You're spontaneous," he said, following it with a kiss. "Sassy."

Another kiss. The corners of my lips flirted with a smile. This was more like it. Next came "smart," "strong," and "sarcastic," each punctuated by a kiss. Then he was at my neck. He kissed just below my ear, then whispered, "Sexy."

When he'd run out of adjectives, he continued with the kisses, dotting my forehead and my cheeks and finally reaching my mouth. I closed my eyes, surrendering myself to the sensation of his lips against mine.

In hindsight, the decision to trade the Town Car—with its roomy backseat and moon roof—for my rental car, had been a bad one. There being no graceful way for a six-foot-tall man to maneuver in the front seat of a compact car, when he leaned closer to me, Colin elbowed the navigation display, jarring the previously dormant Nancy back to life. "Wrong turn," she said, though the car wasn't moving.

I hit a button to silence the mechanical meddler, but she seemed to be stuck on replay. "Wrong turn, wrong turn, wrong turn."

Maybe she's trying to tell me something, I mused. I'd asked her advice on which to choose—Los Angeles or New York, Colin or Tom. Maybe she was weighing in with her answer. *Get a grip,* I told myself. I must have been drunker than I thought if I believed the navigation system was giving me relationship advice.

Now Colin was pressing Nancy's buttons. Suddenly, she was silent.

"Let's go back to my place," he said, nuzzling my neck.

Things were moving fast—much faster than I was accustomed to, but spending the night together was the logical next step, I told myself. Tom and I had spent six months working up to the big event, an event that hadn't even happened in the end, despite extensive preparations on my part—figure-flattering lingerie, a wide array of contraceptive options, and the infamous bank-busting red dress. Maybe it was best to just take the plunge. No life preserver. No testing the waters. No waiting an hour after eating.

Just take the plunge.

I opened my mouth to speak, but was interrupted by the *buzz-buzz*ing of my cell phone. *Ignore it,* I told myself. But what if it was Carter, I wondered, calling about the baby? I'd never forgive myself if Max was sick and I hadn't taken the call. The phone buzzed again, and Daltry whispered into my ear, "Answer it. I'll still be here."

I flipped the phone open without looking at the display.

Ronnie was sobbing. "You . . . ruin . . . everything," she sputtered.

"Huh?" The phone cackled, and for a moment, I thought the connection was lost. I pressed the phone closer to my ear. Between the static and Ronnie's tears, I could barely make out her words. From what I could piece together, she'd called with the purpose of cataloging every injustice she'd suffered at my hands from the age of six onward, from the Easy-Bake Oven incident to something involving Eddie.

"What about Eddie?" I shouted. "I can't hear you."

Colin lifted his head, eyebrows raised. "Who's Eddie?"

"Nobody," I whispered.

"Why didn't you tell me?" Ronnie cried.

"Tell you what?" As far as I was concerned, there was nothing to tell. Aside from my brief preoccupation with Eddie's balls, we'd had a purely platonic relationship. "This really isn't a good time—"

"Your apartment . . . was here . . . He dumped me. . . ." Her staccato sentences were punctuated by bursts of static. It took me a while to get the gist of her latest complaint against me. Apparently, after several dates in which they'd met in public places, Ronnie invited him back to my place, which she tried to pass off as her own rather than admit to Eddie that she still lived at home with her mother.

When they got there, he naturally recognized my apartment. A man doesn't forget the place he met a plaster-coated, cinnamon-scented, bruised-and-battered woman with a monkey. I took comfort in the fact that, if Eddie didn't consider me datable, at least I was memorable.

Colin leaned back in his seat. I held the phone out so he could hear Ronnie's sobs and rolled my eyes in a gesture of helplessness. "I'm sorry."

"Take your time," he said, fishing a pack of cigarettes from his coat pocket.

"He said if I lied about where I lived, he didn't know what else I'd lie about," she said, beginning to regain her composure. "You have to help me."

"What do you expect *me* to do?" I said. "I'm in Los Angeles." Geographic location notwithstanding, I had absolutely no desire to help her out of her self-inflicted dating dilemma. "Besides, you'll get over it. You always do."

"Not this time," she said, her tone serious. "Eddie is special."

Colin climbed out of the car, shut the door behind him, and walked several feet away. He stood staring over the canyon as he lit up a cigarette.

"This isn't a good time, Ronnie. I'm in the middle of something." She sniffled. "You doing Daltry?"

"None of your business," I snapped. "And thanks a lot for telling Tom. How could you do that?"

"You said you were through with Tom," she said. "He's better off knowing you were lying to him."

"Then isn't Eddie better off knowing that you were lying to him, too?"

There was stunned silence on the other end. "That's different."

"Why?"

"I love him."

"Well, I love Tom." The ease with which the words came out of my mouth took me by surprise.

"Then what are you doing with Colin Daltry?"

I looked at Daltry's imposing profile outlined against the night sky. "It's complicated."

Colin let himself back in the car and dialed up the heat another notch. "Your cousin need a shoulder to cry on?" Daltry asked.

"More like a scapegoat to blame."

He leaned over to kiss my neck. "Your lips are cold," I shrieked, shivering at his touch.

"Help me warm them up."

This time it was Colin's phone that broke the mood. "Talk to me," he said into the BlackBerry.

He grunted a few times, then disconnected.

"Girlfriend?" I asked.

"Mick, my driver." He laughed. "I don't have a girlfriend."

"What about Velveeta?"

He cut a sideways glance at me. "Velvetina and I broke up."

"Does she know that?" I asked. "She acts awfully territorial for an ex."

"She wants me back," he said with a shrug. "But I'm not interested. We had some kicks, but it's through."

I blew out air, wondering if he'd say the same thing about me in three weeks. Then I remembered the phone call I'd overheard earlier in the week.

"But you love her, don't you?" I asked. "I heard you on the phone telling someone that you loved them. I presume it was her."

"You thought . . . ?" He clucked his tongue. "That wasn't Velvet. I was talking to my kid."

"You have reached your destination," Nancy said. I looked out the window. We were on the street in front of Carter's apartment.

The building was dark aside from the lights illuminating the front entry.

Colin's expression was inscrutable. We hadn't spoken the last mile of the drive. After babbling about still feeling a little light-headed and having an early call, I'd run out of excuses. Not that I should have needed to explain myself for not wanting to sleep with a man on the first date. In truth, I couldn't pinpoint any single reason for turning down his invitation. Not the fact that when he looked deep into my eyes, he called me "Lola" instead of "Holly." Nor even his revelation that he had a son who lived with his mother in Aspen, whom he only saw sporadically. Perhaps it was a combination of all those things, along with the fact that I kept hearing my own voice echoing in my mind, saying, "I love Tom."

I was about to open my mouth to speak when Colin's Town Car slid to a stop alongside my rental car. Daltry nodded to the driver.

"Your friends are safe and sound back at their hotel," he told me. "Mick says they were shitfaced but seemed like they'd had a good time."

He was fiddling with Nancy's touchscreen, pressing buttons with expert precision. "My home address," he said with a wink. "In case you change your mind."

He removed the keys from the ignition and handed them to me. I took them without comment.

"See you tomorrow, Lola." He opened the door and climbed out of the driver's seat.

I stood on the sidewalk, watching him drive away.

Carter was still awake when I crept in at three a.m. I heard her voice over the baby monitor, warbling the "Monkey Star" song. So she'd learned the lyrics after all. Now maybe she'd stop calling to ask me to sing it at inopportune moments.

I slipped my shoes off and hung my jacket on a hook near the door. Carter emerged from the bedroom on tiptoe. "Good date?"

"Ask me again tomorrow, when I've had a chance to process the evening." I sank into a recliner. "You figured out the words," I said, gesturing to the baby monitor.

"I Googled it," she said. "Didn't find anything at first. I spent hours on the Library of Congress Web site, checking out every copyright registration with the word 'monkey' in the title."

She was like a dog with a bone. She wasn't going to stop digging until she found it. "Yeesh, Carter, in a few weeks he'll have grown attached to something else. 'Itsy-Bitsy Spider' or 'Twinkle, Twinkle Little Star.' Why don't we go out tomorrow and buy him a stack of CDs?"

She shook her head. "It's bigger than the song now. Much bigger." She was pacing from one end of the room to the other, full of energy despite the hour.

"Why are you obsessed with this stupid song?" I asked.

"It's not stupid," she hissed. "It's my baby's song. And yours. It's ingrained in your psyche, whether you know it or not."

I breathed a heavy sigh, knowing it was best not to argue with Carter when it came to metaphysical matters. She was probably more in tune with my psyche than I was. "Ingrained, huh?"

"Indelibly," she said. "I searched the online registries of BMI and ASCAP—they're the two main organizations that control licensing rights for songwriters. You'll never believe what I found."

"I'm listening."

She walked to her computer workstation. "Wanna know who wrote it?"

I shrugged again. I didn't know many children's songwriters. In fact, I couldn't name a single one.

She handed me a sheet of paper from her printer's output tray. I scanned it, saw the title "Monkey Star," the year of its registration, 1980, and the author's name. *Richie Heckerling.*

Heart to Heart

I'd never known my dad went by Richie, which might be why, in my own periodic attempts to locate him online, I'd always come up empty. I'd been searching under his full name, Richard. I wondered what else I didn't know about him. Then I remembered Betty saying he'd been "trying to be a songwriter" when I was born.

I'd gotten little sleep, my dreams punctuated by images of my date with Colin and questions about my father, disconnected thoughts converging to the chorus of the "Monkey Star" song. My father had written it for me. A man who'd once been the world to me but whom now I barely knew.

They were worlds apart, but Colin and my father had each left a child to be raised by someone else. I thought of Max—tiny, helpless, utterly dependent on those around him. Holding him evoked protective instincts in me that I never would have imagined I possessed before. My father must have felt similar emotions when holding me as an infant, emotions that inspired him to write that song. *Promise me, monkey, you'll never fade away.* But he'd been the one to fade from my life.

As I drove to the ranch, I dialed Betty's number. I wanted to know everything she knew about my father, especially his songwriting career. But my questions would have to wait. Bernie said she'd gone to the pharmacy. "She went to buy some more Pepto," he said. "She was up all night with agita."

There were more vehicles parked at Mike's ranch than usual, including a large pickup truck I'd never seen before. Mrs. Mike was standing in the doorway to the house, wringing her hands. I pulled around back and saw Mike entering the compound with a balding, bespectacled man dressed in black jeans and a red Windbreaker.

I locked my rental car, bid Nancy farewell for the day, and walked toward the warehouse. Today was the last day I'd be working with Monkey. She was doing a scene in which Colin proposes to Kelly by having his pet chimp deliver the ring. The simple scenario would be a cakewalk for Monkey. Aside from the fact that she had to do it clothed in a ridiculous flowered jumpsuit, she'd be a natural.

As I approached the primate compound, I heard somber voices. Chewy and two other ranch hands were blocking the doorway.

"What's going on?" I asked them.

"Está muerta," one said. "She's dead."

"What?" My knees buckled. I grasped the doorframe for support. "Who?" *Please don't let it be Monkey.* In the short time I'd known her, I'd grown quite attached to the little chimp.

Chewy was talking but I couldn't hear him over the pounding of my heart. I pushed past him, racing to the chimp cages as fast as my wobbly legs would carry me.

My breath caught when I saw Monkey sitting in her enclosure, curled into a ball and rocking. Morty was swaying back and forth beside her, his mouth wide and teeth bared.

In the next enclosure, Mike and the balding guy—who I presumed was the veterinarian—were inside Mona's cage, crouched over her lifeless body. Mona—the mother of Monkey, Migas, and four other acting apes, whose droopy lip and sad demeanor had made her unsuitable for stardom herself—was gone.

"Where's Migas?" I asked, just as Robyn emerged from the cage cradling the infant in her arms. Her cheeks were tearstained, her nose bright red. "What happened?" I asked her.

She bit her lip and shrugged her shoulders. Then she hurried past me toward the main house, murmuring to Migas that everything would be all right.

Monkey was still rocking. I tried to get her attention, but her eyes were vacant, as though she'd retreated to an inner world. Morty was pounding on the steel bars and bouncing off the cage walls. The hair on his body was puffed out, making him look much bigger than he really was. I wanted to go inside to comfort Monkey, but knew it wasn't safe to enter while Morty was in such an excited state. The average chimp is five times stronger than a human. Even a little guy like Morty could be dangerous if he felt threatened.

The door to Mona's cage was ajar, so I went inside and offered my assistance to Mike and the vet, who both told me there was nothing anyone could do at this point.

"What happened?" I asked.

The vet pushed his glasses up on his nose. "Most likely a heart attack. Won't know for sure until we run some tests."

"Nobody knew she was sick?"

Mike shook his head. "She seemed fine. But she didn't touch her food last night, and this morning, Chewy found her down. She was already cold."

I looked over at her food chute, which was filled to the top with monkey chow.

"Did she have a heart condition?"

"Appeared healthy at her last annual," the vet stated authoritatively. "We had no reason to suspect heart disease at the time." He stood and regarded Mona's body with clinical detachment. "Animals can't tell us what's hurting them. If she'd been human, she'd have been complaining. Heartburn, chest pain, edema, that kind of thing. Pity these guys can't talk."

Morty had settled down and was sticking his lips through the bars of the cage, hooting softly.

Mike glanced at his watch. "Shouldn't you be going?"

"Where?" I said, ready to help in whatever way I could.

"Don't you and Monkey have an eight o'clock call?"

My mouth fell open. "Her mother just died. You can't expect her to go perform."

"Why not?" Mike asked. "You think they're gonna hold up filming so a chimpanzee can mourn its mother? It's not like there's gonna be a funeral."

I couldn't accept the fact that Monkey was expected to report for duty as though nothing had happened. "At least give her a few days to grieve," I pleaded.

Mike put one hand on my shoulder. "Best thing you can do for her is to get her out of here. Sooner she sees life goes on, better off she'll be."

Morty was clutching Monkey from behind, rocking in tandem with her. With each back-and-forth motion, they inched forward. As I watched them shuffle across the floor like a chimpanzee choo-choo, memories of my own mother's death floated to the surface. Snippets of conversation swirled in my brain—the adults around me insisting that maintaining my normal routine would help me cope with the loss. Instead it had made me feel that her death hadn't made a ripple in anyone else's life but mine.

Mike slapped my back, jolting me back to the present. "The show must go on."

As I drove to the set, I found myself wondering not just about Monkey, but also about Migas. His life couldn't be expected to go on as usual. He was still dependent on his mother. He'd have to be hand-raised and bottle-fed. There were no other adult chimps at Mike's ranch. No aunts to fill the gap left by Mona's death.

A low wail emanated from the back of the van. I winced at the sound, feeling like a heel for bringing Monkey to work. A call to Gio had confirmed Mike's prediction that postponing the scene with Monkey would be prohibitively expensive. "If Monkey's not up to it, have Morty do the scene," he'd suggested.

"Won't people know it's not the same chimp that's in the rest of the movie?"

Gio snorted. "They're the same size. Trust me, no one will notice. Especially when we put him in the costume."

I'd initially agreed it might be wise to let Morty go on as understudy. He'd been trained to do the ring scene as a backup. And while he'd clearly been agitated by the morning's events, he would probably recover sooner, as he wasn't Mona's offspring. He had joined the acting troupe six months earlier when another trainer left the business and sold him to Mike.

But when I'd let myself into their cage to retrieve Morty, he retreated into the den box above my head, while Monkey leapt into my arms and clung to me. She was trembling, but calm, while Morty was banging on the den box with such force I thought the wood would splinter into pieces.

After a hasty consultation, Mike and I had agreed Morty should remain at the ranch, while I'd take Monkey to the set alone. Robyn had been scheduled to work with me, but she couldn't tear herself away from Migas.

I parked the van and unloaded Monkey, who, aside from clinging to me tighter than usual, seemed to be faring well. I picked the flowered jumpsuit up from the costumer and fitted it on Monkey, then sat in the animal holding room awaiting our call.

"Morning," Angela said, poking her head into the room. "Is she good to go?"

I nodded. "Unless there's something in the AHA rule book about not working after witnessing your mother's death."

She stepped in the room and closed the door behind her. "What?"

She listened with one hand over her mouth as I recapped the morning's tragic events. "I'm so sorry," she said.

"Everyone seems to think the show must go on," I grumbled.

She watched Monkey, who had picked up a purple ball and was rolling on the floor with it. "If she's in distress, I can shut down filming," she announced. "But I have to say, she seems okay."

I nodded glumly. On the surface, Monkey appeared to be fine. But who knew what was going on inside? "Animals can't tell us what's hurting them," I said, repeating what the vet had said about Mona.

Unlike the excitable Morty, Monkey was calm by nature, which made her a good performer. She was unperturbed by the lights and commotion on a movie set. So I wasn't surprised she carried out her part to perfection. It was Daltry who wasn't on his game, flubbing take after take, calling Kelly by her real name instead of her character's. After several botched takes, Hal called a five-minute break.

I gestured to Monkey, who obediently scurried over to where I stood on the sidelines. She stretched her arms over her head, wanting to be picked up, and I obliged.

"Why the long face?" Daltry asked, approaching. "Still stewing over last night?"

I shook my head. "Monkey's mother died this morning."

"Oh, is that all?" he said, reaching over and patting her on the back. "She'll get over it. Circle of life, right?"

He's not an animal person, I reminded myself, trying not to be chilled by his callousness. "What about you? You don't usually have any problem remembering your lines."

He furrowed his brow and shook his head. "Not sure. I'm having trouble staying in the moment. I keep thinking about last night."

I flushed crimson. I'd been too preoccupied with Mona's death to focus on the events of the prior evening. But with Daltry leaning close, the memory of his lips on mine sent a shiver down my spine.

"What's the Sock Man up to today?" he asked.

"More of the same, I expect." I'd called Gerry first thing in the morning, to see if he and Monica wanted a lift into Beverly Hills, but he'd said they were hungover and wanted to sleep in. I promised to pick them up at five to drive them to the airport. He'd insisted they could take a shuttle, but I wanted to give them a ride, partly so I could give my cousin a proper farewell, and partly out of self-preservation. My future in Hollywood would never be secure as long as Gerry and Monica were in town. "They're leaving this afternoon."

"Good." Daltry leaned in closer. "How about dinner tonight?"

I shook my head no. I wasn't up for another late-night dalliance with Daltry, having not quite recovered from the first one.

He lowered his gaze to my lips and leaned in for a kiss. I felt my resolve weakening along with my knees. "Come on," he whispered into my ear before nibbling on my lobe. "It's Friday night. Let me take you out on the town."

It had been a long time since I'd been out on a Friday night. Unless you counted bingo night at Havencrest Senior Center, which I didn't. Now that they were new parents, it would be a while before Danny and Carter returned to the club scene. Back in New York, Tom would be home with Nicole, watching Disney flicks and eating corn dogs, while I'd be at my place doing someone else's hair or taxes or typing. Or watching someone else's kids or pets so they could go out and have a life, while I put my own on hold.

I looked up at Daltry, a smile flirting with the corners of his mouth as he waited for an answer.

"Sure."

Someone called Daltry's name and he winked at me and turned on his heels, shouting over his shoulder, "It's a date."

Two more takes and the scene was in the can. Monkey's role in the movie was officially complete. My own days on the set were numbered, as there were only a handful of scenes involving animals remaining to be shot.

I carried Monkey piggyback style to the elevator. As the doors opened and we stepped in, I heard someone call, "Lola."

I turned to see Kelly Ripa hurrying toward us. I held the door open for her.

"Thanks," she said, hitting the button for the first floor.

"No problem. My name's Holly, by the way," I told Kelly. "Colin calls me Lola because of my ring tone. 'Copacabana.' But seriously, Lola? It makes me sound like a trampy showgirl."

She put one hand on her hip. "My daughter's name is Lola."

"Oh." Talk about putting one's foot in one's mouth. "I'm sure she's not a tramp."

I decided to go for broke and ask for her autograph for Tallulah. Fear of public embarrassment, and desire for job security, had prevented me from making the request thus far. But I'd just called her daughter a tramp, so I had nothing to lose. "My friend's monkey loves your show. Could I get your autograph for him? He's a quadriplegic."

Her mouth fell open. "The monkey's a quadriplegic?"

I shook my head. This wasn't coming out right. "My friend David is quadriplegic, which is irrelevant, except that he has a helper monkey. And the monkey is obsessed with *Regis and Kelly.* Mostly Regis, but she likes you, too."

"She does?" I could tell by her tone that she didn't believe a word I was saying. "She told you that?"

"No, but she does this thing when she likes someone." I tilted my head to one side and stuck my curled-up tongue in Ripa's direction, mimicking Tallulah's trademark sign of affection. "She does that when you come on TV."

Monkey blew a raspberry as if to indicate what she thought of my story.

The elevator doors opened and we stepped out into the lobby. Kelly asked, "And what does she do for Regis?"

Tallulah's overtures toward Regis Philbin's onscreen image verged on pornographic. "Trust me. It's not something I can reenact in public."

The primate compound was eerily quiet when I returned Monkey to her cage. As soon as I set her down, she rushed over to Morty and the two embraced. I watched them for a moment before heading for my car. Mona's body had been removed; her enclosure stood empty. The triumph I'd felt in procuring Kelly's autograph for David, along with a pair of socks for Gerry, seemed trivial in comparison to Mona's loss.

My rental car was blocked in by a large van, brown with no markings. I saw Chewy watering some plants and asked him about the van's owner. He pointed to the big house just as two women exited through the back door. One appeared to be in her sixties, tall and wiry, with long gray hair pulled into a ponytail. The other looked half her age, with close-cropped brown hair. The younger woman held Migas in her arms. He was sucking on a baby bottle and wrapped in a cloth blanket.

The scene reminded me of Max's homecoming from the hospital. I wondered where Migas's new home would be.

Robyn was watching from the doorway, arms crossed against her chest.

"Can you get the door, Dot?" I heard the younger woman ask her companion. The older woman walked ahead, unlocking the van and sliding the side panel open.

I came closer, stealing a glimpse inside the van for clues as to its ownership. "Where are you taking him?"

The older woman glanced at me, shielding her eyes from the sun with her arm. "Bakersfield. Gotta get moving or we'll hit rush hour traffic."

"What's in Bakersfield?" I asked, partly out of genuine curiosity and partly out of a desire to delay Migas's departure, my heart breaking at the certainty that I'd never see the little chimp again once the van pulled out of the drive.

"My place," she said. "You work here?"

I nodded and stuck my hand out. "Holly Heck—"

"Heckerling," she said, finishing for me. Recognition struck us both simultaneously.

"Dotty!" I shouted, wrapping my arms around her in a hug. Dotty Nixon had been my supervisor at the primate sanctuary I'd worked in during college. Her hair had been darker then, her face unlined, but otherwise she looked essentially the same.

She hugged me back. "How are you, Holly?"

"Had better days," I admitted. "What are you doing here?"

"I could ask the same of you. You're a trainer?"

I nodded, smiling despite myself. "I just fell into it. Turns out I'm pretty good. I'm working on a feature called *Vets in the City* with Colin Daltry and Kelly Ripa. Today I did a scene with Migas's older sister. Her name's Monkey, which is a stupid name for a chimp, but—"

"I know Monkey," she interrupted. "She's a sweetheart."

"Are you adopting him?" I asked, gesturing toward Migas.

She smiled, wrinkles creasing her face. "I have my own sanctuary now. Outside Bakersfield. About twenty chimps and four orangutans, most of them retired from showbiz. I'm not used to having infants. I usually get them when they're older. He'll be a handful at first, but I'm hoping some of the older females will take to him."

"That'd be great," I agreed. "Does that mean he won't be in the business, then?"

"No." She shook her head. "He'll be spared that life."

"It's not so bad," I said defensively. "I used to think it was, but the animals are treated very well."

"I'm sure they are," she said, touching my arm, "especially with trainers like you. There are so many bright-eyed people coming out of the schools, using the newer techniques, operant conditioning and reward-based training, that the old ways are practically unheard-of these days. Every now and again, I hear reports, or I get a chimp into my facility that's obviously been abused. But it's rare."

I nodded in agreement.

"But even if you give them the best possible treatment," she continued, "is it right to exploit them for the public's amusement?"

I cringed at her question. Some of the things I'd seen animals—especially primates—do onscreen or in circuses was ridiculous, perhaps even borderline degrading. But people love monkeys and apes, and if they sold greeting cards and movie tickets, and were treated well in the process, was there really any harm? And if the public enjoyed seeing apes on TV and in movies, then they'd care about what was happening to them in the wild and hopefully support conservation efforts. My own interest in primatology had been sparked by seeing movies like *Gorillas in the Mist*.

"Let me ask you something," Dotty said. "The film you're working on, *Vets in the City*?"

I nodded.

"Cute title. I imagine you're getting a good salary for your work. Mike gets his fee, too, and we all know the stars make a tremendous amount of money. Everyone on the film is getting paid—the director, the crew, the hair and makeup people, the costumers, they all make their money. And then the film studio, the production companies, and the investors will get their share, and the movie theaters will sell their tickets and their popcorn and soda. Then there'll be overseas sales, DVD rentals, merchandizing. It goes on and on, with everybody from the top down making their cut. But what about Monkey?"

I furrowed my brow. Surely she wasn't suggesting Monkey get an actual paycheck. "Well, I guess Mike's fee covers her food and housing and vet care . . ." I trailed off.

"That's fine for now," Dotty said. "But working chimps have a shelf life of six or seven years before they become uncontrollable, and then what? She'll live another forty or fifty years beyond that. It costs ten thousand dollars a year to care for one chimpanzee, and that's just for the basics. Once they stop earning their keep, the owners don't want them anymore. So where do they go? My facility is filled to capacity, but I get calls every day from people wanting me to take more chimps, from circuses, stage shows, roadside zoos, or pet situations that have gone bad."

She gestured at the big house. "Mike's been wanting to retire."

My eyes bugged at hearing this news. While I'd been struggling with whether to make my career move a permanent one, Mike had been secretly planning to close up shop? "He has?"

She nodded. "He's tired of the business. He certainly doesn't want to hand-raise a baby chimp at this stage of his life, and neither does his wife. So rather than wait until he retires, he asked me to take Migas now. I already have his big brother, Macho, who had to be retired after he bit a trainer."

I rolled my eyes, remembering how Suzanne had waved her nubby finger in my face. "I know the trainer," I said. "I'd have bit her, too."

She chuckled slightly. "Have you given any thought to Monkey's retirement?"

"I haven't even given any thought to my *own* retirement," I said truthfully.

The younger woman emerged from the van. "Crusading again, Dot?"

Dotty introduced me to Sylvia, a keeper on her staff, who shook my hand and apologized for interrupting, but insisted they get started on their journey back to the sanctuary. "Nice meeting you," she said, before climbing into the passenger seat.

I followed Dotty around to the driver's side. She paused with her hand on the door handle. "I'm sure you're a good trainer, Holly.

But I have to be a hardliner about this issue. I don't think there's any place for apes in entertainment. Period."

She gave me a quick hug and told me to keep in touch. "Come up some time and I'll show you around the facility."

I nodded numbly and watched her drive away, the van kicking up dust along the dirt driveway.

I was still standing there, staring into the distance, when Robyn came up beside me. Her eyes were red-rimmed and puffy. "It's been nice working with you," she said, extending her arms to give me a hug.

"What do you mean?" I said, wondering if Mona's death had accelerated Mike's decision to retire. "What's going on?"

"I quit," she said, pulling away. "I'm going back to vet school."

"You made up your mind, then. Good."

Her eyes filled with tears. "I should have known something was wrong with Mona."

"You couldn't have known. No one knew. It's like the vet said—animals can't tell us what hurts."

She shook her head. "I noticed she was holding herself funny the other day. Kinda clutching herself, like this." She reached her right arm up over her left shoulder and squeezed tight. "I didn't say anything."

I patted her back. "Don't beat yourself up. There's no way you could have known it was her heart. Don't they call heart disease the silent killer? Symptoms go unnoticed, or they get attributed to something else. Even if she could talk, she'd probably have told you she had—" I strained to remember the symptoms the vet had re-cited that morning: heartburn, chest pain, edema, angina.

As I spoke, I felt a heavy pressure closing in on my own heart. The symptoms had a familiarity unrelated to the vet's comments. My recent conversations with Aunt Betty raced through my mind, my pulse quickening with each complaint I'd ignored—heartburn, swollen ankles, dizziness, nausea, shortness of breath—symptoms I'd chalked up to a hysterical pregnancy. I'd brushed her off, never considering that her complaints could have a real cause.

I flashed back to our Lamaze demonstration at Ronnie's birthday dinner, during which Betty experienced one of her "contractions." I'd attributed the episode to a fanciful imagination and a flair for the dramatic. But instead of clutching her abdomen as someone experiencing a real contraction might, she'd gripped her chest. Perhaps what she was experiencing was angina, episodes of stabbing pain or tightness in the chest.

"Oh, my God," I said, my knees buckling. "I'm such an idiot."

"You?" Robyn was saying. "I'm the one who was studying to be a vet. I'm the one who should have known something was wrong with Mona."

"Not Mona. My aunt. She has all those symptoms, and I brushed her off." I fished my keys out of my pocket. "I have to get home."

Robyn gestured to her four-wheel-drive. "Hollywood, right? I'll drive you."

I shook my head. "New York."

In Due Time

"Does this mean you're moving back to Manhattan?" Carter asked. She stood in the doorway to the guest bedroom, watching as I haphazardly tossed my belongings back into the duffel bag I'd packed to come out west just a few weeks earlier.

I shook my head, scooping my sports bra off the floor and stuffing it into the bag. "I don't know." Danny had left for the studio, so I wouldn't be able to say good-bye to him.

On the drive back from Mike's, I'd tried calling Betty, but there was no answer. I was about to curse her for not having a cell phone when I realized she did have one—and I was using it. If she'd had an emergency and was unable to call for help, it would be my fault.

I'd called Kuki's, where there was also no answer. I'd even tried my place, hoping Ronnie would be home, but the machine picked up. I didn't know who else to call. Gerry and Monica were still in Hollywood, their flight home a few hours away.

I wasn't sure why Betty's condition had taken on such a sudden urgency in my mind. I'd been dismissing her complaints for weeks, after all, making her feel foolish for believing she might have been pregnant, telling her to cancel her doctor's appointment.

But I knew in my gut that time was critical. Too much had passed already.

Inching down the freeway, cursing the Friday-afternoon traffic, I realized why I couldn't reach anyone in my family. It was bingo night. Bernie and Betty and Kuki and Leo liked to hit the early-bird special before going to the senior center. They would have already left the house.

At least she's not alone, I told myself.

She'd be in a crowded bingo hall, surrounded by people too deaf to hear her scream, too focused on their cards to notice her gasp for air, too wrapped up in their own complaints to take hers seriously. If she did have a heart attack, right there in the bingo hall, who would help her?

Eddie.

I hit REDIAL on my cell phone. As I waited for my answering machine to pick up, I prayed that Ronnie hadn't erased Eddie's message. If she was anything like me in the early stages of a relationship, she'd have saved the message so she could replay it over and over again, savoring the sound of his voice. I entered the code to retrieve my messages and waited for the tape to rewind.

The time stamp for the first message was eight p.m. on Thursday evening. David's voice filled the line. "Hi, Ronnie. I wanted to say thanks. I have thirteen MySpace friends already, not counting you. Call me back, okay? I can't remember what time we're due at Lincoln Elementary tomorrow. Margie picked out a new dress for Tallulah."

Ronnie was doing another classroom gig with David? Why didn't I know anything about this?

There was a series of beeps, then a message from one of my hairstyling clients, wanting to schedule a set-and-style. Another series of beeps, then Eddie's voice. "Hey . . . um . . . I hope you don't mind, but I got your number from your aunt. Well, I got my uncle Angelo to ask your aunt for the number. . . ." Eddie's faltering speech had seemed charming the first time I'd heard the message, when I'd thought he was speaking to me. Now that retrieving his phone number could be a matter of life and death, it was just annoying.

"Grow a pair already," I yelled into the phone.

"I'd really . . . I mean, I'd like to . . . I'd love to take you out sometime," he finally spat out before reciting his phone numbers.

As he enunciated each number with a crispness honed by his years of bingo calling, I committed the digits to memory. "Five five five," he said, pausing a moment before continuing, "six zero three—"

Then the message stopped abruptly and Ronnie was on the line. "Holly?"

"Hey, Ronnie, I need Eddie's number. Quick."

She huffed. "Why?"

"It's important, Ronnie. Just give it to me."

"You want to bad-mouth me to him, don't you? You always ruin everything."

"It's Aunt Betty," I yelled. "I think she's sick—" But Ronnie was gone, a dial tone filled the line. I hit REDIAL and the line was busy.

Three tries later, the line was still busy. *Damn Ronnie and her petty jealousies,* I thought, inputting the six digits I'd gotten from Eddie's message into my phone. I might have to make ten calls to do it, but eventually I'd figure out the number.

On the third try, I'd gotten through to Eddie, catching him at the senior center. He was doing his pregame ball check, he told me. In a less stressed state that would have struck me as funny, but now it only merited a halfhearted smile.

"I'm worried about my aunt," I told him, breathlessly cataloging her complaints. "We didn't pay any attention at first, thinking it was all in her mind because she thought she was pregnant. But then this chimpanzee had a heart attack and her symptoms sounded just like Aunt Betty's." The ridiculousness of my words struck me the moment they left my mouth. "I sound totally crazy, don't I?"

"Not really," he said somberly. "Except maybe the chimp part.

Those symptoms could indicate coronary disease. Congestive heart failure, maybe."

He agreed to keep an eye on Betty during bingo, but balked at my suggestion that he whisk her away to the hospital at once. "They'll riot if I cancel the game," he said, promising to personally examine her during the first break.

Next I'd called Gerry, asking him to call the airline to see if he could book me on the same flight as Monica and him. He'd called back to say the flight was full but I could go standby.

I related all this to Carter as I hurriedly packed and kissed her and Max good-bye.

"You don't even know she's sick," she was saying. "Why don't you wait and see?"

I shook my head. I wasn't sure of much these days, but I knew with bone-chilling certainty that Betty was ill and I needed to be by her side. "If I don't get on the next possible flight, I may never leave."

"Would that be so bad?" Her lower lip quivered. "You, me, Danny, and Max. It's been great, hasn't it? Being together again?"

I nodded. "Except for the moratorium on Frappuccinos."

She laughed. "I'm sorry about that. My hormones were haywire. You can have all the coffee you want if you stay. I'll even try to get my job back at Starbucks."

"Really? You'd do that?"

She nodded. "Will you stay?"

A day earlier, free Fraps would probably have tipped the scales in favor of staying in LA, but not today. "No. But you should ease up on Danny. Let him have his coffee back." I squeezed her hand. "And don't worry. He's not cheating on you."

"I know." She snorted. "What was I thinking? Danny and Jennifer Aniston?"

"I went on a date with Colin Daltry," I countered. "Anything is possible."

I slung my duffel bag over my shoulder, kissed Max's fuzzy-wuzzy head, and walked out the door.

Gerry clutched his carry-on bag as though it contained his most-prized possessions, and perhaps it did, for he'd shown me Colin's socks, sealed in a quart-sized Ziploc bag along with Colin's autograph on a cocktail napkin from the Hyde Lounge. Velvet Montana's socks were in a separate Ziploc in Monica's carry-on suitcase, Gerry explained, so that if something happened to one of the bags in transit, they wouldn't lose both pair of socks. "It's called diversifying your assets," he said, tapping his forehead with his finger.

It's called cuckoo for Cocoa Puffs, I thought, but I smiled and said, "Good thinking."

As we waited in the check-in line, Monica scrolled through the pictures in her digital camera. She showed me one of her and Gerry posing with the Four Frigidaires in front of Daltry's Town Car. "I still think we should invite Colin to the wedding."

My cell phone rang. *Probably Eddie,* I thought, glancing at the display. The number was blocked.

"Hello?"

"Lola, doll," Colin said, his voice tender. "You weren't going to say good-bye?"

My heart did a little flip-flop. I'd been so consumed by my desire to get back to Betty that I hadn't allowed myself to think about what I was leaving behind. "I'll be back," I said, knowing even as I said it that I wasn't sure it was true. "How'd you know I was leaving?"

"Danny. He told me about your aunt. Where are you?"

"At LAX. My cousin's flight leaves at five. I couldn't get on it, so I'm on standby, waiting for something to open up on another flight."

"That could take all night," he said.

"I know," I groaned.

"Don't go," Daltry said. "Movie wraps in a few days. Stick around. Then we'll go to New York together. We have a date tonight, remember?"

Traveling first-class with Daltry would have been a far sight better than sleeping in the terminal waiting for a seat to open up in coach. But some things were worth suffering for. "I can't," I said. "I like you—I really do—but family comes first."

"Family comes first," he repeated, the words sounding foreign coming from his lips. I wondered if Daltry had ever put anything or anyone ahead of himself or his career. Including his son. "You'll never get anywhere in this business with that attitude."

"Probably not," I agreed.

He wished me well and disconnected. I felt a hollow knot in my stomach as I inched forward in the check-in line, trailing Gerry, Monica, and their mounds of luggage. My battered duffel bag was dwarfed by Gerry's Samsonite suitcase and Monica's five-piece leather Liz Claiborne set. You'd never guess I was the one who'd practically lived in LA, while they'd been short-term guests.

I was about to ask them how a two-day stay required a boatload of baggage when my cell phone rang.

"It's all taken care of," Colin said. "I pulled some strings."

"Strings?"

"I have a fantastic travel agent. She put you all on the same flight and bumped you up to first-class. And she'll have a driver waiting for you at JFK when you land."

Oh, yeah. I could get used to the perks of stardom. "Thanks. For everything."

"I'm going to miss you, Lola," he said. "Who's gonna coach me?"

"You'll be in good hands," I said. Before tearing out of Mike's ranch, I'd talked Robyn into staying on as a trainer for a few more days, just long enough to finish up the *Vets* shoot in my place. Mike agreed to the plan, adding that as long as he remained in business, there'd be a job for me at his ranch.

"I'll miss you, too," I told Daltry. I was going to miss everything about Hollywood—the animals at Mike's ranch, Gio and the rest of the crew, Angela and her trusty rule book, most certainly Carter, Danny, and baby Max. I'd even gotten a little misty-eyed when dropping Nancy off at the rental car company. But Daltry was in a class by himself.

I powered up my cell phone the moment our flight landed. There was a message from Eddie. He'd noticed Betty leave her table during the fourth bingo game of the night, shuffling toward the restrooms. While midgame bathroom breaks were almost unheard-of at Havencrest Senior Center—most of the seniors would rather risk wetting themselves than miss out on a jackpot—he hadn't worried until her seat was still vacant fifteen minutes later.

He'd enlisted his uncle Angelo to take over as bingo caller and burst into the ladies' room, but found it empty. He located Betty in the men's room, standing in front of the urinal, her head bowed as she dipped her fingertips into the fluid pooled at the bottom of the urinal and made the sign of the cross.

When he'd asked what she was doing in the men's room, Betty had responded, "Men's room? That's a funny place for a baptismal font."

Based on her cold, clammy skin, rapid heartbeat, and disoriented state, he'd decided to take her to the hospital immediately, over Kuki's objections that she was always cold, clammy, and confused.

A second message, this one from Kuki, urged us to come straight to the hospital from the airport. The emergency room doctors pronounced that Betty had suffered a mild heart attack, perhaps more than one, due to severe blockage in two of her coronary arteries.

Gerry and Monica were pressing their own cell phones to their ears, shouting out snippets of messages that had been left by Bernie, Kuki, and Ronnie. By the time we deplaned, we'd all shared the news and our joint conclusion that things looked bad for Betty. She'd been whisked into surgery, an emergency double bypass.

My arrival at JFK was accompanied by the same urgency as my LAX entrée had been weeks earlier, but the anticipation of welcoming Max into the world had been replaced by the dread of having to say good-bye to Betty.

My spirits lifted slightly when I saw a half dozen drivers lined up, holding placards bearing the names of the passengers they'd been dispatched to pick up: Ginther, Gates, Egglefield, Abbey, Heckerling. The driver gathered our carry-on bags and ushered us out to a waiting limousine.

Even onetime cabbie Gerry was impressed with the speed with which the driver conveyed us to our destination, Bensonhurst Memorial Hospital. We raced past a bulletin board advertising Lamaze lessons and other community education classes, and took the elevator to the cardiac intensive care unit.

Kuki was in the corridor by the nurses' station, wringing her hands. Gerry and Monica hugged her simultaneously, then hurried into the room where Betty was recovering from double bypass surgery.

My own heart was racing as I faced Kuki, surprised at how small and frail she appeared. She'd always seemed about ten feet tall, never more imposing than the night I'd hurriedly left town after wrecking Ronnie's birthday, when she'd stormed from the dining room without even saying good-bye. I was acutely aware she'd blamed me for that night, as well as for Ronnie moving out. It was also my fault Betty had been so preoccupied with pregnancy that she misread her symptoms, my fault she didn't have a cell phone with her when she'd gotten disoriented in the men's room. Everything was my fault.

Kuki opened her mouth to speak, and I braced myself for the

barrage of accusations that would surely follow. Instead she took my hands in hers and pulled me closer.

"I can't lose another sister," she said, folding me into her arms and squeezing me tight.

Despite the late hour, and the hospital's limit on the number of visitors allowed in the cardiac care unit, my entire family was crowded around Betty's bed. Bernie held her hand in his as he stared blankly at the cardiac monitor, probably taking comfort in the repetitive zigzagging motion of the green lines. Ronnie was on the other side of the bed, smoothing Betty's hair out of her face. She was shivering even though her full-length overcoat was buttoned to her neck. Gerry and Monica had moved in next to her, while Leo was in a chair by the door. At the foot of the bed, Kuki fingered her rosary beads, her lips moving in a silent prayer.

Eddie entered the room. I thanked him for getting Betty to the hospital so quickly. The doctor had told us that Eddie's fast response, along with the aspirin he'd given Betty at the senior center once he suspected heart trouble, might have saved her life. "Holly tipped me off," he said. "She's the hero."

I was as uncomfortable with the "hero" label now as I had been after I'd inadvertently been responsible for saving Mrs. Mete. "I should have known sooner." Despite my relief that Betty's prognosis had been upgraded to good, I was still overwhelmed with guilt at having ignored her symptoms for so long.

"Don't be so hard on yourself," Eddie said. "In a younger woman, the same symptoms could have been confused for pregnancy. Shortness of breath, nausea, dizziness, swollen ankles. And if she'd never felt a contraction before, it's conceivable she could mistake an angina attack for one."

Betty was stirring. She opened her eyes and looked around the room. "What happened? Where am I?"

Kuki took her hand. "You had a heart attack. But you're going to be fine."

"How did I get here? Last thing I remember, I was at church. It was a lovely service." She looked over at Eddie. "Hello, Father."

The doctor appeared and briefed Betty on her condition and postsurgical care. He listed the warning signs of heart failure and urged her to seek medical attention anytime she had symptoms, no matter how strange.

She'd listened carefully. "You mean everything I've been feeling, it was all 'cause of my heart?"

The doctor nodded. "Even your weight gain could have been caused by buildup of fluid in the abdomen due to circulatory congestion."

"I was never pregnant?"

Kuki squeezed her hand. "No, dear."

"What about the hemorrhoids?" Betty asked.

The doctor shrugged. "Sometimes a hemorrhoid is just a hemorrhoid."

I was slurping stale coffee in the hospital cafeteria, where I'd retreated upon learning that Betty was out of the woods.

"David and I have been talking," Ronnie said, sinking into the chair across from me. "You could do more Critter Comedy gigs if I take over your bookings."

I sputtered as coffee shot up my nose. "What?"

"I've already got us—I mean, you—booked solid the next three weeks." She flipped her hair over her shoulder. "I have a persuasive phone manner, not to mention bitchin' computer networking skills."

This was too much. She'd invaded every avenue of my life while I was away. Now I was back and she was still trying to take over. "You did one classroom visit for me." Uninvited, I might add. "That's it."

"We did three," she corrected. "The first two just with David and Tallulah. For the third one, I brought your other animals, too."

"How could you do that without my permission? What if something had happened?"

"Get a grip." She rolled her eyes. "The schools are willing to pay more for more critters. Lincoln Elementary School's paying us a hundred bucks. That's fifty bucks apiece. But I guess now that you're back, you'll want a cut, too."

How generous of her to offer me a cut of the earnings from my own business. "No deal," I said. "I want you out. Out of my business. Out of my apartment. Out of my life."

Her eyes widened. "All I've tried to do is help you. I fed your pets, kept your business afloat. Why do you hate me?"

"I don't hate you." "Hate" seemed like too strong a word to use on a family member. Even a food-flinging, apartment-stealing, label-making sneak like Ronnie. "You're the one who always hated *me*."

"I don't hate *you*," she said, her voice cracking. "I might be jealous of you. A little."

"Jealous of me?" I laughed. Miss Flushing Beauty Academy, with her flawless complexion, silky hair, and Barbie-doll figure, was jealous of me. "Right."

"Everyone loves you. You're smart and funny and you have a great apartment and cool friends and everything always goes your way."

Excuse me? I thought. *Have we met?* "Then why have you been such a bitch to me ever since we were kids?" I said. "My mom died, my dad abandoned me, and you went around putting your name on everything, making me feel like I didn't belong."

She was bawling now. "Everyone always liked you better than me. Then your mom died, and it got, like, ten times worse."

I choked on my coffee. "I'm sorry my mother's death was such an inconvenience for you."

She exhaled forcefully. "Grandma, Aunt Betty, my mother, they all fell over themselves giving you whatever you wanted, even if it was mine. My room, my toys, my books. If I didn't label my stuff, I'd have lost everything."

I felt my eyes water and willed myself not to cry. Years of lip snarling over the dinner table had hardened my heart to Ronnie. I didn't know how to react to her admission. I couldn't believe she had really felt overshadowed by me in her own home. It didn't make sense. I was the one who grew up living in *her* shadow, catching whatever crumbs I could. I was the one who'd been wronged.

And that was when it struck me. Ronnie's intrusions into my life hadn't been born of spite, but old-fashioned envy. While she'd been hung up on our childhood rivalries, I'd created a life for myself. It was problem-plagued and topsy-turvy at times, but it was mine. I wondered if Ronnie knew what she really wanted. Even her career in cosmetology had probably been driven by the fact that Kuki kept badgering me to work with her at the barbershop.

Maybe Ronnie hadn't been trying to outshine me, but rather to emerge from my shadow.

Kuki arrived, setting a plate of pastries between us. Ronnie and I both instinctively reached for the biggest one. The patterns of pseudosibling rivalry were long ingrained.

Kuki pulled up a chair. We sat in silence for a while. Then she asked if I was home to stay.

My time in Los Angeles flashed through my mind as though I was watching it on fast-forward. It had been a wild ride, and one I wasn't eager to see end. The money I'd made would pay my bills for the next few months, while I'd live off the high of working in Hollywood for years. But as many doors had opened for me in LA, I'd never been ready to close the door on my life in New York.

"For now," I said, staring wistfully into my coffee cup.

Had Betty's illness not hastened my departure, I'd have lingered a few months longer, maybe even traded my rental car for a leased vehicle and Carter's futon for a studio apartment. Certainly pursued a relationship with Colin, despite the probability that it would have followed the pattern of my pre-Tom relationships, coming to a crashing halt just before the three-month mark. It would be a thrilling three months, and would probably ruin me for other men, but was a three-month relationship worth risking everything I had in New York?

Kuki leaned forward, elbows uncharacteristically on the table. "They make movies in New York, don't they? Can't you do your monkey business here?"

"I'm not sure animal training is the right career for me," I said. My last day on the *Vets* set had taught me that no matter how caring the trainers and how humane the treatment the animals receive, show business is still a business after all—a business that puts six-year-old apes out to pasture, and for which I'd coerced a two-year-old chimpanzee to perform hours after witnessing her mother's death.

Now that Dotty had opened my eyes to the lack of funding for retired entertainment apes, I'd resolved to donate a percentage of my *Vets in the City* earnings to the sanctuary, where, if she was lucky, Monkey would live out her golden years in the company of her brothers, Morty and Migas. But my contribution would barely make a dent in the half century of care Monkey would require after outliving her usefulness to the film industry.

"Maybe I'll expand on my classroom talks," I said, wondering if I could somehow incorporate the lessons I'd learned in Hollywood into our presentations. Perhaps even enlist the children's help in raising money for the sanctuary.

I reached into my back pocket and pulled out the printout Carter had given me the night before. "Aunt Betty said my father was a songwriter," I said.

Kuki's nostrils flared at the mention of my father, but her tone was measured. "Writer, artist, dreamer. He never got anywhere with it."

I slid the paper across the table. "Carter found the copyright registration for one of his songs online."

She picked it up and studied it, her expression softening as she scanned the wrinkled sheet and read the title aloud. "Your mother called you her little monkey," she said finally. "He wrote that song for you." She closed her eyes. "I'd forgotten all about it."

"Me, too," I said. "Almost."

She handed the paper back to me. "There's an address. Are you going to contact him?"

I nodded, folding the paper and returning it to my back pocket. "In due time."

"Don't wait too long," Kuki said, standing. "You never know when it could be too late." As she left the cafeteria, rhythmically rubbing her rosary beads, I knew she was thinking about both her sisters.

Ronnie was fingering her bingo-ball necklace. It was obvious who *she* was thinking about. "You really want to win Eddie back?" I asked her.

"Of course," she said. "I really like him, Holly."

I exhaled slowly. It was time for the old patterns to change, I thought, draining the last of my coffee. I was always willing to go the extra mile to help a friend or relative. Why not help Ronnie win back the hunky paramedic?

She leaned forward. "You have an idea?"

"Better than that," I said. "I have a dress."

As I described the silky body-hugging dress and its as-yet-untested powers of seduction, she stood and unbuttoned her overcoat, letting it fall open. "You mean this one?"

★   ★   ★

I slipped into the cardiac unit without stopping at the nurses' station. It was past visiting hours, but I wanted to kiss Betty good night, to see her one more time before going back to my apartment and reclaiming my life.

I passed Gerry and Monica in the hallway, where they were debating whether to have a buffet-style reception or a formal sit-down meal.

Betty looked weak, but color was coming back to her face. Bernie was still at her bedside, holding her hand. His resemblance to a bloodhound had never been so striking—the rheumy eyes, long face, and sagging jowls combining to give him a mournful expression. I wondered if Betty had known, when they met, that he was the one who would be there, forty years later, holding her weather-beaten hand in his. Their life had been filled with heartache, but at the end of the road, they had each other.

I moved closer to the bed, pushing aside an empty chair. A sweatshirt that had been draped over its back fell to the floor and I stooped to pick it up. I recognized it even before spying the familiar university logo. Tom's NYU sweatshirt, the one I'd given Betty when escorting her home from Lamaze class.

"Don't worry, sweetie. I washed it," Betty said from the bed, her voice thin and raspy.

I hugged the sweatshirt tight, surprised that the downy fabric still smelled faintly of Tom's cologne. He'd given it to me one night as we walked hand in hand through the Village, after catching a movie at the IFC and dinner at Hong Kong Palace. We'd talked about Nicole and Tallulah, laughing at the fact that while both had boundless energy and could be bribed with sweets, Nicole, at least, would grow out of her candy cravings and hyperactivity.

Memories of that night were now inextricably linked with the recollection of Betty's Lamaze incident. Maybe Betty's accident hadn't killed the sentimental attachment I felt for the shirt, after all.

"Keep it," Betty said. "I'm too old to be a coed anyway."

"Thanks," I said, tucking it under my arm protectively. "I think I will."

Betty kicked off her sheets and was struggling to sit up.

"Lay down," I told her. "You need to relax."

"I know, but I want to show Bernie my incision." She tugged at her hospital gown. "The doctor says he split my sternum right down the middle. I wanna see." The gown's Velcro fasteners were no match for her determination. One last tug and the fabric went flying over her head.

A large square of gauze covered the center of her chest. She began peeling back the adhesive tape.

"Don't—" I said, but it was too late.

It was like driving past a car crash. I felt compelled to look even though I knew I wouldn't like what I saw—an oasis of patchy pink skin, bisected by a six-inch-long incision held closed by surgical staples. The area around the incision was red and raised. I bit my lip and averted my gaze.

Bernie's jaw drooped further. He let out a single, startled utterance. "Ugh."

24

That's Amoré

I spooned another helping of mashed potatoes au gratin onto my plate and made my way back to my table, skirting the dance floor, where Betty was leading a long line of bunny hoppers, despite her recent release from the hospital. Her double bypass hadn't slowed her down; if anything, she seemed to have a new lease on life. I resisted the urge to pull her out of the line and coerce her to sit and rest, knowing the attempt would be futile.

Besides, as long as she was hopping like a bunny, she wouldn't be showing off her surgical scars. She'd flashed nearly everyone at the ceremony, with the possible exception of the priest, unbuttoning her blouse to reveal the midline chest incision and hiking up her skirt to show where the veins for the heart graft had been removed from her upper thigh.

While family events typically sent Bernie into a catatonic state, this time he watched Betty attentively from the sidelines, duty and devotion evident in his gaze.

Kuki intercepted me before I reached my table. "Seconds?" she asked, one eyebrow arched in disapproval. One of Kuki's steadfast rules was that family members didn't get a second helping until all the guests had had their fill. Even when there was clearly enough food to feed all of Bensonhurst, we had to wait patiently until the guests were sated before daring a second trip to the kitchen.

"Sorry," I said, lowering my gaze to my greedily overfilled plate.

She smiled. "I'm glad you like my potatoes."

"They're delicious." I nodded vigorously. "Plus they make a killer hair conditioner."

I left Kuki wrinkling her nose over that remark and returned to my table, which had been abandoned as most of the guests had made their way to the dance floor or the head table to congratulate the happy couple. I sat at the seat designated as mine by the sock-shaped place card bearing my name. The seat that had been reserved for my date was empty.

"Woo-hoo, Holly." I looked up from my plate to see Mrs. Mannisto shuffling toward me, thrusting a copy of the *Star* in my direction. "Can I get your autograph?"

I rolled my eyes but accepted the tabloid and the pen she also proffered. Though the caption identified me only as Colin Daltry's "unidentified female companion," and my face was obscured by the burly bodyguards, Aunt Betty had made certain every one of her bingo cronies knew it was me.

"Too bad they didn't get your good side," Mrs. Mannisto said.

I scribbled my name across the page and handed the magazine back to her. "It wasn't my best moment."

Over the wedding band's rendition of "That's *Amoré*," I heard the faint strains of "Copacabana" emanating from my purse. I'd switched my ring tone back as a reminder of my time in Los Angeles. I retrieved the phone and flipped it open.

"Hello?" I pressed the phone against my ear to hear over the hubbub.

There was a brief pause and then Daltry's voice filled the line. "Lola," he drawled. "How was the wedding?"

"Perfect." Perfect for them, that is. After struggling with the decision of whether to call his bride by her given name during the ceremony, or stick with the name he'd come to know and love her by, Gerry had stumbled so badly he'd called her neither Monica nor Esther, but Mesther. The priest either hadn't noticed or didn't mind the blunder. Monica had rolled her eyes but otherwise kept her cool, promising to love, honor, and cherish my cousin for the rest of her life.

While that thought used to fill me with dread, I'd come to realize that love is not always what you go looking for, but rather what finds you. I even got a little misty-eyed, watching her limp back down the aisle, arm in arm with Gerry.

"Did they like the present I sent?" Daltry was asking.

"They loved it." Earlier that morning, a FedEx box had arrived, filled with socks once belonging to the biggest names in showbiz.

"How did you get George Clooney's socks? And Ellen DeGeneres's?"

"Ellen wanted me to do her show, and I said I'd give her an exclusive in exchange for her socks. The rest came from a celebrity poker match. I was down to my last chip and put my socks up as a marker. The other guys threw their socks in the pool as well. What they didn't know was I was sitting on an outside straight flush."

There truly is no business like show business, I thought, shaking my head in wonderment.

"Did you do your snake-charming bit yet?" he asked.

"You would have loved it," I said. "Rocky's not the showman Reba is, but he had everyone squirming in their seats." I felt a slight flush at the memory of Reba slithering across Daltry's chest and snuggling inside his shirt.

"I may be in New York soon," he said. "My agent is negotiating for me to do a film that would shoot in Westchester County in the fall."

Daltry in New York. That would make life interesting.

"Guy's a horse trainer. I may need some coaching. Think I could hire you on?"

"Perhaps," I hedged. "Have your people call my people."

He chuckled. "You have people?"

"Actually, I do." I surveyed the room. Eddie was spinning Ronnie around the dance floor, while David was holding court in the center of an eager group of children, who'd lined up patiently to pet Tallulah. "David and I have gotten pretty popular. My cousin Veronica is handling our bookings now."

"It would be nice to work with you again," Daltry said. "I've missed you."

I was about to respond in kind when I felt a tap on my shoulder. I turned to see Tom standing behind me, his arm extended in invitation. "Can I have this dance?" Behind him, I caught a glimpse of Nicole, her hands on Betty's hips, her curly hair flouncing up and down as she jumped in tandem with the rest of the bunny hoppers.

At the sound of Tom's voice, Daltry said, "Boyfriend?"

Tom's slightly crooked smile sent a familiar but still exciting surge of heat through my veins. I hadn't seen him since the night of our six-month anniversary, when the three little words I'd longed to hear were replaced by one that had haunted me ever since. But taking a page from Betty's book, I'd learned that The One Who Said Ugh can also be The One.

"Yes," I said into the phone, before clicking it shut. "Yes, he is."

Photo by Norman Abbey

ABOUT THE AUTHOR

Brenda Scott Royce is the author of five nonfiction books, including *Hogan's Heroes: Behind the Scenes at Stalag 13* and *Party of Five: The Unofficial Companion*. A former book editor, she is Director of Publications for the Greater Los Angeles Zoo Association and editor of the Zoo's award-winning quarterly magazine, *Zoo View*. It's the ideal job for this animal lover, who once worked as a chimpanzee caregiver at a wildlife sanctuary.

Brenda earned a bachelor's degree in anthropology, specializing in primatology, from Cal State Fullerton, where she was awarded a Think Different Technology Scholarship and a Humanities and Social Sciences Life Achievement Award. She's also the recipient of a California Predoctoral Scholarship and numerous writing honors.

Her writing credits include magazine articles, encyclopedia essays, film reviews, short stories, DVD and video liner notes, and more than one hundred audiobook adaptations.

Like Holly, Brenda has a debilitating Starbucks addiction, a mortal fear of snakes, and a working knowledge of power tools. She lives with her family outside Los Angeles. You can visit her Web site at www.brendascottroyce.com.